COMING HOME

Fifteen year old Thomas Elkin engages in the turmoil of the First World War. Accepting the blame for the death of his recently conscripted brother, Elkin switches identity with his dead sibling and enters into the conflict. His burning ambition is to die a glorious death in his brother's name. Believing that, in fully submitting to the reality of war is atoning for his sins, he faces all the attendant horrors with a steel will and a poignant resignation. His personal conflict sees itself mirrored in the wider events and soon the two are inextricably linked, raising issues of mortality, morality, guilt and faith.

COMING HOME

COMING HOME

by

Roy E. Stolworthy

Magna Large Print Books
Long Preston, North Yorkshire,
BD23 4ND, England.

British Library Cataloguing in Publication Data.

Stolworthy, Roy E.
    Coming home.

    A catalogue record of this book is
    available from the British Library

    ISBN   978-0-7505-3890-9

First published in Great Britain in 2012 by Claymore Press
an imprint of Pen & Sword Books Ltd.

Published in Large Print 2014 by arrangement with
Pen & Sword Books Ltd.

Magna Large Print is an imprint of Library Magna Books Ltd.

Printed and bound in Great Britain by
T.J. (International) Ltd., Cornwall, PL28 8RW

In Flanders Field

In Flanders fields the poppies blow
Between the crosses, row on row
That mark our place; and in the sky
The larks, still bravely singing, fly.
John McCrae, 1915

Prologue

London 2010

Joshua Pendleton felt the cold air slap his face and steal his breath away. It was late October and summer already a brief memory, like the days when he roamed the shingle beaches of Brighton with his father, Moses, searching for washed up treasures from faraway places. Now with his father long since passed away he continued, as promised, to undertake the annual pilgrimage to pay his respects to Thomas Elkin, the soldier who had saved his father's life in the Great War of 1914-18. His eyes flickered with uncertainty and he chided himself as he did every year for being too mean-minded to pay the fare for a taxi.

In his mind, contrary to what others thought, London was an intimidating city full of a bristling urgency concealing dark brooding secrets, a place where method and reason battened down chaos. He hesitated and allowed his mind to slip and tried to relax. For a fleeting moment he recalled a panorama of memories, and fixed his eyes on the busy London traffic interspersed with the inevitable red London buses moving briskly over Westminster Bridge.

Beneath the comforting tones of Big Ben ringing thirty minutes past the hour he glanced upwards, and waited patiently for the rapid beating of his heart to slow to an easy rhythm before resuming his journey. Neither late nor early for sixty-eight years he'd shared the intimacy of time, now it felt like a faceless stranger intruding on what should have remained private.

Fatigue came quickly without warning, invading his limbs like an incoming tide washing over a shifting beach. He winced, scowled up at the sudden downpour then shook the rain from his crinkly grey hair.

He slowed and for a brief moment paused, allowing the thinning vaporous trails of his hot breath to become less frequent. It was the wrong kind of day to linger, already the air hung heavy with diesel and petrol fumes, and rising puddles filled with dirty water barred his way. Free at last from the pattering rain he passed through the great north door, flanked either side by grey arched portals. Inside Westminster Abbey his eyes automatically shifted upwards in unbridled awe. Grey stone pillars resembling giant fingers thrust skyward into the tangled intricacies of the magnificent vaulted ceiling. Groups of sightseers, with heads huddled close together, spoke in hushed voices in a mantle of secrecy for fear they disturb the breath of God. The cloying ecclesiastical aroma of incense and burning candles laid siege to his nostrils, lifted his inner strength, and he felt a satisfying sense of eternal security take over his body.

With a long drawn out sigh he stooped to massage the joints in his knees. He arched a brow. It was no more than a futile gesture born of habit, at his age living flesh offered no protection for aching bones. Then, pushing his ailments to one side and with a hint of humility twinned with a sense of inconsequence, he clasped his hands in front of him in a gesture of reverence and looked down at the tomb of the Unknown Warrior. The black marble surround glistened in a sudden shaft of light spearing from the stained window depicting Abraham, Isaac, Jacob and fourteen prophets. Laurels of fresh greenery, combined with vivid artificial red poppies framed the tomb. The intensity of the colours appeared to isolate the tomb from the surrounding sombreness, like a fresh rainbow against the backdrop of a dull sky. To him the tomb had always seemed out of place and incongruous; unnatural in its surroundings, an inglorious memorial to a magnificent sacrifice. For a moment he stood in silence, then slowly untied the heavy red woollen scarf from around his neck, folded it neatly and knelt with it under his knees for relief from the cold concrete floor. Glancing furtively from side-to-side to see whether anyone was watching him, from his jacket he took a pocket watch attached to a silver chain and placed it on the edge of the tomb. And like so many times before he read the last part of the tribute chiselled into the black marble.

They Buried Him Among The Kings Because He Had Done Good Toward God And Toward His House.

'Hello, Thomas,' he whispered. 'How are you this morning? It's raining outside, as usual. Although I hear the forecast is better for tomorrow.'

Chapter One

Yorkshire 1916

Stark memories of swishing canes and stinging buttocks pierced the mind of George Allen when he stepped hesitantly into the small classroom opposite the church of St Luke. His Adam's apple bobbled and he gripped his worn cloth cap tight in his hands, the clinging smell of chalk dust mingling with tingling fear brought back vivid recollections of the not-so-happy days spent in the classroom on the edge of the Yorkshire Moors. Even today, over twenty-two years later, he would have to admit three times nine would still take him an eternity to calculate.

Inside the gloomy classroom, dominated by a huge oak desk overlooking the classroom like the captain's deck on a ship, Mr Webster sat frowning. He did not trouble himself to look up, but instead listened to the brief message then waved a hand at George Allen, dismissing him.

For twenty-seven years Mr Webster had taught at the village school, with never a day missed through illness or otherwise. It was a record he was rightly proud of. He stood tall and lean with slight drooping shoulders, his face pale yet kindly. He glanced briefly at Joe Allen sitting in the front row of the class, and a hint of humility twinned with a sense of inconsequence leaked into his body. Gradually he felt some clarity return and he breathed deeply. They had employed him to bring education and knowledge to the children, not bad news. Instead several of the village elders, in their crass ignorance, thought differently – best the children learn the meaning of war collectively, they said. Not for the first time that year he asked for God's forgiveness for what he was about to do.

'Pay attention children,' he said in his deep baritone voice. 'I'm afraid I have bad news.'

Thomas Elkin's breath came quickly and his heart sucked at his chest. His head felt empty, like a balloon attached to piece of string, and his eyes darted across to the seat where Joe Allen sat. He knew what was coming next, and time came to a standstill.

'It is my misfortune to inform you that Joe's brother, Brian, has died serving his country in France, and while offering our sorrow and regret to both Joe and his family, we may comfort ourselves in the knowledge he died fighting bravely for the freedom of others,' Mr Webster said in a hushed voice. 'Prayers will be said in church on Sunday, and I shall expect you all to attend.'

Joe squeezed his ears tight shut, aware that everyone's eyes were upon him, and stared down at the scratched desktop. He'd worshipped his elder brother, and in his boyish innocence had always adamantly refused to acknowledge this day might come. With childish simplicity he ignored the pencil rolling onto the floor and fought to maintain a look of calm on his face. When the stream of sickly bile reached his throat he gulped and thought he might retch the contents of his stomach over the rickety wooden school desk. Amy Pascoe, the youngest at ten years of age, broke first – a choking sob burst from her chest and she cried openly without shame.

Joe's head nodded back and forwards, and folding his arms tight to his body he crossed his ankles and pulled his legs under his chair. Small beads of sweat glistened on his upper lip and salty tears readily streamed down his face, forming a wet patch over the raggedy sleeves of his hand-me-down shirt. He wanted to cry over the loss of his brother. He wanted his brother to know he had cried for him before his heart broke. A loud intake of breath hissed through his nose. His eyes welled and he began to shake. Harsh sobs racked his small body and fourteen children cried with him.

At one-forty that warm, sunny afternoon, Mr Webster dismissed the class. There would be no more schooling that day. Thomas glanced across at the hunched shoulders of his friend Joe. He wanted to go to him and tell him everything would be all right. But he knew it wouldn't, it would never be same again, not for Joe.

'Hey, Thomas, maybe I'll see you at the gravel pit later,' George Spikes called, with a wave of his fleshy hand.

Thomas looked up, angry at George for his lack of remorse. 'Aye, maybe you will, maybe you won't.'

By rights Thomas should have finished his schooling eight months ago. Yet his mother, adamant he make up the time lost waiting for a broken leg to heal, insisted he complete his education. Today, his mind was filled with nervous thoughts for his brother Archie who, that night, was due to leave for a place called Catterick, somewhere up north, to be trained as a soldier. Later, they had told him, he would be sent to the same war responsible for the death of Brian Allen.

With a chilled sense of foreboding Thomas recalled the not so distant past when many young men had left the surrounding villages amidst the cheers and stirring sounds of a brass band. Some never returned; others did, often minus a leg or an arm. Some came with a stare so vacant and listless that they seemed unable to recognise their own families. They never spoke of their experiences and instead shuffled around like frightened strangers, keeping their own counsel and suffering in silence. They were brave men, all of them, heroes to some. 'Buster' Matthews had just turned eighteen when he lost his right arm on the Somme. For weeks he sat in his mother's scullery staring into the grated fire, never uttering a word, even when he was spoken to – until the day a neighbour's cat jumped onto his lap and dug its claws into his leg.

'Bugger off, you scrawny git! I've seen bigger newborn rats than thee!' he bellowed in pain.

From that day on, for reasons no one ever knew, he'd visited the village pub every night until he learned to play the piano one-handed. He made a fair living playing at weddings, birthdays, christenings and any other events where music was needed. Not that he was any good, but folk thought they owed him a debt of gratitude.

Thomas tried to shake off the black thoughts and

paused to button up his frayed hand-me-down black waistcoat and pull on his flat cap. With a down-turned mouth he made his way over the hill to the small farm where he lived with his parents and Archie on the edge of the Yorkshire Moors.

On the brow of the hill he slowed and desperately attempted to unravel his distorted thoughts, his mind full of confused images.

Archie's easy going nature had changed since the day he foolishly let Vernon Parker's prize bull out of the meadow for a prank. The bull quickly turned on him and gored him so violently the doctors feared he might never recover. From that day, he'd become morose and a bad-tempered bully, and quickly grew to despise everything about the countryside.

'It may be some time before he recovers,' the doctor said. 'The attack has left him traumatised. Strange piece of equipment the mind. Not much I can say really, except take it easy with the lad and hope for the best.'

Since then six long years had passed, and regardless of whichever way his family looked at it the best never came. The army, desperate for men, considered him fit and able for active service.

Halfway down the hill Thomas gazed at the trails of wispy white smoke spiralling into the air. His sombre mood melted and he smiled. His mother must be baking Archie's favourite dark-brown ginger biscuits.

Ruby was there waiting, like always, stamping and snorting, throwing her head from side-to-side showing off. Her coat, wet from the brief

16

downpour, gleamed in the fresh sunlight. At the sight of Thomas she wheeled and galloped towards him, her jet-black mane thrown by her gait and the hairs on her fetlocks flared, black and glistening like a crow's wing. Her mother, a champion Percheron plough horse, died during the birth and Thomas bottle-fed the foal until she was able to graze and a strong bond had immediately grown between them. He'd named her Ruby – not for any reason he could think of other than the name just seemed to come to him.

Casually glancing around the unusually quiet farmyard he listened to the snuffling pigs snouting around for a missed morsel of discarded food. He arched a brow, and with his hand shielding his eyes against the glare of the sun glimpsed his father clearing a blocked stream away in the bottom field. The pony and trap were both missing, a sign his mother must be in the village shopping or maybe visiting a friend on a neighbouring farm. She wouldn't be gone too long, though, with the ginger biscuits in the oven. Ruby muzzled into his chest and snorted her hot, sticky tongue licking at his face. He laughed and grimaced at the same time.

Startled at the sound of a slamming door, he turned and watched Archie swagger from the farmhouse. His thin pale body shirtless and his trousers suspended by a pair of faded brown braces. In his hands he juggled hot ginger biscuits and continually blew on his fingers.

'Hey, I've got something for you. Look after it,' he sneered, holding out a bone-handled penknife. 'Now piss off.'

17

Thomas stared at the knife, his forehead creasing with disbelief.

'Are we friends now?' Thomas asked eagerly, accepting the knife.

'I told you once, sod off,' Archie sneered raising his fists.

The smile left Thomas's face and he backed away. Although a little over two years younger than Archie, in size he matched him pound for pound. Archie lashed out with his fist and caught him square on the side of his head, knocking him down on one knee. In a flash he was on his feet, crouching, circling, his fists balled. As usual Archie's kindness came with the smell of the beast. Nothing ever changed. Momentary fear flickered in Archie's eyes and he hesitated, stopped, then altered direction and made his way towards the stone barn. Ruby pawed the ground and snorted.

'Take no notice,' Thomas said rubbing her nose. 'He's just worried about going to war.'

Gently scrambling onto Ruby's back and touching her flanks with his heels he steered her out of the farmyard. Behind him the sound of Archie's high-pitched laughter followed by a woman's giggle resounded from the stone barn. Instead of kicking Ruby forward, his face hardened into a scowl. Slipping from Ruby's back he crept determinedly towards the barn and pushed his face tight against the rotting slats of the wooden door, and through slitted eyes he peered into the gloom.

Josie Davis, from the next village, was lying on a bed of straw half-naked with her legs apart, and Archie grunted and groaned as he pumped in and out of her. For a moment Thomas stood rooted to the spot listening to her breathless moaning, instantly aware why his brother had wanted him out of the way.

'You dirty sod!' he shouted angrily, pushing the door open. 'I'll tell Pa.'

Archie looked up quickly and wiped the sweat from his forehead.

Josie Davis sat up and struggled to pull on her clothes and ran sobbing, white-faced and shoeless from the barn.

'You'll be in trouble when Pa finds out. He's told you about doing that with her.'

'Tell him what you like, now bugger off before I kick your arse.'

Thomas felt a raging turmoil surge into his body and a pent-up fury streamed from his body. His mind conjured up past dark images of Archie's cruelty. His response was instantaneous and he lunged with his fingers outstretched. Archie waited, crouching and ready, then stepped nimbly to one side. Thomas stumbled and bounced off the side of the stone wall, grimacing at the pain searing into his shoulder, and with arms flailing he struggled to keep his balance. The back of his hand collided against a long wooden-handled scythe hanging from a metal hook fixed to the wall. In desperation he twisted and reached out to prevent the scythe from falling. Too late, Archie raised his hands to protect himself as the grinning razor-sharp blade arced down and slashed across his neck. His trembling hands clutched at his throat as the warm, sticky blood spurted and bubbled through his fingers. His sallow complexion drained to white and his eyes dimmed.

'Bloody hell, you've done for me, you stupid little bastard! They'll put a bloody rope round your neck and hang you for sure now.'

Thomas stood motionless, staring down at the gashed neck, his palms moist and glittering with sweat. It wasn't real; Archie was playing one of his cruel games, like he always did whenever he wanted to frighten him. Behind the barn, next to a small cultivated patch of garden where his mother grew vegetables, the huge pigs in the metal-railed sty caught the scent of blood and their strident squealing split the air.

The blood froze in Thomas's veins. Ruby snorted, shaking her head from side-to-side she backed away, her legs frantically pawed the air and her whinnies turned to piercing screams.

'Stop it! Get up, you great fool, I was only joking. I promise I won't tell Pa, please, Archie!' Thomas cried pulling at Archie's body.

Like dull glass marbles, Archie's lifeless eyes stared into the roof of the barn. Thomas stumbled back feeling the strength drain from his legs. His lips turned blue, and he gasped for breath.

'Don't die, Archie!' he screamed. 'Please don't die; I don't want you to die.'

The pigs ceased their squealing and there was no sound save for the rapid beating of his heart hammering against his ribs. Tears stung his eyes and the muscles in his face jerked in snatches. He felt isolated, as though he had blundered into another world not yet known to him, a world where he would not go unpunished.

Dazed, he lurched towards the farmhouse and sat limp like a child's discarded doll in his father's chair, all thoughts of sense and ceremony erased from his mind. With twitching fingers he wiped his knuckles across his clouded eyes to restore his vision. There, on the table next to Archie's uniform lying neatly folded he saw the ready-packed brown cardboard suitcase. He reached out, the uniform felt rough and coarse, not unlike the coat his pa wore in the cold moorland winters. Outside, the pigs resumed their squealing and his mind dulled with fear, certain the whole of Yorkshire would shortly come to investigate.

'Keep away from them pigs,' his father had told him a hundred times in the past. 'Those buggers will eat you alive as soon as they look at you, bones and all.'

For a moment he sat repulsed at what he had done, his hair clamped to his scalp by hot sticky sweat as hopelessness fogged his mind. Then a thought so macabre it could only be borne of despair coursed through his mind. His toes clenched in his boots. In a desperate attempt to keep his sanity he squeezed his eyes shut to block out the raging floodtide of foolishness choking him. A cold shudder heaved through his body, and he knew what he must do.

He made his way back to the barn and swung open the door, then began pulling the clothes from Archie's dead body. Finished, he stood with his mouth sagging open and panting for breath. With one last final effort he dragged the naked body by the ankles to the pigsty and heaved it over the metal railings. Squealing and screaming

21

the pigs surged forward, slashing at the flesh with their razor-sharp teeth. He turned away, his face contorted into pantomime hopelessness and clamped his hands tight over his ears to block out the sound of slurping and grunting.

For a moment he swayed drenched from head to toe in blood, and waited for the dizziness to pass, then he staggered to the water pump and, with both hands on the handle, sent a gush of cold water sluicing over his head and shoulders. The rasping sound of a flapping crow overhead startled him and his knees buckled in sheer terror and he clutched at the pump for support. Nothing was real any more.

Inside the farmhouse he burned Archie's blood-stained clothes in the lighted oven and wrapped the uniform in a soiled tablecloth. Then with trembling hands reached for the mantle above the fireplace and took down an earthenware jug, five shillings in small change was all he took, then he left a note written in pencil stating that he'd gone swimming in the gravel pit. Outside he hesitated and felt the rapid patter of rain on his face. Suddenly the rain came down as though some malevolent deity had opened a tap in the kingdom of heaven. It came down in sheets, torrents, displaying no mercy. It rained like no man since Noah could remember. With a deep shudder he hunched his shoulders up to his ears and made his way across the moors to the next village.

Thankful no one stood at the bus-stop by the crossroads he waited shivering, the pale light in his eyes flickering with despair. His mind a disarray of emotions, unable to push away his torment he questioned his actions of the past hour. Perhaps he should return to the village and visit the church of St Matthew opposite the schoolhouse to seek God's forgiveness. Forgive us our trespasses and forgive those that trespass against us, it said in the Lord's Prayer. He knew the words, he'd heard them many times, but he wasn't sure of their meaning. Then tiredness swarmed over him and lingered. It seemed as though every tiny grain of strength had trickled from his body. When at last he boarded the bus he took the one remaining seat next to an elderly man who smelled of sickly sweat and sucked noisily on an empty charred briar pipe. Between stops he stared at the passing countryside, all the time fighting against his rising fear until he thought he might succumb to madness. Archie's haunting words: 'They'll put a rope around your neck and hang you for sure,' hung in his soul.

In Leeds he skulked from one shadow to another wandering aimlessly from street to street with his nerves teetering on a knife edge, certain that condemning eyes watched his every move. Finally, darkness pushed away daylight; the pale streetlights threw a haunting dull yellow over looming carriages and scuttling pedestrians. For a long time he searched for somewhere safe to rest until he found an alley separating a public house and an ironmonger's shop. At the bottom of the alley he saw a dilapidated tinker's wooden caravan with broken wheels. Too exhausted to care, he slapped away the dust from the front of his waistcoat and ignoring the flurry of rats climbed inside and closed his eyes.

Shortly after sunrise he woke with a jerk and squinted as the morning sun streamed into his face. When at last he managed to force a gob of saliva into his mouth, he spat on his knuckles and rubbed the dried salty tears from his eyes, then changed into his brother's uniform. Slightly broader than Archie, he carefully holed each button afraid that at any moment the uniform would split in two. Finally he stepped tentatively into the street and asked an elderly lady for directions to the railway station.

On Platform Two he waited for the early morning train to Catterick.

Chapter Two

At Catterick he fought the overwhelming desire to rip off the offending uniform that scratched and chafed at his skin. Everything went cold within him and, seized by fear of discovery, he wanted to run for the nearest cover and hide. He had never seen so many people or heard such an awesome cacophony of voices in one place at one time. Everything seemed hustle and bustle. Men of all shapes and sizes wearing ill-fitting uniforms mingled and stumbled around in confusion.

Head and shoulders above those around him a huge sergeant waited with practised perseverance for four hundred conscripts eager to take part in the great scrap against the hated Hun. His flaming-red hair matched his carefully manicured moustache and he strode up and down like a farmyard dog, barking menacingly at anyone unfortunate enough to fall under his gaze.

'All right, you misbegotten bunch of motherless sons, get into line!' he screamed.

His eyes twitched with a frenzied energy and spittle flew from his mouth. Corporals marched up and down looking for someone to vent their fury on. With beady eyes staring beneath slashed cap peaks they seemed madder than a box of frogs as they shoved the raw recruits into abortive rows of threes.

'You heard the sergeant!' a corporal hollered. 'You don't want to fall into his bad books, by God you don't. Life won't be worth living, will it, not with your heads stuck up your arses it won't.'

Time passed quickly and the chaos reverted to a fearful near-semblance of military order. Thomas stood with anxious eyes, every sinew knotted. Hell could be no worse. Afraid any moment his frailty would betray him he gritted his teeth and prayed to God he might suddenly become a man. If there was a God, he never bothered to answer. Then despite himself, he pulled his shoulders back and with the back of his hand wiped-away the stream of snot dribbling from his nose.

A small breeze licked across his face and suddenly he found a courage he didn't know existed within him. He straightened himself. If God refused to help him he would become a man of his own accord.

To avoid looking suspiciously out of place against grown men he knew he must remain as inconspicuous as possible, to shun confrontations

25

that might lead him to betray the dark morbid secret that gripped his insides.

He knew how to right-dress, how to stand to attention; in fact, he knew most military movements. Mr Webster had drummed into them at school the necessities of discipline. Physical exercise had been hastily discarded and reluctantly replaced by what Mr Webster called 'war training'. With broken broom handles representing bayonets, they had hurled themselves with boyish fervour at an old, dirty, smelly mattress hanging from a tree that had once held their swing.

'The world cannot function without discipline,' he'd instilled in them. 'History will confirm that.'

Once again, Thomas prayed to God, wishing he were back at the school this moment.

'Aha hun!' the sergeant bellowed.

A few men made a perfunctory attempt at standing to attention. The rest stared vacantly at each other in mindless distraction.

'Get to attention!' the corporal screamed. 'Heels together, shoulders back, chest out, chin up. If you can't look like soldiers, try and pretend, you bunch of fairies. By God you lot are in for a shock.'

'Ha yef hun!' the sergeant screamed again.

Thomas made a left turn, his boot crashing down on the tarmac. The remainder stared through quizzical eyes as if he were from another planet.

'Right clever little bastard, aren't you? Want to be sergeant's pet, do you, fucking arse licker,' a voice grated from the ranks.

He remained still, waiting for the moment his brief charade would be uncovered. Nothing, it

26

seemed, not his gnawing hunger or the warm rays of the sun disappearing behind dark clouds, could halt the paralysing terror of discovery. Sooner or later they would discover the truth. He was the boy who slashed his brother's throat open with a scythe, fed his body to the pigs and ran like a coward.

'Silence in the ranks!' the sergeant roared. 'You'll have plenty to complain about when we've finished with you. My God, some of you are the ugliest things ever to fall from a fanny.'

Wilting under a barrage of obscenities some quickly came to the conclusion that soldiering might be a dangerous occupation, and not just a reason to wear a smart uniform to impress the girls. Mumbled protestations fell on deaf ears. Piled into a convoy of open-back lorries like cattle ready for market they were transported to the stores where, to add to their misery, the heavens opened. Ill-fitting uniforms clung heavy and wet. Tormented men already about to give up the ghost complained in loud voices.

'Quiet!' the sergeant bellowed. 'From now on you will keep your mouths shut unless spoken to. The bands are gone now, no more young ladies and wet kisses; only shit, muck and bullets from now on. Shape up, or you're in for some bloody big shocks, by God, you are.'

Beneath the all-seeing eyes of NCOs, in straggled threes soaked to the skin, the hapless recruits shuffled in muted obedience into the stores, harassed at every step. Bullied into line with never the hint of an apology, some trembled so violently they lost control of their limbs. They were

27

issued with a PE kit, a tin helmet, a mess tin, a tin mug, a water bottle, a knife, fork and spoon, along with a roll of cotton and needles called a housewife to repair damaged kit. The corporals smirked with pleasure. The breaking-down process had already began, the re-building of the men into a fighting force now just a matter of time.

Lined up outside the wooden huts the acrid smell of fresh creosote lingered in the air like a malignant cloud, filling the nostrils while bringing stinging tears to smarting eyes. In the distance the sound of boots hammering onto a parade ground carried like the approach of disgruntled giants lost in a heavy fog. Orders followed by counter-orders screamed by frustrated drill instructors echoed and re-echoed throughout the camp, readying squads of recruits for the unspeakable nightmares in far-off foreign countries.

Thomas joined nineteen other men in hut number twenty-three. Inside, twenty ramshackle metal-framed bedsteads with loose springs held mattresses, each smelling worse than the breath of a dying badger. In the centre a gleaming black cast-iron potbelly stove stood upright and resplendent. It wouldn't be lit, regardless of the weather; it was summertime and the coalbunker remained empty.

Away from the others Thomas claimed the bed in the corner and sat with his hands on his lap, unsure what to do next. Nervously, he glanced around at men in various states of dress. Born and bred in the confines of towns and not the rough open countryside, most looked puny and weak. Others were no older than him. His spirits

28

lifted when he quickly realised his levels of energy along with his physical strength would more than suffice in the company of these men.

Then a shadow crossed his face, it was his mental resourcefulness that would be found questionable. In silence he watched as men from every walk of life introduced themselves to each other. Tailors, clerks and coffin makers, even a poet named Rimes from a village outside Ripon stood beaming at those around him. Friendships became quickly sealed with a warm shake of the hand. Jokes surrounded by friendly banter were thrown back and forth as if they had known each other all their lives. He'd never heard a grown-up tell a joke before, and despite his best attempts, he failed to grasp the connotation. Nevertheless, he laughed when they did, and thankfully they paid him little attention. Later, many of the men, him included, exchanged badly-fitting tunics, ballooning baggy trousers and throat-choking shirts in a bid to find a more comfortable uniform. Gradually he became adept at keeping himself as unobtrusive as possible by mirroring the others. When they sat, he sat; if they lay on their beds, he lay on his; when they cleaned their boots, he did the same. Soon the cold unfriendly feeling of forced loneliness became a way of life.

Whenever the opportunity arose, he paid particular attention to stories of the war in France bandied around, and wondered whether or not they bore any credence to the truth.

'Bloody suicide, that's what I heard, thousands blown to pieces in one day,' someone said.

'Shut your bloody gob,' another retorted.

'Aye, keep them daft thoughts to yourself,' a nervous voice called. 'We can do without know-alls like you, you silly bugger.'

At last daylight faded into night and the plaintive call of a bugle sounded lights out. He had survived the first day and lay shivering, staring up through the darkness at the wooden rafters, listening to the wind whistling through the draughty roof. As hard as he tried he could not stop the flow of tears trickling down his face staining his pillow. He shouldn't be here, he did not belong here. It was Archie's fault that he found himself forced to exist in a room full of strangers. Every bad thing that ever happened to him had always been Archie's fault. Archie: the archangel of misery and suffering, the patron saint of maliciousness. There was no way back now, he was in the hands of God and destined to wait for the mayhem of life to plot his path.

Compared to the chorus of men's flapping palates thundering into his ears, Archie's past snoring resembled a soothing lullaby by Handel. The cacophony of noise sounded like a hundred hogs choking to death in a thick cloud of black smoke. Men talked, broke wind and gabbled incoherently; one man cried for his mother.

'Shut your bloody racket, you silly great tit!' someone hollered.

Thomas tried hard to smile but couldn't, and fell asleep.

Six o'clock the following morning the sun appeared over the rim of the earth to herald a new day. The hut door crashed open and he stood there like a ghost silhouetted in the doorway. His beady eyes glistened like burning coals, his lips curled in a snarl fit to frighten the ugliest gargoyle from the highest spire.

'All right, you beauties, hands off cocks and on with socks! My name is Corporal Woollard. They call me Hammer cos I come down hard on fools. For the next ten weeks I will become your worst nightmare before I hand you over to Fritz, for those who don't know, he is the enemy waiting to put a bullet up your arse in the beautiful countryside of France. Into your PE kit! Let's work up an appetite for breakfast, shall we? I don't want to see walkers, talkers and wankers, runners only. Don't want to get fat, do we? Course we don't, can't have Fritz sticking his big sharp bayonet in your bellies, can we?'

Thomas took a deep breath and revelled in the fresh air caressing his face as he ran as hard as his legs would allow. He ran to escape his dark secrets. He ran in the hope of abandoning the past, to leave it trailing in the dark uncharted lanes of eternity. Then, remembering his vow of anonymity, he slowed to allow the others to catch up.

'Eh, lad, slow down for God's sake,' a voice panted behind him. 'That bloody mad corporal will have us out all morning till we can keep up with you. Make out you're knackered, there's a good lad.'

Thomas turned barely able to breathe and looked into the pleading eyes of Stan Banks. Pale, thin and scrawny, he held the appearance of a man in need of a proper meal, and he moved with a slight stoop. His teeth, black and stained, matched his hands. His fingernails were long broken and jagged from constant chewing and biting.

Since the age of twelve he'd worked with his father delivering coal in Liverpool. Aged seventeen, Stan'd seen his elder brother Eli resplendent in his uniform and become dazzled at the sight. Immediately he came to realise that there was more to life than humping coal for a living. Yet for all his efforts frustration followed disappointment when recruiting stations repeatedly turned him down for the sake of his appearance. Disillusioned, he came to fear he would never wear the king's uniform and stand proudly beside Eli.

'Come back next week, lad, when you're two years older,' they laughed. 'And don't forget to have a bath, you dirty little sod.'

In spite of the continual rejections, he purchased a stiff brush and a bar of carbolic soap and spent days scrubbing his body until his skin bled in an attempt to remove the ingrained coal dust. It had little effect. With his head in his hands he prayed to God for the opportunity to become a soldier.

A few months later, he had made his way to Rotherham deciding this was his final chance of signing up. With his cap in his hands he told the recruiting sergeant he'd stopped to help an old lady put out a chimney fire before her house burned to the ground. He couldn't go home to wash and change because he didn't possess any clothes other than those he stood in. The sergeant patted him on the back and signed him up immediately.

'Just the kind of man we need,' he said.

A week later, his father sat him down in the parlour and informed him that Eli had died of wounds received during battle.

Thomas slowed, sat down beneath a horse chestnut tree and stretched out his legs. The last time he'd felt this way was the day he'd run in blind panic from the farmhouse. Immediately he became irritated by the power of his memory and silently cursed as his unwanted past returned as crystal clear as the spring water he drank from the farmyard well. He tried to stem the flood of recollection souring his mind. It stayed, stubborn, and refused to leave.

'Old Hammer, he'll want to know our names now, lad. Fatal that is. Keep your ears open and your head down, that's my motto,' Banks said with a Liverpool twang. 'Never push yourself to the front in the army. My brother Eli told me that. Died of his wounds at a place called Marne, he did. Made him into a sergeant, they did, the bastards. That's what bloody killed him, being a sergeant. He had to go up to the front to lead his men and he were first to get it, poor sod.'

'You men stay where you are,' Woollard's voice rang out. 'I didn't reckon you'd last long at the rate you were going. Trying to be clever were you? What's your name, lad?' he asked, staring at Thomas.

'Thom ... er, sorry, Archibald, Archibald Elkin, Sir,' Thomas stuttered, feeling the flush spreading over his face.

'Do you not know your name, lad? Well, I'll tell you, shall I? It's Private Elkin, and my name is not Sir, it's Corporal Woollard. Remember that,

33

lad. Now get back and join the rest of the useless items, and get some breakfast; and you, Banks, I know who you are, get yourself in the bath. I can't tell what bloody shade of white you are under that grime.'

Banks allowed the remark to pass. His interest instantly aroused by the thought of Thomas stumbling over something as simple as giving his name. His mind alert enough to realise Archibald Elkin wasn't all he made himself out to be. Lies never came unaccompanied. He'd ducked and dived long enough during his life to know when something wasn't as it should be. Nevertheless, he found himself liking Thomas.

Thomas turned away feeling the rising panic start to choke him.

'Strange that, you not knowing your own name, lad,' Banks said watching closely for Thomas's reaction. 'And you're never eighteen years old, lad; you might be a big lump, but never eighteen, and Archibald isn't your real name either, is it? It's Tom, or Thomas. Don't fret, lad, your secret's safe with me. I'm called Stan Banks, you can call me Stan.'

Thomas felt the flicker of uneasiness. His plan to remain anonymous had crumbled like the stones of an ancient building attacked by time's teeth. He neither desired nor felt the need for the friendship of others. And now another bone of contention had now been forced upon him. His age had been questioned. Certain that Banks and Corporal Woollard would eventually relay their suspicions to others, he felt his confidence slip and waver. He would need all his wits about him

34

to survive the coming weeks and hoped he might be sent to France, or a place the men called Belgium. There, with a bit of luck, he might be fortunate enough to get shot: it was better than hanging. Anything was better than that.

Week after week they marched, and when they were finished they marched some more, until some suffered with blisters oozing yellow pus.
Left right, left right,
Why did I join the army?
Left right, left right,
I must have been bloody barmy.
'Bathe your feet in cold salty water,' Corporal Woollard told Brush Wigley, who suffered more than most and wilted under the corporal's withering stare. 'And learn to accept pain and hardship if you want to survive the war.'

Brush Wigley carried the nickname because his hair stood on end like a char's scrubbing brush each time Corporal Woollard entered into one of his frequent shouting and screaming pantomimes. Stan Banks, who possessed a bent for discovering the meaning of surnames, couldn't contain his excitement and chuckled when he heard the name Wigley.

'Make wigs, that's what his family does for a living, I'd bet on it, better watch your hair, lad, there's always a story behind a name. I had a cousin once called Birkenhead Bill whose father was never the same after falling off the end of Birkenhead Pier while the tide was out. He called his firstborn Birkenhead in memory of the occasion,' he told Thomas. 'Like I said, there's always a reason for a name, lad.'

'This weapon is your best friend, remember that at all times. If it jams or you lose it, Fritz won't give you time to find another, he will kill you where you stand, remember that. Without this weapon you're useless, no good to anyone,' Corporal Woollard explained issuing Lee Enfield rifles to the squad.

Detailed lectures on handling and cleaning the weapon were quickly impressed upon them. They sloped, ordered, presented, trailed, reversed and piled arms; they did just about everything possible with the weapons, except fire them. With the same rifles they marched, counter-marched, wheeled right and left, inclined, formed squads and about-turned until they streamed with sticky sweat and buckled at the knees from exhaustion.

'Fat lot of good this'll do us in a fight,' Stan Banks complained.

Finally, they were taken to the firing range where fifteen rounds a minute would be expected, more for an experienced rifleman. Marksmen able to place five rounds at fifty yards into a circle the size of a penny would receive extra pay and a marksman arm badge for their uniform. To his surprise Thomas excelled in marksmanship. So did Stan Banks and a bear of a man from Northampton called Leslie Hill.

Chapter Three

Dusk dropped rapidly over the still waters of the quarry. Lizzie and James Elkin's shadows grew longer as darkness spread its mantle. Multi-coloured dragonflies, like strips of coloured ribbon skimmed and flitted above the surface before retiring to the safety of the nearby reeds.

Hopeful, they waited, watching the men silhouetted against the skyline row towards them. There were three boats in all and they were returning empty-handed. Police Constable Charlie Halfpenny glanced at Lizzie holding her hands close to her mouth, locking and unlocking her fingers, the weariness in her face evident.

'I'm sorry, Mrs Elkin,' he said respectfully, 'not much more we can do now. Time to call it a day I reckon, it's too deep to continue.'

He purposely refrained from telling her a body would eventually rise to the surface when the gases built up from decaying tissues. James Elkin looked at him gratefully and nodded his approval. He didn't want his wife to know either.

'Would you like us to contact Archie at Catterick or would you prefer to do it yourself?' he said to James Elkin.

'No, leave it be for the time being, we'll let him know in good time. Thanks for all your help, Charlie, I appreciate it.'

Lizzie Elkin moved closer to the edge of the

bank, and in the half-light of the red dusk she gazed sadly across the shimmering water.

'He's not here,' she said.

'Steady, lass, he can't be anywhere else or we'd have found him by now. No good thinking foolish thoughts,' James Elkin answered gently.

He caught the sudden flare of anger in her face and her eyes flashed dark and accusing. He understood her anguish yet flinched at her expression, and wondered what he should say. He could think of nothing and remained silent.

'I'm not being foolish. Thomas isn't here, in the gravel pit, I'm certain of it. We need to speak to Archie. Why did he rush away without saying goodbye?'

'Aye, don't think I haven't thought on it often enough. But you know as well as I do, Archie has the devil's spawn in him. Don't fret yourself, lass, I'll write to Catterick first thing in the morning.'

Chapter Four

Five weeks of terror and deprivation passed as though time itself stood still, so they could hardly believe their ears when Corporal Woollard informed them they were to be issued with thirty-six-hour passes. Thomas listened to promises of carnal debauchery and inducements of boisterous beer-swilling encounters and decided he would steer well clear of those straining at the leash. In Catterick he slipped away unnoticed and sat on a bench in a small park. Away from the claustro-phobia of military life he immersed himself in the opportunity to be his real self and refused to allow the past to spoil the moment. It was past mid-afternoon when he made his way into the town centre. In the streets and lanes an unending cavalcade of noisy young men in uniform found a brief contentment singing bawdy songs and indulging in harmless horseplay with the local women. Two young women giggled when drunken soldiers pulled them into a shop doorway and lifted their dresses before slipping groping hands into their drawers in broad daylight. With his mouth gaping open in disgust, he turned away feeling the heat burning into his face.

How far he walked he didn't know or even care. Eventually the rack of fatigue stretched into his legs and he felt numbness creep into his feet. Outside an inn he paused and looked up at the sign creaking and swaying in the breeze: The Fiddler's Elbow. For so long he had wondered how it felt to drink with grown men in a public house. He sniffed, wiped his nose with the palm of his hand and pushed his way through the veil of thick smoke and stench of stale beer and leaned on the bar. Around him people laughed and milled in crowded contentment, some drunk, others almost. A thin man with a long mournful face leant on the bar with one foot resting on the brass foot-rail. He turned and looked him up and down with suspicious eyes. Thomas nodded and the man sullenly returned the greeting.

'Pint,' Thomas said, displaying a false bravado to the barman. 'Give me a bloody pint of your best piss.'

He'd heard Archie say the same when Pa had sent him to fetch him from the Melbourne Arms in the village.

'Coming up, lad, best piss it is,' the barman chuckled.

Thomas watched the beer foam to the top of the glass and suddenly felt different. He didn't know why, he just did. He felt a strong determination. A new-found confidence flooded into his body and for the first time he knew what he must do. He must die; he must force death's hand to touch his shoulder. Somewhere, somehow, he must plan his death and forfeit his life to atone for the crime he had committed against his family, against his friends and against God.

The last five weeks of hard training had toned his body and burned away any excess fat leaving hard muscle. Upright, he stood one inch short of six feet and was still growing; in a few weeks it seemed unreal that he would reach only his sixteenth birthday. Nevertheless, it seemed a good age to die, he told himself. Better to do it before he got much older and suffer a change of heart. With a self-satisfied smile he downed the drink without pausing for breath and slammed the empty glass on the bar.

'Fill her up, landlord,' he spluttered.

Three times he repeated the process, until the foaming beer made an unexpected bid for freedom. With his hands clamped over his lips preventing the liquid escaping, he stumbled to the door. Too late – like a fountain gushing beer, he sprayed everyone in close proximity.

'Bloody hell you clumsy drunken bastard!' a soldier roared, backing away with puke dripping from his uniform. 'I'll bloody kill you, so I will.'

Thomas never felt the blow that caught him flush on his jaw. Under the mind-numbing influence of alcohol he staggered back. His heavy boots clomped and scraped across the wooden floor and his arms whirled out of control. For a moment he tottered and swayed, then fell backwards over a table sending the occupants cursing and crashing to the floor. Clumsily he scrambled to his feet and gazed through glazed eyes at the man dancing towards him with his fists raised, ready to strike again. Without thinking, he raised his balled fists to protect his face, the way his father had taught him.

'Can you not finish me, lad?' Thomas snarled. 'Because I'm going to bloody finish you, you bloody cock-strangler.'

People sensing free entertainment turned and shifted tables and chairs to one side, eager to form a circle for a better view.

'Go on, hit the drunken bastard,' someone called out.

Shaken by the venom in Thomas's remark, the man paled and backed away. A flurry of prodding hands pushed him forward and his eyes sprouted fear. Thomas lashed out sending the man cannoning into the crowd. With his lips pulled back in a twisted sneer he pummelled his fists into the man's face like a blacksmith striking an anvil. Then strong hands gripped his shoulders and pulled him off the man already lying unconscious on the floor.

41

'That'll do, get out of here and don't come back. Save it for the trenches, you young fool. On your way!' the landlord bellowed at him, swabbing the bloodstained floor with a wet mop.

The nauseous taste of vomit gagged him and soured his mouth. His eyes refused to focus. His world dipped and swayed and his brain spun out of control, from the waist he bent with his arms dangling and swinging like those of an ape. Streams of saliva hung from his mouth like a teething child. In desperation, he attempted to focus his glazed eyes on the man telling him to leave. He'd go when he was good and ready.

'Go on, lad, the police are on their way, unless you want to spend the night in a cell,' said the barman, guiding Thomas outside.

Fumbling for his cap, he stuck it crookedly on his head and made his way through the door, away from the gut-wrenching stench of stale beer and fetid cigarette smoke. Outside he stopped and sucked in the cool, fresh air and cleansed his lungs. In spite of his haziness he stumbled across the uneven cobbles and perched unsteadily on a fountain cascading water into a huge concrete receptacle. For a few seconds he blinked and waited for his mind to clear, then splashed cold water over his face. He felt only a fleeting respite from his first ever foray into the mind-numbing world of alcohol. His right hand ached, and blood seeped from his knuckles – the blows must have been harder than he imagined – and he plunged his fist into the cold water.

When the pain eased he wrapped his hand in a wet handkerchief. He knew drink changed men, but he'd never known why or how. Most men he'd seen leaving the village pub sang bawdy songs and continually fell over, roaring with laughter each time they lay flat on their backs in the middle of the road. Apart from Archie, he became even more nasty and violent than usual. He'd return home, staggering and lurching clumsily into the bedroom they shared, his voice slurring as he belched and broke wind. Then, for no reason, he'd become aggressive, tearing the bedclothes from the bed in a frenzied fit of rage.

Thomas quietly left and made his way to the barn and snuggled between Ruby's legs and warm belly fell asleep, wondering how drink could make one man so happy and another so violent. It had made no sense then, and it made no sense now.

The water in the trough settled, smooth like a mirror and he gazed at the bright reflection of the moon next to that of his own face. Suddenly, he shrank from the images staring back at him, like the accusing eyes of a judge about to pass a death sentence. He felt fear and shame, and suffered the self-imposed agony of his own stupidity in the stark knowledge that drink had brought him closer to his brother. He had discovered that drink made him angry and vicious like it had Archie and he trembled at the thought that his life might mirror that of his brother. Archie, the bully who had isolated him from everything in his life he'd ever loved. He belonged where he was, locked inside a pig's gut, away from decent folk. Thomas flicked the water with the back of his hand, disturbing the reflections, and watched the circular ever-widening ripples. There was one thing certain about fate: it never asked for an opinion or considered another's needs. He vowed he'd never drink again.

The next day his stomach felt like a storm drain and his head thumped like a bandsman's bass drum on parade. Bullied into line the following morning by his ever-present tormentor, Corporal Woollard, he stood nervously to attention, waiting for whatever form of medieval torture lay in store for the squad that day. Today they stood in full battledress. On their backs they carried sixty-six pounds of extra equipment. Each man held his own counsel, this was going to be a day when they would be faced with the impossibility of sustaining their dignity, in a situation so often degrading.

'Rumours say the company is about to weed out the no-hopers,' Stan Banks sniggered. 'Those not up to scratch will end up as clerks or officers' batmen behind the lines. No medals or glory for those buggers, only the opportunity to remain alive, lucky sods.'

'Oh aye, well, that bugger will go down a treat with me. I've no bloody wish to get me bloody arse in a sling,' Joe Cavanaugh said.

The previous night Cavanaugh, a man possessed with the dubious curse of being unable to stop talking, laid his hands on one of the national newspapers that occasionally found their way into the huts, extolling the horrors of France and Belgium. The headlines reported the story of the monumental loss of life caused by incompetent leaders responsible for thousands of troops dying needlessly. Lions led by donkeys, the headlines proclaimed. He had fretted so much that he worked himself up into a lather of sweat and lay on his bed, foaming at the mouth.

'Take no notice of that rubbish, they have nothing better to do than stir up trouble. Load of arse-licking pen-pushers, that's what they are,' Corporal Woollard said, quickly confiscating the newspaper and stuffing it into the unlit stove.

Rubbish or not, Cavanaugh, a county cricket umpire, was adamant that no donkey was going to lead him to his death.

'I'm not going to be killed for something I know naught about,' he declared, his eyes wild and staring up at the roof.

'War will be over in no time; aye, we're on top now and Fritz is on the run back to bloody Berlin where he belongs,' Corporal Woollard intervened. 'You lot, you'll be lucky if you see aught of the war. Might easily be finished, the rate you lot arse about instead of getting on with it.'

Stan Banks watched Corporal Woollard stride away, swinging his arms like he was on the king's birthday parade, and smiled.

'He's a rum bugger, he is. Story is he got blown out of a trench at Mons; bloody great shell landed in the trench and killed everybody but him. All he got were a perforated eardrum; deaf as a gatepost he is, so they sent him here to torture us day and night.'

Thomas baulked at the words and a cold surge of anxiety leapt into his mind. The war mustn't end, not yet; he needed a few more weeks. He wore fear like he wore the shirt on his back – no matter how many times he changed it, it would always sit close, rustling, rubbing and staining.

Some grumbled when they were refused permission to discard the heavy cumbersome greatcoats.

'Let's be having you! I've seen clothes-horses move faster than you lot!' Corporal Woollard roared.

Hot sticky sweat poured from their backs leaving spreading black stains clinging to their shirts and tunics. In single-file they followed the tortuous route along the hedgerow; stumbling and cursing while they attempted to adjust the straps of their fully-laden backpacks to prevent them cutting into their shoulders and drawing blood.

'Fix bayonets!' Corporal Woollard screamed. 'At the double, you lazy bunch of arseholes; charge!' he screamed, obscenities sliding from his mouth like they were greased with dripping.

The men surged forward, shouting and yelling, rifles slung low at their waists. Some fell from exhaustion and Joe Cavanaugh, discovering a way out of unnecessary exertion, took the opportunity of falling with them. NCOs screamed and shouted abuse at them to get to their feet. A piece of tarpaulin stretched over a large hole concealed its existence from the struggling soldiers, and yelling with surprise and fear the troops fell head-first into three feet of muddy water.

'Out, out, move yourselves! Load rifles!' Corporal Woollard yelled. 'I never told you to stop, load on the run, you useless buggers, and you, Cavanaugh, you useless miscreant, I reckon the best part of you ended up squirted on your

46

mother's belly! Come on, move, move!' he screamed repeatedly.

'I can't, I can't go any further,' Cavanaugh moaned, lying face down.

'Can't, what do you mean can't? Am I going deaf or am I hearing voices in my head?' Woollard roared, his face turning scarlet. 'Two of you men, take him by the feet and drag him to the top of the field.'

Leslie Hill led the charge. Like a mad bull he ran hollering and screaming, thrusting and jabbing with his bayonet flashing at an imaginary enemy. Sweat flew from his face in a spray so thick that some men reckoned they saw a rainbow form over his head as he thundered over the green field. A rousing cheer erupted from the men behind, and renewing their efforts they took after the big man. At the top of the field, Hill stood with his chest heaving, his face red and flowing with sweat. He stood erect, with his rifle by his side, and the men took their dressing from him, waiting in columns of threes. Every man had passed the test.

'Well done, Private Hill, we might make a soldier of you yet,' Corporal Woollard grinned.

'Thank you, Corporal, it's very kind of you to mention it,' Hill answered shyly.

Hill, from a small village outside Northampton called Duston, had spent his working life in a small printing company as a typesetter. Although a big man with a heart to match and of great strength, he possessed a mild manner until aroused. He was one of the breed looking forward to the war out of boredom, and with a zest for excitement he felt the need to test himself under

47

fire. With a feisty wife half his size, he failed to mention to anyone that he was also severely henpecked at home. He also failed to mention that he harboured a lifetime of hankering to join a travelling circus as a lion tamer.

By now, the army had finally succeeded in re-building and moulding the men into a reasonable semblance of militia fit for the trenches of France. They were now pliant and totally sub-servient, and the constant humiliation and use of indecent language had stripped away their pride and reduced them to a condition in which they were amenable to any command.

Thomas revelled in the fact he had successfully managed to remain impartial to the remainder of the men, apart from the effervescent Stan Banks from Liverpool. Yet unselfishly he assisted Thomas with everything connected to army life, aware he hid a dark secret. He never probed or asked awkward questions. Most nights he slipped silently from his bed and threw the thin blankets back over Thomas's shaking and trembling body, then placed a comforting hand on Thomas's shoulder and waited until the trembling stopped.

Finally the training came to an end and the men were guaranteed to take orders without thought, which ordained them to be passed as 'trained'. It was the last week in October, and lawyers, cobblers, bakers, thieves and rogues were shaped into a fighting force ready for the worst the war might throw at them. The training, coupled with the Spartan lifestyle, had made Thomas lean and muscular, and he was no longer mistaken for a boy. He

48

had become a man before his time: an immature man, maybe, who would never know the dis-appointments of boyhood or experience the frailties of growing into manhood. He held himself erect with a self-assured confidence that matched the other men, and with unashamed pride revelled in the knowledge that they addressed him as they would any other grown man. He listened and glowed with pleasure when they told him of their families, the names of their children and where they were born. Not least, of their hopes and aspirations if they survived the horrible burden of living through the war.

'Hey, lad, you don't know how bloody lucky you are, raised in an orphanage myself, hard times they were, I can tell you. Life in the army is a bloody picnic,' Thomas lied bravely, when questioned about his background. When they asked him what he wanted from life, he didn't tell them he wanted to die.

The following day he was told Corporal Wool-lard wanted to see him, his face paled and fear darted into his chest. With a fearful expectation he straightened his cap and swallowed before rapping on the office door and waiting at attention. An orderly appeared, stared at him like he had the plague and ushered him into the small room.

'Stand easy, Private Elkin. I've been handed a letter from your parents, lad. Seems it's been lost in the post for some time,' he said, his eyes boring into Thomas's face. 'They want to know why you haven't written in all the time you've been here. They also make reference to your fifteen-year-old brother, Thomas. They say he's missing, pre-

49

sumed drowned on the day you left to join us. Seems a strange set of affairs after your insistence you were raised in an orphanage. Explain, lad, in your own time.'

Corporal Woollard sank back into the chair and stretched out his legs, his eyes probing Thomas's face.

Time came to a standstill, Thomas felt his breathing increase and the blood pound into his temples. At last his deception was over and he would go to the hangman as guilty as the day is long. He opened his mouth to speak but dryness welded his lips together. Distraught, he pushed his tongue between them in a vain effort to prize them apart. For what seemed an eternity, words failed to come, then, suddenly, he began to stutter and stammer words that Corporal Woollard failed to understand.

'Settle down, lad, you're finished with the army. I believe you are Thomas, and maybe your brother's deserted and you are taking his place, I don't know for sure. Best take your uniform and kit to the stores and return home, lad. The police will want a word with you. I'll speak with the commanding officer later,' he said.

'No!' Thomas cried, his nerve starting to crack as a paralysing terror gripped his body. 'I'm a soldier ready to fight. I'll not go back, you can't make me. I want to stay with the rest of the men.'

Woollard watched his eyes, devoid of compassion or anger. In the past he'd often turned a blind eye to under-age boys looking for excitement. Morris, Earnshaw, White, Malpas, Goode; the names splattered into his brain. All brave young men who came like lions and ended up like sheep, screaming for their mothers when the first salvo poured into their trenches. Most ended up shovelled into sandbags and dropped into a communal burial pit.

'Nay, it can't be done, lad, I'm sorry. Come on, I'll give you a hand.'

A low moan escaped from Thomas's mouth, beads of perspiration formed on his upper lip. He was surrounded by barriers closing in tighter and tighter until his chest heaved for release. He backed away towards the door, his breath froze in his lungs and tears blurred his vision. His hand reached for the door handle. For a second he felt foolish and wiped his face with the back of his hand. The door swung open taking him by surprise and he stumbled outside.

'Don't be stupid, lad, stay where you are. That's an order!' Woollard called.

Fear rammed into Thomas's mind like a cannon shot and exploded, sending a sensation of pins and needles coursing through his legs. In blind panic he turned and ran, pursued by Corporal Woollard, his breath mixed with sobs rasping and bubbling from his chest. Between the huts he ran absent of any sense of direction, and headed towards the road bordering the square. In the background he heard the rattle of the cook's lorry returning from the stores laden with heavy sacks of porridge and he slowed to a trot. Corporal Woollard reached out. He ducked and twisted to avoid the outstretched hands and watched in horror as the corporal fell beneath the front wheels. The cook, white-faced, pushed down hard on the brakes too late. When the lorry finally drew to a stop, Corporal Woollard lay motionless in a pool of blood.

'Bloody hell, bloody hell, I couldn't stop! Where did he come from, for Chrissake, the deaf bastard? You'll tell them up there it were an accident, won't you?' the cook cried, staring at the crushed remains of Corporal Woollard's head.

Thomas gulped, feeling no sensation of remorse, only a comforting moment of respite.

'Aye, I will that, lad, have no fear. I saw it with my own eyes; it was definitely an accident,' Thomas mumbled, picking up the letter Woollard had dropped and slipping it into his pocket.

Later that afternoon, they marched a nervous Thomas before Colonel Felce to verify the cook's version of the accident. There was no mention of the letter. When Colonel Felce dismissed him he found a quiet spot behind the latrines and fought to restrain the pent-up feelings torturing his insides.

Chapter Five

At last civilians became soldiers, and in the eyes of the army they had earned the right to be called men. Ten weeks of torture, degradation, abuse and near abandonment of life itself had finally drawn to a welcome conclusion. Some, so dazed by the perpetual brainwashing, believed the only time the sky was blue was when someone with stripes on

52

his arm told them so. Yet by this time they had been welded together into a fine body of men, with each believing himself equal to at least three Germans. On the parade ground they waited proudly to be transported to the nearest railway station for departure to Folkestone and then France.

'Right, you horrible lot, seems Fritz isn't ready for you just yet, and due to a lack of transport to France you have been granted five days extra leave,' the ginger-haired sergeant bellowed. 'After which you will make your way to Folkestone; rail passes are available at headquarters.'

Thomas happily left Catterick and headed for Liverpool with his friend and self-appointed mentor Stan Banks. Now they were free to enjoy five days of liberty before leaving for France and whatever the gods held in store for them.

For ten weeks he'd survived with men who'd never questioned or resented his presence while they prepared for war. Like them he too was a soldier trained to kill people: people he'd never met, people who had done him no harm and probably never would nor even wanted to. All that remained for him to do now was to devise a means of ending his life by his own hand. In a moment of childishness, he clamped his eyes shut and wished he was going home to Ruby.

In the home of Stan Banks he was welcomed as a hero for no other reason than being under their roof and wearing the same uniform as their son. Silas Banks called him a southern 'scally' and watched him scoff three plates of scouse, a Liverpool dish made with chopped meat, potatoes, onions, carrots, tomatoes and celery, with a bay leaf added for taste. Molly, Stan's seventeen-year-old sister, found it difficult to tear her eyes away from him and made him nervous. He knew nothing of women nor showed the slightest interest in their existence. At mealtimes, Mrs Banks continually tapped the back of Molly's head and told her to stop staring.

'It's rude to stare, Molly, mind your manners,' she said, and kissed Thomas on the cheek just to tease her. Molly threw down her spoon and ran upstairs, shrieking with anger.

If they mourned the death of Eli they kept it to themselves, his name was never mentioned in Thomas's presence. With the fuel business being so close to the Liverpool docks it provided Silas with the opportunity to make a good living, supplying the dockworkers with coal and logs to keep the fires burning throughout the cold winters, and at mealtimes the table was always full. As a family they were content, good-humoured and quick-witted with a strong sense of fun synonymous with the people of Liverpool, who invariably discovered an amusing side to the idiosyncrasies of life.

Only on one occasion did Thomas witness a form of anger in the house: the time Stan misguidedly brought home a newspaper extolling the horrors of the war in Europe splashed across the front page.

'Get that rubbish out of the house, lad,' his father seethed. 'I'll not be a party to lies and propaganda from some bloody reporter who's never fired a bloody bullet in his life,' he said, snatching the paper and tearing it to pieces.

Already he'd lost one son and he didn't relish the fact that the war now had its claws into another.

On Saturday night, two days before they were due to leave for Folkestone, Thomas insisted he treat the Banks family to the City Picture House on Lime Street to see a Charlie Chaplin film. Dressed in their Sunday best, they sat in the circle surrounded by decorated plasterwork overlooking the dark oak-panelled orchestra pit, and laughed and cried at the little tramp. Molly embarrassed him by holding his hand all through the performance and refused to let it go even when the show came to a close. Contrary to what Molly thought, he was afraid of her and her advances and didn't know how to respond when she touched him in places she shouldn't, causing him to jerk up in surprise and blush a deep red. It was a woman who had been partly responsible for Archie's death and the reason for him being on the run to escape the hangman's rope. Women, he thought, were best left alone until he knew what they were for.

Sadly the five days drew to a close all too quickly, the time to leave arrived. The following morning he and Stan left quietly without waking anyone or saying goodbye and made their way to the railway station. On the kitchen table Thomas left a slip of paper leaning against an empty milk bottle. It read simply, Thank you.

Such was the wonder in his eyes that he stood with childish simplicity staring at the gleaming black locomotives panting on the silver lines at Lime Street railway station, their tenders piled high with shiny black coal waiting to gorge the hungry red-hot boiler into hot scalding steam. The station was a hive of activity crammed full of frowning soldiers with sagging shoulders and doleful eyes. Row after row of tearful women wearing pastel dresses and carrying colourful parasols thronged the platform alongside freshly-painted railway coaches. Coach windows dropped open and men thrust out their heads, allowing wives, sweethearts and well-wishing families to hold them close for perhaps the last time. Throughout the whole of the station the sweet cloying smell of steam gelled with oil and grease ready to crank up the huge iron wheels attacked the senses. Then, one after another the sound of carriage doors slamming shut could be heard like the clacking of a falling row of dominoes; whistles shrieked and shrilled like a horde of imprisoned spirits seeking freedom, signalling the departure of the railed giants. People moved from a walk to a trot in a futile attempt to keep abreast of the coaches for one last glimpse of a loved one. Soon they became no more than tiny specks trailing in the distance as the train picked up steam and swiftly departed from the station, conveying unwilling passengers to a war most didn't want. Embroidered handkerchiefs fluttered from pale, elegant wrists waving the final farewell, then dabbed away moist tears from carefully mascara-brushed eyes.

'Change at Manchester for London and Folkestone,' the platform officer said, slamming the door shut. Twelve soldiers in full kit scrambled swearing and cursing into a crammed compartment designed for six.

'The British Army knows how to treat its

soldiers,' someone complained. 'If there are any generals present, best get off your arse and give me your seat, me bloody legs are killing me.'

'Aye, lad, you'll not see them anywhere near a bloody Tommy. They'll be sitting on their fat arses miles behind the lines, drinking fine wine and filling their stupid faces,' another voice said.

The crowded coach rocked and swayed, billowing clouds of acrid cigarette smoke tortured Thomas's eyes until they smarted red raw. He baulked at the smell of heaving bodies sweating and farting accompanied by loud raucous remarks offending his ears, and felt his temper shorten. Thankfully, the journey was short and quickly over.

At Manchester the cafeteria did a brisk trade and after twenty minutes spent queuing a hot, sweet mug of tea and a week-old pork pie full of gristle quickly improved his demeanour. Further down the platform he listened enthralled to the band of the Grenadier Guards playing *It's a Long Way to Tipperary*, and soldiers joined in. With their arms wrapped around each other's shoulders in a display of patriotic fervour, they drowned out the hissing sound of the waiting trains. Thomas recognised the time at once – the men in the village pub always sang the song just before closing time – and he gazed in awe at the bandsmen's resplendent scarlet and gold uniform and huge bearskin Busbies. He'd never heard a military band before; the sound stirred him to the marrow of his bones and he stood erect and proud in his uniform.

Then, without warning, the band droned to a halt and an eerie quietness descended over the station; people stood as though frozen in time. The only audible sound came from the gentle rustling of starched dresses and squeaking leather shoes, as dozens of uniformed nurses, with their warm smiles fixed firmly on their faces, walked quickly and efficiently to meet the arriving train easing slowly into the platform with a loud hiss of escaping steam. Some pushed empty invalid chairs; others carried crutches and walking sticks. Porters moved hurriedly along the length of the train, pulling open carriage doors and disappearing momentarily in clouds of white steam escaping from the engine's pressure relief valves. For several seconds time stood still, onlookers waited expectantly and wondering: no one stirred until the nurses stepped forward. The first man helped from the carriage had his khaki trousers tied and folded above the knees. A gasp rose from the silent crowd as another man with only one leg and his arm in a sling hopped unassisted onto the platform, followed by another. One man lost his footing and crashed heavily onto the wet concrete station floor without a murmur of complaint. He lay on the cold platform, his face disfigured and expressionless save for the haunted eyes that had witnessed something man was not born to see. Two porters rushed forward to pick him up, and a nurse carrying a wooden crutch chastised him in a gentle voice.

'You have nothing to feel embarrassed about, young man,' she said softly. 'You have done your duty to your country with courage and dignity, and as harsh as it may sound, you must now come to terms with the fact that you have lost a leg and live your life accordingly. May God forever bless you, and all those like you.'

They came with their broken and bleeding bodies rapidly filling the platform. Wounded and dismembered men with bloodstained bandages wrapped tightly around their faces were slumped into invalid chairs; others stood blind, waiting to be guided in the right direction. Nurses smiled and gently took them by the arms. Men confronted by the sight of such appalling injuries watched wide-eyed in disbelief. Women stood in the crowd with their hands over their mouths, some so overcome they crumpled and fainted. Thomas stood white-faced, his mouth hanging open in shock at the sight of over two hundred men bent and maimed for life, hobbling awkwardly in a line of deathly silence. Still they came, on sticks and crutches or were wheeled with their heads slumped loose on their chests. Staring hollow-eyed, they lowered their heads as if ashamed of being seen in such a condition. There was no ring of feet or swing of shoulders; they came dry-eyed and without complaint, like soldiers who had performed their duty to the best of their ability. The fine gallant young men of England were coming home, broken and shattered, the cream of a generation lost forever in a conflict, the reason for which hardly anyone understood. Amidst the horrific scene, someone clapped. The sound echoed and resounded through the hushed station. Another joined in, and then another, and then the applause grew to a great crescendo drowning out all other sounds. The band struck up with Pack up your Troubles. Men whistled and cheered and raised their hats; women stepped forward to place kisses on the mutilated and startled faces. Britain's heroes were returning home.

'All aboard.'

Stan grabbed Thomas and the pair of them rushed to get a seat, but it was too late: they would have to stand like sardines crammed into a tin.

Chapter Six

Sergeant Cromwell Bull waited stiff at attention for them at Folkestone railway station. He was a small man with a withering look and manic ice-blue eyes, said to be capable of turning the bravest of the brave into stone faster than Medusa herself. When he walked his body jerked, like his bones were disjointed, and a rumour went round that he never went on parade on account that he couldn't march in step, and spent the time lecturing defaulters in the guard-house. In another life he'd been a gentle man, living quietly on the outskirts of a small town in North Yorkshire, repairing bicycles for a living. On Sundays, he acted as head bell-ringer in a small church, and led the church choir with a voice capable of uplifting even the coldest heart.

'My name is Sergeant Bull,' he said, staring along the ranks, 'and for your sins you belong to me; lock, stock and barrel. Do as I say and we will get along fine; disobey me and I'll have your guts for bicycle clips.'

Under the cold scrutinising glare, Stan Banks's smirk slipped from his face quicker than a striking snake.

'Har-tenshun. Move to the left in columns of fours, a left hun, habuy the right, haquick ha-march!' Sergeant Bull screamed. 'Pick it up there, you horrible, dirty little man. Next time you have a wash, remember to use water.'

Stan Banks gulped and swung his arms like they'd been lubricated with a gallon of axle grease.

Before lights out they were ordered into lines of threes for a visit from a medical officer.

'Keep your wedding tackle in your trousers,' he warned them. 'Gonorrhoea is rife in France for obvious reasons; anyone contracting venereal diseases will be punished and incur loss of pay. Married men's allowances will be stopped for the duration of the disease, and your wives will probably guess the reason why.'

Thomas listened with a puzzled look on his face, uncertain whether he should let anger or fear take control. From the corner of his eye, Stan watched him with a small smile playing on his lips and said nothing.

That night Thomas raised his rifle and peered down the barrel. Satisfied it was sufficiently clean to pass muster at morning inspection, he rammed home the bolt and leaned the weapon in the rack. With his legs astride his narrow bed, he watched his comrades, their faces wrapped in frowns and ever-deepening creases, struggle with the chore of writing home to their nearest and dearest. Some of the men with a more apprehensive nature, acting on advice from Sergeant Bull, took the precaution of making out a will and called out for payment from those who owed them money. Shifting his mind away from heated arguments of a fiscal nature, he recalled it had been less than three months since he'd left his village. With his lips pressed tight, he tamped down the rising urge of melancholy. His sixteenth birthday had passed unnoticed two weeks previously.

More pressing were the pretence and continual lies that had become a perpetual unwanted fragment of his existence, methodically squeezing and choking the life from his soul. Each time he opened his mouth to utter words that concerned his past, only nonsense immersed in foolishness tumbled out. It seemed past events had cruelly discarded the power of truth.

'Hey, lad, are you not writing to anyone? Might be your last chance,' Stan called.

'Nobody to write to: I'm an orphan. I told you once,' he lied, cringing inwardly.

'That's right, lad, so you did, I'd forgotten. Why don't you write to Molly? She'd like that; I've loads of paper and you can borrow my pencil. Hey, lad, you can write can't you?'

Thomas smiled a sad smile. He could think of no good reason, nor had the faintest desire, to write to Molly. Regardless of how attractive she was, her crush would be short-lived and soon pass when another came along. Still, he was sensible enough to know Stan would never relinquish his constant badgering until he finally agreed. Stan's attitude, at times, seemed almost paternal; forever fussing and worrying as if he were a small uneducated child. Occasionally Thomas smiled and went along with it for the sake of peace and quiet. Other times, he ignored his advice and longed for solitude.

'Maybe I'll drop a line to Ruby,' he blurted out.

Stan Banks jerked his head upwards, his eyes widened and Thomas immediately realised he'd just committed a grave error.

'Ruby? You never mentioned her before, you dark horse. Talk about still waters.' Stan looked eagerly around the room for support. 'Did you hear that? Archie's got a young lass called Ruby.'

Thomas glanced away and his heart sank – there was no escape.

'Come on, Archie, what's she like, does she have big boobies?' Robert McCaughey called out, running his hands over his chest.

'Have you got a picture? Come on, lad, let's have a look, pass it round,' John Felce laughed.

Thomas sensed his face glow red at his shameless lying and, turning his head to avoid their stares, cringed, wishing he'd remained quiet. Piece by piece his life was slowly turning into a never-ending uncontrollable nightmare.

'Take no notice, Archie. Going home to Ruby, that's all you need to think about, lad. Going home to Ruby,' Ian Lewis called out.

The following morning at nine-thirty, accompanied by a Highland regiment in swaying kilts and skirling pipes, the company marched proudly down the steep, narrow path from the cliffs to Folkestone docks. Streets full of backslapping well-wishers cheered and pretty girls threw kisses from crowded windows. Offshore the men saw the destroyer escort belching black smoke and waiting at anchor, the first sign of the insecurities of war.

Bare-arsed jocks, the men called the Highlanders.

'Always shitting where they shouldn't, and too lazy to drop their trousers. That's why they wear them fancy-coloured skirts with no knickers,' someone from the rear cackled.

At the overcrowded dockside the mood swiftly changed and men stood subdued, waiting to be loaded aboard dull grey-painted channel steamers swaying and rolling in a heavy swell. Nearby, separate from the others, a group of soldiers waited morosely to be returned to the front line after a spell of home leave. Thomas watched them through puzzled eyes, immediately struck by their untidy appearance. Some wore grubby, matted sheepskin coats, some army-issue greatcoats with the skirts, casually hacked off for manoeuvrability in the trenches, hanging in tatters. The equipment strapped to their shoulders seemed dull and unpolished, and worn with little concern for any form of military correctness. Rifles, with bolts and muzzles wrapped and tightly-bound with oily rags, lay scattered in nonchalant disarray on the ground. Each face seemed leaner than the next, taut and stretched to the limit. Even after two weeks home leave their eyes held a peculiar look: strangely worn, yet determined, almost barbaric. Beneath the grotesque array of clothing, their bodies were hard and tireless. They were like beasts ready to go about their business because they had been told to and it had to be done. Before

64

the call came to board, Thomas's mind had already left England.

And then, as though by a silent order, screaming NCOs hurled incoherent commands and sent worried men shuffling obediently into an orderly military scramble. Grey-faced and cursing beneath their breath, they allowed themselves to be herded aboard the SS *Empress Queen*, a paddle steamer capable of carrying over two thousand troops. Their destination, Boulogne, France, and for ten miserable hours the men suffered the curse of seasickness, hurling their insides over the side. With blood-drained faces they prayed to God for a quick release from the misery of the black, churning waters.

Thomas ate enough cold bully beef sandwiches for three men and drank hot, sweet tea until he could drink no more. Unaffected by the never-ending rise and dipping of the *Empress Queen*, he found a warm spot in a converted saloon and sat next to a gangly youth wearing wire spectacles. The youth never spoke nor offered any form of acknowledgement. His cheeks appeared to be a breeding ground for large, red spots with yellow purulent heads. Thomas shrugged, closed his eyes and rode the angry heaving waters of the English Channel and dreamed his way to a hopeless oblivion.

At Boulogne, under a misty dusk he was pushed and propelled forward by the surging wave of troops impatiently disembarking from the ever-plunging hull of the *Empress Queen*. Grateful to be on terra firma, warm blood seeped into bloodless faces and chased away the ghostly white pallor,

65

and men exhaled with deep breaths on lighted cigarettes or sucked noisily on charred pipes.

'Stone the bleedin' crows, you can stick that for a larf. I reckon Davy Jones has got half me bleedin' insides,' a cockney voice chirped.

A jumble of emotions rattled the insides of Thomas's skull and he gripped his rifle tighter, afraid it might tumble from his shaking hands. Officers screamed and hollered orders at thousands of men too confused to realise whether they were meant for them or others, and failed to respond. Wild-eyed NCOs with strange looks on their faces stalked the columns like predators, pushing and prodding bewildered soldiers into line. Suddenly, from nowhere, boys as young as seven or eight approached in hordes, and dodging between the ranks extolled the virtues of their sisters and sometimes even their own mothers.

'You come now, mister, not take long for jig-a-jig. She very good in bed, mister, very cheap for Englishman, only pennies,' they cried, tugging at sleeves and flapping tunics.

Thomas swayed on the edge of nowhere and shivered in disbelief. The sight, the sound, the smell, in its infinite horror, smashed through his weakened defences and lodged in his soul, as though it might leave him scarred for eternity. Men closed their minds and refused to acknowledge what their eyes revealed – it must be the result of a bad Channel crossing they whispered in shock. Others timidly lit cigarette after cigarette with shaking hands and gazed down with their mouths hanging open in silent shock, and refused to accept what their eyes showed them.

Thousands upon thousands of soldiers milled and jostled around row after row of tents. In the cold failing watery light of evening, men stripped to the waist heaved and cursed, knee-deep in clinging mud, while positioning huge barrage guns ready for limber to the front line. Makeshift field hospitals struggled to treat the never-ending queues of gassed men brought from the front, standing blindly with their hands resting on the shoulder of the man in front. Score upon score of men minus limbs lay on makeshift stretchers, moaning forlornly, while others screamed in pain or mumbled to an absent God for the quick relief of death. All the time dead-eyed stretcher-bearers hurried to and fro, quickly loading the dead onto horse-drawn carts for a mass burial somewhere on the other side of the woods.

'Bloody hell, seems they spend more time burying the dead than fighting,' Ian Lewis said nervously.

Thomas turned at the remark, grateful for any kind of contact with the living, and caught Stan Banks staring at him through frightened eyes. He nodded and gave a small smile. Stan's expression never faltered, then his mouth twitched and Thomas couldn't distinguish whether the movement represented a smile or a look of sheer terror.

Away in the distance from the rows of tents and corralled in a quadrangle of ropes, five thousand snorting and whinnying horses from an artillery division pranced nervously. Covered in steaming foam, they produced forty tons of manure daily, providing an ideal breeding ground for swarms of huge flies. Thomas had never seen so many horses in his life, and he covered his mouth to escape the nauseating stench.

Disillusioned and tormented, the chilling shock of their surroundings lingered and haunted the soldiers' minds, and they became jittery and shaky. Continual vomiting became commonplace. Some produced crucifixes and made the sign of the cross while pleading with God to make things right. As usual he never listened. Everything remained as it had always been. When darkness fell the horizon lit up with intermittent red, orange and vivid yellow gun flashes, like a far-off firework display, and men watched from the corners of their eyes with fidgeting minds and paper-dry lips.

By now the complement of Yorkshire Rifles numbered in excess of nine-hundred-and-fifty men: almost a full battalion. Sergeant Bull said they were to await orders before being sent where they were most needed. Thomas, Stan, Robert McCaughey and Ian Lewis huddled together and decided to make a pact.

'We'll stick together us four, look out for each other, and God willing, we might come out of this hell in one piece,' Robert McCaughey said, aware the worst was yet to come.

The following morning it sheeted down with cold rain and the men queued in silence to draw rations of tea, biscuits, jam and sugar. An air of discontent, which didn't seem normal, mixed with disillusionment – mild rebellion, even – threw its mind-disturbing canopy over the men. Grouped together for warmth, they spoke of mutiny or at least of running away to somewhere safe.

'And where the hell do you think you're going to bloody run to?' Robert McCaughey growled.

'Anywhere, for Chrissake, I've had enough; bloody cattle get treated better than us. Fuck Kitchener and his bloody big pointing finger,' a skinny man with gimlet eyes whined.

'Right, men, pay attention!' Sergeant Bull roared the following day. 'We are moving to place called Etaples where for the next five days you are going to be put through a training routine harsher than anything you've ever endured in the past, in preparation for life at the front. Get stuck in, listen and learn.'

Under sleeting rain they were transported to a huge grassless field of sand holding enough tents to house one hundred thousand soldiers. And so began a five-day training regime so harsh that no one thought they would have the strength to finish. The instructors wore yellow armbands and were nicknamed Canaries. They made the late Corporal Woollard seem like the Sugar Plum Fairy. The routine was fixed: breakfast at five-forty-five in the morning, at seven the training began, until seven at night. At the end of the day, after last post was blown, the sound of wailing men swirled over the encampment. In a fierce vindictive atmosphere, they were drilled and taught unarmed combat with boots, teeth and knees, followed by bayonet training and hill running while carrying supplementary kit.

Memories of Catterick were replaced with a vicious and barbaric savagery unheard of in England as men sneered and snarled through the

69

stench of their own sweat and filth. Tempers became short fuses, burning rapidly and ready to explode. Gradually complaints disappeared and men's eyes stared a terrible, unnatural look, incomprehensible, like the eyes of a dead rabbit. Now they took on a tense and tetchy attitude, and slowly a hatred for the enemy who had brought them to this place festered inside their minds, consuming their aches and pains. Thomas recalled the taut faces of the soldiers on the dockside at Folkestone. Perhaps they were no longer men, just something put together merely to play out an act of warfare.

'War is about killing, nothing else, remember that. There is no honour or glory in dying, there is only death and eternal damnation,' a whippet-thin sergeant told them. 'Train hard, fight easy; train easy, fight hard and die quickly – the choice is yours. The only way to win this war is to kill the Germans, every bloody one of the bastards.'

Thomas listened, his expression set in stone. His natural inclination was to fight back against the cruelty of war, yet he knew that of all the men present only he deserved to be punished. When the time presented itself he would seek out death until it stared him in the face and embraced his very soul; he would lean towards it, beckon it, until he encountered the eternal damnation the whippet-thin sergeant had mentioned. Now for the first time in weeks he felt calm and in total command of his senses; all that mattered was for him to formulate a simple plan to bring about his death.

By the last day, men were on the verge of refusing the gruelling tasks set them on the grounds of cruelty.

'Come on, move!' the instructors screamed. 'This is a picnic compared to the real thing. If you last a week it will be a bloody miracle.'

At last, faced with the impossibility of sustaining even the slightest hint of dignity in a situation so degrading, the men compensated their misery with bouts of vulgar humour aimed at their tormentors. A few responded by not admitting any humiliation.

At last it was over, their torment complete. Shortly after making their way into the cathedral city of Rouen, news filtered through that three of their battalion had purposely shot themselves in the foot in the hope of repatriation back to Blighty. Rumours ran rife they were to be executed for cowardice.

'Seems a waste of bloody life,' Stan grumbled to Thomas, 'bringing the poor buggers all this way to shoot them. Who the bloody hell do they think they are? Shooting poor sods because they're scared shitless – nowt wrong in being scared. I've shit enough bricks in the past hour to rebuild Liverpool.'

A roar of laughter rang out and frayed nerves settled for a fleeting moment of respite.

'I'll have no more of that kind of talk, Banks; keep them thoughts to yourself in future,' Sergeant Bull snapped at him.

Stan Banks's furious gaze drifted across to the sergeant; he wanted to tell him what he thought of him. Instead, he stared down at his mud-encrusted boots – one had a split toecap and both

71

feet felt like a fire had been lit under them. A shadow flitted across his face, he was frightened and his insides continually turned to water at the sound of the guns; and to make matters even worse, the feeling of fear irritated him. He found it irrational to think that when the time came he wouldn't be able to function as a soldier. His natural impulse was to dismiss the thought, yet no matter how hard he tried, the feeling wouldn't go away. In disgust he clicked his teeth in the dim light and hummed a tune; it didn't help. Other times while in the company of other men, he took great care to keep his hands out of sight, lest they noticed the sporadic trembling and shunned him. Soldiers felt uncomfortable in the company of men who displayed the slightest outward signs of fear; they believed it brought bad luck, and moved away to the sanctuary of those who solidly held their fear in check. He would fight, he promised himself that, and they would never have reason to label him a coward. All he needed was some means of occupying his mind, something that would help to keep him calm and distracted until his nerves settled. He thought of Archie. Maybe if he continued to watch over him like he did at Catterick, dedicate himself and his time to his well-being, there was a distinct possibility it might disrupt his own doubts and distract him from his own fears. Not for a moment did he consider himself a better man than Archie, nor Archie a better man than he. Deep down he admired him for his strength and fortitude. With this hopeless thought in mind, he clasped his hands together and waited for the trembling to stop.

It is said that hope gives the soul cause to rest, yet Rouen proved to be no different from Boulogne, except they were drawing closer to the front and the big guns sounded louder and more threatening. There was a risk that things would run out of control and men eyed each other, hopefully seeking a tiny particle of comfort, a reassuring smile, even a wink. On occasion fights broke out and Sergeant Bull took it upon himself to break them up by firing over their heads. The horse-drawn carts of dead bodies multiplied tenfold, and men no longer bothered to turn and look the other way. Life flourished for the sake of death and men's minds became dry and bleached, fit only for orders.

Now with a slavish obedience to orders they moved on to Amiens and the River Somme. Those who thought conditions might improve were quickly disappointed, despair ran rampant, morale dropped to an all-time low and no man spoke unless to voice a complaint or a grievance. Hygiene became non-existent, a hot shave a luxury, a bath only a faded memory.

'Get a grip of yourselves and stop whining like big girls; learn to live with the mud and shit around you, the darkness, and trust your instincts to do what is right, because that is the right thing to do,' Sergeant Bull told them in an even voice. 'Look after the man next to you and he will look after you; fight for those around you and they will fight for you. Do I make myself understood?'

Some accepted his advice eagerly; others mumbled under their breath and clamoured for news from home.

'The sergeant's right you know, he knows what he's on about, he does. He's got more balls than Midas had gold,' Leslie Hill said, raking up a low ripple of laughter. 'How about you, Stan, what do you reckon, mate?'

'He can't be right, can he? He's a bloody sergeant for Chrissake, and they're never right. What I don't understand is how he manages to be everywhere at once. You can't have a crap in the middle of the night without him turning up with a handful of paper to wipe your arse on, enough to make a miser leave his gold, he is,' Stan Banks answered, turning the ripple of laughter into hearty guffaws.

Gradually everything smelled of army and the men, with their mysterious ways, learned to bond and pull together as one unit. It seemed a shame that it took a war to give man that which he needed most: love, comradeship and self-respect. Occasionally a passing smile greeted with a broad grin invited good-natured banter, and passing inconveniences were ignored as an everyday part of life. Stan Banks and Leslie Hill became the company's comedians. Hill, with his dour well-meant intentions, became the perfect foil for Banks's rapier-like Liverpool wit. Sergeant Bull looked on with a fatherly contentment at the change in behaviour.

Although the improved attitude affected most, it didn't affect all. Over a period of two days two men went missing at roll call. All the men were aware the punishment for deserting was death by firing squad, yet it seemed to matter little to

74

some when the mind hung by the slenderest of threads. The first was quickly caught and tried and sentenced with the minimum of fuss.

At dawn the following morning the battalion reluctantly lined up to witness the execution. Thomas stood uneasy watching the man sitting in a chair. The accused's eyes rolled like a drunk's, and every muscle in his body trembled and jerked in spasms. Two men told to lash him to the chair with rope struggled with the knots and were eventually ordered by a cavalry captain wearing polished boots and shiny spurs to allow the man to sit freely and await his death. From out of the misty gloom an overweight padre with dark stains down the front of his tunic appeared, slipping and sliding in the mud. With a Bible in one hand he uttered a blessing in a loud falsetto voice in a wasted effort to comfort the man. The accused looked towards him and smiled, the mumbling incantations drowned out by the harsh crack of rifle fire. Each man in the firing squad had been given one bullet, some blank and some live so no one knew for sure whether they had fired the fatal shot. The man, or boy, no more than eighteen years of age, jerked and twitched and blinked. The pale-faced captain in charge gulped and withdrew his pistol, and with an apologetic twist on his face performed the coup de grâce with a shot to the head.

'Best way to go, matey,' a cockney voice said behind Thomas. 'Poor bastard never had a dog's chance of getting out of here alive anyway. Stone the crows, look at the blood! Go down as killed in action he will. Just arrived have you, mate? Don't stand and stare, it won't do you any good. You'll see worse than this at the front. Just move on and forget about it; he's at peace now, God bless him. I'll tell you something though, matey, old Fritz deserts by the hundreds he does. Honest, they all run off over the border to Holland, eh, start a bloody war they do, and then run away. What kind of people are they, eh, you tell me?'

Thomas stayed silent. Tiredness poured over him like a heavy blanket. He needed to sleep. His shoulders slumped, his mind and body empty and hollow, like he'd been squeezed dry by a huge hand. As he turned away to make his way back to his tent Robert McCaughey dropped in beside him.

'Is something bothering you, Archie? You seem a bit distant, lad,' he said, in his soft northern brogue. 'Whatever it is, best get it off your chest while you can. This isn't the place for loneliness, or bottling things up inside.'

Thomas snapped and his temper flared into his face. Weeks of tension had weakened his resolve and his vulnerabilities speared through like nettles under a hot, bright sun.

'I'll thank you to mind your own bloody business. I don't interfere in your life so don't interfere in mine, you bloody great know-all,' he raged, fully aware that it was naked fear of the environment and the uncertainty of his sanity. He'd tried his best to digest the words of Sergeant Bull – he knew they were good words, the right words – yet like everyone else he felt lost, adrift in a situation he didn't know how to handle. For days he had tried pushing everything to one side, but it always slid back worse than before and refused to shift

76

from his mind.

'Aye, lad, I'll do that. You know where I am if you want me,' McCaughey said in the same soft voice with a shake of his head.

Thomas sat apart from the others that night, listening to the sound of the big guns certain each explosion brought them ever nearer. As usual sleep hid its face and refused to come when needed most. Instead, he looked at the men around him, their faces grey and weary, most already resigned to the inevitability of death. Overhead a few solitary stars hung in the black sky and the night air bit cold sending shivers down the spine. Flurries of heavy snow gently drifted to the ground forming a white blanket. In another world it might have been a scene from a Christmas card. All that was missing were rosy-faced children and the sound of carols.

Soon the mud would harden, perhaps making life a little more comfortable by the time they reached the front. The ever-present flashes from the big guns in the distance were now taken for granted, like day following night. Some other poor bastard would be on the receiving end tonight, and his turn would come soon enough. Thomas allowed himself a wan smile and turned away. He harboured no intention of waiting for a lingering painful death in some shithole of a trench.

As time passed by the snowstorm gathered momentum, floating down like a wall of im-penetrable whiteness, and pulling on his greatcoat he left it unbuttoned. A shadow flitted across his heart and he swallowed. He clenched his fists afraid that the next ten minutes wouldn't go ac-

77

cording to his hurriedly concocted plan. It was so easy, all he had to do was walk across the snow-covered field in view of the nervous sentries and wait for the bullet reserved for deserters, and his long wait for death would be granted. Nothing could be simpler, nothing less complicated. With his hands plunged deep into the greatcoat's long pockets, he stepped out onto the mud-rutted fields.

Stan Banks stared like a man under hypnosis and watched him stride out across the open countryside. Holding his breath, he climbed to his feet. Abruptly his mind was hurled into a fever of anxious anticipation. He'd always suspected Thomas held a dark secret, something that should have been buried long ago that was not yet dead. A terrible picture flashed into his mind, and he visualised Thomas lying face down in the falling snow with a bullet lodged in his head. The trembling in his hands started and wouldn't cease, and he almost lost control.

'Deal me out, lads,' he said, allowing the cards to slip through his fingers and nodding to Robert McCaughey to follow him outside.

Out of sight on the perimeter of the tented city nervous picket guards with jerky trigger fingers patrolled vigilantly twenty-four hours a day, with orders to shoot on sight at anything out of the ordinary. Thomas headed directly towards them.

Subjected to sweat intermingled with heavy flakes of melting snow coursing down his face, he tried to push away the fear sticking in his throat like a piece of stale crust. What if the bullet only left him injured? Perhaps they would tend his wound merely for the sake of placing him before a firing squad to act as a deterrent against other would-be deserters.

'Come on, come on,' he gasped, 'surely you can see me now.'

He wanted to sing out, wave his arms and draw attention to himself. Suddenly he felt light-headed, disjointed, the rumble of guns made him feel happy and contented. He started to hum a made-up tune in his head while he walked on a bed of air. Of course he'd hear the crack of the rifle as the bullet travelled to its target: nothing on earth is faster than the speed of sound. He stopped, smiled and loosened the pressure of his gritted teeth, and stretching his arms side-ways, he called out: 'I love you, Archie, I love you.'

'There, look, over there, wait for a gun flash, there, see him?' McCaughey said, staring through the snowstorm. 'Christ, the daft bugger's asking for it, he's as good as dead.'

'We've got to try and stop him,' Stan said, breaking into a trot.

In spite of the cold, he flung his greatcoat and helmet to the floor and ran as fast as the wet snow beneath his feet would allow. From behind, he heard a shout and ignored the sound of air rasping into his burning lungs. Twice he sprawled headfirst into the clinging mud, and twice he pulled himself to his feet and continued after Thomas. At the first crack of a rifle he automatically ducked his head and heard the whine of the bullet pass close by; the second crack was followed by a loud groan. From nowhere two men appeared from out of the snowstorm and wrestled him to the ground.

Twisting his head to prevent the mud clogging his nose and mouth, he cried out, 'Stop him, he's a chronic sleepwalker, he doesn't know what he's doing.' It was the only thing he could think of to say.

'Och, laddie, is that reet? Well your other wee friend will never know that, will he? He's back there wi a bullet in the back of his head,' the tall Highlander said. 'Get back to your lines, we'll deal with this, and take your sleepwalking friend wi you. You dinna know how lucky you are, you Sassenach bastard.'

Thomas chewed at his bottom lip, the anger inside him burning white-hot. Why the hell had Banks and McCaughey followed him? If they hadn't interfered he might have been dead by now and it would be over. He shot Stan a glazed look of naked hatred and pushed him to one side before making his way back to the lines. A few yards away Robert McCaughey lay with his face looking up at the stars, his open eyes staring blankly into the harsh dark night, Stan dropped to his knees and cradled the shattered head in his hands. Remains of brain and skull lay in a pool of bloodstained snow, yet still McCaughey refused to die. Raising his head in his arms, Stan looked down at the pleading eyes struggling feebly to cling to life, and he spoke gentle words that meant nothing nor gave any hope of survival. Seconds later, the writhing body jerked and lay still. Thomas heard the low moan escape from Stan's lips and stared vacantly out over the blanket of snow covering the stark countryside. He did not look down at the twisted face buried in a puddle of dirty brown slush turning blood red, his anger prevented it.

Stan struggled to his feet, his gaze boring into Thomas's face. Rage gushed from the bowels of his body. He wanted to smash his fist into his face and beat him to a pulp. At that moment he hated him. He considered him an insipid fool, a dullard with an unsound mind that possessed no feelings for anyone but himself. The thought unnerved him. He had his own malignant spirits constantly tormenting him to contend with. Satisfied the Scottish guards were out of sight and no longer able to control his rage, he turned and faced Thomas, and sent his fist into the blank unflinching face.

'There's something fucking weird about you, Archie Elkin, or whatever your fucking name is, and I want nowt to do with you anymore. You're a bloody jinx. First Corporal Woollard, now Robert,' he said gasping for breath. 'We made an agreement to look out for each other and already you're responsible for Robert's death. What the bloody hell were you doing walking away in the first place? How many other poor buggers have died because of your stupidity?'

Thomas climbed to his feet, and wiped the streaks of mud and blood from his expressionless face. He shared Stan's fortitude, but not for the death or love of Robert – Stan was right, he felt only for himself.

'I never asked you to follow me, and I'll thank you to keep your nose out of my life in future,' he sneered. 'I'm sick of your interfering, I'm sick of your bloody lies and bullshit. Just piss off and leave me alone.'

81

He felt his breath accelerate. Stan treated him like a pet Cocker Spaniel, babying and fussing over him twenty-four hours a day. He needed to find contentment in the solitude of his own company and God only knows that was hard enough, he had learned that deep down he struggled to suffer the intense grip of loneliness.

Robert McCaughey's death was noted as 'shot while deserting'. Stan asked Sergeant Bull permission to bury Robert somewhere he might be found later. They found a spot by a copse of elms where Sergeant Bull solemnly spoke the right words over his grave. Afterwards Stan lost no time in telling the rest of his company what had really happened, and with sneering stares they quickly turned their backs on Thomas. Their contempt rose to the surface of their skin and lay bare, if they had been elsewhere Thomas might have found a bayonet pushed into his gut and left to die in agony. For the time being, however, Stan chose not to tell Sergeant Bull the real reason for Robert's death. The time would come when he would extract retribution in his own way, if only to salvage his own conscience.

Inclement weather rarely stops soldiers from soldiering and although the snow fell heavier the following day, Sergeant Bull marched each man fit enough to carry a rifle out for rifle practice. Wet, slushy mud invaded every crevice of their bodies and clothing, trying its damndest to freeze and make them even more uncomfortable. With desperate raw courage and numb with cold they fumbled with stiffened fingers to fill the ammunition magazines, frequently cursing like cow herders when bullets slipped from their hands and disappeared into the quagmire swirling around their ankles.

'I'll shoot the next man who drops his ammunition in the mud,' Sergeant Bull threatened. 'Fritz won't be waiting for you to fool around scratching your arses. He'll have his bayonet stuck in your guts within seconds. Now, listen to me, the regiment needs four snipers for special training. There will be a shoot-off for all those interested in crawling through No Man's Land up to your ears in shit and muck, looking for enemy machine-gunners to kill before they kill you.'

Heads turned and nodded with quizzical looks, and half-a-dozen stepped tentatively forward followed by approximately forty more, Thomas and Stan Banks included. Thomas, already easily the best shot in the regiment, was pulled to one side immediately. Two hours later, he was joined by three others. To his disappointment Stan Banks had made it through, along with Leslie Hill from Northampton and Neil Letts from Harrogate.

'Right, get your kit packed. Tomorrow you'll be taken to the 1st Army sniping school at Linghem, near Aire, north of here,' Sergeant Bull informed them.

That night Stan Banks held court to those who would listen to him in the mess tent next to a field kitchen, sitting on a table with his legs resting on a broken chair he gave his account of Robert Mc-Caughey's death for the fourth time in as many days.

'Archie bloody Elkin, bloody well deserting he was, as plain as the nose on your face. We should

83

have let the bastard go. Instead, poor old Robert took a bullet meant for him while trying to save him,' Stan Banks sneered.

'Perhaps he was just plain scared, like the rest of us,' someone said. 'He's not a bad lad.'

'Aye, there's not a man here who doesn't shit his pants when he hears them bloody big guns,' another voice called.

'Yeah, well I reckon he's got a bloody death wish,' Stan Banks said scratching the back of his neck.

Chapter Seven

For the first time in weeks those chosen to be trained as snipers walked on a bed of firm grass instead of floundering knee-deep in a morass of stinking mud. Close to the small town of Linghem, Thomas happily found himself billeted in one of the many farmhouses scattered throughout the countryside of northern Belgium. The buildings were always one storey high and made of brick, built around a midden providing fuel. The floor was of beaten earth, with wooden shutters covering the windows instead of glass and a roaring fire blazing in an open cooking hearth. It was like heaven from hell.

The following day he lined up with twenty-three others before the sniping school instructor, Major Ryan.

'Welcome to the suicide squad. Any smokers,

belchers and compulsive farters among you may leave now. I promise you the Hun will detect the stench of tobacco and shit from a hundred yards, endangering any of you unfortunate enough to be in the vicinity. Any slacking or complaining and you'll be back in the trenches dodging the shellfire and dining with the rats. Do I make myself clear?' he boomed.

Raised in South Africa, Ryan had taken the same path as his father as a big game hunter and safari leader, and his only reasons for serving in the war were his unquenchable sense of adventure and the unique opportunity to hunt men to their death in the name of war. The fact that he found reconnoitring the enemy more difficult than stalking a springbok in the African bush never diminished his enthusiasm or appetite for the kill. Over six feet tall and clean-shaven he walked with the easy gait of a man used to being obeyed. A reasonable man, with the enviable knack of making people like him just by talking to them, the men quickly responded to him.

'Patience in stalking and concealment define a good sniper,' he continued. 'It is not just about firing a rifle. Remember, gentlemen, that unfortunately, despite enthusiasm and application, poor field craft will see you victim of a well-aimed bullet from better-trained opposition. You will work in pairs, so get to know each other like brothers. Your lives will depend on the ability to read each other's minds. And I think it's only fair to tell you that the life expectancy of a sniper is a matter of weeks only, so anyone uneasy with these odds can leave now without any feeling of shame.'

Men shuffled their feet uncomfortably and scratched their heads with doubtful fingers, casting dubious glances at each other. No man moved out of line. Thomas found himself paired with Neil Letts, a man with a habit of closing one eye whenever he spoke, and a cleft in his chin so deep he could hold a penny between the creases. Yet, he was a pleasant man with a large moon-shaped face and a dry sense of humour, and Thomas quickly came to like him. Stan's attitude remained unchanged, and Leslie Hill, who seemed to follow Banks's lead, also chose to keep his distance. Thomas smiled and shrugged. For the moment he felt content with his own company. Too young to be a man himself, he some-times thought other men immature.

The first two days were spent stripping, assembling and maintaining their Lee Enfield .303s until they could literally do it with their eyes closed.

'Map and compass reading is vital. The ability to report the strengths and position of the enemy is more important than killing machine-gunners,' Ryan began. 'Wooden sticks painted various colours will be placed at different locations in the surrounding countryside. Using map co-ordinates you will recover the sticks and write a detailed report on the area, for example, cover, camou-flage, imaginary movement of enemy troops and gun emplacements. Thousands of men's lives may depend on the accuracy of your reports, so get it right.'

'Some of us ain't too good at writing, Sir,' someone called out.

'Then make sure you have a good memory. One of you will carry a telescope or a pair of field glasses to identify targets and give accurate range distances. Can anyone speak German?' Nobody moved. 'Pity, sometimes verbal orders might be overheard behind the lines, enabling allied troops to be ready for a surprise attack.'

After days spent firing at targets set at different distances, the men improved under the watchful eye of Major Ryan and his second-in-command, Sergeant Christopher. Eventually the pairs made their way towards mocked-up enemy lines. When thirty minutes had passed, they reversed their roles, one spotting, the other shooting, always alert and working as a well-oiled team. Sometimes they used portable camouflaged hides made from hessian and turned at an angle to avoid detection from the gun flash. Weather became an important factor: whenever it was still and frosty, gun smoke hanging in the air gave away their position. In sunlight, a glint from a barrel betrayed them, drawing fire from snipers; rain would make a bullet fly high, and a slight breeze could drift one six feet either way over one thousand yards. On a good day, a sniper could easily kill ten of the enemy.

'Snipers fight a dirty war, so if you ever get captured, best to keep your mouths closed,' Sergeant Christopher told them. 'A single sniper can demoralise a whole enemy battalion; his presence makes them nervous, and they walk around with their heads down, expecting to be the next target. They are reluctant to do guard duty and become edgy. I once saw a man in a trench take a bullet in the back of his neck; he was so nervous he leapt five feet into the air from a standing position and was dead before he hit the ground.'

Ryan demonstrated various methods of discovering the enemy's position, and one of the most effective, which brought smiles from the trainees, was the use of a dummy's head. Looking almost lifelike from a distance, it was placed on the end of a periscope with a lighted cigarette placed in the lips connected to a rubber tube. Hidden below in the bottom of the trench, a soldier would puff and blow in the tube giving the impression of a careless soldier having a smoke. Maintaining the periscope in line the bullet holes revealed the position of the enemy sniper, allowing the threat to be eliminated. The men learned rapidly and effectively, and time passed quickly. When Ryan felt satisfied that they were competent enough to be employed in the field, he shook each man by the hand and they returned to their respective battalions as accomplished snipers.

Gradually Stan Banks reluctantly came to admit to himself that he'd made a grave error in turning his back on Thomas. He'd tried unsuccessfully to inspire confidence in himself, and he realised that watching out for Thomas had merely been a foil for the fear gnawing and tearing at his own insides. Yet, for the time it lasted it had worked, and he'd felt gratified by his good fortune. Now circumstances had changed for the worse. His nerves dangled unfettered, loose and out of control, his emotions no longer responded and he had changed almost beyond recognition: his hair hung lank, streaked grey at the temples, and he continually chewed at his bottom lip. He had always considered himself immune to sentiment, a jack the lad, a cock of the north, with an answer and a reason for everything. But it was no longer so. The rumble of the guns and the sight of blood turned his bones to jelly. Even worse was the sound of wounded men screaming in pain and crying out for their mothers, or pleading to their mates to finish them off with a bullet to the head. Those sounds haunted him relentlessly during the day, and he looked around for something else to occupy his mind. Without him realising it, Thomas had become more than just a friend; he had become his rock, his covenant in which he could conceal his fear. Now he floundered ensnared in a trap of his own making, from which it might be impossible to escape with dignity and honour. Relaxed only by the privilege of sleep, his hands continued to shake from the moment he woke.

Finally the training was over, and the four men rejoined their battalion on the front line between Carnoy and Montauban, in the southernmost sector of the British Army. Already half of the original conscripts were missing or blown to pieces. Thomas glanced around for faces he might recognise only to be met with hollow stares from men he'd never seen before. They were quick to mingle on the whole, most as hazy and anxious as the next man about what the future held for them. When not on sentry duty most of them slept – something that was not easy to do. Sometimes they played cards. Some sat deep in concentration staring down at a chessboard, an opposing bishop threatening a vulnerable queen more important than raining shells and exploding shrapnel. A passable mug of tea might break the monotonous boredom and sever the sense of smell from the foul-smelling heaps of human waste. For others, time passed by in a sleepless blur. A few sat quietly folded up neatly, fearful to stretch out their legs in case they got trodden on by all those who passed up and down during their mind-sapping shifts in the trenches. Others, afraid to sleep for fear of freezing to death and being devoured by rats listened reluctantly to someone reading passages out loud from the Bible.

'Stop that bloody claptrap or go and tell it to Fritz. You give me the bloody creeps, you Bible-bashing bastard!' someone roared from further down the line.

Tempers frayed and rifles were cocked, threatening death. Some smiled a greeting, pretending to be calm, contemplating the sound of the officer's whistle and the fear-instilling order to go over the top to a certain death in a hailstorm of bullets. If fortunate enough to survive the onslaught, an enemy shell might hurl them like ragdolls twenty feet into the air to land broken and bleeding until night fell and stretcher-bearers from both sides searched for those still alive. Those with missing limbs might survive long enough to be patched up and sent home, where women at railway stations would faint at the sight of them, whilst others would go to field hospitals to recuperate until ready to be returned to the trenches. The less fortunate had their remains shovelled into empty sandbags and dropped into unmarked graves.

'Oy, Horace, give us that song about the three

90

old ladies locked in the lavatory. Old Fritz likes that song, he does. I bet you a fag he joins in.'

'Yeah, on account they don't have any of their own songs, too bloody miserable to write them, they are.'

So Horace started up the first chorus and, sure enough, old Fritz joined in and sang the second. When the singing finally came to an end, both opposing sides applauded each other with clapping and laughter.

'Quiet now, lads, no fraternising with the enemy, you know the rules,' Sergeant Bull said, appearing from the gloom like a bobbing ghost.

'Come on, Sarge, while we're singing we're not shooting the shit out of each other, are we?'

Sergeant Bull turned without a word and continued his rounds further down the trenches. He knew their courage and quiet determination were never in question.

After dusk, when darkness cloaked No Man's Land, Thomas and Neil Letts left to probe the enemy's defences. Crawling less than twenty yards from a German machine-gun emplacement they lay listening to the sound of sizzling sausages and the smell of hot coffee.

'Come on, I'm going in,' Letts whispered, drawing his bayonet.

'It's not our job to fight them in the trenches, you know that,' Thomas hissed.

'Yeah, well, fuck 'em, I've got a hankering for some of those sausages. Are you with me or not?'

Thomas chewed at his lip and sighed. 'If you want to go I don't suppose I have any choice.'

Through a hole in the German barbed wire they dropped silently into the trench. Immediately Thomas felt uneasy at the lack of sentries on duty and the hairs on his neck bristled with caution. He'd half-expected the trench to be manned every few yards by patrolling Germans armed to the teeth, and he felt certain something bad was going to happen if they remained too long. Instead, they were met with a wall of silence, broken only by the idle chatter of the three men cooking sausages over a fire in a split fuel can. The three Germans turned and looked up, their faces clouded with fear and surprise. A few frantic moments later they slipped to the ground with slit throats.

'Christ, they live like bloody lords, and look at these trenches, bloody bone dry they are. So how come we have to swim around with bloody rats day and night? Ought to get our donkeys down here to show them how it's done,' Letts grumbled.

'Donkeys, what donkeys?'

'Officers, for Chrissake Archie. Sometimes, talking to you is like trying to change a fan belt while the engine's running.'

Thomas, not having the slightest idea what Letts was talking about, nodded and began pulling the greatcoats and boots from the three bodies. Letts crouched and slid into a narrow dugout, minutes later he emerged with a sandbag full of tinned peaches, packets of French cigarettes, pipe tobacco and something Tommies prized most of all, razorblades and shaving soap.

'Here, hold onto these while I collect those spiked helmets. Cooks and pen pushers sitting on their arses behind the lines pay a bloody fortune for them. Tell those at home they captured them single-handed, they do, the lying sods.'

Satisfied they had all they could carry they made their way to their trenches. Glum faces relaxed into happy smiles when Letts tipped out the contents of the sandbag. Morale soared one hundred per cent.

'Good old Fritz, nice of him to allow us a few luxuries free of charge. I hope he doesn't miss them,' Leslie Hill grinned.

'Nah, I don't think he'll mind too much,' Letts smirked.

'Soon be going home to Ruby at this rate, eh, what do you reckon Archie?' a voice called from the darkness.

Like lightning the remark quickly became a byword running throughout the battalion. Something the men adopted and clung to as a form of comfort to remind them that life in the trenches wasn't the only way of existence in an otherwise cruel world. Later, the byword spread down the trenches, and when conditions became unbearable and shoulders wilted and drooped, the men would shout, 'Come on lads, chins up, we'll soon be going home to Ruby.'

That night they perched the spiked helmets on bayonets and ran up and down the trenches taunting the Germans.

'Well done, Letts, and you, Elkin, bring us back Kaiser Bill tomorrow and we can all go home to Ruby,' Sergeant Bull said with a rare smile. 'But be careful, lads, best not to strain your luck.'

Three days later Thomas sat on the wet fire-step

cleaning bullets and re-stocking his ammunition pouches. The time they dreaded had finally arrived – they were going over the top, the greatest test a man will ever face, the old-timers told him. When he finished, he greased the rifle bolt one more time and worked it back and forth until satisfied only an act of cruel misfortune would give it cause to jam.

In the trenches there was no warmth, only the damp and stench of human habitation. Seized in a grip of uncontrolled desperation he squeezed his eyes tight shut as fear clutched at his heart and prayed his impending death might come quick and clean. Overhead the chill hung like a black cloud concealing the darkest thoughts. Not one of the men knew an inch of the terrain ahead or where the Germans were entrenched. Frightened they huddled together for comfort, yet oblivious of each other, waiting like chess pieces to be moved at whim to join in the final push on the Somme. Their cynical ribaldry now gone yet not unmissed. Hot breath vaporised in great steaming clouds like that of men chain-smoking cigarettes, and time stood still listening to two men arguing whether it was Monday or Tuesday – it was Sunday morning. Liberal helpings of fiery tots of rum scorched their gullets and curdled in their stomachs while they waited with haggard faces, gaunt with fatigue and fear of a cruel death. From once youthful faces bristly beards sprouted, and eyes sunk so deep in black sockets it was impossible to tell their colour stared unseeing into nowhere. At the scrape of a man sharpening his bayonet eyes raised and muscles stiffened involuntarily. The time was seven-twenty-five in the morning. Photographs and snapshots appeared from pockets. Men with moist eyes kissed the smiling paper faces, uttered words of endearments and mumbled a prayer. Tormented by jangling nerves they waited, clutching their rifles, minus their backpacks and dressed for battle. Strapped to the back of every fifth man was a pickaxe or shovel that would keep him upright and unable to dodge the enemy fire.

Lieutenant Robert Blackie, a tall raw-boned man from Oxford, glanced nervously at his watch for the fourth time in as many seconds. If his heart could possibly feel any heavier it would surely sink to his feet, making it impossible for him to walk.

'God, give me courage, please,' he whispered. 'Don't let me fail in my duty.'

He looked along the line of waiting men licking their lips after the liberal rum issue clotted like treacle in their stomachs. A few caught his eye, like injured children looking up at their mothers for a morsel of comfort. He tried his best to smile, but encountered difficulty forcing his lips back over his teeth. This was his first time in the trenches. Three weeks, he'd been told, was suffi-cient for men and officers to learn the rules of safety and the degree of danger in the trenches. After two months they would attain a peak of efficiency; after that, decline came rapidly. More than anything in the world he'd ever hoped for, he prayed that his brave men would fail to see his nervousness. Somehow he managed to brace his shoulders and he stood erect. Like those around him he struggled to ignore the fear coupled with nausea washing through his body, and turning his bones to rubber.

'Steady, men, not long now, steady. Remember, walk, don't run, or you'll be blown up by our own creeping barrage. Take no prisoners unless you want to go on half rations to feed them. Kill the bastards,' he called, forcing the words from his mouth, and then whispered, 'God, I'm busting for a piss.'

Checking his watch, he gazed across the unknown terrain of No Man's Land – he hadn't expected to be ordered to attack in broad daylight.

Damn stupid generals, he thought. Close their eyes, stick their fingers anywhere on a map and say, how about we attack there, chaps? Before brekkers of course, can't have the Earl Grey going cold, can we?

Whistle in one hand, pocket watch in the other, he watched the seconds of his life tick away through blood veined eyes. At precisely seven thirty he would put the whistle to his lips and lead his men over the top into battle. He fought to visualise the map he'd studied so thoroughly at headquarters. He could see it now as plain as day. The German trenches were eight hundred yards away over No Man's Land, devoid of vegetation and cover. Bomb craters fifteen feet deep, filled with freezing mud and oozing thick fog-like ghostly spectres, waited to suck a man down to a horrible death. Row upon row of splintered trees blackened and stumped by continual shelling stood stark and threatening. After came rolls of thick barbed wire waiting to trap the advancing soldiers like flies in a spider's web. Once entangled, soldiers screamed in agony and cut to shreds by a hail of machine-gun bullets. If God is all forgiving, why is there a hell? he wondered.

'God, I hope this blasted whistle works,' he panicked, licking his lips with a dry tongue. 'Can't allow the men to see I'm on the damn verge of pissing my pants.'

'Fix bayonets!' Sergeant Bull roared. 'Prepare to deploy in extended order.'

Men sniffed and wiped away the dribble running from their noses with their cuffs. The hollow clicking of bayonets being attached to rifles resounding along the line was like the sound of a thousand Spanish castanets. Cold and miserable, soaked and sick, and at the extreme limit of their fear, they waited. Some turned and shook the hand of the man standing next to them.

'Blimey, luv a duck, this is a rum lark this is, ain't it? All the best, mate.'

If a vision of hell could be planted into a man's mind this was it, and it was firmly embedded into the mind of Lieutenant Blackie. He knew German machine-gunners were waiting ready with their Maxims to mow them down like wheat beneath a harvester, the hot zinging bullets separating lumps of flesh and limbs from helpless bodies. If the Germans didn't know already, they would when he blew the damn whistle warning them of his intentions.

'Might as well send a bloody telegram,' he muttered.

At precisely seven-thirty he put the whistle to his dry lips and blew. Men swallowed, crossed themselves and said one more silent prayer.

'Advance!' Sergeant Bull roared.

'Come on, men, follow me!' Lieutenant Blackie roared, brandishing his pistol. The German snipers would be watching for him; the only man not carrying a rifle is the officer-in-charge, making him their prime target. Without him the advancing men would be leaderless.

Fear visited Thomas like an unseen aggressor and, pressing his chalk-white face against the dank-smelling sandbags, he peered though the slit. An enemy shell landed yards in front of him, a blinding flash and a great column of flame erupted into the sky hurling stinging sand and ripped sandbags into his face. He felt himself hurled down into the thick clinging mud. All around him the constant scrabbling and darting movements of rats moving in shifting swarms, like rippling black water, unnerved him. Any sudden display of faltering weakness and they'd swarm over warm bodies, biting, nibbling and gorging on living flesh. Quickly scrambling to his feet he took up his position and rubbed the stinging sand from his eyes. From the disgorging trenches men slowly clambered, cowering and bent double, attempting to make themselves as inconspicuous to the enemy as possible. He shuddered as men lost their footing and slithered to the bottom of the trench and lay covered in soaking wet mud. Rats as large as dogs scampered over their faces. Those on the parapet first halted for a few long seconds and like statues waited until they were in alignment before starting forward.

He held his breath – this couldn't be real. But it

was, it was war: spectacular, thrilling and unbearable. Like lemmings the human race rushed stupidly and needlessly to a death of no consequence, intent on only displaying a frivolous existence in a sea of blood and pulpiness of flesh. With their weapons at the port the soldiers pressed forward led by the magnificent Highlander's pipers. The sound of skirling bagpipes echoed over the scarred countryside as though it had never been beautiful. When the second line started out, tears sprang from his young eyes at the futility of it all. The third line immediately followed by the fourth and the fifth by the sixth. Wide-eyed and unable to turn his eyes away from the carnage he lost his grip on logic as they were mowed down like slender stalks of wavering corn. Then, seized by anger his temper rose to the surface, pushing all other feelings aside as the cut of guilt reared its head. Shame tangled with his conscience. He cowered behind the cover and safety of sandbags gouged and split by huge swathes of shrapnel while men walked to a cruel death.

'Why me, dear God, why me?' he cried.

With a sob, he rolled over, squinted down the sights of his Lee Enfield and squeezed the trigger. The German helmet with a spike protruding from the top ricocheted from the German's head in a scarlet fountain of blood. Working the bolt he rammed another bullet into the breech and watched as another German threw up his arms and disappeared from sight. Suddenly, he shook away the mantle of despair and felt elation buzzing through his body like a charge of electricity. Two shots, two dead, no one could do better. All around him German shells crashed and whizz-banged overhead. Bodies separated from limbs catapulted into the air, screaming with fright and pain. Shrapnel shells exploded above their heads sending out a deadly shower of metal balls, ripping into supple unresisting bodies. His sudden rush of elation rapidly reverted back to naked fear and he closed his eyes to stop the tears blinding him. His young mind became strangled and unable to comprehend the reason for the savage slaughter.

He recalled that Mr Webster had once shown the class pictures of Roman soldiers. They carried shields and wore armour for protection against swords and arrows. The British soldiers carried no protection against bullets and exploding shells, and he didn't understand why. Limbs and heads were blown from bodies and rolled grotesquely over the blood-red snow carpet of No Man's Land. He blinked away the misty shroud of tears, squinted down the sights again and could see nothing. Men on the front line heard the screams from behind and faltered, then pressed forward, unseen in clouds of smoke. Their heads cocked to one side, their bodies coiled like springs and holding their breath, they waited for the bullet to end their lives. Then, at the roar of an order they started running from one shell crater to another hurling Mills bombs at the barbed wire. A few exploded, the remainder rolled to a stop, harmless, leaving men out in the open and exposed to the ever-present deadly chatter of the German machine-guns.

With no regard or thought for his own safety, he climbed to the top lip of a bomb crater and scanned the German trenches. German machine-gunners' helmets flew into the air as his bullets found their marks. When the gunners were re-placed, they were treated with the same contempt. Squeeze the trigger and work the bolt, squeeze the trigger and work the bolt, squeeze the trigger. Thomas moved forward, never faltering, upright, calm and collected. He stared death in the face, nose-to-nose, eye-to-eye, and laid down his chal-lenge, neither flinching nor giving ground. A sense of warmth enveloped his body and his vision cleared. Overhead the sky shone blue and cloud-less. He smiled. Any moment a bullet, a piece of shrapnel, a burst of hot lead would rip him to pieces. Squeeze the trigger and work the bolt, squeeze the trigger and work the bolt. To die in the company of such brave men would be an honour and his atonement would be complete. Something grabbed at his ankle and he looked down at a man with one half of his face missing, exposing bare cheekbones and teeth. One pleading eye hung from the empty socket, and working his mouth in a silent protest he rolled over and disappeared into a bomb crater filled with liquid mud. A trail of dirty brown bursting bubbles marked his final resting place. Neil Letts watched Thomas from the safety of the trenches and a streak of cold sweat ran down his back. He pulled himself over the parapet and, raising his rifle to his shoulder, entered the field of death. Behind him, one by one, the remaining snipers followed suit.

Advancing soldiers squared their shoulders and stood upright, cheering as the German gunners slowed under the deadly, accurate hail from the snipers. Suddenly, as though obeying a silent command, the attacking soldiers rose as one from the field of slaughter, dripping with mud and filth, and charged. Eyes glittered from grimy faces, lips pulled back into barbaric snarls revealing stained teeth, and bayonets flashed in the bright low winter sun like polished mirrors. Into the trenches they poured like interlopers of sanity, treating death as a passing fancy while seeking horrible retribution. Germans cowered and screamed in high-pitched pleas. Some fell to their knees holding pictures of their loved ones above their heads, seeking impossible mercy from the unforgiving as the bayonets flashed and slashed into their quivering flesh. Today humanity laid its soul bare. Today there would be no mercy, only the bloodletting of the bastards that came seeking war.

'Remember, lads, no prisoners, kill the bastards. Think of those lying dead and dying behind you,' a voice screamed above the cacophony of death.

'Aye, the only rations these bastards will get from me are six inches of cold steel,' another voice snarled.

Hand-to-hand battles broke out. Men fought like animals, kicking and biting off fingers trying to strangle them. No holds barred, only survival mattered. Thomas cringed and shrank at the sound of screams and shrieks. His legs refused to function and he stood stiff and frightened. The enemy broke and ran screaming to escape the carnage, only to be brought down by a hail of bullets in the back. Lungs filled with smoke and cordite coughed and gasped as bare hands choked the life from wriggling bodies. Others twitched and jerked under the savage blows of rifle butts smashing into faces, sending splintered bones piercing the brain and a quick death. Then silence, broken only by the sound of a sea of rasping breath – the blood lust was over. Men glanced down at themselves to check if they were still alive, unable to believe they were capable of the slaughter piled up around them.

Thomas sank to his knees and looked down at his muddy blood-spattered uniform. He felt numb and cheated. He was still alive. It wasn't fair, why wasn't he dead? Why hadn't he died a hero's death in the face of the enemy? Overhead, small wispy clouds glided serenely over the blue sky. Larks dived and swooped. He felt angry and denied of that which was his, and in a fit of temper he hurled his rifle to the ground. A burning determination entered his body, maybe next time he would finish the job himself.

'Private Elkin, pick up your rifle and fall in for roll-call, there's a good lad,' Sergeant Bull called gently. Now was the time for Sergeant Bull to pull on the velvet glove, to temper cold fear with warm compassion. With red eyes he watched the men feeling as a father would towards his troubled children and pondered how he might wipe away the horror locked in their hearts. He knew how they felt, but who would ease his mind?

Thomas stood in line and, with his head bowed, listened in silence.

Each time Sergeant Bull called out a name twice and received no answer, in a quiet voice he repeated the same question.

'Anybody know anything?'

103

No one answered, and Thomas clenched his fists tight until they became numb. Some sobbed openly and unashamedly. Others stared mutely, still unsure whether they themselves were dead or alive. Those men, seventy per cent of the battalion, who never answered roll-call that day, would never stand in line again. Not in this world.

Victory belonged to the living, as empty as a tin of used beans rusting on a rubbish tip, and the cruel face of fate had spared them to die another day. How many died that day he didn't know, but he knew it amounted to tens of thousands. When he saw Stan Banks talking to Leslie Hill he wanted to go to them, to talk, even argue, anything to loosen the image of what he'd just witnessed from his mind. Banks turned and held his gaze with an expressionless face; the tenuousness of their past alliance exposed once again. He gave a small nod and turned away.

The wounded were brought in by stretcher-bearers, assisted by soldiers, on stretchers rigged from two poles and greatcoats. Brave men were buried where they fell that day. Thomas helped plunge their rifles bayonet first into the ground, their helmets, balancing on the upturned butt, glinting, as a solitary reminder of where the brave warrior fell. Remains of men past recognition were shovelled into empty sandbags and taken away to be buried in unmarked graves for the rats to feast on. Tonight, for a brief time, the living would thank God for their lives and celebrate with watered-down, over-proofed rum.

'Christ all bloody mighty,' Ollie Love muttered angrily, spitting out blood from a mouth wound.

'Bloody Fritz jabbed me in the gob with his rifle just as my bayonet slid between his ribs. Cruel buggers these Germans. They ought to be more careful where they stick their bloody weapons. Come on, lad, let's get a brew on.'

'Aye, I'm up for that,' Thomas grunted.

Love loaded a fresh belt of ammunition into his Lewis gun and began firing until the water-cooled barrel heated the water enough for a lukewarm brew. Men drifted over in dejected groups and sat silently over Dixies set on Tommy cookers. Hunched down with the mess tins in their hands they waited for God's gift to soldiers: a hot tin of tea and a couple of drags from a dog-eared cigarette pulled from behind the ear to settle the mind and still the nerves. Some men ripped off their blood-covered tunics and set them on fire.

'Do you know something?' Trigger Timpson said between slurping his tea and pulling on a crushed cigarette. 'You never see a bloody officer when the killing starts. You can hear the buggers yelling orders, but you never gets to see one, strange that.'

'Aye, they sling their bloody hooks quick enough when trouble starts, the poncy bastards,' Love said, sticking a grubby finger into his hooked nose and inspecting the proceeds.

'They piss off to the generals and report how they captured the trenches single-handed,' someone laughed.

'Those up there? The bloody useless generals who cower miles behind the lines, flicking particles of dust from their polished boots and toasting their hard-fought victory with fine porter and awarding themselves medals,' Love moaned.

'Bloody Haig never took the time to visit the front, bloody coward. "Lest the sight of the wounded affect my judgement", that's what he said, eh, can you bloody believe it?'

Then, suddenly silence. The banter ceased. Men sat in a calm stillness and stared at the twinkling flames heating the petrol can of water, their minds forging hushed pictures of fallen comrades. No man mentioned names or expressed sorrow, that wasn't the way it was done. Slowly, the adrenaline of battle faded and the unwelcome coldness burrowed its way deep into the marrow of tired bones. Thomas shivered, still uncertain if what had occurred only moments ago really had happened. He closed his eyes. It was a bad dream, a nightmare. He tried to visualise his actions and his memory stalled, like an engine without fuel.

Lieutenant Blackie survived the day, the shadows beneath his eyes deeper and darker than ever before. Alone in his dugout, with a single lighted candle for company he recalled something he once read.

A hundred thousand killed you say, and more,
Tell me, what did they kill each other for,
Ah, that is something no one knows, says he,
But it will dwell in history, as a famous victory.

He raised the monogrammed silver-plated whisky flask – a farewell present from his wife, Lorna – to his mud-caked lips with trembling hands. Most of the fluid dribbled down his chin onto his tailor-made tunic and he wiped it away with his sleeve, fighting like a chastised child to keep the tears from his eyes. Tonight laudanum would provide him with the respite of a night's sleep and null the devils that danced and whirled in his confused mind.

As a result of his outstanding bravery Thomas was deducted three days' leave and two days' pay for leaving the trenches without permission. Lucky to escape a court martial, they told him. Seven days later he was promoted to Lance Corporal. Stunned, and for the sake of peace and quiet, he accepted the promotion, still craving for a quick death.

'Well done, Archie,' the men shouted. 'You'll soon be going home to Ruby.'

'Aye, the sooner the better, best not keep the lass waiting,' he smiled wanly, cleaning the mud from his rifle in the trench dugout.

When he finished he ignored the dampness and stripped to his waist. Shivering with cold, he lighted a candle and attempted to burn the lice from his clothes, paying particular attention to sewed seams where lice eggs lurked, waiting to hatch and gorge on his blood. Turning his clothes inside out, he dressed. It didn't help to get rid of the lice, but it was better than nothing. He could not remember the last time he bathed. It must have been a long time ago and he felt his feet hurting; maybe frostbite was setting in. He needed dry clothes. Tomorrow night, alone, he'd go close to the German trenches further north and infiltrate their lines, confident he'd find decent clothing.

There was no moon the night he slipped unnoticed through the German lines alone. As he went further, he felt his breathing grow faster and he slowed. At Mametz the sudden hoot of an owl startled him, sending the hairs on his neck tingling. He stopped, crouched, and strained his ears, and then slowly made his way north into the dark interior of Quadrangle Wood. Behind a thick clump of hedgerow bushes he knelt and gently levered the branches apart for a better view of a German heavy gun emplacement hurriedly making ready to pull back behind new lines.

To his right the sudden yellow flicker of a sentry lighting a cigarette illuminated a brief burst of green vegetation and, dropping belly down, he waited. Ten minutes passed into what seemed an eternity, as the sentry dutifully patrolled his allotted section with expected Teutonic thoroughness. With the palm of his hand he wiped away the stinging sweat blurring his eyes, and crawled away on hands and knees, then began to silently work his way round to the sentry's flank.

Without thinking, he recalled his training in armed combat: no hesitation, only commitment, they had ground into him. It seemed so simple performed on men who had no intention of resisting. Immediately he loomed to his feet with his bayonet gripped tightly in his hand, he felt himself trembling. The sentry looked no older than himself, and his protruding Adam's apple jerked up and down while he struggled for words. The cigarette fell from his mouth, and making no attempt to raise his rifle he stood stock-still, rigid like a statue, with fear raking his face.

'Nein Kamerad, nein!' he shrieked.

Thomas stood rooted to the spot. The bayonet hung limp in his hand like a ton weight. The German recovered first, his eyes narrowed and his lips curled into a sneer. Raising his rifle, he slipped off the safety catch. Time faltered and the world slowed. The fear on the German's face transformed to naked hate. His finger whitened and pressed against the trigger. Without thinking, Thomas lunged and sunk the bayonet between the German's ribs, pushing and twisting, he searched for the heart. The sentry stiffened and, exhaling a great breath reeking of spices and cigarettes, he shuddered, fell to the damp grass and lay still.

Thomas quickly pulled off the boots and socks, and stuffed the socks into his pocket. His breath came fast and he wiped away the warm tears running down his blackened face. He'd just killed a man with his bare hands for a pair of dry socks. A man who could have been the solution to his anguish and released him from the nightmare of life if only he'd waited a moment longer. Instinctively he'd chosen life over death. He let out a shuddering breath, cleaned the blood from the blade and hated himself. It was war, and it didn't matter, he told himself, other opportunities would arise. Instead of walking away he rummaged through the dead German's pockets and took a bar of black chocolate, an opened packet of cigarettes, a Swiss knife and a letter written in German, which he crumpled in his fist and threw away. Still feeling rattled, he made his way farther behind enemy lines.

Crouched in a half-filled ditch he listened to the sound of jingling harnesses while sucking on a piece of the black chocolate and watched a fat sergeant breathlessly hitching horses to a huge 77mm field cannon. Angry at his brutal treatment of the horses, he squinted down the sights of his rifle and curled his finger around the trigger. Then he changed his mind and moved away to a row of tents glowing like yellow ghosts from the thick white candles burning inside. He hesitated and listened for the sound of voices. Silently drawing his bayonet he slit the canvas and peered inside. Propped against a low wooden camp bed he saw a rifle with a tube attached above the magazine where the rear sights were normally situated. Curious, he took the weapon plus three pairs of socks, a thick green woollen jumper, a packet of small cigars, a photograph of a woman wearing stockings and little else, and half a bar of white perfumed soap. From under the bed he took a coalscuttle helmet, grinned, and urinated in it, and then contentedly headed back to his own lines.

'German Mauser 7.92mm sniper with a telescopic sight, that's what that is, lad,' Sergeant Bull told him when he showed him the rifle. 'Fine weapon, eh, give Fritz a bit of his own back.'

Thomas hefted the weapon onto his shoulder and smiled with pleasure at a blackened tree stump a thousand yards away. It looked less than a hundred yards.

'Get down to ordnance, bound to have cases full of captured ammunition to fit the rifle,' Sergeant Bull told him.

He was right – Sergeant Bull was always right – so he gave him the woollen jumper.

'Eh, right good fit that is, lad, bit on the baggy side mind you, but I'll overlook that, ta very much.'

Although the Mauser was slower to load than

the Enfield and held only a five-cartridge magazine, its unerring accuracy made all the difference. After closely studying the photograph for what seemed an eternity, Sergeant Bull said he didn't recognise the woman.

'Best throw it away, lad. Looking at it for too long will send you blind,' he said. 'And if you intend to use that perfumed soap, don't bend down in the trenches.

That night Thomas stared at the photograph wondering what part of the woman would cause him to go blind. Unsure, he threw it away to be on the safe side. The remark about not bending down in the trenches left him feeling nonplussed.

For days snow fell and froze and entrenched men suffered. Some endured the hardship in silence. The majority sat morose, shadow boxing in their minds whether to attempt desertion. Without restraint frostbite and trench foot quickly depleted the platoons, and extra guard duties were pulled by men already tired from sleepless nights beneath the continual bombardment of the German guns. Those who had signed up to fight because others did and they didn't want to miss the fun found ample time to regret their misguided stupidity. Not that it mattered that much. Conscription would have taken them anyway.

Christmas neared, morale sank and talk of mutiny once again began to circulate. The arrival of tanks caused a stir of hope and they were welcomed as wonder-weapons by the infantrymen, until they were discovered to be unreliable, prone to breaking down and unable to cross trenches.

Men considered the drivers blind when they failed to avoid the wounded, and crushed many allied troops to death. But they frightened the life out of the Germans, and most were only too happy to surrender at the sight of them.

'Got no stomach for a fair fight, the Hun. Bunch of bullies, that's all they are,' someone grumbled.

'Yeah, they drop their weapons quicker than a London tart drops her drawers,' Slippery Stewart chipped in to a muffled round of laughter.

Content to be busy the four snipers found themselves continually employed in keeping the Germans' heads down, thus lowering their morale. Occasionally Thomas ventured alone into No Man's Land accompanied with his newly acquired rifle, and wearing a white camouflaged suit against the backdrop of snow he wreaked havoc with the German gunners. Wherever possible, he stole anything of use he could lay his hands on before returning. Often, he walked slowly back to the British lines in full view of the German snipers, hoping for a bullet in the back of his head, but with bullets zipping around and troops cheering he never received a scratch. Soldiers hailed him as a lucky charm.

'Good on you, Archie,' they called. 'You show the bastards, eh, soon be going home to Ruby.'

Sergeant Bull watched him through quizzical eyes and thoughtfully rubbed his stubbly chin with the palm of his hand.

The following morning sat in the trench on an empty ammunition box Thomas drank tea brewed from a cut-down petrol can. Should someone be foolish enough to strike a match, there was a good chance he would go up in a ball of flames. Even so, it tasted good, so he persevered until he'd had his fill. All around the air reeked of stale tobacco smoke, burning candlewicks and brews of Oxo cubes flavoured with the less pleasant stench of an overcrowded dugout. Overhead the grey sky offered a slight breeze and he gave a small shudder in defiance and smiled at two men arguing noisily over a packet of Woodbines. There seemed no point, cigarettes were plentiful enough. But a heated argument always provided a means of forgetting the war for a fleeting moment, and after a time the protagonists would invariably shake hands, light up and go their different ways. Such was life in the trenches, where No Man's Land sat dark and friendless, impatiently awaiting its next victims.

Pale-faced replacements drafted in to bring the battalion up to strength were shown little interest and given short thrift. Some would cry themselves to sleep every night, others would defecate daily in their trousers, most would be lost to German bullets, and occasionally one or two would attempt unsuccessfully to instigate a sing-song. He arched a brow and turned his mind to the past few days, the force necessary to drive him to his death had waned and spluttered to a halt. The small part of his mind that remained calm accepted this as his good fortune. The larger part accused him of blatant cowardice. He had cheated his way to the trenches in a bid to make reparation for the death of his brother, yet when death became inevitable he instinctively chose life.

The thought provoked him and he thought that perhaps he was a coward; his promises made of dust and ready to blow away at the slightest whiff of a breeze. His face reddened with shame and like most others he needed someone to comfort him, and he could tell himself it was merely a lapse due to the excitement of war. But that wasn't about to happen. Softness was played upon and ridiculed in the trenches. Firmness and strength, when the occasion demands it, was taken for granted. Or perhaps he hadn't tried hard enough to fulfil his promise. The heat ran down his shoulders and through his arms until his fingers tingled. His mind was made up. Tomorrow he would desert again and this time there would be no mistakes like before, when Robert McCaughey had paid with his life. To make sure everyone knew of his intentions, he went looking for Neil Letts. Not that Letts spoke much, but when he did it surprised people so much they never failed to listen.

'I'm going to desert tomorrow. I've had enough of all this shit. If I can reach Holland before I'm captured, I'll be safe,' he said, watching Letts clean his rifle with Vaseline.

'Aye, lad, and best of luck,' he grinned. It wasn't like Archie to tell jokes.

'I'm serious, Neil, I mean it. I've had enough of this shithole.'

Neil looked up, still grinning. 'Aye, send us a postcard.'

At daybreak the next day, Thomas slipped away before roll-call and headed south, with no idea where he was going. Three days on the run would be sufficient to prove his intentions of desertion and warrant a court martial. On the fourth day, he'd give himself up.

Chapter Eight

He stood for a long time, not knowing his whereabouts or what to do. The gentle rustle of green fields and trees trapped in a chilled breeze were things of the past. He gazed at the lapping waters of a small lake and imagined he existed in another far-off world. Gone were the blackened battlefields cloaked by drifting clouds of cordite, stinging unwilling eyes; no more screams of the wounded. Hunkered down on a dry patch of grass beneath a beech tree he pulled out a half loaf of thick brown bread and chomped hungrily at the crust. Then all at once it was there, on the other side of the lake with his head held high, antlers pointing to the sky. He watched the black-tipped ears twitch, his back, a reddish brown in the dim forest light, sloped gently and rose to the head, proud and alert. For a moment he stood suspended in time then his stiff forelegs splayed out like stilts, he reached down for the water, his head bobbed for seconds and then he was gone.

Contentment came quickly and, slumping back against the trunk, Thomas closed his eyes and allowed himself to imagine the farm on the edge of the Yorkshire Moors: the pungent smell of carbolic soap wafting from the stone-floored scullery and the tin tub, so small that when he bathed his chin rested on his bony knees. Large, succulent hams suspended from metal hooks in the outhouse that tasted grand with boiled potatoes and fresh vegetables from his mother's small garden. Even the dust and chalk of the classroom and the maddening charge of eager bodies escaping the trauma of learning at going home time stayed clear in his mind.

Then he remembered why he was here and he wanted to shout and scream, demand forgiveness. But who would forgive him? Who would want to? He was destined to die, unloved and un-mourned.

With a sigh he forced his mind to relax and stretched out his legs, the torpor of the afternoon lulling him from his torment. In the distance he thought he could hear the tolling of a church bell. Closer by the brisk resonant sound of birdsong raised his mood by the smallest of notches.

Late in the afternoon, roused from his solitude, he strained his ears. The voice sounded harsh and biting and he struggled to make sense of the words. Completely unprepared for the sight standing before him his breath swamped his throat. The glistening steel tip of the bayonet pressed into his throat, forcing him back tight against the tree to escape the stinging pain.

'Stay where you are, Englander.'

'Jesus Christ!'

The prick of the bayonet punctured his skin, and he felt the warm trickle of blood run down his neck.

In disbelief his body twitched with fear. The German glared at him as though he'd never set eyes on an English soldier before. Thomas noticed the olive-green riding breeches and knee-length boots. Over his uniform he wore a sheepskin shaped like a jacket with the fleece on the outside.

'Where are your comrades?' the man snapped.

'I don't know, I'm lost,' he stuttered.

'Lost? You fool, how could anyone be lost in this Godforsaken country? For you, my friend, the war is over; you are now a prisoner of the German Imperial Army. Disarm him,' he said, turning to one of his men.

'Jawohl, Herr Hauptman.'

They kept all they found: the rum they drank immediately and hurled the empty bottle into the woods.

'You are a long away from your lines, perhaps you have run away, eh, perhaps you are a coward, a British deserter?' the Hauptman sneered.

Thomas stayed silent. The officer shrugged his disinterest and at gunpoint pushed Thomas through the wood until they reached a narrow, rut-filled track covered in deep, thick mud. Immediately, rough hands grabbed him and two German soldiers hurled him down onto the track.

'I will shoot the next man who ill-treats this man; he is a prisoner-of-war and will be treated as such. Do I make myself clear?' the Hauptman intervened.

With his hands tightly lashed behind his back, the soldiers shoved him into the back of an open lorry. The wind blew bitter and cold, and hardly able to maintain his balance he struggled to remain upright while the vehicle lurched and skidded over the pockmarked road. Finally, when darkness smothered the landscape and his muscles screamed for release from the ropes that held his hands, they juddered to a, halt. Untying his hands, they shepherded him at bayonet point though a wooden gate criss-crossed with thick rusting strands of barbed wire into a muddy enclosure measuring approximately twenty square yards. A small windowless wooden building with a mixture of coloured tarpaulins covering the roof stood in one corner; a trail of wispy smoke rose and drifted lazily from a metal chimney stack into the freezing still air. A German soldier wearing a grey balaclava beneath his helmet hammered impatiently against the door and shouted words he couldn't understand. Seconds later, the door swung open and two men dragged him inside.

'Bladdy hell, cobber gave you a bit of a going over. Where did they pick you up?' one said.

'I don't know. Where am I?' Thomas said, wincing at the pain.

'Your guess is as good as mine, mate, you're a prisoner-of-war now. On your own are you?'

'Yes, they caught me trying to desert.'

'Did they now? Sounds like a bladdy good idea, and I can't say I blame you. Let's get the wet clobber off you before you catch your death. Barnes is my name, Digger Barnes, 3rd Australian Division. This is my mate Ned, the rest of us are all Aussies. You're the only Pom, and seeing as there's a war on we won't hold that against you,' Digger grinned. 'Fritz will come for you later and take you down to their medical station, wash you down and de-louse you. More like bladdy torture it is. Mind you, they'll give you clean clothes and

118

some tucker. Don't know why we're fighting them. Treat us better than our own bastards do. Ain't anybody here looking to get back in the bladdy war,' he rambled, raking the ashes of a small log fire with a charred stick. 'It might be different for you though, being bladdy English.'

'What's your regiment?' Ned asked in a reedy nasal whine, going through Thomas's pockets. 'Don't you bladdy smoke, mate? Strewth, a fat lot a bladdy good you are.'

'I'm a sniper in the Yorkshire Rifles,' Thomas answered, crawling towards the fire.

'Whoa, best keep that to yourself, son,' someone said in the background. 'They'll string you up and use you for bayonet practice; snipers put the fear of Christ in them.'

'They use snipers as well as us,' Thomas answered sharply.

Digger threw a fresh log onto the fire and watched the sparks dance up through the narrow piping acting as a chimney.

'Course they do, we all know that, but Germans don't like an even fight, they haven't got the stomach for it. They like to kill easily, and when they can't they do one of two things, chum: run away screaming or bladdy surrender. You'll learn soon enough.'

Thomas raised his head and gazed around the room. Twenty-five Australian prisoners-of-war existed in the hut, each assigned to a wooden bed with a metal-sprung mattress and one thin blanket. The fire offered sparse comfort and little heat, but it was better than nothing.

'Christ almighty, mate,' Ned said, screwing up

his nose. 'You smell like a bladdy Abo's armpit.'

For the first time in months Thomas looked down and inspected his bare arms and legs, shocked at how much weight he'd lost. His toenails were long and deformed, his feet and bony legs were filthy and streaked with black dried mud. His body the same, with ribs protruding through his skin, and he couldn't remember the last time he'd seen a mirror. Suddenly, all eyes turned towards the door when it swung open, revealing two German guards and a non-commissioned officer.

'Aus!' the non-commissioned officer roared, pointing at Thomas. 'Schnell!' he roared again, aiming a kick at Thomas's head and catching him in the chest. They hauled him up by the arms and pushed him head first out into the freezing snow.

Half naked, Thomas pulled himself to his feet and, at bayonet point, they kicked and prodded him in the direction of an old farmhouse, the roof riddled with holes from cannon shells. Inside a group of untidy men with long hair and vacant eyes, like men who'd suffered long spells under fire in the trenches, waited, dressed in white smocks. One of the men pushed him down into a wooden chair and began to hack at his hair with a large pair of scissors. When he was finished, he clumsily shaved his head with a razor, paying no attention to the cuts and gashes oozing bubbles of blood. Then, armed with a large sponge, he covered him from head to toe in slimy oil that reeked of petrol. Shivering uncontrollably and hardly able to remain on his feet, they frogmarched him outside and along a pathway of icy duckboards.

Now so cold, his head dipped and swirled and he lost all feeling in his body, and slipping to the freezing ground he felt the dull thud of a boot against his flesh. Despair ripped away all feelings of humanity and he groaned and rolled over, staring into the swirling grey sky.

'Kill me, kill me,' he whispered hoarsely. 'Please kill me.'

The German sergeant stared down at him, his mouth twisted into a sneer. 'Pick the English pig up and continue,' he grunted.

Like a sack of rags they dragged him by his ankles and entered a building with frozen puddles of water scattered around the floor and icicles hanging in rows from rafters, like dragons' teeth waiting to chomp into his thin undernourished frame. He prayed for death. So desperate did he want to die, to escape from the darkness that had become his world, he felt as though he was confined to a coffin alive. All feeling of humanity drifted from his body, tiredness came and stole away his strength.

From the gloom two soldiers wearing green gowns and squeaking thigh-length rubber boots, one bandy legged and the other stooped as though he carried a great weight across his shoulders, entered the room carrying brushes, sponges and rough brown towels. From a tank of cold water they began to soak him while the men in white scrubbed and brushed him clean. For over an hour they repeated the process until he thought his skin was on fire, as though it had been scraped with heated sandpaper. By now his swollen knees refused to support him, and reaching out he

121

grasped at fresh air to stop himself from falling. His fingers became stiff and useless, and every joint in his body bulged and ached. Even the slightest movement became unbearable and he wanted to scream, to chase away the excruciating pain. He crumbled down onto the freezing cold floor, whimpering and whining like a newborn pup. When he tried to rise, the concrete floor scraped the skin from his knuckles and finally the joyful bliss of unconsciousness released him from further torment.

The men in white, seemingly completely devoid of human kindness, ignored his suffering and continued until satisfied that their work was as it should be. Rough hands pulled him to his feet. His eyes flickered open and he felt himself being dressed in a clean pair of trousers and a thin cotton jacket. Hardly able to stand for more than a few seconds and with sunken bloodshot eyes staring vacantly into nowhere, they dragged him back to the hut and dumped him outside in the snow. Inside, two Australians quickly stripped him, and in front of the fire they began rubbing and slapping his naked body with their hands, fighting to get his blood circulating.

'Christ, he's done for that's for sure,' Ned said, panting for breath. 'He'll never come out of this; poor little bugger.'

Two hours later he lay shivering and alone in front of the fire, blocking the heat from the rest of the prisoners-of-war. He twitched first and then groaned.

'Here, get this down you, you tough little sod,' Digger grinned, handing him a half cup of weak coffee. 'Saved it for emergencies, we did. Should have known a bladdy Pom would get his greedy hands on it.'

'Glad you made it, son,' Ned laughed, dragging on a scrawny cigarette. 'First time I've set eyes on that bastard of a sergeant, or whatever he is; maybe things round here might be changing for the worst.'

'Yeah, you might be right there; if the war's not going well for them it might be time to think about getting out of here. They won't think twice about shooting us,' Digger said, holding out his hand for the cigarette. 'You greedy bastard,' he said, when the burned-down cigarette singed his lips.

It was seven o'clock the following morning when the soldiers came for him once again. With a bayonet point prodding between his shoulder-blades he stumbled into the German trenches and was ordered to wait outside a dugout hacked into the side. Strings of electric light bulbs pinned to the clay walls lit up the gloomy dawn turning the darkness into a dull light. He noted the neatness of the German trenches, dug deep and shored up with sturdy logs. Strong wooden platforms had been built high to keep soldiers free from the filthy mud and scampering rats. For a moment his mind drifted and he wondered why the British never did the same.

One of the German guards pushed him though a wooden door separating a roomy dugout from the trench. Fixed to the walls were four rows of wooden shelves holding dozens of books, almost like a small library. Three thick white flickering candles provided adequate light for a person to

123

read. Behind a scarred, heavy mahogany desk, on which stood a gilt framed picture of a pretty woman sitting on a bicycle next to a drinking glass full of paper roses, sat a German officer smoking a pink cigarette pushed into an ebony cigarette holder. His fair hair, shaved close to his skull, and a monocle perched uncomfortably and unpractised in his right eye prompted Thomas to smile.

'So, you are enjoying the war, no?' the officer asked, leaning back and stretching his legs onto the table.

Thomas frowned and remained quiet, unsure of the best way to answer. During his time in the trenches he'd never met anyone who freely admitted to enjoying the war, although he knew there were those who thought at one time they might. Perhaps Germans were different from other people and found some abject form of pleasure in the misery of others.

'Me, I hate the war, it has no point. Nevertheless, I must perform my duty to the Fatherland to the best of my ability. I wish only to return to my studies as a doctor,' the officer continued, beating a tuneless tattoo with his fingertips on the tabletop. 'I studied for six months in London you know, St Guy's Hospital, under Dr Crabtree; perhaps you know him? No, I'm sorry, of course you don't, you are only a common soldier, how silly of me. Tell me, what were you doing outside Verdun alone when one of our patrols picked you up? Are you a spy? I think you are; perhaps I should have you shot.'

Thomas stared at him feeling a new rage fire into his body. Was this it? Were these the pompous overbearing idiots that day after day slaughtered his friends?

'Suit your fucking self, you German arsehole,' he grunted.

The officer jerked his head up and narrowed his eyes at the unexpected response. 'You want to be shot, why is that I wonder?'

Thomas curled his top lip. He'd heard stories in the trenches of Germans who thought they ruled the world – men with large heads that housed tiny brains – and he had no intention of feeding this man's ego. Barking dogs seldom bite, his father had once said.

'Maybe you'd be better off thinking instead of wondering, or maybe you find thinking a little too hard,' Thomas snapped, feeling the agony of the previous day and an automatic determination instilled itself in his body. 'You might have been to London, but I've no bloody wish to go to Germany. Seen enough of you buggers here, I have.'

Once again the aggressive nature of the answer caught the German by surprise. He had hoped the Englishman might cower and plead for his life. In London they had accepted his arrogant manner as though they were afraid of him, and had allowed him to do and say as he pleased with no fear of reprisals. But he didn't know the English as well as he might. Born the son of a Prussian general he considered himself ruling class and therefore privileged to ride roughshod over the less fortunate. In his own manner he had studied the British and come to the conclusion that the Welsh were the best songsters, the Scottish the best educated, the Irish the most unpredictable and the English the most tolerant. He took tolerance as a form of cowardice.

'I wonder if you have the intelligence to know the meaning of the word "bugger"?' the German snapped, sparks flying from his eyes.

'Oh aye, it means some brainless bastard that fucks animals. Why do you think we call Germans buggers?' Thomas snapped back.

The officer paled, and with a face fit to skin a crocodile he leapt to his feet.

'Guards!' he screamed. 'Take the Englander back to the hut.'

A rifle butt crashed into the base of his spine and he stiffened with a dull groan; the darkness sounded full of guttural noises, and with a tearing anguish he slumped to the ground. Like a dead carcass they dragged him down the trench by his shoulders and hurled into ankle-deep mud used as a latrine. A heavy boot pressed down on the back of his neck, forcing his face into the filthy rat-infested excreta. In desperation he struggled and fought for air to escape drowning. Thankfully the pressure eased, leaving him gasping and choking for breath. Nearby a group of Germans laughed at him and tapped their fingers to their heads.

'Englander idiot,' they scoffed.

Thomas bore the taunts along with the raucous laughter, and such was his anger from that moment he vowed he would never forget the humiliation heaped upon him that day. There could be no forgiveness for men such as these, no place in heaven next to God. Something in their pitiless faces evoked a primitive urge for revenge, and his mind festered into a hatred for the

German race that would never diminish. He promised himself that, if he survived imprisonment, he would kill as many Germans as the war would allow him before he died.

That night, in a fitful sleep, he was haunted by a great predatory monster with dripping fangs waiting to feast on his iron guilt. Archie's face, as white as Arctic snow, stared down at him, and in his hand dangled a noose. His empty laugh coursed through Thomas's body and, slipping the rope over his head, he pulled the noose tight.

In the morning he felt as if sleep had passed him by. His tongue felt like a bullock's, blocking the passageway to his lungs. Blackened bruises surrounded the cuts and lacerations covering his body and still his bones felt as though they were filled with ice. A few hours felt like fleeting minutes. He would have risen if only he possessed the strength, then, without warning the bullying German sergeant kicked open the hut door and smirked purposely waiting for the tiny amount of heat to be displaced by an icy draught. Two men helped Thomas to his feet and half carried him outside. Shivering, they lined up in silence under the drifting snow for the daily roll-call and answered to their names. With hollow eyes and blue trembling lips each man waited to return to the meagre heat of the hut.

Thomas's mind became a blank darkness, an eternity of nothing and he swayed with weakness, only the thought of another beating gave him the strength to remain upright. Then, through tired veined eyes he looked up and noticed a golden hue from a string of glowing light bulbs suspended above the trenches. He searched his memory for times he thought he might have long forgotten. The sight reminded him of the village baker's shop at Christmas time, and his mind wandered into a past life away from the horror of the present.

At Christmas Mr Bridle had always decorated the bakery window with gold tinsel and silver tinfoil, and multi-coloured lights shone and twinkled over the delights he produced like magic from the warm ovens at the rear of his shop. Just the sight of Father Christmas made of currant cake and covered in red icing had made the juices in his mouth run like sweetened water. A snowman with a happy smile on his face and chocolate buttons pushed onto his thick creamy coat stood surrounded by shiny green holly. Finally, the Christmas tree, with gaily-wrapped sweets tied to sagging branches, and a fairy complete with gossamer wings and a halo glowing above her head smiled down from the top.

On Christmas Eve the children stood in their best Sunday clothes on the village green, singing carols under candlelit lanterns glowing gold in the crisp night air. Later they ate freshly roasted chestnuts and baked potatoes that burned their fingers and heated their throats in front of a roaring bonfire before going home, too excited to sleep. Boxing Day morning, children trying to suppress their excitement gathered from surrounding villages to form a quiet, orderly queue outside the bakery and wait for a free slice of the snowman, or perhaps even Father Christmas himself.

At six-thirty in the evening the prisoners waited to be herded out like cattle for a meal of thick gruel and a thin slice of black bread. Later one man would tussle with the freezing conditions and accompany a guard to fetch logs for the fire from a nearby wood. If he survived, he would be allowed time in front of the fire to control a bout of shivering. With typical Germanic thoroughness, exactly on time, the door swung open and the men filed out as they had done so many times before. This time they stood pinioned to the spot, and their mouths sagged open. In the centre of the compound a small Christmas tree with four white candles burned a warm glow against the backdrop of fresh snow, and a tray full of hot black sausages and brown bread stood beside a steaming pot of coffee and two tins of Craven A cigarettes.

'Merry Christmas, Tommy,' one of the guards laughed, slamming the gate shut.

It was Christmas Day – even amidst the relentless carnage and slaughter in the freezing slime. For men dying and screaming in agony under the light of the dull yellow flares, the sacred day of Christianity could be remembered and celebrated. Thomas watched, unable to halt the sneer crossing his face, and wondered what gave these men the right to celebrate Christmas. How could they justify such hypocrisy? How dare they consider themselves Christians?

Later, each with his own thoughts, the prisoners sat with tears streaking their dirty faces, remembering past Christmases spent in the company of those they loved. Melancholy eyes stared down at irreparable muddy boots to the sound of the enemy singing *Silent Night*; some hoped they might one day see another Christmas under different circumstances. The sneer on Thomas's face refused to budge and, for some reason unknown even to himself, he thanked God he was still a boy and not yet a man.

For the ensuing months Thomas, more than any other prisoner, suffered bitterly at the unforgiving cruel hands of the Germans. Day by day he grew even thinner and gaunt, and immersed into a world full of despair and misery. His breath became ragged, gasping, an explosive panting, like someone about to choke. Yet he clung to life like a barnacle to the hull of a ship. A festering hatred formulating in his heart helped keep him warm, with a certain belief that his day of reckoning would one day come. The Germans would rue the day they treated him worse than a rabid dog.

Overnight trenches quickly filled knee high with swirling snow and the prisoners-of-war were put to work clearing away the drifts. Like ponderous windmills they shivered and threw their arms around their bodies in a futile attempt to keep warm in the worst winter ever recorded. A few of the older German soldiers, unhappy at the treatment, kindly handed out worn-out greatcoats to help keep away the cold. Later the younger soldiers, pale with fury, ordered them to remove the coats and confiscated them. The only privilege they were allowed was that of closing their eyes at night and sleeping in shivering fits, in the forlorn hope they might survive and be alive the following morning. Hopes soared when a British bombardment started up and continued day and night. Thomas sat in the hut rocking on his haunches, praying a stray shell might hit the

130

compound and blow it to kingdom come.

In the morning, shovels were thrust into their hands and they set to work repairing the damage caused by the allied bombing the previous night. Now the Germans treated them worse than before, and beatings became a daily occurrence for no apparent reason other than that they were the enemy. Thomas and two other men were issued with wooden buckets and ordered to remove the water from melted snow that rose steadily in the bottom of the trenches, and for long hours they toiled until every sinew and muscle screamed for pitiful release from the torment as they hurled bucket after bucket over the side of the trenches.

When the water failed to subside the Germans screamed and demanded they work faster, until eventually the inevitable occurred. A slightly-built man from Alice Springs swayed and collapsed with fatigue. Beaten half to death with gun butts, he lost the will to live and passed away quietly during the night in the cold hut. Thomas had tried to intervene – flinging a German to one side he sent him head first into the clinging mud, slipping and cursing he got to his feet, pointing his rifle at Thomas's stomach.

'Go on, shoot, you German bastard!' Thomas roared at him. 'Go on, finish it.'

If the German didn't understand English he quickly got the gist of the remark, and his finger tightened on the trigger. Thomas leaned forward, a sneer ripped across his face only inches from the German.

'You fucking cunt, you haven't got the fucking guts!' he screamed, hurling a mouthful of phlegm

131

in the German's face.

'Halt!' the German officer called. 'Lucky for you, we don't shoot prisoners-of-war,' he said flatly. 'Curb your tongue, Englander, or maybe you will become the exception.'

'Fuck off,' Thomas sneered.

From that moment on the Germans stepped up their reign of brutality and singled him out at the slightest pretence, he was beaten and degraded at every opportunity. Slowly but surely his hatred deepened beyond the bounds of reality for the Germans, devouring every cell of his existence for revenge until it finally overtook the gargantuan desire for his own death. The day would surely come when he would wreak his revenge tenfold, even if he needed to rise from the grave.

Months passed and in the course of time the weather eased and the driving sweep of snow and sleet turned to heavy rain. Now mixed with a rise in temperature, the countryside turned into a morass of slime and mud, impossible to move artillery and horses the fighting became sporadic and all but ground to a halt.

'Soon, you are to be moved to a camp in Germany, where perhaps the conditions will be better. If it were left to me, I would shoot you all,' the sergeant sneered.

Sure enough, two days later they were informed they were to be transferred to a camp called Giessen, inside Germany. Thomas's heart plummeted. No matter who won or lost the war, should he survive, he would, in all probability, be returned to England and his regiment. The blackness hovered in his mind for a moment, but clamping his eyes shut he failed to block out the image of standing in the dock at the Old Bailey, with Archie's grinning face peering over the judge's shoulder.

Over the following days the British shelling increased and spirits in the cold hut were considerably raised at the prospect of an early release.

'I reckon the allies are building up for a big push, I can feel it in the air,' Digger said.

'Oh yeah, well while you're up there in the air, see if you can find me a sexy little blonde, you bladdy drongo. Sit down and keep quiet,' Ned grunted.

'Might be better to sit the bladdy war out, not our bladdy fight anyway,' someone remarked. 'I've got a missus and kid at home.'

'I wouldn't be too cock sure about that, mate, bladdy good chance these bastards will kill the lot of us if they think they're going to lose the war,' another argued.

Quickly, the discussion became heated with the promise of turning into a free for all.

'All right, all right, settle down,' Digger called out. 'The way I see it, we don't have much choice in the mat...'

His words were cut short as a loud explosion rocked the hut. Beneath them the ground shook and heaved with bursting shells and the chimney crashed from the roof in a shower of hot sparks sending clouds of choking black dust billowing from the rafters. The prisoners lay on the floor with their hands locked over their heads for protection, waiting hopefully for the hut to collapse. Thomas lunged and tugged vainly with all his might at the door handle, forcing the tips of his

133

fingers under the door he wrenched with all his might. The door held firm and with his guts twisting into knots he cursed and blasphemed with every expletive he could lay his tongue to. Still the door held and outside the stillness returned.

'Chrissake, that was bladdy close; almost turned me underpants inside out!' Digger muttered.

'Yeah, I reckon you're right, we might be out of here any minute if Fritz has done a runner,' Ned answered, turning his attention to Thomas inching closer to the fire. 'Get away from the bladdy fire, you bladdy Pom, you know the rules. Nobody hogs the fire.'

Thomas rubbed his hands together and moved away.

As still as a ship on a painted canvas they waited expectantly, shivering in silence in the forlorn hope that someone might arrive to release them, take them somewhere they could bathe in hot water and eat a hot meal. No one came, and with sad reflective smiles on their tired faces, they shuffled patiently back to their beds and lay staring morosely up at the damaged rafters. Less than an hour later their hearts dropped as the hut door swung open, the bullying sergeant stepped inside scowling and scanned the faces glaring back at him through hostile eyes. Thomas sighed. The event he dreaded most was about to happen, he felt the slip of hope drift away and be replaced by cold despair.

'Aus, Aus, schnell.'

Reluctantly, he climbed into the rear of the first lorry of two and found himself next to the bullying sergeant sitting by the tailgate. Knowing how long the journey might take, he knew at some stage they would have to stop, when the opportunity arose, however slight, he would make his bid to escape, or die trying.

Hours passed and day crumbled away to dusk. Shivering in their thin uniforms, and with all hope washed from their eyes they approached the lights of a French village. Thomas listened to the driver grate the gears and the vehicle slowed to negotiate the narrow cobblestone streets. Bright candlelight danced and flickered, masked by delicate white lace curtains from scattered windows. With his throat as dry as a limekiln and his nerves tingling on edge, he tensed and waited, his mind made up. By the roadside next to a drinking trough lay a dead horse with its front legs hacked off, bloated and swollen with one side chewed away by the hungry dogs that scavenged the countryside in search of food. No doubt the villagers would have taken their share.

For some reason known only to him the sergeant leaned out and bellowed with laughter at the sight. His grip on his rifle momentarily relaxed. Thomas seized his opportunity and, snatching the rifle from the sergeant's hands, threw himself from the back of the lorry, narrowly missing being crushed by the one following. He ran, crouching between the houses and dipped down behind a burned-out car, red with rust and full of roosting hens next to a wooden barn. The drizzle ceased, replaced by a light breeze whipping up small ripples over deep puddles reflecting the distorted lights from the nearby houses. To prevent his warm breath vaporising in the chilled air and revealing his position, he held his hands over his mouth and waited. If they wanted him they would have to take him dead, but this night he would not die alone.

In a disorganised melee, panicking guards leapt from the vehicles shouting and screaming orders, each aware an escaped prisoner meant a death sentence, or worse, a transfer to the sub-temperatures of the freezing Russian front. The Germans would show him no mercy; only his death would satisfy them. They were not far behind him and he possessed little strength for a fight. When he glanced up, one by one the glowing candles from the windows were extinguished and the houses resembled ghostly shadows under the waning moonlight. Behind him the staccato yapping of dogs excited by the sudden commotion echoed through the narrow streets, a dart of apprehension rippled through his body. If they were loose, they might find him and give away his position.

His body tensed and he squinted against the darkness. The sound of crunching boots grew nearer and his finger tightened on the trigger. Elation filled his mind and a quiet courage gripped his heart, he was ready for the men who had treated him worse than an animal. The first German guard came, bent and stooped, making his way cautiously towards the burned-out car. His eyes wary and alert, swivelling first left and then right, slowly he withdrew his bayonet and snapped it onto the muzzle of the rifle. The click resounded through the village like a warning of impending death and Thomas swallowed. He

136

waited, ready, his teeth bared in a snarl. For a split second the guard hesitated, unsure of himself. Slowly he moved closer until Thomas could see his frightened blue eyes below a helmet too large to sit squarely on his head. With the rifle tucked securely into his shoulder and his cheek resting on the butt, Thomas squeezed the trigger. The German stopped in his tracks as though frozen in time and surprise flooded his eyes; in astonishment he looked at the blood pumping from his chest and crumpled to the ground.

Thomas sprinted across to the body, snatched up the German's rifle and entered the barn. Now he had extra ammunition, and stuffed the spare magazine into his pocket. The convoy consisted of six guards and two drivers. Unless they killed him first, they were about to meet their maker.

And so he lay concealed from view beneath a thin layer of straw facing the entrance to the barn. The smell of the old hay and fresh manure revived memories of his childhood. From across the farm-yard he heard the sound of music from a radio and he frowned. Then they came, as he knew they would, in a crouch, one slightly ahead of the other, their eyes hesitant with fear at the unexpected turn of events. He smiled with joy at the coarse face beneath the helmet leading the way: the bullying sergeant, his beady eyes flickering and snotty streamers hanging loose from his nose.

The bullet entered his mouth, blowing out the back of his neck sending a scarlet mist of blood splattering over his companion's face. The companion stepped back, dropped his rifle and, screaming with fright, attempted to wipe away

137

the blood. A snarl of naked hatred twisted and contorted Thomas's face. All thoughts of tiredness evaporated from his mind and he remembered the small Australian beaten and worked to death in the German trenches.

The man's large waxed ginger moustache caked with blood twitched below crazed eyes. Thomas pointed the muzzle at the man's right eye and pulled the trigger. In the background the dogs' barking turned to bloodcurdling howls echoing into the night. Three down, five to go. Automatically he remembered his sniper training and slipped from the barn searching for a new position to resume his destruction of the enemy.

His blood ran cold at the sound of a chilling scream reverberating through the night air, followed by another. The third scream sent such a torrent of fear through him his legs weakened and buckled, and he slid down behind a pile of weathered logs chopped and ready for burning. His hands trembled, he couldn't hold the rifle still.

Suddenly a German darted across the yard and disappeared behind a rotting outhouse. Sucking in air, he steadied his nerves and gripped the rifle, then cautiously worked his way round to the other side of the building. He halted and listened to the German labouring to catch his breath, mumbling in a low, incoherent voice.

The wind altered direction and the cold stench of the decaying horse pushed its way into his nostrils; he turned his head. Rage stoked through his body like a blazing bush. He wanted the German to suffer; he wanted them all to suffer the same way they had made him suffer, without pity or remorse. He saw the German kneeling with his hands clasped together, muttering in prayer. He stared, unable to believe his eyes. How dare a German pray like a Christian in the same manner he did in the small village church? His temper ignited into fury. Gripping the rifle by the barrel and with all the force he could muster, he darted over, swung the butt at the praying man's head. The German's head struck the outhouse wall, splintering the rotting wood and sending his helmet spinning into the air. With a low groan he slumped down on the wet grass. Thomas disconnected the bayonet from the rifle and sat astride him, pinning his arms down with his knees. With his teeth bared like a wild animal he stared down into the German's face, stretched long and ugly with protruding stained front teeth. He neither screamed with fear nor roared with anger, but wailed like a hungry baby, plaintive and heart-rending. Yet still he was a German. When he broke wind and filled his trousers, Thomas retched at the smell and pushed the tip of the bayonet slowly into the man's throat. The German's legs kicked and jerked, and Thomas watched with a contented smile until he lay still.

For too long he stared at the dead German, and a great whoosh of disgust devoured his body and numbed his mind. He felt lonelier than at any other time in his life. For a moment, he sat still, digesting what he'd done, and from the darkness the image of Archie loomed into his subconscious, leering, mocking and waving the inevitable noose. He didn't care: fuck you, Archie, fuck the Germans and fuck the war. The sword of justice is double-edged and, for the time being, he would wield the sharp edge.

'Monsieur, come quickly, please,' a voice called from out of the darkness.

He spun round and saw a Frenchman jogging across the grass towards him. The sleeves of his striped collarless shirt were rolled up to his elbows; on his head perched a flat cap and his bootlaces were untied. In one hand he held an unlit clay pipe, in the other a butcher's cleaver with fresh blood staining the blade.

'Monsieur, you are in great danger. The German drivers are dead and one guard has escaped. We must hide the two vehicles. German patrols will be along shortly and we must hurry.'

Thomas approached the two vehicles standing unattended by the roadside and pulled back the canvas flaps, surprised at the sight of the Australian prisoners waiting patiently for a turn of events. He grimaced and thought perhaps they might have shown a little more imagination.

'You waiting here for the Germans or going home?'

'Crikey, you're a bladdy handful, you are,' Ned said, climbing from the back of the lorry and getting in the cab. 'Right, all of you in the back, let's get out of here.'

Thomas smiled and slipped away unnoticed, waiting for the lorry to disappear into the night. The thought of desertion and the repercussions still held the sway of his mind, as did the death of the Germans. He was in no mood to return just yet.

Egged on by the gnawing fear of recapture, Ned

140

gunned the lorry forward until dawn fought the darkness turning night into day. Two hours of skidding and sliding on the treacherous wet roads while he grappled with the steering wheel caused his aching arms to feel as though they were in danger of being wrenched from their sockets. At the sound of gunfire he twisted his head round as the windscreen exploded, hurling shards of flying glass into his face. In panic he let go of the wheel, and throwing his body beneath the dashboard he waited for the lorry to come to a halt.

'Right, let's be having you, out you get, you Fritz bastards!'

Ned wound down the window and pushed his head out.

'You bladdy drongos blind,' he hollered. 'We're bladdy Aussies, escaped from a prisoner-of-war camp. Got a load more in the back. Take a look if you don't believe me.'

The nearest two British Tommies hesitated then cautiously made their way to the rear of the vehicle, ripped the canvas to one side and ordered the occupants out.

'Who's in charge?' a thickset corporal asked lowering his rifle.

'I suppose he is, he's the one who got us out,' Ned said, looking around for Thomas and then frowning. 'Where is he? I thought he was in the back with you.'

'We thought he was up front with you,' Digger said. 'Bladdy hell, he's as slippery as a billabong full of eels. He can't have disappeared into thin air; he's the one who set us free, for Chrissake. He ought to get the biggest bladdy medal you lot can

141

muster, if the Germans haven't already got him.'

'Give me his name and regiment. We'll keep an eye out for him,' a sergeant said.

'Says his name's Archie, that's all we know about him. Yorkshire Rifles, he said, a sniper. Germans brought him in alone, in a bad way he were, no one else with him though. He's a plucky little sod, I'll tell you. Looks like he might be twelve years old next birthday, he does. Don't suppose they feed 'em right in England. The Germans worked him over good and proper. He wouldn't let them break him though. Fair dinkum lad, I reckon, what do you reckon, Ned?'

'Yeah, reckon you're about right there, Digger, ain't seen many better, not outside of Australia anyway.'

'Yeah, well, it took an Englishman to rescue you bunch of thick kangaroo shaggers, didn't it?' a soldier prodded, working the bolt on his rifle.

Assisted by the villagers Thomas threw the dead Germans into a disused ditch and covered them with soil and rotting branches. The remaining German trying to escape was quickly caught frothing at the mouth. He clasped his hands over his ears and fell to his knees screaming for mercy. The Frenchman raised the cleaver and sliced open his neck.

'The Bosch, they are shit. They rape our women and steal our food and anything else they can get their filthy evil hands on. Then scream for mercy when we do the same to them,' the Frenchman said offering his hand. 'My name is Paul. You are a brave man, mon ami, welcome to our village.'

The villagers cautiously left their homes and, gathering round, stared at him in puzzlement, taking in his wild-eyed stare and emaciated body under the prisoner's threadbare uniform. They asked no questions. Content with their brief encounter and victory over the hated Bosch, they shrugged their shoulders in the Gallic way and boiled water. Alone at last he eased his body into the tub of hot water and for the first time in months took a hot bath. Wincing with pain he washed the filth from the cuts and bruises that covered his body. Later they burned the prison uniform and he smiled at the soft feel of ordinary clean clothes nestling against his stretched skin.

Like a man who hadn't eaten for months he threw himself into a meal of freshly cooked pork and hunks of black bread, and anything else he might stuff into his mouth. Politely he refused the wine, and stayed with clear spring water. Satisfied he'd eaten his fill, he sat hunched like an old man rocking on his haunches before a warm fire.

An elderly woman called Fleur gently bathed the sores on his head and wiped away the congealed pus before applying a soothing cream from a green bottle. Maybe she never had been an attractive woman: black hairs sprouted from a wart on the side of her nose and her lips were thick and cracked, like those of a hooked trout. Yet she possessed the touch of an angel, and her murmuring, combined with the cool cream, soothed away his pain. In a moment of unguarded weakness, her kindness nestled in a corner of his youthful heart and he loved her like a boy might

143

love his mother. Before she left, she brought hot water and a shaving razor and, placing the back of her wrinkled hand against his cheek, she spoke words he didn't understand. With a warm, comforting smile, she left him alone.

For the first time in months he looked at his reflection in the mirror and didn't recognise the person peering back: he seemed to have aged twenty years. His eyes, lifeless and sunken in dark sockets, stared from the deep recesses of his skull, a gaunt witness to the war and horror spent on the battlefields of hell. The lines on his forehead were deep and furrowed above hollowed cheeks, skin pushed tight against his jawbone bristling with a sparse, unkempt beard. His legs were white and thin and his ribs protruded like a man on the edge of starvation. The sobs came uninvited and un-aided, the tears ran freely and his body trembled and racked, not unlike a man on the verge of in-sanity. Yet he wasn't a man but a boy in an environment invented by the madness of men. Tonight he would take one step closer to a manhood he didn't relish and take his first shave, and scrape away the coarse hair that gave him so much discomfort. At sixteen years of age he didn't consider himself old enough to shave. Only men shaved he thought.

He leaned forward with his face in his hands and tried to make sense of his tangled life. Man, boy, what is the difference? He was just flesh and blood like everyone else, he hurt and ached like everyone else, and in his mind he believed only the conclusion of death would give him a welcome release. But when he leapt from the lorry he'd automatically feared for his life. He'd shook and trembled with naked fright in his bid to remain alive and survive to live another day. This time he hadn't killed in the name of self-preservation but in the name of cold-blooded revenge, and still his stomach ached and knotted for more. He swore he would have it. He no longer knew who he was, or cared. He was lost in a maelstrom from which he felt he would never escape, because there was nowhere else to go, except oblivion.

That night he shaved without the enjoyment or thrill of such a major step into the hallowed halls of manhood. The act meant nothing to him and held no significance. He merely scraped away unwanted hairs from his face for the sake of comfort. No band played and no cherubs appeared, showering him in masculine stardust. With a sardonic smile he wiped the soap from his face, abstractly aware that he would have to do the same again tomorrow, and the day after, and the day after that – it seemed fruitless.

Surrounded by a deafening quietness after the imprudent sound of shelling and gunfire he felt strange and unsure. Habit caused him to slow his breathing for fear of his presence being revealed to an imaginary enemy lurking nearby. For the best part of the night he forced himself to remember he was far away from the battlefield. Twice he woke with a start and left the bed to check outside, ever fearful of a sudden attack. The second time he dressed and fell into a deep, untroubled sleep, fully clothed. Better to be prepared than dead, he thought.

On a soft mattress he pulled the clean sheets

over his head like a child afraid of the dark, and dreamed he was safe in his mother's arms.

'S'il vous plait,' Fleur said the next morning, gesturing to the chair facing the table. The warm kitchen smelled of a distant past that he found almost too difficult to recollect without straining the archives of his memory. He took off his jacket and waited as Fleur busied herself over a hot stove with his breakfast. With saliva filling his mouth he thought his patience might expire and he would rip the hot food from the oven in his overwhelming desire to satisfy his hunger.

Fleur sat and watched in open amusement while he devoured fried eggs, black sausage and freshly baked croissants, until he could eat no more. She glowed with pleasure, clapped her hands at his hearty appetite and watched him slurp four large cups of black coffee. For five days he basked in all-consuming luxury. It seemed as though the whole village had turned out to shake the hand of the brave Englishman who had fought and beaten the Germans singlehandedly. When he felt ready he gladly helped to repair broken farm machinery, like he did at home on the moors with his father. To be allowed to clean out the barn was the greatest pleasure of all, and the smell of animals brought back the pleasant memories of the times he spent with Ruby. When alone, he would pretend that she stood behind him waiting to play the bullfighting game they enjoyed so much, and he whispered her name out loud and revelled in the sound.

His burning hatred of the Germans neither

wavered nor diminished. A primitive abyss of revenge and lust for blood pulsated through his veins like a raging river about to break its banks. Slowly but surely his strength returned and, silently under the cloak of darkness, made his way across the rain-covered fields. Like an avenger from the deepest corners of hell he searched for retribution.

Night after night, week after week he killed indiscriminately using rifle, bayonet and the meat cleaver borrowed from the butcher. Sifting through his victims' pockets, he took what he wanted and destroyed everything else. Sometimes he left them naked, tied and bound to freeze to death; others, he sliced off the top of their heads like an Apache Indian would scalp an enemy. On his return, he shared the spoils with the villagers, apart from the black chocolate, which he split equally between Fleur and Marie, the sixteen-year-old daughter of the baker who lived on the edge of the village.

Her long black hair and flashing dark-brown eyes confused him and dragged him under her spell. He couldn't tear his eyes from her tight-fitting dress, struggling to contain the heaving body of a young woman. After a time they became inseparable. Her father, although grateful for all that Thomas had done for the villagers, knew the relationship would one day inevitably lead to trouble. Then one morning, under a warm spring sun he stood with a sad and mournful expression, he twisted his cap with nervous fingers and faced Thomas outside the wooden barn.

'It is with regret, Monsieur, that we have come

147

to a decision that breaks our hearts, but we must be sensible. If the Germans return and find you here, Monsieur, we will be in much trouble,' Marie's father said. 'They will fire the village and kill us all. Women and children will be raped and killed also. I am sorry, and it is with deep regret we must ask you to go. We thank you from the bottom of our hearts, and will always remember everything you have done for us.'

Thomas listened for a moment he felt hurt at the sudden coldness. His personal knowledge of German cruelty and bestiality cut deep, yet he harboured no desire to bring reprisals to the village. Reluctantly he promised to leave the village the next day. That night in the barn he met with Marie to say goodbye. There was a chill in the air and everything seemed calm and quiet – the war might have been a million miles away. The straw felt soft and warm when she leaned over and kissed him softly on his lips. He remained motionless, confused, his body taut. His breathing came faster when she gently squeezed his cheeks with her fingers, causing his mouth to open. She kissed him again and he felt her tongue probe into his mouth. He pulled away, unsure what he should do next. When he noticed she had closed her eyes he followed suit.

A pigeon fluttered noisily in the loft, sending him bolt upright with nervousness, like a man on a scaffold unsure when the trapdoor would spring open. She smiled. It was going to be his first time and she felt glad it was with her. André, the carpenter's son, had stolen her virginity twelve months previously, and often ever since. She had quickly learned that making love was far more enjoyable if the initiative was hers. Taking his hand she placed it on her warm heaving breast. He squeezed gently. Undoing the buttons holding the thin cotton blouse she allowed it to fall. Gently cupping her full breast in his hand, he ran his thumb over her chocolate-brown nipple and listened to her soft sigh. She pulled his head down allowing his tongue to replace his thumb, as though he'd done it a thousand times before. Her sighs became more urgent, and holding him tighter he sucked and licked greedily, driven by a frantic haste.

For the first time in his young life he felt the fire in his groin and her darting fingers released the buttons of his trousers. His whole body became engulfed in a tempest of primitive desires and all thoughts were swept from his mind. When his hand automatically sought the moist treasure between her legs she brushed it away, and with her body trembling and more urgent she lifted herself over him and engulfed him. He felt her warm and moist, and seconds later the sky opened and the stars exploded. He jerked and bucked, his body spiralling out of control, and in a sublime frenzy he felt the surges from his body. He lay back, drained and exhausted, bewildered that something so natural could be so wonderful. When he opened his eyes, she was gone.

That following morning Fleur pulled his jacket collar tight around his neck, like a mother would with her child about to venture out into the cold. Again, she spoke words he didn't understand, and kissing him lightly on both cheeks she handed him a hunk of boiled ham, a slab of cheese and a loaf of freshly baked white bread wrapped in white cloth.

Chapter Nine

It was the time in England when nature begins to break into beauty, a time when heavy scented roses peeped shyly from unfurling green buds and fairies could be seen flitting from blossom to blossom at the bottom of every garden. It was springtime.

In France, for three days the flashes of the thundering guns drew closer and shellfire destroyed nature's efforts indiscriminately and without conscience. Yet Thomas felt his mind calm and untroubled, his thoughts unshackled and crystal clear. Satisfied that German flesh had felt the press of his revenge for the brutal treatment they had meted out, he calculated how many had died by a swift stroke of the meat cleaver he'd borrowed from the village butcher, or those who had died with a bullet in the skull. At least fifty, possibly more – he hadn't thought to count.

Then there was Marie, with the dark eyes that had transported him to a world of ecstasy and pleasure such as he'd never known, and perhaps might never know again. He felt certain he'd made love to her, but couldn't remember because it had all happened so quickly. From now on he held the right to consider himself to be a man. After all, what else must a boy do to attain manhood? He smiled.

A vision of his parents sprang into his mind. Only six months had passed since he'd left the small village on the edge of the Yorkshire Moors, more than a hundred thousand lifetimes on the Western Front.

On the fourth night a cold wind penetrated his skin and he found shelter under a small wooden bridge spanning a slow-running stream. With lips blue from the cold he tried to rest. Reluctantly plagued by constant shivering and accompanied by scurrying rats he finally gave up the remote hope of ever snatching a few hours sleep. Throughout the night he huddled as best he could to keep out the cold and listened to the sounds between the rumble of cannons – the cry of a fox, the hoot of an owl. Then with his eyes closed he recalled every swear word and expletive he'd ever heard, and repeated each three times out loud over and over again; until sleep eventually came.

When he woke he listened to the non-stop sound of hungry ducks and hissing geese; overhead a bright sun shone in the sky and he smelled the burning wood of a campfire nearby. Seized by fear he pulled the rifle close and slipped off the safety catch, pulled back the bolt and slowly pushed a bullet into the breech. Not far from where he lay he heard the whinny of tired horses accompanied by the jingle of harnesses followed by the deafening rumble of heavy artillery crossing the bridge. For a moment panic rushed into his heart at the thought of being captured once more by the Germans. He fought to find a reason to live and cursed Archie beneath his breath. First his hands, then his legs, then his whole body trembled and he lost control. The rifle slipped from his hands, slithered down the bank and disappeared into the clouded water. In a panic and blinded from any semblance of reason he climbed from under the bridge and pulled himself up onto the bank.

'Come on then, you German bastards, get it over with!' he roared, raising his arms sideways and clamping his eyes shut.

The four men in shirtsleeves brewing tea on a makeshift fire turned with startled eyes and stared up at him. A fifth man stepped from behind a row of tethered horses with his rifle aimed at Thomas's head.

'What are you waiting for? Fucking do it, shoot me!'

'Who do you think you are, you noisy big bastard?' the man said, lowering his rifle.

Thomas frowned and opened one eye. 'You're not Germans,' he said in a bewildered voice, 'you're English?'

'Bloody hell, he's quick off the mark, ain't he? Can't be a bloody officer, that's for sure,' the man grinned. 'Who the bloody hell are you, and where did you get them clothes from?'

'Stone the crows, he's a bleedin' frog,' one of the men crouched round the fire said. 'That's what he is, I can tell.'

'You might be right, Bert, you always was a clever sod, too clever for this army. Take his shoes off and make sure he ain't got web feet,' someone chuckled.

'I'm a deserter,' Thomas said, staring into the grimy black face.

'Well, you didn't get far, mate, you're in the middle of the British lines, you daft sod. What's your name then, and where's your uniform?'

'I'm Lance Corporal Archie Elkin, 3rd Yorkshire Rifles. Uniform? I threw it away.'

A small crowd of soldiers curiously aware of the disturbance gathered round and nervous fingers fondled cold rifle triggers.

'Hang on, hang on. Elkin, did you say, Archie Elkin?' someone asked.

'Yes.'

'It's him, ain't it? I recall the name. They've been looking for you for bloody ages, mate. Stone the bloody crows, never thought I'd ever set eyes on you. Kangaroo shaggers said you were dead. Shot by Fritz trying to escape. Come on, him up there would like a word with you,' the man with the cockney accent said.

'Up there? Who's him up there?' Thomas frowned.

'Him up there, that's what we call the bloody useless officer ain't it, him up there, them up there, what's the bloody difference? They're all bloody officers and that's what we call them, when we don't call them donkeys. Ain't lost your memory, have you? Blimey, that's a turn up that is,' the cockney said, pushing his cap back and scratching his head.

Thomas pushed out a long sigh of relief – at last his war was over, and rising like Samson in his blindness, he set his mind on his death.

'Come on then, matey, my patrol's nearly over,

some other poor bugger's turn to wander round freezing his balls off half the night,' the cockney said, slinging his rifle over his shoulder.

They passed the burned-out and gutted remains of a large roofless farmhouse, still smoking, and dropped down into a narrow trench. Even with duckboards piled three high the water reached their ankles. As they moved forward row upon row of shivering dejected men leaned belly down on the sides of the wet, greasy trench grasping rifles with fixed glistening bayonets tight to their chests as though they offered a last bastion of comfort. Their filthy uniforms, now a familiar sight on the Western Front, hung soaking wet and water squelched from their boots like squeezed sponges at the slightest movement. In another time they might have been shadows of his imagination if it were not for the utterance of oaths and curses falling from their downturned mouths. Some turned with a disinterested glance at those passing; others, with a cigarette dangling from their lips, coughed and shook their heads to escape the stinging smoke blurring their sight, and prayed to God they wouldn't go over the top tonight and God would spare them to see another dawn.

An assortment of dirty canvas sheets and box-wood covered in a thick layer of earth concealed the dugout serving as officers' quarters. Two old splintered decaying front doors, still complete with brass door knockers and handles taken from a bombed house, lay over the canvas to prevent the wind from blowing it away. To the left an annexe had been hacked into the side of the clay trench, similar to the one used by the arrogant

154

German officer with a penchant for pink coloured cigarettes. Two thin candles hung from the roof offering minimal light, flickered over the pages of an opened book describing the art of fly-fishing. Lieutenant Devonshire, wearing his cap back to front, sat at a small table studying a map through a magnifying glass. He turned and looked up when the sentry came to attention.

'Brought in an escaped prisoner-of-war, Sir,' he said. 'He says his name is Elkin, Sir. Lance Bombardier Elkin. If you cast your mind back, Sir, you might remember they've been looking for him for weeks. A deserter, Sir, that's what he is, Sir, or that's what he says he is. Says he deserted months ago, Sir, from the 3rd Yorkshire Rifles.'

'Thank you, Private Knowles, that will do for now, carry on. Come in, Elkin,' the officer said, noticing Knowles' reluctance to leave. 'Carry on!' he bawled at the soldier.

'So you're Elkin? I've heard quite a bit about you, old chap. The Australians look upon you as a hero. We all thought you'd bought it, you know. Captured while out on a sniping mission, eh, to bring a few captured goodies back for the boys? Jolly clever ruse of yours telling them you were a deserter. The Germans are not over fond of snipers. I imagine Fritz gave you a bad time. By all accounts they have an unsavoury reputation for torture and ill-treatment of prisoners. Well, they've got it coming jolly soon,' Lieutenant Devonshire boomed, 'but organising the escape of over twenty Australian prisoners-of-war, capturing enemy vehicles and killing the guards

155

... the stuff of heroes, that's what this is, and I won't hear any different – responsible for sending the morale in the trenches sky high. Even the papers back home are having a field day. Be a medal in this for you, that's for certain, and a promotion most likely.'

Thomas sat with his mouth open, his mind as clear as a blinded window. Promotion, medals, what in God's name is he talking about? His spirit spiralled into his boots. Which part of this army didn't he understand? He was a deserter not a bloody hero. He desired death not medals. Perhaps he should go home, break into Buckingham Palace and shoot the king while he's on the crapper. Maybe that'll make them sit up and take notice.

'But, Sir, it's true, I was trying to desert, Sir,' he stammered.

Lieutenant Devonshire cocked his head to one side and ran his hand across his mouth.

'Hmm, give you a bad time did they, eh? Rest, that's what you need, old boy. Get some food and a good night's sleep. They moved your lot up the line to a place called Serre, I think. We'll sort it out in the morning. Anyway, well done, lad, been a pleasure to meet you. And one other thing, pop along to the stores for a new uniform – can't have you wandering around dressed like that, old chap, against army regulations.'

Chapter Ten

1917

On the top deck of a red double-decker London bus converted to carry twenty-five fully kitted soldiers, Thomas sat in his new uniform feeling like a teat on a bull. More than one hundred buses made up the convoy for Serre that day and the air quickly grew heavy with choking diesel fumes. With unrelenting regularity, soldiers exercised their God given right to complain about anything that moved and grumbled at everything that didn't. In joyous unison they hurled obscene insults as a long tailback built up and lorries hooted impatiently trying to queue-jump horse-driven wagons loaded with supplies for the front. The majority of the troops were from the 12th Battalion Durham Light Infantry in the process of being moved to new positions. The minority, aware of where they were going, made it un-commonly plain to the drivers that they were in no rush to reach their destination.

As usual Thomas continued to keep a low pro-file, content to listen as some ignored the furore while eating tins of bully beef and singing the tunes of the day in loud, confident voices. Some showed scant regard to his new uniform; others threw a brief enquiring stare and then turned their interest to three-card brag or pontoon. It wasn't their place to interfere with another man's thoughts, most were too intent on wiping away gruesome memories of their own.

Although he didn't agree Thomas accepted that the released Australian prisoners had taken it upon themselves to over-elaborate the events relating to their escape. Men liked to exaggerate their exploits in time of war, it made them a figure of respect in the eyes of other troops, and through their splendid accounts he had been reluctantly pushed to the fore as a hero.

All along the front line the landscape remained unchanged. The big thaw was taking place and thick mud and slush replaced the frozen earth. Men stripped to the waist and bathed in sweat heaved and cursed with every expletive known to man, and slowly field guns and cannons were manoeuvred into position for the next onslaught. Outside the graveyard, marked by helmets atop bayoneted rifles, lay the heartrending sight of dead cattle and horses, prone and bloated, their legs pointing grotesquely towards the sky.

As far as the eye could see the countryside resembled a charcoal etching on a dull grey background, a place where gaunt black branchless trees stood stark, cold and forbidding holding up a bleak sky. Hills and mounds where proud men once stood and fought and died magnificently were now unprepared burial sites roamed by the spirits of warring soldiers, and in the mist alone and cold they waited for the Valkyries to transport them to the halls of Valhalla.

After a cold journey of several hours the convoy slowed to a crawl. The sickly smell of blood, gangrened wounds, iodine and chloroform mixed with the stench of death penetrated the air, dulling the senses. Men quickly lit cigarettes allowing the smoke to drift up their noses in a vain attempt to neutralise the nauseous odour. Those that never smoked held dirty rags over their mouths to prevent from retching. Ahead, a medical station full of mutilated and dying men with red and pink stumps where strong limbs once grew waited for attention, some covered in masses of wriggling maggots gorging on the rotting flesh. A soldier with his head wrapped in a bloodstained bandage moved slowly among them offering words of comfort, while swabbing the maggots away with stinging disinfectant. It seemed extraordinary that in this tented house of pain and misery there was no outward expression of moans or complaints. Most of the wounded and dying asked for no more than a smoke, some never lived long enough to finish the cigarette. Men left the buses and searched their pockets and kitbags for small titbits of food, and perhaps a packet of cigarettes or a sticky boiled sweet for the fallen soldiers.

'There you go, mate, all the best. Ain't you the lucky one, going home to Blighty? Chin up, pal,' they mumbled holding back the tears and handing out all they could spare.

Shuffling to one side they bowed their heads in humble silence and fumbled with the buttons of their uniforms, each man aware he might be next to die a long lingering death. All around young nurses with matted, straggly hair and blood-stained uniforms swept to and fro with empty, vacant eyes caring for their charges. Their pretty faces were drawn and tired yet never without a brief semblance of a smile. Some sat with men calling out for their mothers as death drew closer. 'Yes, dear, Mother's here, rest now,' a nurse whispered, taking the man's hand. For a moment he looked young again, the pain drained from his boyish face, and with a final upward glance his head rolled to one side and he left this hell for a better world.

When night-time fell each man had to fend for himself: no hotels, no beds, no feather mattress. Throw your kit down anywhere. Sleep wherever you can lay your head and be grateful if it still remained on your shoulders when you woke in the morning. Tired men slumped fully-dressed on the seats of the red London buses, their faces black and grimy, and with clothes and boots caked with wet mud they shivered without complaint into a fitful night's sleep. Perhaps tomorrow would be a better day, a day when a nightingale sang, a day when the battlefield turned into a golden meadow and all the things nature intended. Instead the morning of disappointment dawned and everything was as the day before, tired eyes rubbed sore with grimy hands. Then it was time for a quick brew and back to the buses and the next port of misery.

Thomas watched Sergeant Bull bobbing along with his jaunty walk. He smiled, feeling as though he had never been away. The time he'd spent suffering in the prison camp he'd erased from his mind and now amounted to no more than a bad dream. Close by Leslie Hill leaned against the wooden timbers supporting the side of the crumbling trench, his grimy face a picture of concentration as he cleaned his rifle with an old sock full of holes. Stan Banks sipped steaming hot tea from a dirty enamel mug with a broken handle. His skin grey, his eyes rimmed red, he looked up with an empty stare displaying no acknowledgment. Ian Lewis lounged against the muddy trench wall staring down with a bored pitiless expression at a rat the size of a mongrel dog nibbling at his boot. There was something in their sad haggard faces that evoked apathy in others and kept at arm's length any introspection. He felt the cold breath of disappointment tug away his smile.

'Eh, lad, it's good to see you in one piece. Had a bad time by all accounts, been expecting you we have, only a few of us left from those who started out with us,' Sergeant Bull said, his ice-blue eyes even wilder than ever before. 'Got a new officer now we have. Other poor lad disappeared under a bomb blast along with Ollie Love. He'll want to see you straight away.'

Lieutenant Tarry gazed at Thomas through dull grey lifeless eyes. His sharpened cheekbones jerked like a man used-up, and his mouth twitched at the corners. In his bony white fingers he clutched a pencil, and his hands trembled and shook in spasms as though they might fall to pieces. He pushed the writing paper away and tried unsuccessfully to work his facial muscles into a smile.

'Lieutenant Tarry, Sir, this is Lance Corporal Elkin, Sir. We were informed some days ago he

161

was on his way, you particularly asked to see him,' Sergeant Bull said.

'Elkin, who the devil is Elkin? Ah yes, Elkin, I remember now. What did I want to see him about, Sergeant?'

'I understand he is to accompany you to HQ Sir, as soon as he arrives, both to be awarded medals, so I've been told.'

'Well, what are we waiting for? Let's go.'

'Best if you put your boots on first, Sir. I'll fix up some transport and we'll leave first thing in the morning,' Sergeant Bull said gently.

'Good idea, Sergeant, till the morning then.'

Outside the trench, Sergeant Bull took Thomas to one side.

'He's lost his nerve he has, poor bugger. He led two assaults from the front. Stepped out in front of the men as brave as a dog in a bone factory and marched with his arms swinging into a hail of bullets without flinching. Aye, then he stood on top of the trench hurling grenades at the Germans from a bag he carried slung over his shoulder. When he was finished with that lot he walked to the second German trench and did the same again. Bloody Germans scarpered like rabbits in a field full of greyhounds when they saw him coming. It finished him though. He knows he's going to die and he's just waiting for it to happen. I've tried to reason with him but he'll have none of it. You're both being awarded medals for bravery tomorrow. I'll come along to keep an eye on the pair of you.'

And so he did. He fussed over Lieutenant Tarry like he was a child, cleaning his boots and uniform – unheard of for a sergeant.

162

Lieutenant Tarry was awarded the Military Cross for Gallantry in the Field by a major general wearing a starched uniform, and promoted to captain. Thomas stood in line with other ranks waiting his turn to be decorated by a bent and decrepit old colonel, who had to shout to overcome his own deafness. Thomas wondered what part they had played in the slaughter of the thousands of men dispatched from the trenches to certain death, or if they even knew there was a war on.

'Well done, Corporal, damn fine show, fine exhibition of soldiering,' the elderly officer rasped, and with fumbling hands spent the next two minutes attempting to pin the Military Medal to Thomas's tunic.

The officer's handshake felt cold and weak, almost without life. He cringed and wanted to be free of him. He wanted neither the medal nor the promotion to corporal. Nor did he wish to be in their company. The only tangible memento after battle was a decoration of some sort, and its tangibility made it highly valued. The only prize for the ordinary soldier was a coloured ribbon to show he had done his duty towards his king and country. Yet, to Thomas this meant publicity, the one thing he wanted to avoid. Later, an army photographer looking for a story tried to take his picture and he ducked away, covering his face. The offer of seven days' leave in Blighty softened the blow, and that evening he caught a train to Calais.

Chapter Eleven

Blighty

The slow train to Calais was packed sardine-tight with sunken-eyed men returning to England. No light or hint of emotion appeared in any of them, not even a dash of hope glimmered faintly in their dimmed eyes, apathy ruled. Most suffered wounds and sat minus limbs on their way to hospitals all over England. Allied field hospitals were no longer capable of coping with the horrendous number of wounded pouring in – men had died who might in a different time have been saved. Gradually the chatter abated.

Tired eyes sparked to a glimmer and gazed in wonder from steamed windows at the sight of trees with rustling green leaves, a spread of lush green grass conquered the manmade desolation. As if by magic a landscape untouched by thousands of screaming shells annihilating and demolishing everything in their path appeared like a dream from another world, stretching for as far as the eye could see. Gone were the blackened battlefields of death. Gone were the decaying bodies, rotting and putrefying in the near-forgotten realms of No Man's Land. Gone were the thousands of upturned rifles holding a solitary helmet, standing in dark silhouette against the dim early-morning dawn, marking the grave of a husband, a father, a boyfriend, a brother, a son or a boy not yet out of his teens. Houses with bright-red tiled roofs clustered together forming a small village, the smoke of house fires drifting lazily into the still air like white columns from stout chimney pots.

'Are we there already? It's gone very quiet,' a man with a bandaged face whispered. 'It's just that I can't see. Can someone tell me what you see?'

'Aye, I can that, lad,' Thomas said, looking at the weeping blisters on the man's hands. 'I can see a forest of a thousand trees. Green they are, like holly at Christmas. The fields are full of golden corn and flowing yellow rape surrounded by neat and tidy hedgerows. In the middle I can see a small village with white painted houses sitting side-by-side with bright-red roofs glistening in the sunlight. Children are playing on a swing watched over by their mothers. Hey, I can see a herd of horses cantering towards a silver lake full of leaping fish. In the distance black-and-white cattle are grazing in a meadow, with larks sweeping and diving overhead in a sun-drenched blue sky. It's a grand sight, lad, one to remember,' he said, reddening at his newly acquired eloquence when eyes swivelled towards him.

'Aye, it sounds like it is, thank you. You've given me something to think on, lad. God bless you,' he answered quietly, and turned his blinded eyes to face the window.

At Calais the ever-present rain sheeted down like the devil's gift to the righteous. Injured and hollow-eyed soldiers stood soaked to the skin without complaint, to be helped aboard the dipping ship waiting to take them home. Thomas looked around for something to cheer him: a peal of laughter, a smiling face, a dog wagging its tail. His optimism unrewarded, the fingers of war and misery reached out like the tentacles of a male-volent octopus, tainting and defiling all in its wake. He was one of the more fortunate: a hero and a winner of the Military Medal. The sight of an uninjured soldier with all limbs intact seemed to be rare. From the gloomy hardware shop doorway, he sheltered as best he could from the rain and watched a young, frail, pretty nurse stagger while attempting to support a burly private twice her size. With only one leg he strug-gled to manoeuvre his crutches without crushing the young woman and they began to slip from his hands. He tottered and the nurse's face creased in pain in a vain attempt to steady him. Thomas caught his arm and slipped it over his shoulder.

'All right, lad, I've got you. Let me take the weight and we'll get you safely onboard,' he said, glancing at the blood seeping from the dressing covering the stumped remains of the man's leg. Through a line of stretcher-bearers with their patients he made his way to the front of the queue.

'Gangway!' he hollered. 'Got a man bleeding to death here, make way.'

'We've people on stretchers here if you don't mind,' someone called. 'Wait your turn.'

'Aye, and he can lay on his arse a bit longer. Now get out me bloody way or I'll throw the lot of you into the bloody sea,' he growled. 'I'll not tell you again!' he roared.

Quickly they shuffled to one side mouthing silent complaints and made room as the two men stepped onto the swaying gangplank.

'Come on, lass, follow me, you're going to be needed in a minute, I reckon,' he called over his shoulder.

Pushing a lock of loose golden hair away from her forehead and with a small grateful smile forming on her lips, she followed him onboard. Thomas found an empty table in the saloon, laid the man on the surface and turned to the nurse.

'Will he be all right, miss?'

'Thanks to you I think he'll be fine, thank you,' she said, searching through her bag for a needle and thread to re-stitch the leg. 'Are you one of the walking wounded?'

'No, miss, thank God, I've just got a spot of leave,' he said sheepishly, walking away to escape the eye-watering smell of disinfectant.

Through tired eyes he watched from the stern of the ship as France disappeared into a heavy mist. White horses leapt from the crest of waves and a stinging spray whipped into his face. He tugged the collar of his greatcoat closer around his ears. Gripping the handrail he leaned out over the side and watched churning foam from huge bronze propellers leave a frothing trail in the grey waters. Overhead shrieking seagulls wheeled and hovered against the biting wind, hoping for the sight of a small fish to ram down their hungry gullets.

Not so very long ago back in the dark doorway at Calais he'd almost made up his mind he wouldn't travel back to England. The French port would have suited him fine, a roof over his head and a dry bed to sleep in would more than suffice. But deep down he knew helping the nurse to get the injured soldier onboard had been the right thing to do. If the situation were reversed, he was certain others would do the same for him.

The miseries of war were a self-inflicted burden waiting to be shared by everyone, and he was no exception. He'd been lucky up to now – or perhaps in his state of mind, unlucky. He held his breath and leaned further out over the handrail, until he reached the point of balance where an inch either way would make the difference between going over the side into the waiting waters or remaining onboard. With his eyes closed, he gritted his teeth and loosened his grip on the rail. Now was the time to repay his debt to the living world.

'Hello, I thought you might appreciate a warm cup of tea.'

For a stunned moment he thought his ears were playing tricks with him. A sense of great joy seemed to leap and flame within him and he was barely able to contain the heat of happiness coursing through his blood. Once again he had cheated death and left Archie floundering and sneering in the black waters below. He pushed himself back and turned to face the young nurse. When she removed her hat to prevent the wind blowing it from her head, he gasped at her golden hair, long and curled it streamed into the wind. Her pale-blue eyes were large and held a permanent expression of disconcerted bewilderment. Her soft flesh glowed young and unwounded with an aura of peace and gentleness, and the tenderness of her smile said, let's be friends.

In an instant he went from man back to boyhood. He felt foolish and awkward, wondering if she knew he had been about to hurl himself into the swirling black sea. He looked down at her small slim body trying to come to terms with the dipping and rolling movements of the ship, the knuckles of her small hands chalk-white as she gripped the ship's rails. Turning his head, he glanced ruefully at the dark waters and fought the malignant forces squeezing his heart. The feeling passed as quickly as it came and he returned to his imaginary state of manhood.

'Eh, you shouldn't have bothered, lass,' he said, forcing a smile. 'You'll catch your death out here in the cold. How's your patient?'

'He's fine, he wants to thank you.'

'No need for that, I would have done the same for anyone.'

'Nevertheless, you should practise what you preach. Now come in out of the cold,' she chided.

The injured man had fallen asleep and she tucked his collar round his ears and briefly stroked his forehead as a mother would a sick child. Sitting by his side she gently pushed his hair away from his eyes. He murmured softly without waking.

Her name was Catherine Banner, she told him, and she lived with her parents in Deal, on the Kent coast.

'Have you always been a nurse, miss?' Thomas asked shyly.

She smiled. 'Catherine, call me Catherine. No, only for a few months. I watched the wounded being brought ashore at Dover during a visit to a friend, and the next day I joined the Voluntary Aid Detachment as part of Kent's care for the wounded. Father wasn't at all pleased. I used to listen to the sound of the guns from my bedroom and thought I might be of use. I'm not qualified, but I do my best.'

'I'm sure you do, miss,' he said sheepishly. 'I reckon you do a grand job.'

'They said I lacked the stamina for nursing at the front,' she smiled. 'I tried as hard as anyone to fulfil my duties, but I grew tired so quickly, so they transferred me to a hospital in Folkestone.'

Inseparable, they spent the journey to Dover talking and chatting about nothing in particular. At first Thomas felt uneasy that someone as beautiful as Catherine would choose to speak to him, a rough, poorly-educated farmer's lad from Yorkshire with only an inkling of manners. Yet he felt a warm glow spread through his body and for the first time in months he felt relaxed and the rewarding feeling of confidence eased his mind. He wanted to tell her about Archie, tell her that it was an accident and he hadn't meant for him to die. He wanted to bare his soul to her and scrape his conscience clean. She would understand, he could see it in her eyes. When he turned to look at her the gusting wind lifted her hair revealing her slender white neck, he felt an overriding desire to reach out and touch her, to hold her in his arms.

'There, there they are,' she cried, grabbing his arm and squeezing, 'the white cliffs of Dover. We are nearly home!'

His thoughts crashed from his mind. He smiled at her excitement and glanced down at her hand clutching his arm. She caught his glance and blushed. Quickly removing her hand she grabbed the ship's rail with both hands. Disappointment cut into his heart. He cursed the moment he had looked at her hand on his arm, he wanted to feel her touch once more, but the moment had passed.

'You should see the moors on a fine day, lass, there's a sight to see,' he said, and cursed himself for his forwardness towards her.

He wondered if men were allowed to make love to nurses, do the things he and Marie had done in the small French village. Most likely not, he reckoned, they're too good to do bad things to, and he felt shame at his carnal thoughts.

'Perhaps one day I will,' she said, watching him from the corner of her eye.

His heart leapt and he felt a great tenderness towards her. The boat ceased to dip and roll in the angry sea, and the waters calmed like the small pond behind the church of St Luke in his village on the edge of the moors. Cautiously, he slid his hand along the handrail and placed it gently over hers. For a long moment she remained motionless, making no attempt to move or discourage the bond. He wanted to speak, to tell her how he felt, to tell her he loved her, but his mind froze and the words refused to enter his mouth. He bit into the side of his cheek and tasted the salty blood as she slowly pulled her hand away.

All along the harbour rows of ambulances with red crosses painted on the sides waited bumper to bumper with engines running to take the wounded away for treatment. Some would recover from their wounds and eventually be returned to the slaughter at the front; others, perhaps, would spend the remainder of their lives staring into a grate of burning embers, trying to forget the past.

171

Whether, like Buster Matthews, they would ever master the art of playing the piano was debatable.

'Will you write to me, Archie?' she said, gazing up at him. 'Visit me one day; you are a good man and I have enjoyed your company, and thank you for helping me.'

Thomas's heart soared so high he thought he might stop breathing.

He watched as she wrote her address on a slip of paper. He wanted to hold her and kiss her, protect her from her own frailness. Then he remembered his previous thoughts – perhaps you are not allowed to kiss nurses. She stood on her toes and kissed him lightly on the cheek. Before he could respond, she disappeared into the back of a crowded ambulance.

Chapter Twelve

London

The address on his leave pass read No. 2 Frith Road, Leytonstone, East London. The clerk at HQ in France told him it was clean and tidy, and Mrs Tuttle, the landlady, served a good meal. Outside Victoria Railway Station he stared as far as his eyes would allow at the mass of buildings protruding upwards into the skyline like a set of uneven teeth in a huge mouth. The rumble of heavy cannon replaced by the discordant sounds of a busy city hummed in his ears, and the hustle and bustle filled his mind. People laughed as though they did not have a care in the world. Men dressed in smart suits with bowler hats walked arm-in-arm with ladies who wore tight-fitting gowns and dresses displaying slim waists and firm, accentuated bosoms. The sight of so many khaki uniforms astounded him and he recalled the forlorn haggard faces cowering in the trenches. Why were these men laughing and making jolly while others disappeared from the face of the earth under an exploding shell? None of it made any sense, and he turned away feeling confused and sceptical.

'Hop on the first bus to stop over there,' an elderly lady selling purple heather on a street corner said, pointing to a bus stop. 'Ask the driver for directions, dearie, he'll tell you where to get off.'

In Trafalgar Square he stared up at Lord Nelson, thinking it was a statue of the king. Slowly, the city began to fascinate him, teeming with life, a multitude of babbling tongues from all corners of the Commonwealth laughing and shouting, and recruitment posters plastered over walls showing the grim face of Lord Kitchener with a pointing finger, reminding the fainthearted that their country needed them. The brittleness of war was evident everywhere. Soldiers from all parts of the British Empire paraded in an array of uniforms in the crowded streets. For the majority it was their first time in a large city and London, the capital of the Commonwealth, had everything: women, pubs, clubs, sex and alcohol were all the requirements necessary for a fighting soldier waiting to go to war.

'Leytonstone?' the policeman outside Downing Street exclaimed. 'You're heading in the wrong direction, son, head up that way,' he said, and sent him along the Strand.

Thomas set off, in no hurry, his eyes darting like a camera taking in and storing all that he saw. Occasionally he stopped to look through shop windows at the numerous goods and wares on offer, and remembered the raggedy children in Leeds for whom he'd bought broken biscuits. He saw no such thing here, maybe people were richer in London. Women dressed in stylish tailored costumes with perky hats sitting jauntily on their heads paraded down the streets. More than one woman smiled at him as he passed by, and he blushed scarlet when two teenage girls blew him a kiss and shouted, 'Hello, soldier boy, show us your bayonet!'

Halfway along the Strand he stopped to admire two magnificent shire horses harnessed to a brewer's dray. Flashing polished brasses jingled and glinted, the leather harness shone in the low afternoon sun and the horses pawed the air and snorted down their noses, eager to be on their way to a nosebag of oats and to slake their thirst from the cool water in a waiting trough.

'I'm looking for Frith Street,' he asked the driver.

'Gawd blimey, General, hop on, I'm going that way myself, so I am,' he said, shovelling a pile of horse droppings into a bucket and wiping his hand down his green smock. 'On leave are you, mate? Well, you enjoy yourself. Tried to get in myself, I did, lost two fingers off me right hand, I

174

did, first day I started work. Dropped a barrel of brown ale on them, didn't I? Blimey, it bloody hurt, did a right bloody dance-and-a-half I did, to bloody Covent Garden and back. Army wouldn't have me, said I couldn't fire a rifle properly with half me fingers missing. Cor blimey, happy as a pig on a bacon slicer I was.'

Mrs Tuttle was a large woman with a strident voice to match and a heart twice her size. She wore her hair pulled back straight and tied in a severe bun with a length of black lace looped in a bow and habitually wiped her hands on her white pinafore before inspecting her fingernails. Her toad in the hole was to be the best he'd ever tasted, although he would never admit that to his mother. She had lost her husband in 1914 at Mons. His name was Archie too, she told him, watching with a satisfied smile as he demolished a plate of stew and dumplings and wiped the plate clean with a hunk of bread.

'You're a corporal, are you? Well, you don't look bleeding old enough to be in the army. That piece of cloth on your chest, that's a medal ribbon ain't it?'

'Not just any medal, Maud,' an elderly gentleman said, sitting in the corner reading a newspaper through a pair of pince-nez spectacles perched on his nose. 'That's the Military Medal, awarded for outstanding bravery in the field. Spotted it soon as the lad walked in; we've got a hero with us today, Maud, better look after him.'

'I look after all my guests, you should know that, Mr Nutt. Treat them all the same I do, always have done. Won't have no conchies though, not bloody likely. My Archie did his bit, so can every other bugger; conscientious objectors they call themselves, bloody cheek, cowards they are, all of them,' she said forcefully in her jerky cockney accent.

Thomas shifted his thoughts back to the trenches. 'I don't know who told you that, Mrs Tuttle. Conchies, as you call them, are some of the bravest men on the battlefield. Medics and stretcher-bearers they are. They go out under fire unarmed and bring in the wounded,' he said, staring into her face. 'Aye, half the British Army owe their lives to them men.'

'Well, that just goes to show we learn something different every day, don't we?' she said with a sullen face, wiping her hands on her apron and inspecting her fingernails.

Next to the window overlooking the street she heaved her heavy frame into a rickety wicker chair, which, under the weight of her over-ample body, creaked and groaned in ineffectual protestation. Tensing, he held his breath, expecting any minute to see her sprawled on the floor kicking and cursing, knowing he didn't possess anything near the necessary strength to lift her. Miraculously, and by the grace of God, the chair held. From her apron pocket she pulled out a charred briar pipe and with a stained finger tamped down a bowlful of golden tobacco, struck a match and sucked on the flame until the contents glowed red.

'Going out later to see the sights are you, Archie? Don't blame you after what you've been through. I'll tell you what, my Dilly will be home

176

from work soon, why don't you step out with her? She knows all the places, she does. She's a good girl mind you, no hanky panky, and you can keep your hands off her ammunition pouch or you'll have me to deal with. I know what you bleeding randy soldiers are like. I ought to, I was married to a bugger, God rest his soul,' she said with a throaty laugh, and disappeared behind a cloud of grey-white smoke.

There was no doubting Dilly Tuttle was a pretty girl: nineteen years old with doll-like features, slim, with curves where they should be, and aware of her body and the effect it had on men. Whenever she moved she would glance over her shoulder and catch Thomas watching her. It was a teasing game she played with him, and each time she caught him he turned red like a strangled beetroot and she giggled. She worked in Covent Garden as an accounts clerk in the offices of a local fruitier. With an engaging smile, she always blew her nose on a large buff-coloured handkerchief whenever someone made her laugh. Whichever way he looked at her, Catherine always remained uppermost in his mind and he kept his secret from everyone in the boarding house.

'I wouldn't be seen dead with a man out of uniform, people will think you are a coward,' Dilly snapped at him when he suggested getting out of uniform and into civvies for once. 'Look at you, Archie Elkin, a great strapping corporal with a medal. Half the girls in London will be after you when we step out together, you big handsome sod, you.'

At Piccadilly Circus he stared in wonderment

177

at the Bovril and Schweppes advertisements lit up with electric lights, and when he told her he thought Eros was Robin Hood, she fell into an uncontrollable fit of laughter and pulled out the handkerchief to cover her face.

'You're a case, you are, you've made my mascara run now, you have,' she giggled. 'Come on, let's have a drink, I need the toilet.'

She knew most of the pubs and small inns around Covent Garden. Smiling and laughing, she joked with everyone they encountered and happily introduced him as her soldier boy, with her arm linked tightly around his. Although a blackout was officially in place as a precaution against Zeppelin attacks, lights and oil lanterns illuminated the workmen unloading vehicles and carts laden with fruit and vegetables from the countryside.

'Look at it,' she said in a serious voice. 'It's not nearly enough to feed us in London, never mind the rest of the country. When I first started working here, Archie, they brought in ten times as much, in a good season, more. There are only the women left to do the work now, young middle-class women with nothing better to do all day than talk about themselves. They volunteer their services to work in the countryside assisting the farmers. They try their best I suppose, but most of them only want to work in the munitions factory – they get more money than you soldiers when they work a twelve-hour shift. Dangerous work, though, especially if there's an explosion.'

When she finished talking, she smiled and watched him slowly sip his beer. 'You don't like drinking much, do you, Archie?'

'No, not much, it doesn't agree with me.'

'Does it make you ill, then?'

'No, it makes me shrink until I'm only nine inches tall and my boots fall off,' he said with a grin.

'You silly sod, you're making me wet myself,' she shrieked, stumbling towards the ladies' toilets.

She warmed to him more by the minute, smiling at his shyness and continual blushing whenever he looked at her. In the short time she had known him a natural tenderness began to nurture inside her for him, and for a split second she hoped it might grow into something wonderful.

'What did you do to win your medal, Archie? Was it dangerous? You didn't kill anyone, did you?' she said eagerly, leaning forward and clutching at his arm with both hands.

'Couple of thousand before breakfast, sometimes a few more – depended how hungry I was.'

'You're a lying bugger, you are,' she shrieked, pulling out her handkerchief. 'You've got a way about you, you have.'

On the fourth night of his leave he decided to spend some time alone. He found himself growing fond of Dilly, yet Catherine remained closest to his heart and he wondered if a man could love two women at the same time. When Dilly had pouted at being left behind, Mrs Tuttle said all men should spend some time alone. It helped clear their minds, seeing as a man's brain didn't have the capacity of a woman's.

In a crowded bar opposite St Patrick's Cemetery

on Claremont Street he watched five young men wearing the uniforms of newly-appointed officers. Showing off and singing, they frequently gave way to raucous bouts of giggling laughter and sent the contents of their beer glasses slopping over anyone close enough to be a victim. He felt his temper rise. Why would they be drinking in a bar in the East End of London when men were dying in filthy trenches less than fifty miles away?

'Take no notice of them, son, they're a bunch of actors doing a show over the road, they are,' the barman said, watching Thomas fidget.

'Think the war's a bloody show, do they, the stupid bastards?' Thomas said hotly.

'Settle down, mate, bit of humour never did any harm. Any one of them lads over there would be happy to buy you a beer every night of the week if you asked him. Most of them tried to enlist but got turned down on account of them being poofs.'

'Poofs?' Thomas said, creasing his forehead.

'Yeh, you know, iron hoofs, poofs.'

'I don't know what you mean.'

'For Chrisssake, lad, they're homosexuals, shirt lifters.'

'Shirt lifters? I still don't know what you mean.'

'Whose bloody army are you in, lad? Where-abouts are you from anyway?'

Thomas frowned. 'I'm from a small village in Yorkshire.'

'Yeah, and I suppose they're short of an idiot at the moment, are they?'

'What do you mean, you silly bugger? You need to get your bloody head sorted you do,' Thomas said, feeling his temper beginning to get the better of him. He pushed his way outside accompanied by a drunken rendering of *Pack up Your Troubles in Your Old Kit Bag*. He'd never heard of poofs and shirt lifters before, and for a moment he felt sure they might be the nicknames of two British regiments he'd never heard of.

Outside, he hesitated and glanced up at the half moon drifting in and out of black wispy clouds and reflecting in the still puddles of rainwater scattered on the cobbled road. An old brown-and-white carthorse, with his head high and ears pricked, pulled an empty cart, the clip of its hooves echoing through the streets. The driver looked up and touched his forehead in a salute.

'Goodnight, young'un,' he said, clucking to the horse to go faster.

'Goodnight, Sir,' Thomas called.

The sound of the horse's steel plates fading into the distance conjured up a picture of Ruby.

'Stay easy on the plough, Ruby lass,' he said softly.

With no particular reason to hurry and little idea of the time, he made his way back to Frith Street, allowing the air to clear his head. As always Catherine filled his mind and thoughts. Her faint perfume of crushed lavender, her smile, her frailness and the touch of her warm hand clutching his arm brought her ever closer to him. Seven times during the short journey he was accosted by different women, each one enquiring whether he wanted a naughty girl for the night. He forced a smile and declined the offers. The first one resembled one of the witches from Macbeth, the remainder a close second. One he gave a sixpence

181

– she looked even younger than he. Thin and pale, and wearing only a threadbare blue dress, she told him that her mother sent her out onto the streets each night to earn enough for bread the following day.

'Goodnight, Mr Soldier,' she said in a plaintive voice. 'Thank you.'

With sadness he stuffed his hands into his pockets and watched her skip away and vanish into the lurking shadows, realising no one was exempt from the cold touch of war. His mind was made up – the next day he would go to Deal and look for Catherine. London had turned cold on him.

Mrs Tuttle puffed on her pipe amidst great clouds of grey smoke that whirled into the air, while the chair struggled and creaked under her weight. One day it would surely collapse and impale the woman, and it would take strong men to raise her before she died from a loss of blood. Dilly sat at the table scribbling letters in a notebook. She jumped to her feet when he walked in, and her face shone bright with a ready smile. A tight black ankle-length skirt hugged her thighs and accentuated the shape of her long legs; the top button of her white lace blouse was undone, revealing her pale, slender neck. He watched her sway into the kitchen and listened to the sound of water splashing into the tin kettle. Seconds later, he heard the scrape of a match and the puff of a flame igniting the gas, followed by the tinkle of cups and the cocoa tin.

'Would you like a sandwich, Archie?' she called. 'Got a piece of cheese left, we have, saved it for

182

you special, didn't we, Ma?'

'Course we did, we have to look after our heroes, or we'd never forgive ourselves,' Mrs Tuttle smiled. 'Well, I'm off to bed now, don't be late the pair of you, going to be a nice day tomorrow, I can feel it in my kidneys. Take Archie to the park tomorrow, he'll like that. Goodnight.'

'Archie,' Dilly called, draping his tunic over the back of a chair when he entered the kitchen. 'Archie, you can write to me if you want to. I'll answer your letters if you do, honest.'

Before he could answer she turned and clasped her arms around his neck, taking him by surprise. He felt the warmth of her body pressing against his groin. She smelled clean, of perfumed soap, and he felt her small, firm breasts push into his chest. Her faced lifted, her lips parted. Was it always this easy? he thought to himself. He wanted to look at her in her nakedness, to eat her with his eyes, like he'd looked at Marie in the French village.

'Archie, you are a naughty man,' she murmured, running her hand down the front of his trousers and holding him. 'We mustn't let it go to waste,' she said, slipping his buttons undone.

In frantic haste, he raised her skirt and looked at her. She smiled. He slipped her silk drawers over her ankles and she lay back on the kitchen table. She was lovely in her excitement, her ragged gasping explosive, her panting like someone choking. He groaned and his eyes feasted on her nakedness, her slender legs encased in fine black stockings. In-between her legs his fingers probed the moist mound. Again, she moaned and her body arched.

183

Sitting up on the table she raised herself and he entered her. His mind swam in a giddy swirl, and throwing her hands around his shoulders she pressed her lips tight against his. In the middle of the room she squirmed and jerked, and her teeth bit into his lips, drawing blood, as she moaned, this time louder. He pulled his mouth away and placed his hand over hers to quieten her.

Outside, the soft rain pattered against the windows like muted drumbeats, disguising the sound of the creaking staircase. They heard nothing but the rasping sound of their own breath. His hands clasped her warm, soft buttocks and he pumped in and out of her, fast one second, slow the next. Marie had been a good teacher and he an eager pupil. Dilly responded, pushing and heaving, her eyes rolling.

'Don't stop, Archie, for God's sake don't stop, oh Archie, harder, harder,' she breathed hoarsely in his ear.

Mrs Tuttle swung open the door, her heavy breasts, freed from the whalebones of her reinforced corsets, hung to her waist, and a thick cotton nightdress hid from view a sight only a blind man would rejoice in seeing. Thomas released his hands from Dilly's buttocks and she slid to the floor. His eyes widened with fear, uncertain of what he should do, and his face turned bright crimson with shame at his semi-nakedness displayed before the large woman.

'Go to bed, Dilly, now,' she said evenly, her eyes not flinching from Thomas's face. 'I'll speak to you in the morning. Make yourself decent, Archie, you and me have some talking to do.'

Dilly wriggled her skirt down and, with a small cry, ran from the room. The stutter of her feet on the stairs filled the house.

Mrs Tuttle sat at the kitchen table, the withering look in her eyes enough to tell Thomas to do the same.

'I'm not going to lecture you, Archie. You're old enough to know what is right and what is wrong, although when I look at you I wonder. Dilly has taken a liking to you. I'm not surprised, you're a good-looking boy with them dark brooding eyes and broad shoulders.'

Thomas's eyes flickered with childish surprise. Bloody hellfire, she wants me as well, he thought.

'I know there's a war on,' she continued, 'by God I do and I know all about live and let live. People like you live only for the day, thinking tomorrow may never come, but it will for Dilly, and she wears her heart on her sleeve. I want better things for her, Archie, better things than a randy soldier who shows no respect for womanhood,' she said, taking off her nightcap and placing it on the table. 'I think it's for the best if you leave, tonight. Get your things together, I want you out within the hour.'

Thomas stared at her, his revulsion for her turning to acid in his stomach. What did he have to do to tell her that he had no desire to live? Tell, her that he only wore the king's uniform to hasten his own death? His heart sank. And what did she mean, go? During the last few days Dilly had helped him forget the horrors of war, the killing, the maiming and the feeling of emptiness as he tried unsuccessfully to end his troubled life.

In a daze he quietly climbed the stairs and packed his case. What did she mean, people like him only lived for the day? From the next room he heard Dilly's racking sobs and raised his hand to knock on the door, then changed his mind. Minutes later he stepped into the dark streets – it was past midnight. A loose shutter turned slowly on its hinges and banged against a window in the darkness, sending an invading echo into the stillness. A tall crouching figure with his hands thrust deep in his pockets flitted by on the opposite side of the road and silently disappeared into the mouth of a dark alley.

'Archie,' Dilly called from her bedroom window. 'Archie, I love you, write to me, please.'

He turned and looked up, smiled and waved back. The window slammed shut and he heard the bellowing voice of her mother remonstrate the facts of life to her wayward daughter. Perhaps he should have felt differently when he realised he wasn't particularly perturbed at being evicted from the house. What had just occurred had served only to bring him closer to Catherine. Sweet Catherine, with the bewildered eyes and warm hands. Suddenly, shame struck him, as cold as a dagger's blade, and his shoulders sagged. What had he done? What would Catherine think? Perhaps he should tell her that it was only an insignificant moment of foolishness instigated by a woman of easy virtue. Women like Dilly took men whenever they wanted to. Maybe he wouldn't tell her, not straight away anyway, later perhaps, when they were more settled. He wondered if his mother was the same with his father and felt a surge of self-disgust.

The rain ceased and the wind died to a gentle breeze, humming its way through the alleys and deserted streets. Tramlines glinted like long twisting serpents winding their way through the streets in the cloaked moonlight. In a side street he noticed two shadowy figures huddled round the glowing coals of a brazier. Like clothed statues perched on wooden boxes, they stared empty-eyed into the crackling embers.

'Mind if I stop for a warm, just for a few minutes?' he asked hesitantly.

'Stay as long as you like, lad, there's plenty here for everyone,' a small man with one leg said, raking the coals with a stick. 'Isn't that right, Alf?'

'Course it is, lad. Pull up a box and get dried out, we won't be going over the top just yet. First thing in the morning maybe, but not tonight,' Alf said in a droning voice.

Thomas forced a smile and sat on a rickety wooden packing case. Neither of the men could have been much past their mid-twenties. Dressed in worn-out jackets with frayed cuffs and collarless shirts, each wore a button-less army greatcoat draped over their shoulders. Thomas fidgeted, wondering whether he should engage in conversation or leave the two men alone in their self-inflicted seclusion. With a childish simplicity he pushed out his hands palms first and felt the heat penetrate his fingertips. The sudden sound of Alf's staccato snoring took him by surprise and his smile widened. His heart missed a beat and he gulped to catch his breath – both men were missing a leg.

187

'Lost them on the Somme, we did, near a place called Thiepval, nine months back now. Bloody nightmare it was, even today I can't believe it really happened,' the other man said, staring hollow-eyed into the flames. 'Left like heroes, we did. Big crowds, young girls throwing their arms around us and bands playing. Nobody cares now; people look the other way if you have a limb missing. They're not used to it, you see. We're lucky if we manage to beg a crust of bread each bloody day, isn't that right, Alf?'

Alf's snoring ceased and he gave a tired shrug. 'Course it is, lad. Pull up a box and get dried out, we won't be going over the top just yet. First thing in the morning maybe, but not tonight,' he said.

Thomas frowned. 'Do you live in London?' he asked.

'Course it is, lad, pull up a box and get dried out, we won't be going over the top just yet; first thing in the morning maybe, but not tonight,' he answered.

'Got caught in a barrage of shellfire, he did. Poor sod's never been the same since he lost his leg – his mind's gone. Still thinks he's in the trenches, he does. His best mate walked into an exploding shell. The force snapped his legs off below the knees clean as a butcher's knife and ripped out his arms straight from their joints. He'll be all right with me. I keep my eye on him. We're mates now, eh, two men with two legs between them, that's a lark, ain't it?' he said, rubbing his brow to hide the welling in his eyes. 'Got a wife I have, in Whitechapel, but I daren't go home with only one leg, frighten the bloody

188

life out of them it would, especially the two kids. Best I stay here with Alf.'

The words numbed him and he didn't know how to respond. Terrible pictures formed in his mind of children asking their mothers for the whereabouts of their missing fathers. He wanted to reach out and put an arm around the two men's shoulders to console them and tell them everything would be all right when the war ended and that people would appreciate the sacrifice they'd made. Instead, he felt an overriding desire to leave and prevent their misery touching him, tainting him like the mark of a branding iron. Then shame engulfed him like a raging virus and, standing, he searched his pockets and handed them two shillings each, enough to keep them fed for a week.

'None of my business,' he mumbled. 'Best you take your friend to a doctor and go home to your wife and kids. Things might not be as bad as you paint them, and maybe the children would rather have a one-legged father than no father at all.'

In the cafeteria on Victoria Railway Station he sat hunched by a window watching the confusion of embarking servicemen each wearing a vague look of uncertainty. Wives and girlfriends stared into their faces with a faint glimmer of hope in their eyes. He turned away from the scene and with his second mug of scalding tea he ate a cheese sandwich with a pickled onion from a large half-filled jar. Shortly he would be rid of the city. Inside his mind, London was an intimidating place full of bristling urgency concealing a mass of dark brooding secrets, a place where both method and reason battened down pending chaos.

Flushed at the thought of making love to Catherine, he fidgeted. Perhaps she already had a man, or a boyfriend who made love to her as often as she wanted, leaving her satisfied and needless of another. He shrugged the thoughts to one side. She wouldn't do things like that. She's a nurse and they're as pure as a nun in a nunnery. His pale face clouded and his mind whirled, casting him adrift from reason, and he wondered why he continually thought such carnal thoughts. Nurse or not, she was still a woman and he'd discovered that women were easy, like predators seeking gratification from any male of their choosing. He decided he would wait and see what happened, which way the wind blew, so to speak.

Then as if from nowhere the station filled with depressed soldiers, some so drunk they could hardly stand, the patrolling military police ignored them. Forty-two days in the glasshouse at Colchester was a poor exchange for men who might die in Ypres twenty-four hours later. Some might be lucky enough to survive and live to be broken cripples, others would be blown to a hundred pieces. Either way churches wouldn't overflow with mourners. Freshly trained soldiers hung around in groups, fidgeting on the far side of the station, all watching from the corners of their eyes. Some clenched their fists and stared down at their feet. None wanted their eyes to fall on the broken retreating figures streaming down the platforms.

'Have you got any timber, mate?' a voice chirped. 'Sorry, I should have said corporal.'

He turned and looked at the two young soldiers

190

wearing fresh new uniforms. He felt older, like a grown-up, like a man who'd seen it all before and been everywhere. They were so alike it was difficult to tell one from the other.

'Timber, what do you mean, timber?'

'A match to light my cigarette, of course,' the chirpy voice said again.

'Sorry, I don't smoke,' he answered.

'No, neither do we really, we just thought we'd give it a try for a bit of a lark. Off to the war too, are you, corporal? Bit of a lark too, isn't it, so we've been told?'

His stomach knotted and he resisted the urge to punch the pair of them in the mouth – to draw blood, to watch them bleed. Don't these people ever learn? Can't they see what's in front of their eyes? He raged inside. Dropping his suitcase to the floor, he grabbed the two conscripts by the scruff of their necks.

'Hey up, lad,' he called to a soldier with a bloodied bandage wrapped round his head and his left arm in a sling. 'These two lads think the war's a bit of a lark, what do you think?'

The soldier blinked and squinted through his one good eye. 'Bit of a lark, eh? Lost ninety per cent of our regiment we did, in one bloody charge, suicide it was. We're the lucky ones, couldn't find the others, blown to pieces they were, heads, legs, arms everywhere. Mate of mine got knocked out cold,' he said, adjusting the bandage on his head. 'Know what did it? A head, a bloody head still wearing a helmet, no body attached to it, just came from nowhere it did and hit him straight in the face. I suppose you might

191

call that a bit of a lark.'

Thomas turned to the two white-faced young men. 'Get out of my sight, you stupid little bastards,' he growled. 'Get out of here before I kick your useless arses.'

Dropping their unlit cigarettes, they turned and scuttled into the crowd. 'Cannon fodder, bloody cannon fodder,' he mumbled quietly to himself.

Like a belching steel monster the train eased onto the platform. Thirty minutes later the rumble and clatter of trolleys carrying baggage ceased. Doors crashed shut, a man waved a green flag, the stationmaster blew his whistle and the train jerked and pulled away slowly, puffing and panting with the raised head of steam. Fluttering handkerchiefs and wet tears on made-up faces shrank into the distance. The tears might be seen again, perhaps next week, perhaps next year, and perhaps never.

Lucky to find a seat by the window he sat and smiled at the banter flying back and forth amongst the occupants heading for the shores of France and Belgium. The sun appeared from behind the clouds and lit up the meadows and green valleys. A river shone like a silver ribbon, snaking its way through the different shades of green before disappearing under a stone bridge. He crammed his eyes with scenes of civilisation, hills, fields, tiny hamlets, winding roads and church spires, anything to fill every crevice of his memory to push out the old, to forget the pain and replenish it with the joy of life.

At Dover doom washed away all his thoughts of civilisation like freshly-fallen rain pouring into the gutter. Morose and saddened by the continual sight of misery and impending death, he made his way to the crowded bus station. Everywhere a sea of khaki milled and throbbed, and he struggled with an overriding need to get away, to escape to normality for the peace and quiet of the countryside he was used to. A vision of Archie sprang into his mind and turned his face to granite. All that was rotten was centred on Archie, the swaggering bully who hated everything and everyone was to blame for involving him in all of this. Why couldn't he have gone to war and died in the first few minutes?

Abruptly he felt ashamed of his rambling emotions and tried to stifle the dark feelings. Unwillingly he admitted that he must live with his feelings. He must endure, resist and adapt to the circumstances that oppressed him and learn to embrace the virtues of life whenever possible. Somehow, he decided, when Catherine undressed him and ran her hands over his body as Marie and Dilly had done, he would resist. He would refuse her advances no matter how hard she tried. He would tell her he loved her, cleanly and honestly.

The large red-bricked house was the third on the left, No. 5, a semi-detached Victorian dwelling three storeys high with dark green ivy smothering the bottom half. The garden, laid mainly to lawn with a rounded flowerbed, surrounded a concrete statue of Pan. Already green shoots heralding spring flowers peeped through the ground promising better times ahead. Of hot summer days and warm, gentle evenings. A tall hedge of striking evergreen Leylandii separated the front garden from the house next door. To the right, a row of beech trees, stiff and unbending, stood like protecting sentinels acting as windbreak and a screen from unwanted prying eyes. Black drapes hanging sombrely at the pulled-shut windows gave a sense that something wretched had occurred and the house seemed deserted.

Making his way down the winding pathway to the heavy wooden door, he tugged the thin rope and listened to the musical jingle of bells from inside. Tentatively he straightened his cap and clasped his hands behind his back, and hoped that Catherine would open the door and smile at him with her bewildered eyes, perhaps even touch his arm with her tiny, warm hands.

A huge grey cat caught his eye. He watched it stretch and stroll slowly across the lawn, without a care in the world. Seized by a mounting sense of impatience, he tugged the thin rope once again. At the sound of withdrawing bolts he stepped back and waited. Finally a small shifty-looking man in his late fifties opened the door. He wore brown overalls and looked like someone who dealt with mechanical problems. His beady eyes surveyed him and there was a weasel-like quickness about his movements.

'Mr Banner?' Thomas asked.

'No,' the man said in a cackling voice. 'Who are you?'

'My name is Archie Elkin. Miss Catherine said I could call on her. We met a week ago, on the boat from Calais.'

'Henry, who is it?' a woman's voice called from inside.

194

'A gentleman in uniform asking for Miss Catherine, ma'am,' the man answered.

There followed an undisturbed silence and Thomas nervously brushed away the creases from the front of his tunic. The cat arched its back and with a short series of purrs rubbed its body against his legs, and Thomas smiled at the man holding the door. He declined the smile and returned a non-committal stare.

'Oh dear, better ask him in.' The voice sounded tired and resigned, with a tinge of sadness.

Reluctantly the man stepped to one side with a look of disdain on his face. Thomas took off his cap and made his way cautiously down the long, dim corridor. Passing a table holding a vase of tired daffodils, by the doorway to the lounge he stopped and peered inside. A woman, tall and slim with gold-coloured hair piled on top of her head and dressed from head to toe in black, met his gaze. Her eyes were wide and sympathetic, her lips full and parted, and her high cheekbones offered a vision of eternal youthfulness. He knew immediately it must be Catherine's mother.

'I'm so sorry. I never caught your name.'

'Archie Elkin, Ma'am, like I told the gentleman, I only met Catherine last week. She said it would be all right for me to call on her. If you don't mind, that is.'

The woman moved away and peered through a gap in the black drapes.

'I'm afraid Catherine was killed hours after she arrived at Dover, during a Zeppelin attack on the harbour,' she said with her back to him. 'She was pulled from the quay with a broken neck. They

195

promised me she died instantly.'

The words struck into his brain, echoing and re-echoing like the sound of a giant bell. His legs felt unsteady, close to buckling, and without invitation he sank into a plush velvet chair. For a brief moment his lungs struggled for air, and when it came he held it, afraid he would never draw breath again. Not Catherine, with the golden hair and bewildered eyes, who had kissed his cheek for helping her with the injured soldier and clutched his arm at the sight of the Dover cliffs. Not the same sweet Catherine whom he wanted to tell he loved.

'I'm sorry,' he said through gritted teeth. 'I shouldn't have come.'

She noticed his discomfort and, looking down at the floor, felt a slither of pity and forced a semblance of a smile.

'I never had the opportunity to speak to her that day, everything happened so quickly. You must have been one of the last people she spoke to,' she said gently.

Thomas never answered, shadows darkened his feelings and his heart sank ever deeper into a void of despair at another part of his life being snatched away from him. He had known her for only a matter of hours and she had been taken from him as though it were only a fleeting dream. Already, he missed her. What harm had she ever done to anyone? How dare they have the effrontery to say she was too frail to assist men dying in agony? Ask the men she nursed in death. Ask the men to whom she became a surrogate mother when they cried out for their own mothers while gripped in the throes of a horrible death. Why is she dead, she wasn't a soldier? Some give some, some give all. Like quicksilver anger flashed in his eyes. He wanted to tell the woman what he was thinking then thought it best not to make a bad situation even worse.

She watched him, sensing his vulnerability. 'You are returning to France today?' she asked, sitting in a chair and facing him.

'No, Ma'am. My ship doesn't leave until tomorrow evening. I'm truly sorry to hear of Catherine's death. I'll leave now, I need to find lodgings,' he mumbled quietly.

'Oh dear, you won't find lodgings anywhere on the south coast while the war's on. You poor man, you must stay here, I have more than enough room to spare and Catherine would never forgive me if I turned you away.'

Dazed, he followed her up the creaking treads of the carpeted stairs. On the first floor she showed him the bathroom and toilet. In the bedroom, with tentative fingertips, he reached out and felt the softness of the bed. He was exhausted. Undressing, he stepped from his clothes and left them where they lay. With the crisp cotton sheets pulled over his head, he sobbed himself to sleep. When he woke, the falling dusk matched the mournful ache in his heart. Immersed in the luxury of a hot bath, he tried to recover his senses and come to terms with his loss, wallowing until the water turned cold. He shivered – it didn't matter, nothing mattered any more.

Naked and dripping water he gazed from the window overlooking the garden. In his mind he saw a picture of dead men fighting a dead enemy in grey trenches overflowing red with blood. He stepped back, fearful he was going mad, and blinked the thoughts away. Why did such thoughts invade his mind? He doused his face with cold water. When a vision of Catherine formed in his mind, he trembled. He wanted to reach out for her, to hold her, to feel the warmth of her body and smell the sweet fragrance of her perfume. He attempted to shrug the thought away, but it remained, teasing and tantalising his nerve ends. Catherine, sweet, frail Catherine, wrenched from his grasp like Ruby, Marie and Dilly. Sometimes love was like a razor and left only a bleeding heart. From that day on, Thomas knew that the only things that really existed in this world were in people's heads.

The light tap on the door disturbed his thoughts. Back in the real world, he pulled on the bathrobe and opened the door. Mrs Banner stood holding an armful of men's clothing.

'You are the same build as my husband,' she said. 'I thought perhaps you might like to be out of uniform for a while. As I said, it was just a thought, the choice is yours. Dinner will be in one hour,' she smiled, handing him the clothes.

Slowly he stroked his fingers across the smooth coolness of the silk shirt. He couldn't muster a smile, and even if he could he really didn't want to.

Dressed in light trousers, a dark blazer and the white silk shirt he discovered the shoes were two sizes too small. Ignoring the pain he tied the laces loosely. With only a passing glance at the striped tie, he felt the flush of self-consciousness and dropped it on the bed. He'd never worn fine clothes before and considered changing back into his uniform. If Archie could see him now he would never have lived down the shame.

On a small table by the door, standing next to an empty china bowl, stood a bottle of men's cologne. Removing the cap, he sniffed at the contents, unsure whereabouts on his body it should go, or how much. The clock on the wall stated it was a further thirty-five minutes before dinner was served. Should he wait in the bedroom or go downstairs? Again, uncertainty filled his mind. Accustomed to eating when he was hungry, and certainly not accompanied by refined ladies like Mrs Banner, he prayed she wouldn't spread a row of cutlery on the table making him look foolish. He became nervous and decided to go down for a recce to work out the lie of the land, like snipers do.

'I've decided on steak, potatoes and green beans, followed by apple pie and cream and a glass of beer from the cellar – man's food,' she smiled, not wishing to appear pretentious. Tomorrow he would be gone and Catherine would approve of her hospitality.

'Yes please, I mean, thank you,' he stuttered. Noticing only two places set, he frowned.

'Mr Banner's in London, on business. He won't be joining us for dinner,' she said, noticing his glance.

'What business is he in, Ma'am?'

'Oh, he owns a carpentry business, but at the moment he has a government contract to produce rifle butts for the army. I hardly see him these days, spends all his time in London. He was called away just before you arrived. I'm sure he would have liked to meet you. He and Catherine were very close. He has ambitions of becoming a politician, but I don't think he's cut out for it. Would you know anything about such things, Mr Elkin?'

'Yes, I do, Ma'am. I'm a sniper with the 3rd Yorkshire Rifles. Would you mind calling me Archie? I can't get used to being called mister. I keep thinking people are talking to someone else.'

'Of course, Archie,' she smiled knowingly, 'and you must call me Sarah, if it makes you feel more comfortable.'

Throughout the meal they struggled with small talk. When Sarah leaned back, her meal hardly touched, he took it as a signal to leave the knife and fork side by side on the plate, like his mother had taught him.

'Please, tell me how you met Catherine,' she said.

Surprised, he found her easy to talk to. She listened attentively, never interrupting, and showed her generosity and graciousness when he stumbled over a word. She was a kind, gentle woman, like he knew Catherine would have been. They chatted while he drank his beer and she sipped small glasses of sherry.

With the meal over she stood to remove the plates, and he got to his feet with the intention of helping. She smiled inwardly at his boyish enthusiasm. Maybe it was the sherry that caused her to stumble. Whatever it was, it happened quickly, and he automatically reached out to save her from falling. She flushed and reddened at the feel of his hands on her body. He felt the warm firmness of

200

her slim frame and quickly pulled away. Still blushing at the contact, she moved backwards, brushing her hands down the front of her skirt. Thomas felt the heat burn into his face and the sudden uncontrollable warmth spread into his groin. Embarrassment and disgust welled in his stomach. He hated himself and wanted to run outside and hide his face in shame.

'Sit down, Archie, and I'll make coffee. We both seem to have been over-excessive with the drink – must be the times,' she said, attempting to diffuse the tenseness. 'You do like coffee I presume?'

'Yes, Ma'am,' he stuttered, dropping her Christian name.

He sat alone in the dining room with only his burning shame for company while she busied herself in the kitchen with the coffee. He couldn't keep his feelings from overpowering his body – he wanted her to be like Dilly, or Marie, to touch him and arouse him. But she was the same age as his mother. He crossed his legs and prayed she took her time.

The following morning at breakfast, he asked for tea only. She seemed happy to oblige and chatted amicably, like the previous night had merely been a figment of the imagination. She looked different, he thought, radiant and relaxed, and the texture of her skin glowed pink and smooth. Dressed casually but conservatively, with no jewellery other than a string of pearls around her neck, she wore a white ankle-length skirt and matching silk blouse with a low neckline. She looked almost angelic, and he couldn't erase the thoughts of the night before. He felt a vague disorganised affection for her and again the juices of desire enflamed him. He seethed with anger and shame, and dared not look at her. Do people only do it when the woman wants to? Doesn't the man have any say at all? he thought. When she excused herself and left the room he heaved a sigh of relief.

Although the sun shone outside the house was dark and gloomy, enveloped in the black drapes in respect for Catherine. Glancing around the room in the hope of seeing photographs of her, he was disappointed by their absence. From the rear window he gazed out over the long expansive garden reaching as far as the row of beech trees. At the bottom, a large greenhouse with moss-covered glass panels stood partly hidden by overgrown St John's Wort bushes, already sprouting yellow. Feeling the need for fresh air he wandered slowly through the garden, urgently in need of a good pair of willing hands to return it to its former glory. A pond, half-full with still, green water caused by an excess of algae, lay before a fancy wrought-iron bench for two, and a weeping willow offered adequate shade during the hot summers. Flowerbeds invaded by weeds waited for the cut of the hoe to halt the invasion, to bloom and become easy on the eye. Inside the greenhouse wooden tables stood bare, empty terracotta pots lay scattered and broken, and a rusty pruning knife lay on a brown wicker chair with a missing leg.

Minutes later Sarah entered carrying a mug of tea in one hand. He took a few sips, purposely avoiding her gaze whenever she spoke to him. When she brushed by him, the smell of crushed lavender wafted into his face – she and Catherine shared the same taste in perfume. When she leaned to replace a broken plant pot on a wooden table, the fabric of her blouse fell away from the creamy skin of her neck revealing the cleavage of her small breasts. He held his breath and gazed at the shadowed gap between silk and flesh, and again felt a tremor spread through his legs. He wanted her, now, not later, this minute, he wanted to remove her clothes and feel her soft cool flesh respond to his touch. Suddenly, unable to control his feelings any longer he strode by her, heading for the house. She watched him walk away, her large blue eyes momentarily clouded with sadness.

Henry appeared later in the afternoon. He had functioned as an odd-job man, butler and fetcher and carrier since she first married her husband twenty-two years ago, and Sarah Banner relied on him heavily. In no hurry Thomas packed his suitcase and prepared to leave. The brief honeymoon with reality was over. Too soon the time had arrived to return to the harsh life in the rat-infested trenches of France and Belgium, and face recompense for his past sins. She packed him ham and pickle sandwiches to eat during the crossing and smiled when he opened his crammed cardboard suitcase to find room without crushing them. In the lounge she felt awkward, knowing that Henry might walk in at any moment. It was impossible to say goodbye to him the way she wanted to.

His presence had given her a renewed strength and, for a brief moment, had filled the empty void in her life caused by the continual absence and lack of attention of her husband – and now the sad loss of her daughter would add to her unwanted loneliness. She had felt the loss of Catherine all the more during Thomas's stay, yet she knew that if he'd offered the slightest gesture she would have gone willingly to him. Even the shortest interlude of love and affection would have brightened her life and made her once more feel like a woman. She wanted to hold him and tell him to take care of himself, to feel his strong arms crush her waist and make her do all the things she shouldn't do and say the things she shouldn't say. He stood before her, his deep-brown eyes staring into her soul, and she felt her pulse quicken. From a small bag hanging from her wrist she extracted a silver pocket watch attached to a silver chain.

'I want you to have this, Archie. It belonged to my father and I have no further need for it. It was meant for the man who would become my daughter's husband. Now that can never be, but perhaps you will remember us both when you look at it.' She blushed slightly and looked beautiful. 'Goodbye, and please take care.'

His tender age of sixteen years sprang back into his soul and he felt vulnerable, alone and sad. His defensive walls crumbled and the forced bravado and effort of acting like a man melted away. With a swish of her loose skirt she was gone, leaving the wisp of her perfume hanging in the air. He was glad she hadn't seen his chest pumping with emotion and felt a tug of relief that nothing had transpired between them the previous evening. She was a lady, both gracious and kind, like his mother.

Gently closing the gate he stepped into the deserted street. At the corner, he turned and looked back. He saw her face at the window, pale and ashen against the blackness of the drapes. The bus arrived at the bus stop the same time he did.

Chapter Thirteen

The port of Dover was busy as usual and he expected no less. A deathly hush hung in the air. He gazed sadly at the rusting ship bobbing up and down at the quayside destined to carry him back to France. With a casual eye he watched men in uniform walk slowly up the gangplank. No band played and a handful of young boys waved paper Union flags in a half-hearted manner as if they preferred to be elsewhere. The soldiers moved in a grim, determined manner with heads bowed, eyes sunken with resignation, anxious faces desperate for reassurance now they knew that the war was a deadly serious business and not a part-time adventure. They had witnessed the return of the wounded: men without limbs; men blinded for life by the swirling gas; men in a state of shock, shivering and trembling like frightened rabbits caught in the glare of a car's headlights. A killing field waiting for the conscripted victims who shook and quivered in their shiny black boots.

The fainthearted had no place in the trenches with only the stink of human shit and the sickening stench of rotting flesh for company.

Less than an hour had passed since he'd left Sarah, yet it seemed a million years ago set in another world far from here. Further down the quayside a ship disgorged its bloody cargo: blood-red bandages, screams of pain, lines of ambulances and the ever-present angels of mercy equipped with permanent smiles and smelling of soap and disinfectant. The sights attempted to blot everything else from his mind. Frantically he pushed his hand into his pocket feeling for the watch and was relieved to feel the cold metal. It was still there, it must really have happened. Sarah and Catherine really had existed and it wasn't merely a passing quirk of his troubled mind. He shivered and felt afraid.

Leaning on the ship's rail, he watched the waving crowd as the ship's whistle whoop-whooped. Water churned and frothed grey-white under the throbbing propellers. Soldiers returned the kisses blown across the oily water from the quay and waved back vigorously. Suddenly, the sound of a splash brought boos and cat-calls.

'You bloody coward,' someone shouted.

'I hope you drown, you chicken-hearted sod,' another voice called.

All eyes fell on the man as he struck out for the shore. In full uniform and greatcoat he floundered and disappeared from sight. Then his head bobbed to the surface, uttering words no one could hear above the noise of the shouting. His hands waved and flailed above his head and he slipped down, disappearing below the murky water. The noise abated as people stood on tiptoe craning their necks, waiting in vain for him to reappear. Only the khaki peaked cap bobbing on the waves marked the watery grave.

'Poor bastard's better off down there than where you lot are going. In a couple of weeks you'll be wishing you were down there with him,' a sergeant called out. 'Now get about your business.'

The sea spread calm like a millpond on a summer's day, making the crossing easy and pleasurable under the warming spring sun. He found a rare quiet spot and ate his cheese and pickle sandwiches and when he had finished he pulled out his newly-acquired pocket watch and checked the time.

The weather changed from sunshine to a steady but not uncomfortable overcast drizzle at Calais. Rolling his shoulders he shrugged away the gloom. Aboard a London bus he entered the blood-letting theatre of war. Soon the green of Mother Nature gave way to the manmade hell, a place where nothing but misery ever grew. At Serre, in northern France, he caught up with the Yorkshire Rifles. Nothing had changed and Sergeant Bull still kept a watchful eye on the newly-promoted Captain Devonshire like a doting mother. Fresh troops shipped in to make up the depleted numbers were ready to face a battle of attrition; their prize, a few sparse fields of rotting turnips and potatoes.

'Glad to have you back, lad. Not a lot going on at the moment so try and take things easy while you have the opportunity,' Sergeant Bull said.

'Good to see you, Corporal Elkin,' Captain Devonshire said, pumping his hand in an unexpected display of friendliness. 'How are you, my man, did enjoy your leave? Rogered a few beauties I'll be bound! Good man, one needs to make up

the population these days.'

To Sergeant Bull's amusement Thomas frowned and failed to understand the gist of the question, so he answered with just a small smile and a nod. The captain still trembled like a sack of frightened jellyfish and Thomas wondered where on earth he found his courage from.

'Get yourself north of the village, lad, there's a large farmhouse with a red roof, you can't miss it, get settled in there for the time being,' Sergeant Bull said. 'Fritz is too busy running to do any mischief for now.'

The next day they were joined by a company of cyclist soldiers from the Highland Light Infantry from a village further south called Vraignes. Their arrival brought good-natured catcalls and whistles, as their kilts fluttered in the air leaving nothing to the imagination and answering the imponderable.

'Only little girls and babbies wear knickers, you heathen bunch of Sassenachs,' they called back.

Both Vraignes and Serre had been razed to the ground in accordance with the Germans' scorched earth policy. The usual trail of devastation and raped women lay in their wake as they fell back to re-group and the men hated the Germans more with each day that passed. When they came face-to-face in the final reckoning the bayonet would sink a little deeper and Fritz would settle in full for his abnormal cruelty. For months they had fought and died, only to be rewarded with the ruined remnants of a town or village that offered less than nothing, no running water and no electricity to heat water for something as simple as a

208

bath. The rain steadily increased, and once again the front resembled a quagmire. Horses left standing overnight sank to their bellies, and officers drew their pistols and shot them where they stood. Groups of men, tired and weary caked in wet clinging mud, watched, hissing and sneering openly at the officers. A beautiful bay mare blinked slowly as an officer raised his revolver.

'Put that bloody gun away, you useless turd,' Neil Letts spat at the young chinless lieutenant.

'Who the hell do you think you're talking to, Private?' the officer snapped, startled by the sharpness of Letts' tone.

'We need those horses a bloody sight more than we need the likes of you, now fuck off,' Letts replied, looking the officer full in the face.

'Sergeant, arrest that man and bring him to colonel's quarters immediately,' the officer said lowering his revolver.

'What man would that be, Sir?' Sergeant Bull said evenly.

'You know precisely who I mean, and that's an order.'

A hush descended over the village and men turned from their tasks – this wasn't the first time conscripted men had turned their anger and resentment towards officers. The young officer raised the revolver and pointed the muzzle at Sergeant Bull's head.

'I shall tell you one more time, Sergeant, arrest that man!' the officer said in a rising falsetto voice.

'I'm arresting no one, Sir. So it's best you pull the trigger, Sir, if you've a mind to,' Sergeant Bull said, staring directly into the officer's face. 'Letts, get some shovels and men and start digging those horses out of the mud before they disappear, there's a good chap.'

The young officer froze. Unsure of his next move he stared at Sergeant Bull. The metallic click of a bolt drawn and slammed closed echoed in his ears, followed by another click, then another. Suddenly he felt his self-respect drain from his body, flushed away in a tide of disgust at his uncertainty. He looked at the rifles turned towards him and gasped, knowing they would pull the triggers. It mattered not a great deal to them, tomorrow or the day after they would die anyway. He grimaced and clenched his teeth.

'You men,' he said, hoping his voice wouldn't break to a shriek, 'get some shovels and do as the sergeant says, quickly now.'

'Thank you for your help, Sir, much appreciated it is,' Sergeant Bull said calmly.

'Yes, well carry on,' the officer muttered, backing away.

Rumours were rife of officers who'd disappeared overnight after incurring the wrath of their men. These men were snipers and he was aware that the same might happen to him one moonless night.

'Bloody hell, Bully's got some bloody nerve, I thought he were a dead man for sure, lad,' Stan Banks said to Hill.

Sheets of blinding rain saturated the men to the skin, doubling the weight of their uniforms and equipment. The skin on their backs and shoulders stung red raw with chafing webbing, and the clinging ankle-deep mud sucked at their feet, wearing them down until their limbs ached. They walked in silence, eyes fixed on the back of the man in front. Some fell and floundered, paddling in the thick mud with cold hands in an attempt to rise. Hands gripped at exhausted bodies and helped them to their feet and a few paces onward the same men would succumb once more. Past tiredness and past caring they sank into a mindless oblivion, all shards of common decency ripped from their shambling existence. Again, without prejudice, the strongest hauled the desperately tired bodies from the filthy clinging swamp, ignoring the screams and wails of broken men eager to die and vanquish the misery forever.

News that the French Army had mutinied against the way they were treated sent British morale plummeting to an all-time low.

'Would you believe it, eh? Only the bloody frogs would do a runner,' one of the newly-arrived replacements said. 'Thirty thousand of the cowards left their trenches and went home.'

'Aye, if I catch one of those red-legged bastards in my sights he's as good as dead,' another man grumbled, referring to the red trousers worn by French soldiers.

'Don't believe everything you hear,' Sergeant Bull snapped, sensing the unrest and growing resentment.

Sergeant Bull knew the men were tired and talk of mutiny had become commonplace for weeks. Months of forced hardship and the constant degradation of living like animals in the filthy infested trenches had stretched their taut nerve ends to breaking point. The night patrols he sent out ventured no further than a few yards from their own lines, and in the morning when they came back they muttered a garbled report invented by their own imagination. A normal night's sleep became almost impossible as men shook with fear at the thought of death or, worse, mutilation. Lately some had been seen waving their helmets above the trenches in the hope of taking a sniper's bullet in the arm. Some even lay brazenly on top of the parapet and raised their feet, waiting for a sniper's bullet in the leg and a one-way ticket to Blighty.

'It's true, Sergeant, on my life. Mate of mine saw it happen with his own eyes,' the conscript continued.

Later the words were found to be true. Four hundred French ring-leaders were tried and found guilty of mutiny and treason. Fifty were executed by firing squads made up of their own friends and the remainder sent to the penal colony on Devil's Island. The French Army, to its disgrace, had offered to defend its own country but refused to leave the trenches and participate in any attacks, leaving the bulk of the British Army to fight alone on the Western Front.

Three days later Thomas watched disinterestedly at the sight of Sergeant Bull approaching. As usual, he displayed the ever-present bobbing head now synonymous throughout the battalion.

'Report to Captain Devonshire's quarters, eight o'clock tomorrow morning,' Sergeant Bull told him and left without another word. Thomas shrugged his shoulders.

The following morning, holding a groundsheet over his head in a vain attempt to keep out the sheeting rain, he dragged his feet through the morass of clinging mud and made his way to the large empty house where Captain Devonshire quartered. He stopped and waited for a convoy of lorries to pass, crossed the road and made his way up a worn gravel path full of deep potholes filled with brackish water. The men told him they had heard rumours that the captain kept two French waitresses as mistresses, and Thomas promised to keep his eyes open and let them know if the rumours were true.

'Sit down, Corporal, no need to stand on ceremony. We all know each other well enough by now,' the captain said smiling, the twitch still visible on his mouth.

Thomas grabbed a wooden chair and made himself comfortable facing his commanding officer. The face beneath the peaked hat was hard with the stubble of a prohibited beard, his eyes dull and set far apart. Thomas felt a twinge of genuine sympathy for the captain. He was a good and decent man who held the safety and well-being of his men close to his heart. He knew many of them by name, those who had a wife or a fiancée waiting for them back home. At burials he could always be relied on to be present with a small white wooden cross for the spot of a fallen comrade, and he would lead the reciting of the Lord's Prayer in a loud, solemn voice. Like the rest of them he'd been forced into a war he wanted no part of, and the men referred to him as a gent and held him in the highest respect.

Sergeant Bull in particular knew the comforting effect the captain had on his men.

'I'm concerned about the number of men we have been losing, and both Sergeant Bull and I have come up with an idea which might concern you, Corporal Elkin,' he beamed. 'How would you feel about taking forty of our best shots and turning them into snipers? Your own little band of merry men, so to speak. It'll work wonders for morale.'

Thomas felt his brow crinkle and gazed in embarrassment down at his mud-caked boots. No officer had ever asked him how he felt about doing anything before. He was used to accepting orders and obeying them. It was always that simple, without fuss and the way he preferred it. Now he was unsure how to respond. He felt a mixture of pride and humbleness, although he doubted whether the men would be merry.

'Don't sit there looking your age, Elkin, answer the captain,' Sergeant Bull said, glaring though narrowed eyes.

'Well yes, Sir, I could manage that, if you think I could, Sir,' he stammered. 'What would we do with forty snipers? We can't have them crawling all over the place. Fritz would soon find out and retaliate in kind.'

Sergeant Bull nodded and smiled his approval at the answer.

'Not if they were to operate in four groups of ten and alternate in different positions at different times. With Hill, Letts, Banks and you with nine men apiece you could cause havoc. With you in overall command I think it's a splendid idea. I've

214

heard what you did with a rifle a few long months back. It'll keep Fritz's head down and give us a better chance of survival,' the captain said.

'You've got three weeks to find and train your men, Corporal Elkin,' Sergeant Bull said. 'I want them up and down the line harassing and skirmishing with the enemy as soon as possible. There's talk a big push is on the cards, starting at Ypres. The weather we are having at the moment is forecast for weeks and I want all the help we can get. Raise the men's morale – we want to send them home, not into graves.'

'Excellent,' said the captain. 'Well spoken, my sentiments exactly. I think that deserves a little drink. Tell me, do you like cognac, Corporal Elkin?'

Thomas threw Sergeant Bull a quizzical look. The sergeant turned away hoping Thomas never noticed the small smile play across his lips while the captain pulled out a bottle from an ornate drinks cabinet with broken doors. With fumbling hands, he attempted to remove the cork, almost losing his grip on the bottle.

'Let me, Sir,' Sergeant Bull said.

Thomas watched the two men drink and threw the cognac down his throat. Seconds later his stomach caught fire and exploded, sending a rush of breath erupting from his mouth followed by a bout of coughing.

'Bloody hell!' he said, forgetting the company he was in. 'That were reet hot, that were.'

The captain laughed. 'What did you do before you joined the army, Corporal Elkin?'

'I helped my father on his farm, Sir,' he said,

struggling for breath.

'Must be an incredibly healthy life, you don't look old enough to be in the army. Still, all that fresh air, eh? Perhaps we can find work for you round here, must be a farm somewhere nearby, eh?'

'Yes, Sir, I'm sure there is, Sir,' Thomas said, glancing at the sergeant staring back expressionless.

'On your way, lad,' the sergeant said, nodding his head towards the door. 'And you might find a use for this,' he added, handing him a new Mauser sniper rifle similar to the one he'd stolen in Quadrangle Wood.

Neil Letts clapped his hands and thought it was a grand idea, so did Leslie Hill. As Thomas expected Stan Banks remained silent. For some reason, today, Banks's petulant attitude annoyed him and, out of character, he rounded on him.

'Whether or not you agree is no concern of mine, Banks,' he snapped angrily. 'I want nine men from each of you in three days, so instead of whinging and whining, get on with it. That's an order.'

'Soldiers like to whinge, it's one of our privileges, but like most of other things I didn't expect you to know that. You are becoming a regular little Kaiser, aren't you?' Stan Banks sneered.

Leslie Hill fidgeted and stared down at his boots.

Thomas felt a coldness cross his shoulders and stared at Banks through the grey drizzling rain. For the first time he was shocked at Banks's dishevelled appearance, his uniform streaked in

216

mud and hanging open, unbuttoned and lank. He'd aged dramatically and his sunken eyes stared back impassively. Even his stoop seemed more pronounced than ever before. His trembling hands pushed deep into his pockets to avoid the questioning looks of the other men. When he ate he bolted his food down whole and when he drank the liquid trickled down his chin like an infant. He'd almost become a recluse, like a hermit in a solitary world of his own choosing. Twice he'd refused the offer of leave and respite from the hell and terror of the trenches. He felt too afraid to go for fear he might lack the courage to return and would be branded a coward. Already the wickedness of war had taken his brother, Eli, and he would heap no shame on his family name.

For a moment Thomas felt a surge of overwhelming pity for the man who had once been his best friend, his only friend. He wanted to extend his hand in everlasting friendship, yet kindness seemed out of place, a mark of weakness in the unnatural surroundings where only raw courage and strength survived. On the day he died, Robert McCaughey had told him the trenches were no place to harbour bad feeling towards each other. He hesitated briefly, and then walked away.

In the farmhouse he removed his helmet and swept his hand across his wet brow, tugged off his boots, threw himself on the bed and stared up at the ceiling. Sooner or later, unless death took either one first, it was inevitable that he and Stan Banks would need to settle their differences. The thought even crossed his mind that Banks might be his saviour, a means to an end, and maybe if he riled him enough he might be the one to pull the trigger. Perhaps one day he might give him the opportunity.

Three days passed and the mud became deeper, in some places waist high, the latrines overflowed and the excrement ran out, mixing with the mud and turning it a sickly orange colour. Every company had a sanitary man. Dan, Dan, the sanitary man they called him, regardless of his proper name. He'd come with a can of creosote on his back, and pumping up the can he sprayed the trenches to keep out undesirable smells. It made little difference and the men took to wearing gasmasks to prevent continual vomiting. Arguments over trivial matters broke out, bayonets were drawn and waved in temper, rifles were raised and safety catches released. The balance of the men's minds became precarious and the trenches were vacated.

In a field behind the lines, Letts, Banks and Hill stood in front of each of their nine handpicked men. Thomas's men waited while he walked slowly along the lines looking at the soldiers.

'I don't want any smokers, farters, troublemakers, shirkers or complainers. I know most of you men. If I tap you on the shoulder, step to one side and return to your companies,' he said.

Some he touched on the shoulder with a negative toss of his head.

'Replace them by tomorrow morning,' he told the three men. 'And from now on you will be referred to as section leaders.'

'He's bloody changed, I tell you, lad, he's gone all high and mighty,' Stan Banks said to Leslie

218

Hill. 'He thinks he's a bloody officer, he'll be riding a bloody horse next, you mark my words.'

'Shut up, you moaning sod. He's doing the right thing. I don't want any bloody fools in my section, not when my life is going to depend on them and anyway, where's he going to get a bloody horse from?' Hill said, walking away and leaving Banks staring after him.

The following day Thomas accepted the replacements.

'One from each group will step forward and fire six shots at the target one hundred yards away, two shots standing, two kneeling and two lying in the prone position, belly down in the mud. If a rat chews at your arse ignore it, or leave the field and don't come back,' Thomas growled at them.

A few of the men were fair shots – a little tutoring would make them better still – others seemed confused as to which end of the rifle the bullet came out. Soon a large crowd of off-duty men watched with a critical eye offering unwanted advice, each one convinced he could do better given the opportunity. They were only halfway through the exercise when the crowing onlookers ceased their good-natured banter and turned their attention to the sound of chanting coming from the trenches. Selected men lowered their rifles and in wide-eyed silence stared at a company of approximately thirty men shuffling into view. Carrying shovels, picks and spades, and with their heads held high, they approached the overflowing trenches. They wore the uniform of the British Army yet carried no weapons. It was the first time most of the men had ever set eyes on a black man.

'Blimey, real live golliwogs!' someone shouted.

'Go on, mate, they're painted Paddies they are,' another laughed. 'Hey, Sambo, give us a kiss.'

'Sergeant Bull, bring those two men to me immediately!' Captain Devonshire roared. 'On the double, if you don't mind.'

'Mind? Not at all, Sir,' Sergeant Bull growled. 'Casey and Lineham, three paces forward, march, quick about it, left right, left right, left right, move it!'

'Starting now seven days' latrine duties, these men are soldiers of His Majesty and you will treat them with respect, don't ever forget that!' Devonshire raged at them, red in the face. Turning to the black sergeant in charge, he called, 'Do with them as you will, sergeant.'

'Yas, Sah, thank you very much, Sah,' the sergeant answered, producing a smile fit to put the stars to shame. He reached out and grabbed both men by their collars and hurled them headfirst into the filthy trench. 'Give dem children a shovel boys, dey is gonna show us piccaninnies how to shovel shit.'

A huge roar of laughter erupted from the watching troops.

'That shouldn't be too hard, most of it belongs to them anyway,' a voice called out, bringing another roar of laughter.

'May I ask the purpose of your visit?' Captain Devonshire smiled.

'Yes, sah, we is here to clean out your trenches, so you little white gentlemen don't get your pinkies wet.'

'Then be about your business, Sergeant.'

'Back to your duties, men, we are here to beat the Hun. The sooner it's done, the sooner we can go home,' Sergeant Bull grinned.

Thomas labelled the four sniper groups simply as sections one, two, three and four, and based the format on the sniper school at Linghem. Competitions were arranged to see which section performed best. Stan Banks's section came out on top and he quickly seized the opportunity to revel in his newly-found fame. Some days his mood improved, on others he reverted to his morose self. Thomas debated whether to replace him with someone of a more dependable nature, then decided against it and let the matter rest for the time being.

As the days wore on he smiled with pleasure at the rapid progress the snipers were making. His anxiety faded and he enjoyed the warm feeling of pride at his accomplishment.

'I think you are ready to be let loose on Fritz, men. Well done all of you,' Captain Devonshire said to them, and added for effect, 'You are a credit to the Rifles.'

Sergeant Bull watched Thomas and listened with a small smile playing across his lips. He felt a liking for him almost bordering on the paternal. Like most others he felt certain the young corporal wasn't old enough to be in the army, never mind serve in the trenches, yet there was no doubting his ability as a soldier. He possessed a refreshing innocence forged with a great inner strength that he'd failed to notice in many other men, something others recognised all too quickly and gladly responded to. Weary yet attentive to the needs of others and always prepared to help, he always listened to a complaint or a grumble and rarely passed judgement.

'Well done, Corporal Elkin, you've done a fine job,' Sergeant Bull congratulated him.

Thomas tried to hide the blush, moving away he felt ten feet tall.

Morale rose quickly and bets were laid as to who would bring in the most German greatcoats, waterproof groundsheets and leggings. These items, along with German boots, were highly sought after to keep out the ever-present rain. The performance of the patrols improved, and under the night-time protection of the snipers the men became bolder and infiltrated the enemy lines, bringing in prisoners for interrogation from right under the Germans' noses.

In the farmhouse Thomas settled into a padded chair with the stuffing hanging out and flipped through a month-old magazine. Trying to read seemed pointless, so he stared at the pictures of cartoons of men with small bodies and large heads, not really understanding their meaning. Outside the rain ceased and a pale moonlight hung over the hillside. Away in the distance the prerequisite rumble of guns and the darting flashes momentarily lighting up the horizon became as common as night following day. Startled, he turned his head at the sound of fluttering wings and stared from the window at a ghost-grey flock of pigeons breaking from the hedgerow and wheeling away to better places – there was another world. When the heavy farmhouse door groaned open, Neil Letts appeared, his face caked in black camouflage from a night-time foray inside the German lines. His boots squelched and oozed mud. In one hand he carried his rifle, in the other a German coalscuttle helmet. Snipers often carried two helmets to confuse the German sentries, and on many occasions the Germans became jittery and fired at their own men.

'Got some bad news, Archie, we've lost Pete Kenny. Fritz got him with bayonets, poor bugger, I saw it with my own eyes, carved him up good they did, the bastards,' he said, leaning on his rifle to get his breath back.

'Had to happen sometime, I suppose,' Thomas sighed. 'We'll find a replacement in the morning, anything else?'

'No, not really, heard rumours that we're moving south to a place called Arras I think, and soon by all accounts. Well, I'm going to get some grub. I'll see you in the morning. Goodnight, Archie,' he said.

'Hey, best get stripped off and dry your clothes in front of the fire before you leave,' Thomas called.

'Thanks, if my bones get any colder they'll fall out my arse.'

Thomas watched Neil strip to his underwear and felt the nip of shame at his nonchalant attitude over the news of Pete Kenny's death, as if life didn't matter anymore. Death came easy, unannounced and without warning to those who stood in its path. There was no wringing of hands, wailing wakes, seldom even a solitary tear. Men lying dead like run-over dogs in a ditch were met with just the slightest of shrugs followed by a faraway look.

Over the following weeks the West Indian Regiment made a first-class job of cleaning up the trenches and lined the floor with a pathway of raised duckboards. For good measure Dan, Dan, the sanitary man made an appearance and left the trenches smelling, as Stan Banks said, 'Like a whore's arse on a Sunday morning,' and for the moment it was possible to walk though the trenches without human excrement disappearing down boot tops at every step. All signs of colour prejudice quickly disappeared, and the West Indians taught the soldiers how to catch rats with a piece of cheese on the end of a bayonet. They even taught some the forgotten art of laughter and even Sergeant Bull's blue eyes softened at their banter. All the time they had spent completing their thankless task there was never a murmur of complaint and they became a familiar sight in the trenches and welcomed by all. It was a different story when they said they skinned the rats and ate them cooked. The men turned up their noses and refused to believe the story.

The occasional break in the sky was a rare treat, and those who were not on duty turned up to witness the shoot-off to replace Pete Kenny. Kenny had been in Neil Letts' section and he felt keen to have a good man take his place. Four of the five were nowhere near up to the mark; the fifth man was border-line.

'Excuse me, Corporal,' the black sergeant in charge of the West Indian Regiment called. 'I've

224

got me a man who can shoot de eye out of a black-eyed pea, and he'll give any of you boys a run for your money. My two shillings say he'll beat any man here.'

Thomas grinned. 'Bring him out, I'll be happy to take your money.'

'He'll be doing the taking,' the sergeant grinned back. 'Moses, get your beautiful body out here immediately, on de double, man.'

Thomas watched the man called Moses step forward. He stood erect and proud, and tinged with an arrogance that was easy to see. A little over six feet, broad-shouldered and weighing around twelve stone, with strong, honest features, he moved in a relaxed manner like a man sure of himself. Thomas stared in open awe. He was the most handsome man he'd ever seen.

'How may I be of service, my good man?' Moses said in a clipped, precise voice, bringing whistles and cheers from the watching soldiers. 'And a very good morning to you, gentlemen,' he responded with a sweeping bow.

'You've fired a rifle before, have you?' Thomas asked.

'On occasion, old chap, on occasion,' Moses answered.

'Two shots each, standing, kneeling and prone, in your own time.'

'Splendid. Am I permitted to see the weapon?'

Moses took the rifle and slid the bolt open. Sniffing the breech he rammed the bolt home and ran his hands down the length of the barrel, feeling and caressing, touching every part as though it was made of the finest delicate china

225

and ready to crumble. Hefting it onto his shoulder he swung it first one way and then the other.

'Any objection to us both using this rifle, old chap?' he asked, catching Thomas off guard.

Thomas stood and breathed deeply on the air. Feeling puzzled, he nodded.

'Fine with me, let's get to it.'

Moses fired first. After the first shot, he stared down at the target one hundred yards away.

'Bull!' Sergeant Bull shouted.

'Sergeant to you,' someone called. A raucous roar of laughter and whistling from the onlookers was brought to an abrupt end with one stare from his manic ice-cold eyes.

Thomas fired next – another bull, and when the shoot-off was over they were even. Six shots each, twelve bulls.

'Damn fine shooting, Sir, if I may say so, damn fine!' Moses extended his hand.

'And you,' Thomas chuckled.

'Bring out the mug,' someone called from the crowd. 'A hundred and fifty yards. I've got a bob on the darkie.'

'I'll take that,' someone else hollered.

Men quickly hammered a five-feet-tall wooden stake into the ground and placed a brown enamel mug on top, behind which they lashed a strip of wood to mark the spot the bullet struck after firing – the aim was for the bullet to pass though the handle without disturbing the mug. Moses stepped forward first, but feeling a breeze sending ripples over the puddles of muddy brown water he hesitated. A blackbird sang from a blackened branch and he lowered the rifle and waited. Men stood in silence, unmoving, witness to a sight and sound infrequently seen or heard on the Western Front. When the bird-finished and flew away Moses raised the rifle, sighted and fired. Silence reigned supreme as Sergeant Bull walked to the target.

'Bull!' he shouted.

Cheers rang out and tin helmets hurled sky-wards. Thomas nodded at Moses and gave a small smile, waiting for the furore to settle. He'd half expected Moses to miss the shot. The patter of rain obscured the muddy reflections in the puddles and the breeze increased, bringing mur-murings of unrest from the crowded onlookers. Thomas raised the rifle and, in one flowing motion, sighted and fired. Silence again. Sergeant Bull walked to the target, turned and shook his head. The crowd groaned and shoulders slumped between heavy shoulder blades.

'Oh dear,' he said, with a twinkle in his icy eyes. 'It's another bull.'

The cheers erupted, drowning out the sound of the rumbling guns in the distance, and the soldiers surged forward to congratulate both men. For a fleeting moment, the cruelty and slaughter of war was forgotten and smiling faces stretched away haggard looks of misery. Men remembered how to laugh, how to enjoy a moment's jollity. It seemed a good time for everyone.

''Ere, he can come out on night patrol with me any time, no bugger will see him in the dark, will they?' Masher Martin laughed.

'Really?' Moses said amidst the roar of laugh-ter. 'Better not let me catch you bending down in the dark then, old chap.'

'What's he mean? Eh, what's he mean?' Masher said, with the smile draining from his face. ''Ere, I don't think I like the sound of that, I don't, I never said nothing about bending down, did I?'

The next day the necessary paperwork was hurriedly completed and Moses became the first ever black Yorkshire Rifleman.

Moses Pendleton had been raised by a wealthy family in the county of Dorset, Southern England. His mother had been head housekeeper to Earl Howard, a wealthy landowner and farmer. His father, from America, served the family as head groom, but died shortly before Moses's birth after being trampled to death by horses while saving the earl's daughter in a hunting accident. The earl, a fair man, showed his gratitude by insisting that Moses should receive a proper education. How his parents ever came to be present at the house Moses never knew, although when he grew older he guessed they were bought as slaves. They were treated well and his gender and origin were never relevant factors in his childhood.

Moses left Dorset shortly after his mother died and headed for London. Time after time he applied for numerous positions in the city and each time he encountered hatred and prejudice. Educated and outspoken, with a mind of his own, he quickly gained a reputation as an uppity nigger. When the war broke out he enlisted in the army, hoping he might be treated with respect and become an officer. Easily passing the officers' board with flying colours, he was sent to an officers' training academy on the outskirts of London. It wasn't long before the constant baiting and insults became intolerable and eventually a young titled officer ended up with a broken jaw and three broken ribs. Brought before his commanding officer, Moses stated that British officers were a bunch of pansies that possessed neither the ability nor the brains to start a fire in a match factory, and should never be allowed to command men in the field. Without awaiting a response, he turned and walked out. Three weeks later, he signed up with the West Indian Regiment as a private and was assigned to digging trenches, cleaning latrines and doing the work no white man had the stomach to partake in.

In the trenches he quickly became popular with the men. Always prepared to help them pen letters home to their loved ones became a regular pastime and on two occasions he helped write offers of proposals, both of which were accepted. Some of the soldiers spent their spare time trying to teach him slang-words and profanities, yet he would have none of it and took their banter in good spirit. He had learned to shoot in the country during his upbringing and his skill with a rifle brought gasps of admiration from onlookers. On his first venture out into No Man's Land he returned with a German greatcoat and, to everyone's astonishment, two piping hot German sausages, which he shared. The banter continued, and he won the hearts and respect of the others.

'Cor blimey, something smells good,' Masher Martin said, holding his hooked nose in the air and sniffing the wind.

'Yeah, I reckon you're right there, and whatever it is it's making me feel hungry,' Leslie Hill said, hunkered down next to Martin in the trench and wringing water from his socks.

'Come along, gentlemen,' Moses called, clanking a spoon against an empty fuel can. 'Anyone care for hot meat and vegetable stew?'

By the time Hill put his socks back on he was last in the queue and knew it would be pointless to push his way to the front because revenge would be meted out later. Left with no choice but to patiently wait his turn, he fervently hoped that enough would be left for him before the pot was emptied. Anxiously, he kept his eyes on the pot, then at the array of mugs and cups the men carried. It would be a tight call, he thought. He might just make it, and then again maybe he wouldn't. Inhaling through his nostrils he held his breath for a few seconds and then ripped out a fart so loud they must have heard it in the German lines.

'Stone the bleeding crows, what a stink, you dirty bastard! I hope you've shit your drawers,' Martin said, moving out of the queue with his hand clamped over his nose. Others followed suit and Hill progressed closer to the head of the queue.

'Sorry about that, lads, it were an accident, honest,' Hill said, holding out his mug for the last ladle of stew. Squatting down with a satisfied smile on his face, he spooned the stew greedily into his mouth. 'You should have been a cook, Moses. This is bloody handsome. Hello, what have we got here? Piece of string, how'd that get

230

in there?'

'Oh dear, how remiss of me, I thought I'd removed all the rats' tails,' Moses said, watching Hill's face turn green. For the second time that day Leslie Hill broke wind. This time, however, it did not come unaccompanied.

For the following seven weeks they did nothing but huddle against the driving rain, drink tea and complain until orders came to pack their kit and prepare to march south to a ridge dominating the Ypres salient. Mid-afternoon they arrived, tired and soaked to the skin. One of the men sighted a mobile canteen, and their spirits soared and complaints were quickly thrust aside.

The next day, after breakfast, Sergeant Bull called the snipers into line. 'Your job is to act as a decoy and hinder the Germans while our boys find their way across No Man's Land. Keep your eyes peeled and remember your training,' he said.

Thomas smiled. The time was fast approaching when he might at last achieve all he hoped for – death. He'd remained patient, never forgetting the vow he'd made to himself. The Rifles battalion consisted of just over nine hundred men, and they had trudged their way south through the worst weather in forty years. The terrain of No Man's Land resembled a badly ploughed field without any cover and near-constant sheeting rain filled bomb craters until they overflowed with muddy slime. The men knew the price of slipping or stumbling into them was certain death by drowning.

'You are not to wait and assist the wounded, do I make myself clear? I don't care if it's your best friend or your grandmother lying there dying. Carry on until all your objectives have been accomplished. I want casualties kept to a minimum,' Sergeant Bull continued.

The drainage system that had once existed long before the event of war had now become non-existent after the continual bombardments from both sides. British and German soldiers fought and died in a man-made swamp of misery while the French cowered in their trenches and watched. Occasionally the snipers took to taking shots at them to while away the time and relieve the boredom. A few days previously the French had been seen drunk with alcohol while brave men fought and died for their country, and the Rifles hovered on the verge of attacking them in broad daylight. Sergeant Bull fought desperately to quell the uprising by sending a few men at a time to a nearby village for de-lousing, which never achieved a great deal. Within days the white lice would once more become rampant. Nevertheless, after an early morning patrol some of the British troops, accidently they pointed out, managed to find their way into French trenches and left the foul-minded occupants in no doubt as to how they felt. With military regularity the British artillery bombarded the Germans day and night for days, and although gains into German territory were being made, men were over-stretched and the casualties numbered in tens of thousands.

At last the day everyone dreaded arrived and with blackened faces like Christy minstrels the snipers waited hunched in the trenches with a hundred-and-fifty-thousand troops as they had done many times before, nervous, exhausted and trembling with fear. Captain Devonshire waited pistol in hand, for the flare to arc into the sky, and ignoring the sweat springing from his forehead he called out his commands. The wild stubble on his chin bristled like the spines of a hedgehog. Some men waited with chalk-white faces and flitting eyes that stared into nowhere. Others held photographs of wives, girlfriends and children in their twitching hands. The youngest and those about to go over the top for the first and probably the last time clutched pictures of their mothers close to their chests. One youth wearing a brand new uniform grinned from ear to ear for some reason known only to him as urine trickled down his leg and stained his trousers. Men turned their backs and moved away nervously, thinking he might be about to turn insane.

'Get a bloody move on for Chrissake, blow the bloody whistle and let's get it over with!' a man roared, with his nerve ends jangling.

'Fix bayonets, prepare to deploy in battle order!' Sergeant Bull screamed, and then added in a calm voice, 'Steady, boys, steady, won't be long now, when it's all over we can all have a nice cup of tea.'

Nobody heard the well-meant remark over the barrage of two thousand British field guns from the rear pounding away at the German trenches. The ground shook and men reached out to steady themselves, blinking to clear the cordite from their stinging eyes. Thomas cringed, his body ramrod stiff, listened to the sound of screaming horses as they tore wild-eyed to escape their halters and bolt to safety. Captain Devonshire gritted his teeth and attempted to control his trembling hands under the concerned eye of Sergeant Bull. Feet away from his head spumes of wet mud spurted into the air on the edge of the parapet as the German gunners found their range with long-distance machines guns. Sergeant Bull sighed. He'd long grown used to the sight and smell of ripped human flesh hanging limp from bodies, and he knew thousands would be cut down before they had gone ten paces. This wasn't a war, it was organised murder.

'Advance!' he cried.

Along the line as far as the eye could see a single line of men climbed out with rifles at the port. With a man every two yards apart, they moved forward.

'Come on, boys, they're all ours now, let's finish the blighters off,' the captain intended to call, but nothing came. The words remained inside him, trapped in the arid dryness of his throat. His hands gripped the scaling ladder and he climbed up to the parapet. The first blast of machine-gun-fire took him full in the face. Jack Maynard stiffened and retched over the men climbing the ladder behind him.

'Move!' Sergeant Bull roared at the top of his voice.

Maynard slithered over the parapet and lay stiff with fear beside the captain's headless body. Someone had removed the lid from hell. The stutter of a machine-gun sent his heart racing as bullets, like a swarm of wasps, hummed over his head. The groans of dying men and curses of those still alive with shattered limbs filled the air, and boots slipping and squelching in the sucking mud drowned out all other sounds. He closed his eyes hoping to shut out the fearful noise. Then he forced his mind to clear, and started to crawl out into No Man's Land ignoring the bloodcurdling screams of agony all around him as men went down kicking and jerking. It was as if a giant hand swept them to one side. Nine days ago he'd sat in a seafront pub in Mablethorpe on the Lincoln-shire coast gently pushing a brand new engage-ment ring onto Maggie's finger. He'd saved enough for a small cottage overlooking Robin Hood Bay, near Whitby and they planned to marry during his first leave.

'Come along, lad, let's get it done,' Sergeant Bull said gently.

'Aye, I'm with you, Sergeant, get nowt done lying here shitting me'sen. See you at t'other end,' Maynard muttered, climbing to his feet.

Thomas spread his men out at fifty-yard intervals down the line, and standing on ramps they continued firing through slits between sandbags until the volume of the advancing allies blocked out the sight of the enemy. Before them masses of advancing soldiers pressed forward at walking pace beneath the creeping barrage of their own guns. When the guns ceased firing, thousands of Germans poured from concrete dugouts and, manning machine-guns, cut the advancing soldiers down in a solid hail of bullets. The allied bombardment had proved useless. Allied soldiers fell like wheat beneath the scythe and slithered into the water-filled bomb craters from previous bombardments. Their hollow screams for help ignored by all, even their best friends. Like bedraggled insects crawling to a certain death, most of the attackers were out into No Man's Land – now they had reached the point of no return and they knew there was no going back. Only the flight of a stray bullet or red-hot shrapnel ripping them to shreds stood between them and their fate. Thomas pushed a fresh magazine clip into the Mauser and sneered. This wasn't the time to remember orders and he heaved himself over the blood-stained parapet.

Beneath his feet the ground trembled and a white flash blinded him and burned into his eyes, a sudden gust of hot air lifted him clear of the muddy trench, wrenching the breath from his body. With arms and legs flailing like a ragdoll in a storm he felt himself deposited facedown ten yards behind the trench. Like a lost puppy dog he whimpered and groped blindly around in darkness, searching for his rifle. Panic tore into his body and he rubbed vigorously at his eyes with slime-caked hands – the exploding shell had rendered him blind. His hand reached out into the filthy clinging mud and touched the rifle. He gripped it tightly for fear it would slip through his fingers and climbed unsteadily to his feet. For a moment he swayed unable to decide which way to turn and stumbled towards the sound of the guns. He felt his feet slide from under him and crashed headlong into the bottom of the trench. Darkness turned to a smoky grey, then light blue. His vision returned and his whimper turned to a high-pitched shriek of joy as he clawed away the mud and filth from his face. Everywhere bloated dead rats lay scattered all over the trenches. Then he stopped and sweat poured from his forehead when his eyes fell upon the grotesque sight staring him full in the face. In sheer desperation he reached out at fresh air for support. A man's head and body, minus his waist and legs, lay embedded in the soft muddy wall of the trench. A look of calmness fixed on its face and the eyes wide and expressionless stared back at him. His companions vaporised, bones and all, into nothing. Vomit snaked up from Thomas's stomach and he sank to his knees spluttering and rasping for his breath. In the pale light he turned his head and felt a pang of jealousy. They were free of the misery.

'Come on, you bastards!' he roared, clambering up the trench and spilling into the mud.

On his feet, he swayed and stumbled towards the Germans' guns firing from the hip. How could they miss him. Just one bullet and his debt would at last be paid in full. He slowed to almost a dawdle and moved out into the open, away from the other crouching soldiers. And standing to his full height he waited.

'Come on, please, come on, do it,' he whispered hoarsely under his breath.

Hans Richter, from the 136th Cologne Infantry, saw him, pushed back his helmet and smiled. 'Come closer, you British pig,' he murmured, thinking of his friend Heinz lying screaming and legless in the bottom of the trench. His chin rested on the rifle's stock and slowly his finger curled round the cold metal trigger.

'Get down, you bloody fool, are you trying to

get yourself bloody killed?' Sergeant Bull shouted, grabbing Thomas by the ankle and pulling him down below the lip of a mud-filled bomb crater.

Richter pulled the trigger and waited. The bullet struck the rim of Thomas's helmet and sent it spinning into the air. Thomas sank to the ground shaking his head in despair. Uncontrollable panic fired into his body and he felt himself sliding down the steep side of the muddy crater. Kicking his toecaps into the slippery mud for a foothold he felt himself sliding closer to the morass waiting to suffocate the life from his body. Frantically, his fingers gripped and scraped futilely at the slime, leaving deep trailing furrows as he fought to gain a hold, and the filthy cold water filled with bobbing human remains advanced up to his waist.

'No, not this way!' he screamed aloud. 'I don't want to die like this, I don't want to die. I'm sorry, Archie, I don't want to die!'

Sergeant Bull's strong hands reached out, gripped his greatcoat collar and heaved him from the water. Part of a body, mutilated from a shell strike, splashed into the crater sending a wave of blood-red water cascading over his head and shoulders. The body twitched and kicked like a man gripped in the throes of a fit before sinking slowly beneath a pool of gurgling bubbles. Suddenly, he heard the sound of running boots slopping through the quagmire and looked up. Thousands upon thousands of British, Canadian and Australian soldiers came spoiling for a fight. A wave of Highlanders ran screaming with their plaid kilts swirling into the air revealing their nakedness, their white bony knees caked in mud.

They looked like dirty raggedy dolls that a child might discard without a second thought. German field guns and trench mortars opened up, and metallic missiles poured down like the drizzling rain. Bodies somersaulted into the air, ripped to pieces. Great lumps of human flesh landed with a loud slapping noise, like someone clapping their hands, as they fell into the mud-slimy earth.

'Get back to your lines, Corporal Elkin. I'll be having a long word with you later!' Sergeant Bull roared above the increasing crescendo.

'Sorry, Sergeant,' Thomas shouted, and climbing to his feet wiped away the blood streaming down his face. The sweat of fear ran down into his eyes, stinging and smarting. Summoning every ounce of strength he reached and grasped for remnants of ragged courage and slithered his way over No Man's Land towards the German trenches. Like a man who had lost his mind he began to laugh – a throaty laugh that bubbled from his chest – and he felt the lightness in his legs carry him towards the death-spewing machine-guns. He was worthless and dispensable, unfit for the company of those around him and no longer placed any value on his life. Death came forever closer, within touching distance. Men were dying all around him, every-one a better man than him. He told himself today was a good day to die and allowed the Mauser to slip from his hands. Empty-handed and screaming and shouting every obscenity military life had taught him he threw himself at the enemy's lines.

Soldiers stood with feet apart hurling grenades into the German trenches, sending limbs and fountains of blood gushing into the air until the ground ran like a river of blood. It was like bedlam in hell. Thomas, ignoring Sergeant Bull's calls, leapt into the German trench. His legs buckled beneath him when he landed on the duckboards, and losing his balance he staggered back and fell across the prostrate body of Hans Richter. Yards away a German officer holding a wounded leg oozing blood raised his hand and pointed his Luger. He pulled the trigger. An orange flash momentarily blinded Thomas, and the bullet entered his left shoulder pushing him back against the trench wall. His laugh turned to a gurgling cackle as the officer levelled the gun once again. The officer frowned and hesitated, then pointed the Luger at Thomas's temple. Thomas closed his eyes and waited – the hangman would not have him. 'Click' – nothing happened. The officer pulled the trigger again and again. Thomas vaguely heard the explosion behind him and the German officer's left eye became a black socket, his right eye staring in surprise as he crumpled to the floor.

'Rather lax, old man,' Moses said, staring down at the dead officer, 'running all that way just to get killed. One would think you had a death wish. Shall we return to our own lines? We seem to be finished here for the time being. Lucky the German's gun jammed, he might have killed you.'

'Why don't you mind your own bloody business?' Thomas shouted, incandescent with anger and ignoring the pain searing into his wounded shoulder. Then from nowhere, and without warning, hordes of German stormtroopers, like an innumerable swarm of locusts began a counter-attack from a reserve trench. The allied soldiers pulled back, scrabbling and clawing their way back over pools of blood and stumps of flesh to their own lines. Some so thirsty they drank from the blood-filled craters, pushing aside the floating human remains. Above the crescendo of war they cried and wailed for their mothers to take them away from the universe of human destruction. Some slipped into the trenches unaware of their missing limbs, as naked fear, the greatest antidote for pain, coursed through their young bodies. It was just another day manufactured in hell.

Moses hefted Thomas onto his shoulder and in an act of blind providence brought him to safety.

'Move your arse!' the stretcher-bearers shouted at Moses. 'We've the wounded to attend to, tell him to take his bloody scratch elsewhere.'

'I'll be all right,' Thomas shouted over the chaos and moans. 'I'll go to the medical station when things quieten down. Anyway, I reckon the bullet passed clean through.'

Moses nodded and turned to look across No Man's Land at the straggling men covered in blood dragging comrades to the Godforsaken haven, where the ever-present rats waited, squeaking and squealing, to banquet on warm human flesh. The unbelievable sight appalled him. Tears turned the whites of his eyes red and trickled down his mud-stained face. He had never felt so lonely and desperate in his life, never so cut off from reality. All perspective of humanity dribbled away to nothing, like piss down a drain.

'Who will dig the graves and say words in defence of humanity?' he cried out. 'Who will tell them why they were born, and for what?'

With unsteady hands he tore open the top button of his tunic, and pulled out a crucifix. A quick wrench snapped the silver chain holding it around his neck and he hurled it into No Man's Land. With sobs beating his chest he raised his head and gazed up at the grey sky, the rain splattered and bounced off his face, and he whispered, 'I have no want of you any more. You are never where you are needed most.'

Thomas struggled to yank the pocket watch from his tunic and with flickering eyes opened the protective cover and glanced at the watch face. Snapping it shut, he replaced it in his pocket. He still didn't know the time, it wasn't important.

That evening during a welcome lull in the inclement weather Stan Banks sat trembling on the firing step sharing a tin of prunes with Leslie Hill.

'I can't stand prunes, they give me the shits, like everything else around here,' he grunted.

'You can't turn down good food in the trenches, very unwise,' Hill answered.

Banks frowned and shot him a look then glanced into No Man's Land. The night chorus of croaking frogs and toads were out in full force – twice on previous nights he'd ventured out to catch one for no apparent reason that he could think of – but he never had. He'd heard them but had never discovered their whereabouts. When someone stated it was German animal impersonators keeping them awake, it had stretched his nerves to breaking point.

'You're not going to make it up with Thomas

then?' Leslie Hill asked suddenly.

Banks glanced up quickly. 'Strange question, what makes you ask?'

Hill stared into Banks's face and worked the muscles in his jaw, searching for a semblance of a smile. He knew Banks's nerves were on the verge of breaking point. Most of the battalion knew and waited for the day when he would finally snap and be taken to the crazy house in Scotland. They were all afraid, afraid of their flesh being ripped from their bodies by showers of white-hot shrapnel, of being left forgotten and headless at the bottom of a gore-filled crater. Light faded, quickly replaced by darkness, and under the moon No Man's Land glowed unnaturally, like a shadowy negative of a land inhabited by devils.

'He misses you and you miss him. Trouble is, the pair of you are too bloody stupid to admit it. You were best friends once, perhaps it's time to make up and allow bygones to be bygones. We've enough enemies on the other side of No Man's Land without falling out with each other. How would you feel if he died tomorrow? Go on, tell me that. You'd cry your bloody eyes out like the rest of us, but be too late then, won't it?' Hill said, struggling manfully to find the appropriate words.

Banks looked down at his boots thoughtfully and raked his head with his fingernails.

'Yeah, I reckon you're right, lad, I might find it in my heart to give him the benefit of the doubt. No good harbouring grudges in the trenches, is there?' Stan said, his eyes flickering out of control. Leaning forward, he strained his ears. 'The German buggers are repairing their barbed wire. Put a flare up, lad.'

They caught the party of Germans working on the barbed wire filling in the gaps. There were eight of them, and six died from gunshot in the ghostly luminous shroud of the drifting flare. They left the other two to suffer, screaming in fear and agony, entangled in their own barbed wire.

Thomas lay on his bed trying to ignore the ache from the bullet wound throbbing in his shoulder and to make sense of the past few days. Why had he cast a vote for life in the water-filled crater and then charged towards the German lines empty-handed seeking death? Why should he be allowed the privilege of picking and choosing the method of his demise? Archie wasn't allowed a choice in the way he died. No one had the divine right to choose. To take one's own life is as bad as murdering someone else, he'd heard somewhere, but he couldn't remember where.

He lied when he said he'd attend the medical centre. Instead, he returned to the farmhouse with the bullet still lodged in his shoulder. In his mind he argued with himself. If the bullet wouldn't kill him, perhaps gangrene might. All he needed were a few days of peace and quiet somewhere he couldn't be found. The next day he found Sergeant Bull and told him the doctor had recommended a few days' rest to allow the wound to heal. Back in the farmhouse he waited until everybody was about their duties and using all his strength pulled up the heavy trapdoor leading down to the dusty cellar. In the corner a pile of hessian sacks reeked of dried blood from slaughtered animals – a legacy from better times when the building had been inhabited by farmers.

Four days later, hungry and detached from reality, he lay in a peculiar stillness, and as time passed the infection set in. First he began to sweat and shake uncontrollably, his teeth chattering like a man freezing to death. Rapidly the infection penetrated deeper and deeper into his body and he dipped in and out of delirium, conscious one moment, semi-conscious the next. It couldn't be long now, he told himself, it was time to persevere, time to give up his life that was once so precious and alluring.

Archie came, like he always did, holding the rope with a noose dangling at one end. He saw Ruby, broken and dejected, herded away to the slaughterhouse. The butcher with the green van cut her up and made a display in his shop window, and people laughed when they fed their dogs on her flesh.

Thomas's initial reaction when he woke with a start to the acrid smell of disinfectant and carbolic soap was one of abject confusion, and twisting his head he wondered where he was. A nurse gently cut the blood-dried shirt away from the wound. She had once been voted the prettiest girl at the summer fete in the Sussex village, today her eyes were red raw, her eye sockets surrounded by dark lines and her flaxen hair pushed untidily under her stained starched hat. Her cup of coffee still waited untouched on the locker – they had made it for her at seven that morning. It was now nine-thirty in the evening. She worked quietly and diligently in a professional manner, her almost angelic smile ever present, as if someone had nailed it to her face. A man with grey hair and a clipped moustache peered down at him. His breath reeked of onions and Thomas knew he wasn't dead. He turned his head and tried to speak, to tell them to leave him alone to die, but no words came and his heart began to race. He mistook the yellow glow of the acetylene lamp for the sun and scowled.

'You're a very lucky man, Corporal. If your friends hadn't brought you when they did, you might well have died,' Dr Burch smiled. 'Another day or so and we wouldn't have been able to contain the infection penetrating your upper body, and that would have been that, I'm afraid. We have cut away the worst, now rest. Careful treatment should see you up and about in four to five weeks.'

Before he could find the strength to answer, they left to attend to others more deserving of their attention than a man consumed by a selfish intent to bring about his own death. He felt the stabbing pain sear across his chest. Christ, four to five weeks!

'Why, why for God's sake won't they allow me to die?' he murmured, wondering how they had discovered him lying in the cellar.

In the evening the pain worsened and on several occasions he grimaced and twisted his head in a vain bid to escape the pain. Men lay wounded, waiting for attention, their features distorted in agony like a grotesque mask. Yet they made no complaint, asking only occasionally for a smoke. His discomfort seemed irrelevant, nondescript, and he lay with his eyes closed forcing himself to remain silent. The man in the next bed gave a long low moan. The spread of his chest displayed an anger of blood-mashed flesh and bare exposed ribs where shrapnel had ripped away half his torso.

'Sorry,' he said, trying to raise his head, 'It's the pain. I'm not keeping anyone awake am I?'

When the young ashen-faced nurse attempted to bathe the wound, he screamed and kicked in agony. Finally she broke down, her nerve ends severed from overwork and raw fatigue. The blood red swab fell from her hands and she ran sobbing from the tent. It seemed hopeless, worse than washing bare flesh in an abattoir. The man jerked once, called for his mother and then passed away. Minutes later he was replaced by a man with his right leg blown off. He clutched the severed limb tight in his arms, holding it close to his chest, and refused to give it up. Finally, when he came to his senses and realised what had happened to him, shock set in and he began to convulse. Kicking and thrashing, it took four male attendants to hold him down.

After twenty-five minutes, the doctor, drenched in blood and trying to administer aid to twenty patients at once, ordered him to be tied down on a stretcher and taken outside. Silence descended like a sea fog when the sound of a pistol shot rang out and the screaming suddenly ceased, patients fidgeted and looked nervously at each other seeking confirmation that their fears were ungrounded. He pushed his raging thoughts to one side, refusing to believe that the British shot wounded soldiers, regardless of how bad their wounds were. The man with the severed leg was

247

never seen again.

That night he clasped his hands together and prayed. He prayed to the God that Moses had denounced to be taken from this man-made hell and left to die somewhere green and pleasant, where it didn't rain, where birds sang in freedom and dogs scratched at flea-ridden hides.

Two weeks later nature gave up its unnatural barrage of torment and the weather began to improve. It grew hotter, soon the slushy furrows were baked into solid ruts, and men stumbled and cursed with dust-blindness and sore eyes. Trenches were cleared and Dan, Dan, the sanitary man made a welcome appearance with his can of creosote. Hygiene and sanitation improved, and men stripped and de-loused their clothing. Nothing was ever perfect, yet morale rose and grim jaws relaxed. Thomas sat outside the casualty clearing station to allow adequate room for the ever increasing incoming wounded. Settled in a comfortable padded chair he watched the sparsely-leafed branches of an elm tree sway and rock in the breeze and the gentle rustle of newly-grown spring leaves sent him into a state of semi-hypnosis. When the nurses changed his dressings he refused to defer his concentration, preferring to fill his mind and soul with a tiny glimpse of the long-forgotten wonders of nature.

When Moses made a surprise appearance it was even more surprising that he came accompanied by Stan Banks. Thomas glared at him, his features no longer as he remembered them – he was even more drawn and paler than ever, his lips bloodless and faintly blue. He barely recognised the gaunt and haunted man standing in front of him and pondered how long before Banks finally succumbed to life in the trenches. He tensed, and waited for the sneering innuendo and barbed insults to assault his senses.

'It is good to see you looking well,' Moses spoke first.

'You're looking well, lad. A bit peaky, but you're looking well,' Stan said nervously, reddening in a fret of embarrassment and wondering how Thomas might react after months of having derogatory remarks hurled at him.

'Thank you, I'm fine Stan. How are the snipers doing?' he smiled, quietly overjoyed at the opportunity to heal past differences with his old friend.

'Not many of us left now. After you were shot it kind of all fell to pieces, nobody really knew what to do. You're missed, lad,' Stan said, his heart singing out with happiness at Thomas's response.

'Keep them up to full strength. It's important for the morale of the others. Tell the section leaders to recruit men from the ranks – it doesn't matter how good they are, just make it look good.'

'Aye, I'll do that. Masher and Neil are no longer with us, can't find hide nor hair of either of them,' Stan said, wringing and twisting his hands.

For a moment Thomas reflected on the loss of his friends and two more faces joined the never-ending hallway of his memory. His sadness quickly evaporated, replaced by a boiling rage. His breathing came with short, fast gasps rattling from his open mouth. Every night he'd prayed for death and upon waking he prayed again. He fumed silently to himself – how can they die so easily, why do they make it sound so damn simple?

'Perhaps Moses can help – he gets on well enough with the lads and they respect him,' Stan said, glancing at Moses.

'How do you feel about that, Moses?' Thomas said, keeping his eyes firmly fixed on the swaying elm. 'Could you take Neil's place?'

'If I can be of any assistance I shall be only too happy to oblige,' Moses said.

'Good, that's settled then.'

Thomas wanted to cry out with sheer joy when the doctor told him he was to be transported with three other men by horse and cart to a first aid station to recuperate. Anything was better than living among the horror and stench of the dying. Nothing too strenuous, they told him. Take it easy and allow time to work its magic. The words gave him reason to smile. Here he was, in the middle of a mindless bloodbath where it seemed a thousand times easier to die than live, and yet he couldn't manage it. After another week they arranged transport back to the farmhouse and warned him to avoid the cellar. The next time he fell down the steps he might not be so lucky and might break his neck. He struggled to stifle a smile. Moses, not so dull-witted as some, watched him from the corner of his eye and kept his thoughts to himself.

Every three days he was attended to by a cross-eyed stretcher-bearer with a limited knowledge of first aid, and fresh dressings were applied to his wound. It seemed a waste of time – the present bandages dried onto the wound, and each time

250

they were removed the wounds opened and bled.

'Maybe if you left me enough fresh bandages, I could change them myself every day,' Thomas suggested.

'No problem, we have plenty of spare bandages. I'll leave you enough for ten days. After that I'll drop by and take look at you,' he said, throwing the used bandages onto the small open fire.

'Do you enjoy what you do?' Thomas asked for the sake of conversation.

'My father forbids me to kill – I'm Jewish,' he shrugged with bony shoulders. 'Anyhow, believe it or not I like the Germans – I have relatives in Dusseldorf – so why would I want to kill them? In Germany there are many Jews in high places responsible for running the country. Germans would never harm a Jew.'

The face of good fortune never smiled for long and against all expectations the rain started again with a vengeance, swallowing the day and filling the trenches ankle high. Extra duckboards were collected by a line of dejected men and piled one on top of the other. This resulted in men moving around hazardously with their heads and shoulders on display above the trenches – an easy target for German snipers. Sandbags were quickly filled and heaped on the parapet to eliminate the danger. Again, cases of self-inflicted injury rose. Some men, desperate to escape the horror and carnage, shot themselves in the foot, others put a bullet through the leg tendons in a bid to receive an early passage back home. Worst of all was the man found minus his boots and socks and his big toe resting on the trigger of his rifle, the muzzle in his mouth as he prepared to blow off his head. He told the Military Police that during the previous evening he'd had a premonition he was going to die, and nothing anyone said could alter his belief. He was taken away and never seen again.

Moses dropped by the farmhouse with a half bar of chocolate he'd traded for a German bayonet. He sat peculiarly quiet watching Thomas seated by the window engrossed in the activity of a bird singing in a tree shading the farmhouse.

'This war is important to you, isn't it, Thomas?' he said quietly. 'It has some relevance to your life. You use it as a form of retribution.'

'How do you mean?' Thomas answered, feeling heat creeping into his ears.

'You treat the war as if it is a form of jury, to judge you. I believe in your own perverse way you see yourself as the judge, jury and executioner, with yourself as the accused. Why is that?'

'I don't know what you're talking about,' Thomas said, shrinking from the question. Inside of him lurked a degree of vulnerability that he seldom gave any thought to, but he knew it was there, waiting to come to life. Moses teetered on the verge of reviving it.

'You disobeyed orders when you left the trenches,' Moses continued. 'You weren't even firing at anyone, you just kept walking, waiting to be shot or blown to pieces. You want to die, and I would like to know the reason for your moral bankruptcy.'

Thomas spun round on the chair feeling the hairs on his neck bristling with anger. He wasn't bright by any definition, nor was he that stupid that he didn't know when he was being compromised. Moses had been the first to put two and two together and come up with four.

'It's none of your bloody business, is it? Anyway, you don't know what the bloody hell you're talking about.'

Moses leapt from his chair taking Thomas by surprise. His hands encircled his throat, cutting off his air supply.

'Listen to me, boy,' he hissed between his teeth. 'Sergeant Bull saved your life out there when he pulled you down. He saved your life again when you were about to be sucked into the crater, and all that time you thought only of yourself.'

'He didn't have to,' Thomas gasped.

'No, he didn't, and I didn't have to risk my life running over No Man's Land to stop that German officer from un-jamming his pistol and finishing you off. You don't care about anyone but yourself, and that makes you a liability and a danger to the safety of others!' Moses roared. 'If you want to die, be a man and shoot yourself. Go away and blow your head off and leave others to survive.'

Thomas felt his defences crumble and struggled to free himself from Moses's grip. 'You don't understand, I have to die, I have to, for my parents,' he cried out.

Limp in Moses's strong hands his resolve drained away like water flowing into a gutter. It was over and he was no longer Corporal Archie Elkin, winner of the Military Medal for outstanding bravery. Now he was just a vulnerable sixteen-year-old boy living a terrible lie in a man's world, a world so full of strange tangled contradictions that his young mind couldn't understand. His options were simple. Die by a bullet or die on the end of a rope. Both frightened him witless and he remembered his father telling him that if a person doesn't know where he's going, any road will take him there. This day, for the first time, he knew the meaning of those words.

'What the hell are you talking about? What have your parents got to do with the war, for God's sake?' Moses roared, releasing his grip.

Sergeant Bull's hand hovered over the door handle. He hesitated, his eyes slitted and instead of moving away he remained still and listened to the raised voices. Thomas exhaled, struggling to hold back the well in his eyes. With the back of his grimy hand he wiped away the snot running from his nose and sniffed. He wanted to fight Moses, to try and silence him before he learned his secret. Instead, he blurted out everything from the beginning. Moses listened in silence. Outside, Sergeant Bull turned his head in the hope he might hear more clearly. He was by no means a man who eavesdropped on other people's conversation, yet he'd always held the view Archie Elkin wasn't the person he made himself out to be. Thomas reached for his rifle, slid the bolt open and rammed a shell into the breech. With the muzzle tight to his forehead he reached for the trigger. Moses snatched the weapon away.

'It was an accident for God's sake, and they don't hang fifteen-year-old boys in England. However, I must admit the episode concerning feeding your brother's body to the pigs is a little extreme. So, you want to die a hero in Archie's name and make your parents proud of him. Both will be lies. Have you thought about that, my friend? Learn to live like a man and you will die like a human being. Because that is what you are, not some hunted rabbit continually haunted by the past. You have done enough in Archie's name. What would Ruby say if she knew of this, or maybe she already knows?'

'Ruby is a horse. I helped her during her birth and treat her as a pet,' he said quietly.

Moses clamped his teeth together and didn't know whether or not to laugh. Thomas felt certain he would, and tapping his toe in the mud he made a small puddle and waited for some kind of derogatory remark – Moses was famous for his quick repartee – but he never spoke and Thomas was glad.

'I suppose you will tell Sergeant Bull now and I'll be sent home?'

'No, Thomas, Archie, or whatever your real name is. What you have told me I shall treat with the utmost confidence and will never repeat to anyone, but I would suggest you begin to live your life the way it should be lived. Death will arrive in its own time, it always does,' he said, turning to leave.

Sergeant Bull pulled away from the door and waited concealed behind a small ramshackle shed. Worry lines creased his brow, an expression of confusion darted into his eyes. He had overheard the full account of Archie Elkin's past and agreed he wasn't guilty of murder, but of unabridged fear twinned with panic. Yet the thought that he had fed his brother's dead body to a sty full of pigs floated in his bowels and sank as though he'd swallowed a ton of bricks.

Thomas watched Moses walk stiffly away. He wanted to feel better, as if a heavy yoke had been lifted from his shoulders, but he didn't, and again his imagination played games with him.

'I am Thomas, not Archie, Thomas, Thomas, Thomas,' he cried aloud clenching his fists. Then he felt calmness, and serenity fill his mind and he knew who he was, he'd always known. No longer would he abandon himself completely, and with only a squirt of despair he pleaded with God to restore his faith.

Sergeant Bull watched, the sound of Thomas's pleadings pressing against his skull, and he tried to calm his thoughts, for the time being he would keep the terrible secret to himself.

Chapter Fourteen

It was for no apparent reason that he could think of that Stan Banks's and Leslie Hill's attitude towards him had changed for the better after they moved on to Messines Ridge. They became more amiable. Not that he cared much – he was a hardened veteran now, and with his newborn zest for life he relished the fight for survival. What use were friends if the next day they would be dead or missing in action?

'Okay, get cleaned up!' Sergeant Bull roared. 'The battalion's pulling back to a Belgium town called St Eloi for seven days' rest. Find some-where to bathe and de-louse yourselves when you get there, and I don't want to hear any bloody nonsense.'

Much to their disappointment there didn't seem any chance of a bath or any other particular form of hygiene to ease their discomfort. And, unfortunately, no bloody nonsense either, as Sergeant Bull had so eloquently put it. Those who had a few centimes to spare and were lucky enough to get a pass made their way to the nearest *estaminet*. Sitting and nursing a cup of coffee they would enjoy the singsongs and company, and round off the evening with a plate of egg and chips. True to form the Hun, in his barbaric sense of reason, had razed most of the small town to the ground. Not that that stopped the American soldiers swaggering and bedding anything that turned a trim ankle, and trim wasn't always neces-sarily the order of the day. MPs spent most of the time carting them drunk from bars and breaking up fights. Yet they were fearless fighters and wel-comed as well as respected by the allies.

As usual, houses bridges and roads had dis-appeared and buildings stood skeletal and pitiful. Out in the street the sight of queues of half-naked men clutching bars of carbolic soap, waiting patiently in the drizzling rain for their turn to bathe in the cold water of the village horse trough, nearly led to a riot. A group of Royal Engineers were quickly drafted in and worked furiously through the night to repair a fountain to allow a flow of running water, having been left smashed to pieces and full of excrement

257

by the Germans before they withdrew. The allies hated them for their barbaric and destructive attitude, but they could wait until the time came to push in the bayonet and twist.

The antics of a cavalry troop performing a gas mask drill on horses provided an afternoon's entertainment, although the horses caused more damage to the handlers than a field barrage.

An elderly Belgian lady called Laura, who never stopped chattering, acted as a hairdresser and shaved most of the men bald to help rid them of nits and lice. Her two fourteen-stone daughters, Fifi and Belle, offered sexual favours but were refused, although it was rumoured their hands and mouths were put to good use.

'Keep well away from them, Thomas,' Stan Banks called. 'It would be like throwing a sausage up an arcade.'

Thomas smiled good-naturedly, wondering what he meant, and shrugged at the laughter.

Moses, in his own inimitable style, somehow managed to produce a bottle of olive oil to massage Thomas's shoulder. It responded well to the treatment, and with a slow wink Moses refused to reveal its source when questioned. When Thomas pressed him he relented and said he allowed the ladies of the village to look down the front of his trousers at what he called his Black Beast. Afterwards they gave him whatever he wanted. Some men tentatively chose to look, but then most walked away quickly with a perturbed look on their faces, wishing they hadn't bothered.

'I've seen them licking their fingers and wiping them down his face and chest, men and women alike. They think he's painted and try to wipe it off,' an Ulsterman said, causing a ripple of laughter.

Despite a thorough search, the bodies of Masher Martin and Neil Letts were never recovered and both were posted as missing in action. The men gathered inside a bombed-out church and listened in silence with raised eyebrows to Sergeant Bull's moving testament to the deceased's lives. When he led the singing not a dry eye remained. Still the war continued, and like others before them they were quickly forgotten and replaced by Alex Taylor and Fred Furlong from York. Under Thomas's watchful eye the snipers were quickly brought up to full strength. Moses chose to keep his own watchful eye on Thomas, still unsure, yet concerned for his state of mind, though he detected a slight shaft of confidence in his manner, a ratification of assurance. He smiled to himself, pleased with what he saw.

Second Lieutenant Bellamy introduced himself as the new platoon commander. Fresh from Sandhurst he informed Sergeant Bull, and not given to nonsense. Twenty-two years of age and an ex-public schoolboy with matinée idol looks, clipped moustache and brown brooding eyes, he came with a smile that almost matched that of Moses. His keenness mixed with inane statements soon became a great source of amusement to the men, and they waited eagerly for his outbursts.

'I say, chaps, everyone cleaned their teeth and changed their socks?' he asked each morning with a happy smile. 'We mustn't let the Hun see us in a state of poor dress. Good grief that would never do, chaps, never, never, absolutely never.'

Spring was drawing to a close, the season of renewal and the birth of beauty almost completely marred by the never-ending rain. Moses said it was Mother Nature washing away the blood that man spilt in his quest for self-destruction.

'It's Mother Nature's revenge more like, pissing over us for damaging her property, I wouldn't be surprised,' Stan Banks said. 'Hey, you don't think this Bellamy bloke's family had anything to do with making bells do you? Never heard that name before, I haven't. I knew someone called Ringer once. He was nothing to do with bells though – his mother took in washing.'

Men tensed when Sergeant Bull bounced in un-announced from the night, accompanied by a tall, thin man looking resplendent in a new uniform with a corporal's chevrons sewn onto his sleeves. In his left hand he carried a small metal box.

'This is Corporal Crumble. He is our new am-munition technician responsible for the distri-bution of ammunition, and from now on you go to him when you are getting low.'

Being in charge of the ammunition was a job feared by front-line soldiers, kept mainly in dug-outs in the side of trenches, it took only a stray spark from a falling shell to send the whole trench and those in it sky high.

Corporal Crumble had a milk-white face, long and angular, and he was so thin that his bones seemed to shine through his skin. His complexion hung sour, almost daring approach.

'Hey up, Corporal, you don't have a sister called Apple do you?' someone called out, followed by loud guffaws and sniggers from those unsure of the nature of the joke.

'Nay, lad,' Crumble answered, with a voice as deep as a grizzly bear with a sore throat. 'But I'll let you into a secret. I'm from Blackpool, that's in Lancashire for those that aren't educated, and I can't stand bloody tight-arsed Yorkshire men with big gobs.'

A few seconds passed in silence, a match flared orange and a cigarette glowed red, and then twenty voices broke out in a chorus of *Oh I do like to be beside the seaside, I do like to be beside the sea.*

Displaying a set of teeth that would shame a carthorse for size and quantity, Crumble grinned and sat down. Pulling out a pipe he struck a match and puffed until the contents glowed red and he contentedly disappeared into a cloud of grey smoke. To the chagrin of the men time passed all too quickly. On the final day of their welcomed rest period, the Scottish entertainer Harry Lauder made a concert appearance with his five-octave piano and brought the house down with such songs as *I Love a Lassie* and *Roamin in the Gloamin.*

Thanks to Moses's oil, the pain in Thomas's shoulder eased and he reported back to Sergeant Bull the following morning, declaring himself fit for duty.

'Pull another stunt like last time, Elkin, and I'll have your stripes, bloody Military Medal or not, do you understand? Going off half-cocked is dangerous, liable to get somebody killed it is, and I won't have bloody liabilities in my company,' the sergeant said, glaring directly into Thomas's face.

261

'It won't happen again, Sergeant,' Thomas answered.

'Bloody right it won't. Right, day after tomorrow I want you to send some of your men up on the ridge and keep an eye on Fritz, see what he's up to. The Royal Engineers along with the Canadians and the Australians are tunnelling below and we don't want Fritz sticking his bloody great nose in. It's your job to cause a distraction.'

'Right you are, Sergeant.'

Two days later Moses gathered the men together. Thomas split each section into five pairs and explained exactly what he wanted them to do.

'Keep out of sight and work your way as near to their lines as you can. Use your bayonets if you have to, but no gunshots. Have any of you got cudgels?'

'Yeah, we've got five between us, and we'll use the buggers if we have to,' Robert Sadler, a new addition to the snipers, said.

Thomas nodded. For some time the Germans had taken to sneaking over to the British lines during the night and splitting the heads of sentries wide open, putting the fear of God up them and giving them cause to fire at anything that moved, and that included their own comrades. Now it was payback time. Dusk fell and the landscape resembled a picture painted in hell: black, stark and forbidding, like Satan's cemetery. The wet summer weather came accompanied by a welcome rise in temperature, allowing the men to discard most of their heavier clothing and carry only the bare essentials, assisting them to move quickly and silently. Stealthily, they moved within earshot of the unsuspecting Germans. The inviting aroma of cooked fat from hot black puddings sizzling in pans wafted into their nostrils and the clinking of beer bottles tested their patience. The guttural sound of a German singing brought a twisted smile to Stan Banks's face.

'You won't be singing that tune in a minute, you fat bastard,' he chuckled to himself, withdrawing his bayonet.

Silently, under a threatening moon darting in and out of the scattered rainclouds, two German machine-gunners died from slit throats, their guns pushed into a slime-filled bomb crater. Two more were despatched in the same manner and relieved of their helmets. Four snipers slipped into the German trenches wearing the stolen German helmets and greatcoats.

'Robert, you go first with your cudgel,' Banks said.

'I can't bloody wait,' Sadler answered hefting the weapon.

'Right, we'll work our way down to the first bend and finish them off as we go, is that clear?'

'Yeah, clear enough for me,' Sadler grunted impatiently.

'Then we fill the swag bags and scarper bloody sharpish,' Banks said, looking at the blackened faces of his three men.

Robert Sadler wasn't a big man, in fact he was slim and wiry yet when he wielded his cudgel it was as though it were part of his body. With a sadistic grin he made his way down the German trench, staving in heads while humming a tune no one had yet identified. By the time he'd finished there wasn't a part of his body or uniform not covered in the blood of his terrified victims. Banks nodded and worked his way along the trench behind Sadler, ripping open the throats of those still alive. They were aware the Germans weren't adept at handling surprise attacks with any speed: their mentality bordered on the offensive with overpowering numbers. Silently they filled the sandbags with food and any objects that might later prove useful. Finally cobblers, bakers, clerks and candlestick makers, covered head to toe in the blood of the hated Hun responsible for a thousand sins, made their way back to their own lines. Tomorrow they could do the same, and the day after, until there were none left.

'Right, tomorrow we'll head away from the ridge and take up positions further down the line and skirmish. We don't want the Hun to think we're hiding something. If they grow suspicious they might discover the mines,' Thomas said.

Sergeant Bull nodded his approval and remained silent.

Contented with their early-morning brew nestling in their stomachs, they left with their respective sections and headed away from the ridge. Their job, to harass the enemy by any method possible; death their first choice, any other would be considered a failure. Each man carried a sneer fixed on his lips, ready to take the battle to the hated Hun and finish him forever. One section at a time went out for the duration of one hour only, and when each returned after wreaking havoc, another section left for a different location. Concealed in No Man's Land they waited level with the enemy trenches picking off nervous sentries at will. When midnight spread her cloak and under the cover of a moonless sky another section made its way across No Man's Land, crawling through the mud and slime over the remains of bodies and severed limbs of the enemy to haunt and torment.

Slippery Stewart, so named because he had a knack of knowing everyone else's business and relished in passing round misinformation to anyone who would listen, was the oldest man in the section. He wore a set of false teeth too small for his mouth and had developed a habit of clicking them together. In the dark stillness of night, without thinking, he began his habit in the middle of No Man's Land. The younger men, unable to control themselves, found it impossible not to giggle and on one occasion one of the men burst out laughing and gave away his position. The patrol was quickly recalled, and the next time Slippery crossed No Man's Land he went toothless.

Corporal Crumble retained the nickname Apple. He took it in good heart. There were more pressing matters like staying alive to worry about than a friendly round of banter.

'How come you've got a new uniform, Apple?' Leslie Hill enquired. 'Just in from Blighty are you?'

'Just in from Blighty? What the bloody hell are you talking about? Been here two bloody long years I have, you cheeky big bugger. Arras, that's where I got this uniform from, bloody Arras, down the trenches I were, dishing out ammo, when a mortar bomb landed smack on top of me stock. Bloody lot went up and killed most of the poor buggers, but not me. Tore every shred of clothing off me it did, aye, lad. I stood there as naked as an ostrich on Derby Day I did, except for me boots, I kept me boots on, strange that.'

'Did you get any leave? You could have worked a stinker there, got a bit of cushy Blighty.'

'Nay lad, that were second time it happened. There's a war on you know, best get it finished and go home for good, I reckon,' he said, snatching up a rat by the tail and hurling it towards the German lines. 'And you can bugger off back to where you belong.'

The men nodded their silent approval at his words. Some stared down at their boots and conjured up images of loved ones waiting for them back home. Others undid tunic buttons and searched for photographs and with melancholy looks gently wiped their muddy thumbs over the paper faces smiling back at them. In the distance the strains of *We'll Keep a Welcome in the Hillside* drifted in mournfully from further down the trenches.

'Hello, the Welsh must be getting ready to attack,' Apple said.

'How do you know?' Leslie Hill asked.

'Cos they only sing when they are shit scared,' Apple laughed. 'That's why they are bloody good singers.'

Signs of an impending offensive became more and more evident over the following weeks and extensive preparations began to take place. Field guns were brought in, ammunition depots were enlarged and additional railways were laid to bring in men and stores in readiness for a big push. When Sergeant Bull bobbed into view, Thomas looked at him expectantly and blinked.

'Corporal Elkin, get your three section leaders and follow me.'

For approximately three hundred yards the five men made their way down the trench in single file, passing men shoring up the damaged ramparts with strips of wood and sandbags. Other working parties re-hung the telephone lines onto the sides of the trenches to prevent soldiers from tripping over. The ledges, where snipers stood and plied their deadly trade, were rebuilt in readiness for the next onslaught. Stopping at a dugout concealed by a canvas gas curtain the sergeant turned to face the men.

'What you are going to see you will keep strictly to yourselves, is that understood?'

They nodded. Stan Banks puffed out his cheeks and wondered nervously what was in store for them this time. Sergeant Bull pulled the canvas curtain to one side and the four men followed him inside a dugout used by the officers of the day to organise and ready the men to attack or defend. On one side stood a chipped wooden table surrounded by three odd chairs sinking in the ever-present mud. On the far wall hung another gas curtain, much larger than the one they had just passed through. Moses shivered and the whites of his eyes were veined red. He hesitated, preventing Leslie Hill from moving any further.

'Come on, Moses,' Hill said, pushing Moses in the back. 'Get a move on, mate.'

'Take your hands off me,' Moses snapped, and

267

stepping sharply backwards he sent Hill staggering out into the trench.

'That will do!' Sergeant Bull barked, turning to Moses. 'Are you afraid of enclosed spaces, lad?'

'Yes, Sergeant,' he answered simply, wiping the sweating palms of his hands down the side of his trousers.

'Good lad, best you told us now rather than hold it back until times of trouble. Wait outside and see if you can scrounge a brew. Hill, stop arsing around and get in here, now.'

The second room was cavernous, eight feet high and twenty feet wide. Piled against the walls stood mining equipment: shovels, picks and spades of various sizes. Strange-looking machines with bellows attached and tubes protruding from both ends were stacked neatly against another wall. Hundreds of lanterns lay next to boxes of candles and electric light bulbs. Strangest of all, the men stared in muted surprise at stacks of small cages containing chirping canaries.

'This way, and get a move on,' Sergeant Bull snapped.

From the centre of the room a shaft dropped almost thirty feet down into a tunnel, running for a further ten yards before dividing and forming three more tunnels leading off at different angles. Each tunnel was lined with electric cables holding light bulbs, and both sides were shored up with vertical timbers high enough for a man to stand erect. Narrow gauge railway lines disappeared into the gloom, and further on were more small cages holding rats and mice.

'Welcome to the underground war, gentlemen,'

Sergeant Bull said. 'Do any of you geniuses know what this is?'

'Yeah, these are the tunnels I've heard people talking about. I didn't realise they were as big as this though,' Hill said.

'What people?' Sergeant Bull said with a suspicious look. 'What people have you heard talking about these mines? Remember I told you earlier, what you see here today you will keep to yourself.'

'Yes, Sergeant,' Banks said.

'Hundreds of men have spent the past two years digging these tunnels. They run beneath the Messines Ridge for miles and now they are almost finished. When the time's right, engineers will blow the mines and send Fritz to hell. The Ridge overlooks the German positions and is therefore strategically vital. Once we have the Ridge under our control, we can start to push the Germans back. That's where you come in. We don't want the Germans to discover our little secret,' Sergeant Bull said, with a glint in his eye. 'It's been a hell of a job and recently the Germans have started tunnelling from their side, unaware of what we're up to.'

'What has all of this got to do with us?' Thomas asked, sucking in the damp for oxygen.

'Our boys can hear the Germans tunnelling and know exactly where they are, and they are worried they might accidently mine their way into our tunnels. Your job is to kill Fritz before he spills the beans. Once that's done, the miners will set off an explosion in the German tunnel. A camouflet they call it, just powerful enough to cause a minor cave-in without disturbing the surface and discourage them, make them think it's too dangerous to carry on.'

'Bloody hell, be a bit cramped for room won't it?' Hill said.

Sergeant Bull ignored the remark. 'Follow me,' he said, descending down the shaft by the ladder.

'I don't like the sound of this,' Banks said, staring into the murky gloom.

Thomas noticed Banks's nervous twitch and watched him tug his collar close to his ears and look guardedly around him. He knew what he was thinking, hopeful that the cavern wouldn't suddenly cave-in and bury them alive. The tunnel narrowed the further they went, and he felt the crown of his helmet scrape against the slimy roof. Beneath his feet a thick layer of wet mud sucked at his boots, forcing him to dig his heels in and walk slowly for fear of slipping. Cut-outs were hacked into the mud walls to allow men to step aside and make way for trolleys and the men removing loose earth to pass unhindered. As the tunnel snaked further into the ridge, brown muddy walls gave way to heavy blue clay. Further ahead they heard the sound of scraping and the muffled voices of men working on the mine face. Stepping aside into a cut-out, they waited for two men pushing a trolley laden with sacks of earth to pass, the trolley wheels encased in rubber to avoid making a noise.

'Next stop, Leicester Square,' one man said, a grin lighting his sweat glistened face.

For a further twenty-five minutes they moved forward until eventually the tunnel widened.

'Bloody hell, it must have taken ages to tunnel this far,' Leslie Hill said looking around.

'Approximately one foot each hour, so I've been told. Fritz might only be feet away from us at this very moment. So, listen carefully, this is the plan: four men will do eight-hour shifts down here with the miners, they'll let you know when you're wanted. You'll be armed with bayonets and pistols, use your rifles as a last resort – if these mines cave-in you'll have half of France down on top of you, keep that in mind.'

Stan Banks blinked in the gloom and felt the cold sweat sting his red-rimmed eyes. Slinging his rifle over his shoulder he stuffed his trembling hands deep into his pockets.

Grateful once again to be outside in the fresh air, they stretched their muscles and breathed deeply to rid the smell of dank clay and chalk from their lungs. Thomas, who had felt reasonably certain the mines were safe until he saw black twisted tree roots like dark witchlike fingers protruding and dangling through the roof of the tunnels, felt a dark feeling of impending disaster creep into his bones.

'We'll take the first shift, that way we will know what to tell the others. Someone will have to replace Moses,' he said.

'Aye, and Bellamy wants the skirmishing with the Germans to continue. You're doing a grand job keeping Fritz occupied,' Sergeant Bull added. 'First shift is at midnight, so best find your replacement and get your heads down.'

Thomas made his way back to the farmhouse, picking his route around the deep puddles and piles of scattered debris. With his quarters in

271

sight he stopped and stood to one side to allow an elderly man driving a horse-drawn cart laden with bulging sacks pass by. The horse, a large well-groomed Piebald, slowed and Thomas held out his hands to stroke the animal's head, murmuring quiet nothings.

The elderly man wore a tattered black overcoat with a matching beret perched precariously on his head. Odd bootlaces kept his well worn boots from falling from his feet. He smiled, exposing a mouthful of rotting teeth that might have represented a crooked row of gravestones in a neglected cemetery. Hercule wasn't partial to strangers and yet he seemed contented to be stroked and fussed by the Englishman. In the past the British had often tried to commandeer the horse to pull field guns or stores wagons. Each time he lashed out with his whip and drove them away and eventually they relented and left him in peace. Late in years and cursed by time's merciless fingers, he slowly eased himself down from the cart and with a grated groan straightened himself up.

'Pomme de terre,' he said. 'Pomme de terre, you like la pomme de terre?'

Thomas shrugged – he'd never heard the words before. The man turned and made his way to the rear of the cart, all the time shaking his head from side-to-side in a fatherly fashion, then pulled a hessian sack from the cart and handed it to him. Thomas looked inside at the large potatoes and grinned with delight perfect, for baking on an open fire.

'Thank you, Sir,' he said. 'Thank you very much.'

Thomas turned to walk away with the sack slung over his shoulder.

'Fromage, you like Fromage?' the man called.

Again, Thomas shrugged his ignorance. This time the man pulled a canvas cover from a wooden box and extracted a block of cheese weighing approximately three pounds. Thomas's face broke from a grin to a wide smile. The man chuckled and climbed up on the cart. Twice he clicked his tongue. Hercule knew it was time to leave and leaned into the harness. Away in the distance the field guns began their monotonous avalanche of death.

'Boom, boom, not good,' the man said, and with a lurch the cart rolled forward.

Thomas watched with mixed emotions and the thought of Ruby filled him with sadness then, like an antidote, the thought of baked potatoes dripping with lashings of creamed cheese momentarily dulled the emotion.

He found Moses barefoot in the trench attempting to dry a pair of socks over a small petrol fire in a tin that had once held hardtack biscuits.

'Bring yourself with Stan and Leslie, and whoever's to take your place, to the farmhouse tonight, about ten o'clock,' Thomas grinned.

He didn't tell him why and it gave him pleasure to leave Moses with a puzzled look etched on his face. With great care he separated enough cheese and potatoes to share with the section leaders, the remainder he gave to Sergeant Bull to distribute amongst the soldiers on sentry duty that night. The sergeant duly took some for Second Lieutenant Bellamy, and then made his way to a

273

dugout beneath a star-clustered sky listening to the men talking between themselves and singing *Pack Up Your Troubles.*

Later that evening Thomas sat impatiently at the table by the window with one eye on the door and the other on the potatoes baking on the sizzling fire. He had considered slicing the cheese into slivers, but then changed his mind – let them take it as they wanted it. Perhaps some didn't even like cheese. They came with groundsheets hanging from their helmets dripping from the sudden downpour, their boots sinking ankle-deep into the thick mud. He knew from the moment the men stepped inside the warm farmhouse they would offer no word of complaint, and he wondered how far a man can be pushed down into the bowels of hell before he says no more, this is enough. Biting his lip he cast his mind back to two days ago when he had witnessed the demise of a soldier finally reaching the end of his tether.

'Sod the bloody war, sod the bloody king and sod the bloody useless generals,' the soldier ranted, throwing his rifle into the mud. 'I'm bloody well going home to my Peggy, bollocks to the lot of you. What the bloody hell am I fighting for, eh, tell me that? The bloody king's a bloody German and the fucking Kaiser's probably his fucking uncle. Who do they think they are? The useless scrounging bastards could stop all this crap in minutes. Fucking Germans are nothing but trouble. And the generals, well I ask you, general bloody arseholes they are, couldn't catch a fish in a jam jar for fear of drowning themselves. Put them in the bloody trenches and they'll soon be

274

sitting round a table out in No Man's Land, with German generals drinking champers and scoffing bloody caviar, and the war will be over without a shot being fired. But us, oh no not us, not the gutter rats, born to bow and scrape to useless arse-holes when we're ordered to, bloody cannon fodder we are, here to provide the bastards with a bit of sport.'

Three Military Policemen quickly moved in and soon scuffles broke out. One policeman received a bayonet wound in the leg and that just about put paid to the disgruntled soldier. Brought before a court martial he was sentenced to be shot. For cowardice they said, although most of the men thought he was the sanest man on the Western Front and deserved a bloody medal for having the gall to tell the truth. After the shots were fired, he sat tied in a chair and blindfolded, unarmed and still alive. After a few minutes the officer in charge dismissed the squad and a new squad prepared, the same thing occurred – no one would shoot the soldier. The officer drew his pistol and shot the condemned man in the head. It took four bullets to kill him. All the way down to the front men threatened mutiny against the incompetent offi-cers and the military decided not to take further action against those in the firing squads. The following morning the officer who had made such a terrible mess of executing the accused soldier was found on the parapet of a trench with two bullets in the back of his head.

They trudged into the farmhouse without knocking, and Moses dumped himself in front of the roaring fire and stared in unabated amazement at the sizzling potatoes.

'You might as well take your wet clothes off and dry them properly,' Thomas said, watching them make futile attempts to brush away the wetness with their hands.

'Eh, lad, you're a right diamond, you are,' Stan Banks expounded, ripping off his wet tunic and hanging it over the back of a chair. 'Must be a grand life being a bloody corporal.'

Thomas looked at him in just his underwear from the corner of his eye and wanted to laugh at the sight of his scrawny white body, instead he said nothing. He had long become used to Stan rarely engaging his brain whenever he put his mouth into gear.

'I must apologise for being unable to accompany you gentlemen on this foray into the unknown,' Moses said on a serious note. 'If there is any way I can repay you by doing extra turns of duty, please let me know. I'll be only too pleased to oblige.'

'Don't worry about it, mate, we'll think of something,' Leslie Hill grinned, already halfway through his third baked potato.

'That's right, lad. Anyway, it's a bloody sight safer down there than it is up here, bloody hell. I nearly forgot, letter here for you, Archie, picked it up this morning. Be from Ruby I suppose. Give her our love when you write back, kept a lot of us going she has, God bless her,' Banks said, pulling the letter from his back pocket and handing it to Thomas's shaking hand.

Thomas glanced across at Moses who remained staring into the fire. The letter felt damp and

276

wrinkled. It was nothing unusual for men to receive mail so wet that the ink ran, making it impossible to read. They were best avoided for a few days until their tempers abated.

'Not going to read it then, lad?' Banks asked. 'Might be important, I'd read it if it were mine.'

'I've no doubt you would read it even if it wasn't yours, so do be quiet about it, there's a good chap,' Moses said, scowling.

Banks drew back his lips in a malevolent sneer. Then, seeing the look on Moses's face, he shrugged and pushed a hot chunk of dripping cheese into his mouth.

'I'll read it in the mines tonight, might help pass the time,' Thomas said, clearing his throat.

Time lingered for Thomas that night and the letter burned a hole in his pocket. He knew it couldn't contain good news and could only have come from his parents. Perhaps one of them was ill, or dying, or even worse dead. Eventually the night slowly eroded and the time came for the men to separate and go about their duties. With their bellies comfortably full and the rare luxury of dry clothes they were as happy as condemned men were allowed to be. Packing needles and wool, Thomas stuffed holed socks and shirts with buttons missing into a swag bag. It might be a good time to do repairs.

'Right, John,' he said to John Burke, the man selected to take Moses's place. 'Time to make a move, might even get the chance for a bit of shut eye.'

'Might be right, lad,' said John.

John Burke hailed from somewhere deep in

Southern Ireland and men speculated why he chose to fight for the British. He spoke rarely, even then few understood his broad Irish brogue. A crack shot with an Enfield he never hurried or allowed himself to become flustered. He said he had learned to use a rifle shooting at British soldiers in Dublin. At times, his odd rhetoric gave a great deal of amusement to the men in the trenches, though most weren't certain what to believe.

'What did you do for a living, John?' Stan Banks enquired one night.

'I cleaned mackerel out of bagpipes,' he answered with a straight face.

Banks looked at him with a furrowed brow and then looked blankly at those around him. They returned his stare with a nonchalant shrug.

'Yeah, well how the bloody hell did they get into the bagpipes in the first place?' Banks said scratching his chin thoughtfully without looking up.

'Ah, that's something I couldn't be telling you.'

Minutes later Banks made his way down the trenches enquiring whether anyone knew how mackerel managed to find their way inside bagpipes.

Nevertheless Burke proved himself to be a good man to have around: steady and reliable, he'd done his share of spilling German blood in the trenches. The soul-sapping drizzle ceased and a full moon drifted in and out of grey clouds, disappearing for minutes at a time and then appearing again for only seconds. Unfortunately it did nothing to quell the fretting in Thomas's mind and he felt himself growing irritable and impatient to read the letter. Similarly at the same time he wanted to rip it to shreds and hurl it into No Man's Land, afraid the contents might be the cause of his existence becoming even more unbearable than it already was. Perhaps he should wait until morning and open it when Moses was present. He would know what to do and always offered a wise solution to a problem. A short time later they made their way to the mines. Inside the first dugout they stopped and watched a man trimming the claws of a canary.

'Bloody hell, lad, are you getting it ready for a bird show?' Stan asked.

'You all right, our kid?' the Brummie answered looking up. 'No, course I'm not, if they gets a whiff of gas they grips the perch with their claws for a few seconds before dropping dead, so we keep the claws cut short and they falls off right away. Gives us a few extra seconds to get out it does, before the gas gets us too.'

'Gas? I've heard no mention of gas,' John Burke said.

'The shelling up top causes pockets of carbon monoxide to escape from the clay, kill you dead that will, kid. We use mice as well – you can't be too careful down here.'

Now grimaced, and with their minds working overtime on the horrors of a gas attack they slowly made their way in single file into the mine, passing rows of candles burning in glass bowls. The flames jerked and danced from the draught of the man-operated bellows pushing in fresh air like gasps from a huge set of lungs. Close to the mine face they stopped and screwed up their noses at the

279

stench of sweating unwashed bodies. Off to the left, men covered in sweat toiled silently and a brisk sense of urgency permeated the atmosphere. Breathing became laboured and difficult, coming in short panting gasps. Thomas averted his eyes from the dangling tree roots protruding from the roof, still it did nothing to help to dispel his jangling nerves from the thought of a cave-in. Leslie Hill led the way. For a man of his size he seemed exceptionally light on his feet and ducking and swinging from side-to-side to avoid the low roof and strengthening timbers he seemed almost at home in the mines.

Eventually, they came to a dead-end and saw three men covered in grimy glistening sweat working the mine face. One man lay on his back on a wooden board with his feet facing the blue clay. In his hands he held a shovel, which he stabbed into the clay, and then using his feet he pushed it further into the face and twisted.

'Clay kicker, that's what they call him. He digs out the clay and the second man pulls it away to pass to a third man waiting behind, who bags it. Three men operate the trolleys and take the bags to the mine entrance to be deposited where the Germans won't see them, or they use them to reinforce the trenches. Another man works a set of manual bellows, pumping in fresh oxygen,' Leslie Hill said.

'How the bloody hell do you know all this?' Stan Banks asked screwing up his eyes.

Hill never got the opportunity to answer.

'Hello, boyos, come to look after us have you?' Taff Palfrey from Cardiff interrupted. 'About bloody time, the bloody Germans are everywhere tonight, boyos. You'll see some action tonight, I can guarantee it. This here is Billy Williams, and this handsome young man is Bryn Evans. Where are you boyos from then?'

'We are from the Yorkshire Rifles,' Hill answered.

'Pudding makers are you?' Palfrey chuckled loudly at his own joke. 'I'm a tenor in the Cardiff Operatic Society, Bryn here is a landlord, owns his own pub he does, lucky bastard, and Bill, well he's a real miner, see. Trouble with the English generals is they think everyone born in Wales digs bloody great holes for a living.'

'Don't you get cave-ins?' Stan Banks asked, looking round tentatively at the dull blue clay.

'All the time, boyo, all the time, but don't let anyone else know, or they'll all bugger off and won't come back,' Palfrey said, glancing at Hill's paling face.

'Don't listen to that silly bugger,' Williams said, shaking his head from side-to-side. 'There'll be no cave-ins while I'm in charge. Safe as a Chinaman in a curry shop we are. The thing is, bach, we can hear Fritz scratching away like a rat in a sandwich and we've arranged a little reception for him.'

Stan Banks looked up, his face a picture of apprehension.

'Mined a special tunnel we have, a dummy tunnel we call it, to keep him away from what's really going on down here, and he's heading straight for it – should break into it anytime now by my reckoning. That's why you're here, bach, to make sure he doesn't get out alive and reveal our little secret. When you've finished with them we'll block

281

the tunnel off.'

'How many are there? Will they be alone or will they have soldiers with them?' Thomas asked anxiously.

'Oh no they won't be alone, boyo, you can be certain of that, they'll be armed to the teeth and have troops with them, might be a whole battalion of them, see. Hard to say how many, but there'll be enough to keep you busy for a while.'

Williams shook his head at Palfrey's exaggerated remarks.

'You'll need to get them bayonets cut down, bach, they're too long to handle properly in confined spaces. You need a six-inch double-edged blade with a sharp point for stabbing. It will be fine to use revolvers, no problem there, but try not to use the rifles if you can avoid it, just to be on the safe side,' Williams said, heaving a bag of clay onto the waiting trolley.

'Go and have a fag and a brew, boyo. We'll tell you when we want you,' Palfrey said, staring at the passive expression on John Burke's face.

John Burke lit a cigarette. 'Jasus! I reckon this tunnel's shrinking.'

'Shut your bloody big mouth,' Hill snapped, looking hopefully at Thomas for sympathy. 'And put that bloody cigarette out, you heard what they said about escaping gas.'

Thomas dismissed the need to look up at their worried faces, he shared their turmoil. All around the walls seemed to close in, and the sticky blue clay clung to his feet as though attempting to hold him down forever and keep him prisoner. His hands became unsteady and he felt the cold sweat forming on his forehead. He pulled his bayonet from the scabbard and scraped the clay from his boots, then wiped the blade clean on his puttees. The others automatically followed suit.

The stillness mixed with a ghostly silence slowly began to affect their minds and fired their overworked imagination distorting their natural instincts. Below ground, the rumble of guns and screams of dying men no longer pounded in their ears and stretched their taut nerves to breaking point. Now only an eerie foreboding silence seeped into their thoughts, magnifying their overvivid fear of burial beneath tons of clinging earth. Their haunted eyes darted around. They felt as though they were confined alive in a dark inescapable coffin.

'Hope we don't have to use our rifles. What do you reckon, Archie, will it be all right to use them?' Hill said breaking the silence.

'If any bugger comes for me I'll use anything I can lay my bloody hands on,' Banks interrupted. 'I've no intention of being buried alive down here.'

Stan Banks found himself becoming increasingly dependent on the safety of the mines. He saw them as the one place where the world seemed at least sane and didn't understand why the men found the solitude threatening or the smell nauseating. To his mind anything was infinitely more tolerable than the carnage and wasteful slaughter committed in the trenches above ground.

Thomas moved away down the subway and sat alone, three sets of eyes watched him in silence. He couldn't be afraid, not Thomas, he was fearless, faced the enemy alone he did, bold as the brass knocker on the mayor's front door, every-one knew that.

I'm glad the bugger's here, Hill thought.

Banks smiled, sitting contentedly on his hands.

Thomas studied the address on the letter care-fully for a few minutes. There could be no escap-ing the fact it was addressed to him. Even the serial numbers matched his own, or Archie's. Frantically, he searched his mind for a valid reason not to open the letter, afraid of what the contents might contain. The smile on his face spread and he felt foolish for not realising earlier. The letter couldn't be for his eyes, it was addressed to Archie Elkin, not Thomas, therefore, the contents were none of his business, he reckoned, and it wouldn't be right to read another person's mail.

He recalled the case of Spenny Harrison, one of his friends in the village who'd read out a letter ad-dressed to his father because his father couldn't read. The letter stated his father had been ordered to attend the local court to answer charges of poaching. When Spenny finished reading the let-ter, his father cuffed him hard round the ears and thanked him to mind his own business in future.

Time waits for no man and in one easy flowing motion he tore the letter open. Holding his breath, he read the address at the top right-hand corner. His breath whooshed from his open mouth and his shoulders sagged. Pushing his head back he looked up at the damp roof and sucked in oxygen. The letter was from Dilly.

'Bloody hell, lad. Must be some letter if it takes your breath away,' Banks giggled.

'How is she, Thomas, how's Ruby? Keeping

your slippers warm for you, is she? Not like my missus I hope, always down the bloody Melbourne Arms she is, drunken little mare,' Leslie Hill complained. 'Good spanking with the arse end of a bedpan, that's what she needs.'

Thomas never had the opportunity to answer or even time to read the letter. Billy Williams scurried into the subway waving his arms like a puppet with broken strings.

'Come on, boyos, the action's about to start!'

Thomas grabbed his rifle and in a moment of lucidity hurried after the others feeling as though a great weight had been lifted from his shoulders. Then he frowned and couldn't remember ever giving his address to Dilly, or his army serial number.

'In here, quickly, they're almost through,' Williams said, darting into a tunnel concealed by an anti-gas curtain.

Palfrey and Evans leaned against the wall, their faces covered in lines of concentration. Pushing flat-sided French water canteens tight to the wall with a rubber pipe attached to the stopper, they held the stoppers to their ears and listened to the magnified sound of the German miners chipping at the clay from the opposite side. Both men moved closer to the spot where the chipping sounded loudest, and when they stood side-by-side they knew the exact spot where the Germans would break through.

'Be sure to kill them all, boyos, we can't have them getting back to their own lines and raising the alarm. Good luck, we'll have a brew waiting for you,' Palfrey said, moving away.

'One on either side, one kneeling and one

standing, wait until they're inside before firing. Use the pistols first, save the bayonets as a last resort,' Thomas said grimly.

Each man then began to arrange himself for the coming combat in such a manner as his fancy took him. Hill swallowed and wiped away the cold sweat trickling from his face with his cuff. Banks stared wide-eyed at the wall as if trying to see through to the other side. His hands ceased to tremble like they always did at killing time. Burke began sniffing as if he'd discovered a bad smell. Thomas held his pistol loosely in his hand and waited patiently. Gradually, the faint scraping grew louder, sounding like a trapped animal burrowing its way to freedom. The wall trembled ever so slightly and a lump of clay fell shuddering to the floor. The end of a shovel appeared, prodding, twisting and enlarging the hole until it became big enough for a man to crawl through. The sound of grunting and heavy breathing dulled by the damp clay walls halted, and quietness descended.

Thomas gritted his teeth and gripped the pistol butt tightly in his hands, turning his knuckles a ghostly white, and waited. Without warning, part of the wall collapsed and four armed German soldiers rushed through the gaping hole. Before they could raise their weapons they were quickly cut down and fell kicking and twitching. Two more rushed in and were metered with the same treatment.

'Right, lads,' Thomas shouted, 'let's finish the buggers!'

He rushed for the opening, firing blindly into the body of men futilely attempting to back away yet forced forward by the men behind. Germans dropped like flies, screaming and yelling in a bid to escape the hail of bullets. For a fleeting moment Thomas thought there might be too many for them to handle. Leslie Hill pushed his way into the tunnel and, drawing his bayonet, slashed at the panicking Germans. A tall hook-nosed officer raised his pistol and took point-blank aim at him. Calm and collected, oblivious to the carnage raging around him, his finger tightened around the trigger. Thomas automatically stepped in front to take the bullet. The sound of igniting gunpowder raked his eardrums and the smell of cordite burned into his nostrils. Suddenly, against all the odds, he felt the grip of life tighten, and more than ever before he experienced the overriding un-wanted will to live, it was too late. Then, yelping in pain, he felt the bullet strike the blade of his bayonet, sending it spinning from his hand.

'Christ that was bloody close! Thanks, mate,' Hill said, slashing open the officer's face and plunging the blade into the gasping chest.

Burke quickly re-loaded his revolver and with his bayonet in his other hand sprinted down the tun-nel to finish off the retreating Germans. Thomas followed, jumping over dead and writhing bodies while loading his pistol on the run. A German stopped, turned, and dropped to one knee. Burke froze and raising his hand made the sign of the cross, certain in his mind that he was about to die. Thomas hurled him roughly to one side, sending him cursing and sprawling headfirst down into the sticky mud.

This is it. At last. From no more than twenty

yards, the German fired and the bullet grazed his shoulder like a red-hot poker brushing against his bare skin. His eyes shone livid with anger and disappointment, still he lived. A second shot struck his chest with the force of a blacksmith's sledgehammer, hurling him backwards. Slammed against the soft wall of clay he slumped to the floor, his sight dimmed into blackness. His ears filled with a sound like a tide flowing onto a sandy beach, and surging rushing waves washed away his consciousness.

Hastily working the bolt, the German fumbled another bullet into the breech and stared at Thomas though hate-filled eyes. His head jerked upward at the sight of Leslie Hill bearing down on him, followed by John Burke. Without aiming, he pulled the trigger sending the bullet flying harmlessly over their heads. The rifle fell from his shaking hands and he backed away then turned and fled. From one hundred yards Hill dropped him with one shot to the back of his head, and it was over.

Palfrey waited with a large smile on his face. Unperturbed by the sight of the bloodstained bodies, he waited until they had removed Thomas from the tunnel and then set a small detonation to block the tunnel off. Now directly over the enemy lines, the miners could begin tunnelling in different directions.

'Well done, boyos,' he said. 'Sorry about your corporal though. Soon be ready for the big bang – it'll send thousands of the German buggers to hell, it will, boyos. Just make sure you don't miss it.'

Banks and Hill carefully lifted Thomas onto the trolley and slowly pushed him to the entrance of the mine. It was six-fifteen when they emerged into the breaking dawn. A heavy mist hung over No Man's Land like a giant cloak and the morning air felt cold. A couple of sentries gave them a cursory look, puffed and coughed chestily on Craven A cigarettes, sniffed and wiped their runny noses on their cuffs. John Burke cleared his throat, unscrewed his water bottle and took a long swig, rinsed his mouth and spat out the taste of the mines. Tipping the bottle upside down, he poured the remaining contents over Thomas's upturned face.

'Get up, yer idle man,' he grunted.

Thomas stirred and roused from his unconsciousness, spluttering water from his nose.

'Am I dead?' he said quickly, glancing around.

'You're no deader than I am. The bullet struck the winder on that pocket watch of yours. You're a lucky man so you are, someone's watching over you.'

Thomas attempted to lift himself and lay back with a yelp.

'Fractured or broke a rib, I reckon. We'll find a stretcher-bearer and get you up to the medical station.'

Stan Banks frowned and peered at Thomas through thoughtful eyes. On two occasions in the tunnel he'd seen him attempt what was tantamount to an act of blatant suicide. His mind went back to Catterick and Corporal Woollard and he remembered Archie struggling to remember his own name. His sympathy, though well inten-

289

tioned, carried with it an indictment of a deep-rooted secret so malignant that he feared for his friend's life.

Unable to walk unaided Thomas sat apart from the others waiting for the arrival of the medics to take him away on a horse-drawn cart for treatment. That night in the trenches sleep would not come and fatigue racked their limbs. Hill attempted to revive his spirits with a shave in tepid water, nicking his throat only once with the dull-bladed razor, he congratulated himself and felt better.

'That Archie, he does some strange things at times,' Stan Banks said, cleaning his black fingernails through the gaps in his front teeth and swallowing the proceeds.

'He took a bullet meant for me, I'm sure of it. Just stood there like a man waiting to be shot,' John Burke mused.

Leslie Hill scratched his head.

'Yeah, funny you should say that. That bloody Fritz officer had me in his sights at point-blank range. Thomas, he steps in front and waits for the bullet as cool as a fresh cucumber. Bullet struck his bayonet and saved his life, and mine,' he said.

Stan glanced across at Moses sitting quietly in the background cleaning his rifle. Moses remained silent, uncertain whether or not to speak, thought he might try to change the subject, or at least put a different perspective on the informal exchange of words. With a concerted effort he pulled himself to his feet and eased the stiffness from his legs before walking a few paces down the trench. Stan watched him sit down on the firing step, take out his bayonet and prod away a rat chewing at his shoelaces. It squealed in protest and disappeared.

'Maybe they were acts of bravery, perhaps he didn't want any of you to die, perhaps he felt responsible for you and felt the need to protect you,' Moses shrugged. 'He is always first in line whenever something needs doing. Perhaps you should celebrate the fact that because of him you are still alive.'

Hill ripped the top from a tin of bully beef and stuffed the contents into his mouth until it could hold no more. 'Yeah, I reckon you're right. I'm going to tell Mr Bellamy tomorrow,' he chomped thoughtfully. 'He deserves another medal I reckon. Where is he anyway?'

'He's up at the farmhouse, lad, with Apple,' Banks chirped in, keeping his eyes firmly on Moses.

'Bloody hell, that sounds a bit dodgy, the number of times Apple's been blown up it's a wonder anyone goes near him,' someone called from further down the trench.

The rib was broken, they told him, and they bandaged him tightly to help the bones knit together properly. He didn't dare think how he'd survived in the mines and his thoughts were no more than black shadows that evaded reason or even common sense. How much longer could he survive aware of the inexorable onslaught on his own ruin? He had promised himself life. Yet once again he had unconsciously tried to end it and struggled to reason why his mind forced him to do the things his heart denied him. He understood he must learn to face his fears, confront them, grasp and bend them to his own will. The past is over and done with, live like a man, Moses had said. But he couldn't because he knew deep down he lacked the inner strength, the moral fibre, and he loathed himself for his weakness. He belonged only to Archie, and no other would ever possess him unless he found the strength to bludgeon down the doors of guilt and wash away the curse of shame.

Without warning his Adam's apple bobbed and stuck in his throat, he coughed and his eyes filled with warm salty tears and flowed unchecked down his grime coated cheeks. Against his wishes he cried like a child and knew only in death, would he find an everlasting peace.

When the tears dried he sniffed and stared up at the roof and searched his imagination for what it might be like to exist in another time, to feel the warmth of sunshine playing over his face. To once more smell the heady scent of fresh heather wafting across the moors and tease his senses. He pictured Lord Buxton standing in his gleaming black boots outside the church waiting for his groom to arrive with the bay horse and trap. From there he would go to the inn and take a gill of brown ale with the parishioners, who would cling to every word he spoke. Not that he ever made any sense, but because he was a lord.

He swung his legs over the side of the bed and pulled himself gingerly to his feet, feeling the pain bite into his chest like dagger points. Somehow he struggled across the room, pulled the letter from his tunic hanging on the back of the door and eased himself into the chair next to the window. Apple lay sleeping silently on his back with his arms folded across his chest like a monarch lying in state, his mouth opening and closing like a goldfish in a bowl at a fairground.

This was the first opportunity he'd had to read the two-page letter properly since the mêlée in the mine. After the first page his hands shook and he felt no need to read any further. The pages slipped from his hands and fluttered down onto the table. His chest heaved, sending spasms of pain darting into his body. In spite of the agony he picked up the letter and read the first page once more. She was pregnant. He was about to become a father. It could only be his. He needed Moses – he would know what to do.

Sleep tormented him that night with a riot of dreams, some of profound happiness, others tangled and twisted with dark flickering night-mares. He dreamed of playing in the top meadow with Ruby, of holding a baby, his baby, standing in front of the altar with Dilly by his side and his mother and father watching with the rest of the congregation. Archie stood holding a noose in his hand on the other side of the church. Something gripped his shoulder and he felt himself being led away. He resisted, he didn't want to go, yet still the grip on his shoulder remained, pulling him first one way and then the other. Sitting up in the bed, he screamed in agony as the pain ripped merci-lessly into his chest. A red mist blocked the light from his eyes and he trembled without restraint.

'Whoa there, lad,' Apple said, releasing his grip on Thomas's shoulder. 'Take this, it will help you sleep.'

In a state of dazed confusion Thomas swallowed the pill without protest and gulped the cold water, while Apple wiped away the sweat on his face.

'You were having a bad one there, son. I've had dozens of nightmares since I was first blown up, never had another after the second time,' Apple said.

'Why, what happened?' Thomas murmured sinking back onto the bed.

'I shit the bed instead.'

Thomas couldn't stop himself from laughing. 'You're joking,' he said, holding his hands to his chest to relieve the pain.

'Get your head down, that pill will work in seconds,' Apple said with a smile and a wink.

Like Apple promised the pill weaved its magic and he contentedly drifted into a deep sleep, feeling warm and at peace with the world, his mind sitting comfortable with his body. Apple stayed awake and made coffee. Raking the grey embers in the fire he threw on a couple of logs and watched the flames lick greedily at the offering and celebrated by sending a flurry of sparks dancing their way up the chimney. With a satisfied smile he listened to Thomas's breathing become deep and even and approached the bed. Lifting the corner of the blanket he stared into Thomas's young face for a few moments. He knew the young corporal was no older than sixteen years of age at the most. If he'd known he was younger it wouldn't have surprised him. He'd seen them before: orphans, abused children cast from their homes by cruel parents, children who stole to live and hid in misery from the harshness of the law, others who were misguided youngsters searching for adventure and glory in a conflict forecast to last only months. To some Thomas might have appeared older, but not to Apple – he saw through the fear and degradation manifested by the uncommon misery invoked by life in the trenches.

Men aged twenty looked fifty, and men of thirty-five looked more like worn out grand-fathers. Thomas looked his age with his eyes closed, the boyishness glimmering through in its bliss and splendour as sleep relaxed his features. Awake, the sunken haunted eyes were surrounded by black sockets and the tautness of fear gazed into a bottomless chasm. Lips pulled back, snarl-ing exposed teeth ready to tear out a throat for the sake of self-preservation while he worked the bolt of his rifle and dealt out death with the same ease as a dog chewing a bone. All these things gave him the appearance of someone twice his age, but without the privilege and longevity of experience.

In the brief time he'd known Thomas he'd felt an intensity lurking within the boy, a hidden agenda, something dark and subliminal skulking and waiting to be released. He saw a boy strug-gling for manhood, who might never swing a pick and leave his mark on the world, yet his bravery and courage could never be questioned – always first into the thick of trouble and the last out, he seemed to exist within an aura such as he had never witnessed before. He turned away and saw the letter lying open on the table, and felt the temptation to read the words. Instead, he folded it neatly, replaced it in the envelope and pushed it back into Thomas's tunic pocket.

Second Lieutenant Bellamy strode into the farmhouse the following morning accompanied by Sergeant Bull. An unusual occurrence in itself, officers and senior NCOs rarely felt the need to present themselves to corporals.

'Stand easy and be seated, Corporal Elkin,' Bellamy said, noticing Thomas wincing. 'This isn't an official visit, by God it isn't. I simply like to keep an eye on my men. Too much slaughter and not enough consideration for the fighting men going on in this war. Now, Sergeant Bull tells me two of the men you spent time with in the mines think you deserve a medal for saving their lives. Is this true, eh, what, what, speak up man?'

'Is what true, Sir?'

'Did you save their lives by a courageous and unselfish act of bravery?'

'I don't think so, Sir. I just did my duty.'

'I'm inclined to disagree, Corporal, by God I am, by God I am. I think you exceeded your duties and were lucky to escape unscathed, apart from the injury to your chest. Mmm, what do you say to that, eh, eh, eh?' he said, rubbing his hand over his jaw and squeezing his lips together with his fingers, then pinching his forehead.

Thomas remained silent. He wanted to avert his eyes from the clownish antics, not from shyness or embarrassment but calculation. It was all put on, a façade designed for everyone to see that he was a caring officer with only the well-being of his troops in mind. Thomas knew it was all bullshit. News travelled fast in the trenches and Bellamy had been recognised by a sergeant from the Welsh guards.

'Tried to court-martial him for cowardice they did. Ordered his men over the top and remained shitting himself in the trenches. When his men won the day he sprang from his trench and raced across No Man's Land without being spotted and dropped into the captured trenches,' the sergeant continued. "Gave them a sound thrashing that time we did", that's what the cowardly bastard said. One of the men had lost all his mates in the attack and wanted to rip his head off. 'Who's we?' he asked him. 'I don't remember seeing you, Sir, apart from the time you slithered back into the trenches and stayed there shitting your nice corded breeches, Sir. Mind you, Sir, nice of you to find time to come over and visit us, Sir, now it's all over, Sir.'

At his court-martial Bellamy had stated that his helmet had been shot from his head and he had suffered momentarily from amnesia. They let him off and sent him to the Yorkshire Rifles.

'Can't blame him for being scared,' Thomas said.

'I've seen more than my share of frightened men in my time, lad, myself one of them. Fear's not a crime. I know that, by God I do, it's a trait of human nature. But the poor buggers still took their turn in going over the top and died gripped in the arms of fear the same as brave men,' the sergeant said, becoming agitated. 'It's the lying sods that falsely claim the success won by others that causes the bell to toll.'

Thomas thought long and hard on the words. He decided it unnecessary to spook the remainder of the men in the battalion, and chose to keep the truth about Bellamy to himself for the time being. If the officer endangered any of the Rifles he would have no hesitation in shooting him.

'Ah well, perhaps a medal's not in the offing after all, pity though, Sergeant Bull informs me you've hardly taken any leave since just after Christmas. You're no good to us at the moment and I think we can manage without you for six days. A few days in Blighty might be just what the doctor ordered. You can leave when you feel fit to travel,' Bellamy said. 'Tell the men. I like them to know I'm always thinking of their welfare, what, what, what.'

Thomas felt he needed no favours from him and, for a moment, felt like telling him where to stick his leave. He wasn't the only one who deserved a break, the whole battalion's nerves were stretched to breaking point. Then his thoughts turned to Dilly.

Raining, raining, forever raining, it became like day is to daylight and dark is to darkness. The raindrops fell, whispering a symphony on the uneven panes of glass, and he thanked God that the fire crackled a smiling comforting hello. Two weeks, they told him, two weeks before he was fit enough to travel, he couldn't believe his luck. Already he'd written to Dilly informing her he was coming back to Blighty. When, he wasn't certain. He'd pass on a letter to a soldier going home on leave to post it for him when he was sure. For two days he wrestled with his mind unsure whether or not he was doing the right thing. To all intents and purposes he supposed he might be too young to get married and raise children, then again, Dilly might not even want him when she discovered his age. Reflexively he raked his fingers through his hair and reminded himself to wash with carbolic soap before he left. He could feel the lice crawling over his body, sucking and feasting on his blood.

Each morning he sat impatiently by the window watching columns of men tramping to Ypres and the front line, their faces smiling as they engaged in bouts of uncouth banter. Others with downturned mouths convinced they were engaged in a one way journey. Ammunition carts and field guns struggled through the clinging mud. Behind them came the baggage column with its long-eared mules, then the field kitchens – black greasy boilers on wheels – and finally, the stretcher-bearers with their little wheeled ambulances. In all the time he'd spent in France and Belgium he'd hardly known the sun to shine for more than a few days at a time. Now he had grown to hate the place, along with the officers, those ineffectual idiots who foolishly sent tens of thousands to a needless death. Above all he hated the Germans who'd started the bloody war in the first place. The sight of Moses plodding through the rain cheered him and he smiled at the thought of much missed company. He filled the pan with water, pushed it onto the hot embers and prepared two cups of coffee with extra sugar.

'How are you this fine morning?' Moses said in his clipped voice, usurping the chair by the window.

'I've had a letter from Dilly. You remember I told you about her?'

'I certainly do, how is she keeping? Very well I hope.'

'She's pregnant.'

'Really, and who's the lucky father?'

'I am.'

Moses's head jerked upwards, and with a solemn face he watched Thomas pour hot water into two tin mugs.

'When did you last see her?'

'Almost six months ago. Bellamy's given me six days leave and I'm going to London to see her. I'd like to marry her. Do you think I'm too young? What do you think I should do?'

'Are you serious?' Moses said frowning. 'She's six months pregnant and you have only just found out, and now you want to get married at the age of sixteen and raise a family. A few weeks ago you were all set to get yourself killed. I think you had better slow down and put things into perspective.'

'I know I can never go home, but I can make a life somewhere else, I can change my name – that's not against the law is it?'

'No, it's not,' Moses said, perturbed by Thomas's sudden change of heart and determination to live. 'If you want to change your name, there are thousands of bodies out there in No Man's Land. Just take your pick and switch identity tags.'

Thomas's eyes sprung open wide. 'I never thought of that,' he whispered excitedly. 'I knew you would know what to do.'

'For God's sake,' Moses snapped. 'Slow down and try to consider things rationally instead of stumbling around like a blind man in the dark.'

Thomas felt his face redden and he turned and

stared out of the window. At times, Moses's cutting attitude placed a strain on their friendship and he felt the bite of anger grip his chest. The child is his, what else is there to consider? he thought petulantly.

'The men out on patrol day and night are really putting the frighteners on the Germans,' Moses said, changing the subject. Thomas only half-heard him as he watched Slippery Stewart, the eternal bearer of bad news making his way towards the farmhouse.

'Hello, Archie. I just thought you ought to know that Stan Banks has a dugout in the trenches full of souvenirs taken from the dead – got quite a thriving business by all accounts,' Slippery said in a whinging voice and avoiding eye contact.

Thomas spun round with his eyes blazing and fists clenched, the thought strangled his heart, and already annoyed by Moses abrupt attitude he snapped.

'Where is he now?'

'Ignore him,' Moses snapped. 'He's just stirring the shit, as usual.'

'He's in the trenches,' Slippery added nervously, turning to avoid Moses's glare.

Thomas pushed aside the pain in his chest and pulled on his tunic, with a sneer on his lips he made his way towards the trenches, followed by Moses. Once there, he made his way to the Rifles' position.

'Give me a grenade, Corporal Crumble, now!' he growled at Apple.

Apple opened his mouth to speak.

'Give me a bloody grenade or I'll blow you up

301

for the last time!'

Apple handed him the grenade and glanced at Moses, Moses shrugged and held out his hands palms up. A queue of men standing outside Stan Banks's dugout turned to see what all the noise was about.

'Hey up, lads, our very own hero's turned up to pay us a visit. Come to buy a souvenir have you?' Banks called out.

Without responding, Thomas pulled the pin and threw the grenade into the dugout.

'Hey up, you baby-faced bastard, what do you think you're doing?' Banks screamed, diving for cover.

'Get out of here, Banks, and don't come back, you weasel-faced rat, you're finished with the snipers. For months I've watched men slaughtered and blown to pieces, many I considered friends, and you want to sell souvenirs and make money from their deaths.' He turned to the men. 'You,' he asked the man closest to him, 'you know anybody who copped it out there, and you, how about you, and you, you lost a brother didn't you?' he said, pointing his finger at a man with downcast eyes. They nodded and dropped their heads in shame. 'Get back to your positions, and you, Banks, fuck off.'

Banks's snarl was instant and his hand reached for his bayonet. Then his shoulders slumped, his arms hung limply by his sides. Thomas felt the coldness of his glare and shuddered. Banks picked up his rifle. His finger reached out and fumbled with the safety catch.

'Who do think you are, eh? Oh, I forgot, you

302

don't know who you are, do you? I'll remember this. You haven't heard the last of me, Elkin,' he growled quietly.

Thomas turned his back, unable to dispel the chill shooting up his spine. The threat had found its mark. They would meet again, he was sure of it and perhaps it wouldn't be on friendly terms.

'You might have been a little offhand there, my friend,' Moses said thoughtfully, watching Banks disappear.

'I don't think so,' Thomas snapped.

'Since wars began soldiers seldom return without plunder. Banks is consumed with the fear of dying, like everyone else, but he does something about it – he invents another world as a diversion to keep his mind off the horror that eats away inside of him. To help allay his fear he brings others into his world and gives them something else to think about apart from dying. When they queued up to buy his souvenirs he knew what he was doing. He knows, as the rest do that they might all be blown to pieces this time tomorrow, and those who survive will queue again the next day, and the days after that. It offers them an alternative to the inevitable,' Moses said.

'For God's sake, speak in English,' Thomas said. 'I don't understand what you're talking about.'

Moses looked him directly in the face, blinked slowly, shook his head from side-to-side and walked away.

Rattled, in the farmhouse Thomas stared grimly into the fire, waiting for his anger to diminish. For some time he struggled to decipher the meaning of Moses's assumed words of wisdom. They made no sense. Ever since they had fallen out over Robert McCaughey's death at Amiens, Banks had sought to re-invent their friendship, yet he was always prepared to hurl a biting insult whenever the opportunity arose. He recalled the time spent training at Catterick where Banks had become his best friend, always looking out for him. He even rightly suspected that he was under-age, but said nothing. He'd taken him home to his family, never doubting his story of being raised in an orphanage with nowhere else to go. With his head in his hands, he sought to make sense of the situation and failed. Maybe he had deprived the men of hope in a hopeless environment, but he failed to see how. He crossed to the window and watched horses straining and heaving to pull carts overloaded with stores. They came in all shapes, sizes and colours. None looked like Ruby, and he was glad.

That same evening, Sergeant Bull sent for him.

'I understand you've had another falling out with Banks?' he asked.

'Yes, Sergeant.'

'Tell me what happened.'

Thomas related the story as he saw it. Sergeant Bull listened impassively without interrupting until he'd finished.

'Corporal Elkin, I don't care if a soldier crosses over to the German lines and makes love to them every night, as long as he kills them before he returns. You don't seem to be able to grasp what war is about and how it affects people differently,' Sergeant Bull said in a patient voice. 'Plundering and pilfering goes on all the time. It's a way of life in the trenches. You yourself always carry an empty sandbag like the rest of the men. You cannot steal from a dead man, you can only take from him, remember that. Men take from their dead comrades in No Man's Land all the time. Watches, rings and other meaningless trinkets go missing, but they are not taken for gain, the men take them to prove to themselves they have survived and are able to do so. Do you understand?'

Thomas frowned and the words tumbled around in his head.

'No, Sergeant, I've tried to understand, but it doesn't seem right,' he said doggedly.

'Then listen to me for a moment, they steal to prove to themselves they are still alive and have made it back safely to their lines. Back in the trench the man will inspect the watch he has taken from the body of a dead comrade and perhaps, out of habit, he will shake it and then check the time against his own watch,' Sergeant Bull continued. 'During those few fleeting seconds, all thoughts of the war are obliterated from his mind. Later, he will throw the watch away, maybe sell it or trade it for something else. Call it an instant tonic, a medicine that wipes away the memory of war and the thought of death. Call it whatever you will, but it works.'

Thomas fidgeted and scraped the toe of his boot over the wooden floor. The sergeant's words verified those of Moses. Nevertheless, stealing was stealing, and stealing from comrades, whether dead or alive, was a crime he couldn't tolerate.

Sergeant Bull stared into Thomas's eyes, curious to see if he'd understood, but he knew that he hadn't and he hesitated for a moment. Then, crossing the room to a small table in the corner, he rummaged underneath a pile of dog-eared magazines and produced a packet of cigarettes. With a small metal lighter he lit a cigarette and inhaled. Thomas watched, baffled, as he sent the grey stream of smoke spiralling into the air. Thomas hadn't realized until that moment that Sergeant Bull smoked.

'Sit down, lad,' the sergeant said in a gentler tone. 'I once had a man from Wakefield under my command. He was a lawyer and he believed the war was illegal and even refused an officer's commission. When the war was over he planned to bring the British and German generals into court for crimes against mankind. So he went to a medical station and took as many small empty bottles as he could carry. Before he went over the top he scraped a piece of mud from the trench, put it in one of the bottles and labelled it. He did this in every trench he found himself in, and even took samples from German trenches he fought in. He called it evidence to be produced in court. Ten bottles should be enough, he told everyone. The whole battalion, aware of what was going on, took it upon themselves to protect him. He filled eight bottles before he was ripped to pieces by shrapnel. He went over the top like a lion, his only ambition to kill the enemy and fill the bottles. The men went with him willingly and fought like devils for a cause that wouldn't stand up for two seconds in a court of law. It was their way of enduring the war without thinking about it.'

Thomas raked his fingers through his hair and a shiver ran down his spine. He smiled, and he understood. Then his smile faded and his gaunt, sallow face grew drawn. In the flickering glow of the candlelight, the words slowly seeped into his anguished mind. What have I done? Who am I to pass judgement on better men than I?

'How do you manage to get through the war, Sergeant?' he asked, his voice barely a whisper.

'Me, lad, I tell everyone what to do, then spend my time worrying that they've done it correctly. I don't have time to worry about dying.'

It was still light, and dusk was in the throes of preparing to close down another day when Thomas left, his mind a kaleidoscope of contradictions, disjointed and ill-fitting – nothing felt simple any more. He thought of his schooldays and Mr Webster – the more you learn, the more you need to remember, he used to think.

From a small wooden bridge spanning a fast-running stream he noticed scattered groups of bright red flowers and stopped to stare. Poppies – he hadn't seen those since his time on the farm. His face creased into a warm smile. At last, something fine flourished amidst the stark cemetery that had once been beautiful countryside. Back at the farmhouse he sat alone and knew what he must do. He must find Stan Banks and make reparation for his foolhardiness. Snared in the trap of guilt at sending Stan away, he knew the feeling would not pass easily. It was neither sentiment nor possessiveness but a way of existing within his own weakness. However, regardless of his enquiries to contact him, all investigations into his whereabouts were fruitless. Stan Banks had vanished from the face of the earth.

Chapter Fifteen

London

'I don't want him under my roof again, and that's final,' Mrs Tuttle rasped, patting her chest and coughing. 'He's a dirty little sod, that's what he is.'

Dilly held her breath certain that at any moment the tortured chair would at last succumb to one final assault.

'Oh, Ma, you don't mean it. He's come all that way, the least you can do is give him a room. He's been fighting in the war, he might even have another medal. We can't just turn him away, what will the neighbours say?'

'Neighbours? Them bleeders have said enough already. Brought shame on the household, you have. You'll have to dig him a trench in the back garden, he'll feel at home there.'

Dilly tossed her head, covered her mouth with her hands and gave a muffled shriek of laughter. 'Ma, that's a horrible thing to say! Let him stay just one night until he finds another room. Give us both time to sort things out. We can't ignore him, can we? Under the circumstances, I'm surprised he even wants to talk to me.'

Mrs Tuttle's dark eyes scrutinised her daughter.

'One night, that's all, and then he's on his way. What time are you meeting him?' she finally relented.

'Half-past-one it said in his letter, under the big clock. I hope he's not late, I hate Victoria Station, always full of dirty-mouthed soldiers.'

'Well you better get a move on girl, it's after twelve now.'

Thomas didn't mind waiting. He'd purposely arrived twenty minutes early, he didn't want to be late because he wasn't certain if pregnant women possessed the stamina to stand for long periods of time without sitting down. He knew little or nothing about women having babies, apart from how they were made and where they came from. After almost six months, perhaps she might already have given birth to the child. He should have asked Moses – he knew the answers to most things – now he would have to play it by ear. The visit to the gents for a refreshing wash and brush-up had raised his spirits. He'd dampened his hair, parted it in the middle and slicked it down with his comb. Pensively he glanced around at his surroundings.

The station was much the same as before: fresh batches of soldiers reluctantly going out in their hundreds to replace the poor shuffling hulks covered in bandages making their way along the crowded platforms. Occasionally some stopped by the wooden-built bank offering to change francs and centimes into pounds and shillings. Foreign money bought nothing in the churlish side streets of London. As ever, always on hand in a crisis, the nurses assisted wherever needed and the Salvation Army handed out free cups of tea and currant cakes to those short of a few pennies. He'd seen the Salvation Army on the front many times, situated just behind the trenches – brave

309

bunch they were, and the troops loved them for their kindness. He fingered the pocket watch and thought of Catherine and her mother. The engineers had made a good job of repairing the winder.

The large station clock overhead clunked one-thirty. It was a bright sunny afternoon and he felt overwhelmed with excitement.

'Hello, Archie,' she said from behind him. 'It's good to see you.'

He spun round, nearly losing his balance, and smiled. 'Well, it's the least I can do isn't it, you know, what with everything?' he said sheepishly.

In a moment of tenderness he wanted to kiss her and could see no reason not to press his lips against her sweet mouth. He leaned towards her, but she made no effort to reciprocate and so he quickly pulled back. Disappointed, he frowned at her reticence and allowed the moment to pass. Maybe later, when she grew accustomed to having him back, she might melt and show him a glimmer of affection. He glanced at her stomach hoping to see a visible sign of a swelling.

'Ma said you can stay for one night, and then you will have to find somewhere else,' she said distracting his attention.

'Oh well, it's only to be expected I suppose,' he said, sensing an abrupt coldness in her voice he hadn't expected. 'Come on, we'll get a cab, can't have you walking around in your condition.'

He'd forgotten how pretty she looked and glowed with pride when men turned to look at her with appraising glances. She looked radiant in a cream two-piece ankle-length suit, with a pink lace blouse and matching hat perched jauntily on the side of her head. He wanted to put his arm around her waist, to advertise to all that she belonged to him, Thomas Elkin, a soldier who'd fought in the war and won a medal and still lived to tell the tale. Now his whole life was about to be shaped forever by a single act – he was about to become a father – and the intensity of his cravings frightened him. The memory of her firm white thighs, her soft pubic hairs curling between his fingers, burned in his groin and disgusted him. He lowered his arm and quickly pushed his hand into his trouser pocket in an effort to quell the offending bulge.

By the time they reached the house on Frith Street and paid the cabby, he thankfully had himself under control and sighed with relief. Mrs Tuttle sat in her chair by the window, as usual the inevitable sound of spittle rattled through the glowing pipe like water pouring down a partially blocked sink as she sucked harder to keep the tobacco alight.

'Hello, Mrs Tuttle, keeping well I hope?' he said.

'Well enough, Archie, how about you?'

'Aye, same as you, well enough.'

Dilly left and busied herself in the kitchen, leaving him alone with a feeling of unease. He held his cap in his hands and fidgeted with the peak, feeling the sweat beneath his tunic. Mrs Tuttle cleared her throat and, turning her head, stared out of the window as though he wasn't there. He struggled to understand her off-handed attitude and thought maybe he should apologise for making Dilly pregnant. Then thought better of it – what is done is done. In his own way he loved Dilly. Well, he thought he did,

311

although he wasn't too sure how being in love felt, until he thought of Catherine.

Finally Dilly returned to the drawing room carrying a tray containing a china teapot and matching cups. Silently, she poured out three cups and passed one to her mother and another to him. All the time his mind raced – he wanted to speak, to begin a course of conversation. Mrs Tuttle murmured something he didn't catch about opening a window, and with flapping hands she waved the pipe smoke away from her face. He turned to Dilly hoping for some form of support; he noticed her hand shook slightly and heard the rattle of cup against saucer. He smiled at her, and she fluttered her eyelids and turned away.

'Well, say what it is you've come to say, Archie. You can stay the night and that's it,' Mrs Tuttle suddenly interrupted.

He placed the cup on the table and frowned, puzzled by her unfriendly manner. In his mind no problem existed – he had come prepared to marry Dilly and do all that was required of him both as a father and a husband.

'If Dilly and I are to be married, don't you think we should try to get on?' he said, staring directly into her face.

Dilly's face turned white, her bottom lip trembled like a child about to cry and the cup tumbled from her hands and shattered on the floor.

'Archie,' she said tremulously.

'There now, no need to fret, lass. Surely you didn't think I would abandon you, I know it's what you want. What would you have expected me to say?' he said gently.

'Archie, you must have read my letter or you wouldn't be here,' she whispered hoarsely.

'Aye, course I did, that's why I'm here, Dilly, to do the right thing. If I'm to become a father we'll need to be married straight away.'

'What are you talking about? You couldn't have read the letter properly. I told you I didn't want to marry you,' she said, clasping her hands to her cheeks. 'I'm engaged to Cyril Beale, a manager at the brewery. He's in charge of the drays and horses, and a little house comes with his job. I wrote about the baby because I thought it was the right thing to do. I'm so sorry, Archie. I wanted the baby to have a proper father – you could be killed at any time.'

Thomas sat stunned. The heat of foolishness and confusion burned deep into his face. His world shattered like the broken cup on the floor. He looked into Dilly's face and saw the tears run unchecked down her cheeks. She murmured soft words and reached out to touch his arm. He recoiled and squeezed his eyes shut, remembering he'd only read part of the first page of the letter. She didn't want him, as a husband or a father to their child. She could make that decision and there was nothing he could do to change her mind.

'Aye, looks like I've made a right fool of myself,' he said, blinking hard and shaking his head. 'You've not had the child yet then? Only I wondered if I might see it,' he mumbled, getting to his feet.

Mrs Tuttle coughed and rasped as she fought

for her breath. The pipe twisted in her hands and red-hot tobacco spilled onto her lap.

'Get out of here, you silly beggar, go on, be gone with you, you daft bleeder! What would Dilly want with the likes of you? I've seen more brains up a horse's arse,' Mrs Tuttle shrieked at him. Finally, the chair gave up the ghost and, with a resounding crack, splintered and disintegrated under her weight, leaving her floundering like a beached whale on a shore of hot needles.

Justice was served and he found himself unable to stifle the grin spreading across his face. For a moment he stood with stilted legs, and then jerkily made his way to the front door. He heard Dilly call his name, her voice plaintive pleading for forgiveness. He ignored the hooting omnibus and crossed the street, pushing his way through the crowded pavements making no attempt to avoid barging into people. For the next two hours he walked without direction or thought, finally he stopped and in an open doorway stamped his feet to relieve the tiredness and hesitantly watched people go about their business. Checking his pocket watch, he saw it was just after three-thirty. The stab of his own foolishness seemed much more painful than Dilly's rejection, even more painful than Mrs Tuttle's tirade at his lack of common sense and intelligence.

Dilly was a nice girl and in all probability he would have married her. Whether the marriage would have lasted is a matter for conjecture. Perhaps if he had something to live for he might have found some solitary haven for happiness in his heart. The baby, he thought, what about the baby? It's mine and I'll never see it. Months of deceit, lies and pretence after the death of Archie had finally taken their toll and he felt himself drowning in a sea of abandonment, unable to keep his head above the waves of existence. The harsh grind of his twisted and tormented life eroded his mind, pulling him further and further down into a bottomless abyss and making him doubt his own identity. He had given life through Dilly who, in return, had rightly or wrongly cast him aside for the sake of security for her and the baby. Now he wanted to experience a life of his own, to make his own decisions, a life he was entitled to embrace like everyone else.

He needed new avenues, but where would he look to find them? When do people start to live a life? How does a person know what to do and when to do it? He thought of Archie and felt nothing: no remorse, no sorrow, only propriety for his right to taste the bitter sweetness of life on earth. Moses had been adamant that Archie's death had been no more than an unfortunate accident born of his own wrongdoing. Why should he torture his own soul for someone like Archie? Why should he suffer the stinging darts of conscience when so-called intelligent men sent hundreds of thousands of innocent soldiers to their death in the name of war?

Outside an inn called The Tramlines, he listened to the loud drunken voices bellowing out the songs of the day. Pushing open the door, the raucous noise slammed into his ears, and changing his mind he turned and left.

When he reached the river and could go no

further, he sat down on a wooden bench overlooking the Thames. Faded green paint curled and peeled off the bench leaving the exposed wood to rot beneath time's unforgiving teeth. Perhaps the man responsible for the care of green benches lay in pieces at the bottom of a bomb crater in a foreign country, leaving a wife and children to fend for themselves. He turned his mind away. His brown eyes flickered and steadied like the flame of a dying candle, and he concentrated on the murky river. The water ran like undiminished time, slipping through unsuspecting fingers.

He didn't take much notice of a man wearing a tight-fitting suit, a worn shiny bowler and scuffed, black boots until he sat down beside him. From a silver tin he pulled out the makings and hand-rolled himself a cigarette.

'All right, mate, how you doing? On a spot of leave are you?' the man said, striking a match and inhaling.

'Aye, just for a few days.'

'I'm the same. I'm a cook on one of the cross channel boats what takes you over there and back. What do you do?'

'What do I do?' Thomas answered, suppressing the need to laugh out loud. 'I dodge bullets, get eaten alive by fucking rats and lice, and live like a pig in a filthy trench full of rotting flesh and stinking shit! Does that answer your question?'

The man flushed, the red spots on his cheeks glowing as bright as a pantomime dame's make-up. He turned his head and looked in the opposite direction, allowing cigarette smoke to trickle down his nose. 'Sorry, mate, that was a stupid question.'

316

Thomas gave a wry smile, pulled out his watch and looked at the time. The sun had started to sink over the horizon and still he had nowhere to spend the night. Tiredness lingered and his flesh seemed to have died on him.

'Aye, aye, here comes the floating meat wagon,' the man said.

Thomas turned his head and followed the man's gaze. Through the early rising evening mist, like a ghost a longboat appeared, rowed by six hatless policemen wearing rubber aprons and boots. Slowly the boat turned in a curving ripple of water and headed towards the shore. A black tarpaulin covered the stern, the corners trailing in the murky water leaving a slight eddy as a breeze skimmed over the river. The policemen shipped the dripping oars and placed their peaked caps on their heads, their mouths downturned and sour below expressionless faces, pale and ashen like a cold winter's dawn.

'Poor sods, suicides they are under that canvas, mainly women and young girls who have lost their boyfriends or husbands in the war. They can't manage on their own unless they go on the street. Police fish them out the river by the dozen every day. There might be a bloody war going on in Europe, mate, but I'll tell you something for nothing. There's a bloody bigger war going on over here. People are starving or dying of influenza every day. Got any family have you?'

'No,' he lied. 'Influenza, what's that?'

'Blimey, where have you been hiding, mate?' he said, frowning and looking at Thomas's uniform. 'Sorry, mate, I shouldn't have said that. It's like a

317

cold, only worse, and it's killing people all over the country, especially up north where it's damp.'

Thomas's face set hard, and what had chewed at his stomach for months like a can of maggots was about to become reality. If there was one thing he needed more than life itself it was to know his parents were well and in good health. He stood and walked away without a word. The man watched and shrugged his shoulders, turning his attention back to the meat boat.

'Bloody hell, had a busy day today, guv?' Thomas heard him say.

'Bugger off, you nosey little sod, before I run you in,' replied a gruff voice.

At Euston railway station Thomas peered through the thick glass of the ticket office window.

'Sorry corporal, there aren't any trains for Sheffield today. Nine-fifty-five tomorrow morning,' the grim-looking ticket clerk said, trying to raise a smile over his half-moon spectacles.

'Thank you, I'll come back in the morning,' he said.

Outside the station, he stared up at the pink-and-lilac-streaked sky hanging over the world's largest metropolis. It was late evening and the pavements glistened, reflecting the street lights and illuminations, London was a city that never suffered from nature's intended darkness. Not even in the late hours of night-time. Streets bustled with people, some dressed elegantly, others poorly attired. Shoeless urchins begged fervently, driving their well-heeled benefactors to lash out with an occasional well-aimed boot.

318

Pocket watches and wallets disappeared into dipping hands, distressed ladies not paying attention to their belongings felt their handbags and purses expertly unhooked or nipped from their elegant wrists. Men in uniform were everywhere, some drunk and others about to become so. Often drinking houses ended up a shambles, drink flowed, arguments flared, tempers fired, tables were overturned and webbing belts whirred while drunken men lurched into the streets fighting and cursing. Slatternly women with scarlet gashes of lipstick plastered over their lips and powdered faces posed like a child's worst nightmare. In a bid to attract men of any colour or tongue, they loosened their clothing like harlots in a devil's inferno. Khaki fever they called it, and women thought nothing of sleeping with men in uniform, doing their bit for the war they said, and spreading VD like confetti at a wedding.

Thomas sneered and shifted his gaze to a stretch of lawn, which at one time had more than likely been a small enclosed park, where mothers and nannies sat with tiny children and watched the world pass by. Beneath the shadows of a group of towering elms, stood a row of wooden benches covered in the acidity of pigeon droppings. Holes that once held shiny black railings heaved full of litter and bracken water, the metal now a salvo of projectiles waiting to be hurled at enemy trenches sending frightened men into a thousand bloody pieces.

Wearily he purchased a bag of hot chestnuts from a street vendor wearing a Tommy's tin helmet and a large grin and sat on the bench least covered by a pigeon's random neglect of hygiene. The evening felt warm and what he had thought dead and reduced to a faded memory began to leap and inflame inside him, and it was not an impulse. This would be his final opportunity to see his parents one more time before he died, unnoticed, in the trenches. Alone in the park, absentmindedly he allowed the hot chestnuts to grow cold, and pushing his hands into his pockets he stretched out his legs and closed his eyes. In the trenches he knew his place – where life was simple and expendable, where you died or lived to die the next day. From one minute to the next the men would never know when the dark angel would come along with a ticket for those about to perish. Outside the trenches, he struggled with life's complications, always feeling like a blind man seeking his way from a maze.

Finally, as evening succumbed to night, he remained on the bench and for the first time in months slept peacefully. No rats gnawed at his flesh, nor did the ground heave and tremble under the thumping onslaught of heavy guns. He dreamed of the place where he longed to be – home. He dreamed of his mother kneading and rolling dough in preparation for the hot oven. In the morning she would produce a mouthwatering loaf of golden bread. He dreamed of his father yawning in front of the roaring fire while he struggled to read one more chapter of Robert Louis Stevenson's *Treasure Island*, before he made his way to his soft down bed. Of Archie, there was no sign. No ceaseless sneering face to torment him, to force unwanted misery down his throat, leaving him to choke on a viscous vitriol. When he woke, he felt that perhaps the nightmare was finally over, extinguished from the Bedlam of his mind.

In the cafeteria at Euston station the following morning he sipped a hot cup of sweet tea and idly spun a penny on the tabletop. The minutes passed and time refused to be stopped, and at last he heard the last call for the train leaving for Sheffield from platform three. He picked up his cardboard suitcase and, taking a deep breath, boarded the nearest carriage. Opposite, a slim young woman sat with a cooing baby of no more than nine months on her lap. She wore a simple pale-blue gingham frock with a low neckline that offered no offence to anyone in terms of decency. When she noticed the stripes sewn on his uniform, she allowed him a glimmer of a smile. He nodded and turned his attention to the passing countryside. When the child made a gurgling sound of contentment, he swivelled his eyes and listened to the woman whisper terms of endearment into the child's ear in a bid to keep him quiet.

'I'm sorry if he bothers you,' she said quietly. 'I think soon he'll fall asleep.'

Thomas smiled. 'It doesn't bother me at all,' he said. 'Babies make noises.'

The child looked up with enquiring eyes and gazed into his face. Thomas took in the small mouth, upturned nose, cherubic face and podgy arms, and with a smile he thought of Dilly. He stared down at the floor, his mouth as dry as dust, and he felt the cold haunt of melancholy and what might have been slip silently into his heart. Without thinking he leaned forward and held his hand out towards the child. His face twitched into a smile and he chuckled when the child gripped his finger. Gently he moved his hand from side-to-side. The child giggled and then laughed out loud. His mother smiled.

'Are you married?' she asked.

'No, ma'am.'

'Pity,' she smiled. 'I think one day you will make a good father.'

Thomas floundered like a herring on the dry deck of a boat. It was a simple enough remark, made with no purpose other than polite conversation, but something in the way she looked at him pleased him.

'What do you call the boy?' he asked.

'Thomas, he is called Thomas.'

'That's my name too, I'm called Thomas,' he said a little too regally, and his face exploded scarlet. For the remainder of the journey he stared from the window and remained quiet.

At Sheffield, he stood and hefted his case from the luggage net.

'Goodbye, Thomas,' he said, tickling the child's chin. 'And goodbye to you, ma'am, have a safe journey.'

'Goodbye, Thomas, keep your head down and your socks dry,' she answered, with a broad smile turning into a cross between a giggle and a gurgling laugh. 'My husband taught me that, he's called Thomas also.' Thomas laughed with her.

He waited on the platform until the train belched greasy steam and pulled away. When he saw the blue gingham arm waving farewell, he waved back frantically. He no longer had any need for the sanctuary of the trenches – he was sane, he was, he knew he was.

That day the slight breeze cooled and flapped the cuffs of his trousers and at the same time tempered Sheffield, at last he felt at home. No more strange accents he failed to understand, no more saying yes or no at the wrong times and feeling foolish. 'The calf always returns to the milk' was an old Yorkshire saying, and from the station he stepped onto the familiar lanes and hesitated. He felt his chest bulge and he wanted to cry out with sheer joy, to celebrate the privilege of being alive. He wanted to shout until the echoes shivered their way through every nook and cranny, proclaiming his presence. Yet he dared not, this was a clandestine visit motivated by the heart, his mind must remain sealed.

From a corner pawnshop he purchased a second-hand grey worsted three-piece suit, a white collarless shirt with light-brown stripes and a pair of nearly new brown boots. In a chemist, he paid for a roll of bandage and a large safety pin and rented a small single room above an inn advertising ponies and traps for hire.

Two hours later he pulled the pony to a halt and stepped from the trap. Concealed from prying eyes in a small copse of bushes, he wound the bandage around his face, checked his appearance in a small handheld mirror and pinned the bandage into position. Recognition would be impossible. With loose reins, he allowed the horse to trot easily and entered the village close to the small farm where he had been raised. In the short time he'd been away he hadn't expected things to be any different, although he thought the village seemed smaller than he remembered. People glanced and some stared with curiosity at the man wearing a smart suit with his head and face covered in bandages. 'Another casualty from the bloody war,' someone said, giving him a friendly nod. In the Longboat Inn he leaned on the bar and sipped a warm half-pint of dark mild.

'From round here, are you, lad?' the landlord asked casually.

'Further north,' Thomas mumbled through the bandages. 'I might be interested in buying a bit of land. Heard a man by the name of Elkin might be selling. Do you know him?'

'James Elkin? Aye, I know him well enough. He's having a hard time by all accounts. His missus is right poorly, got that influenza or whatever they call it. Aye, she'll not last long unless she gets help. He doesn't have the time to care for her with a farm to run, and she won't sit still for five minutes since she lost her youngest son. Eldest one's a war hero, so I've been told. I'll not dwell on that though, none of my business.'

Archie hailed as a hero caused him to smile inwardly. Confident of his disguise, he gathered up the reins, headed for the Post Office and withdrew five pounds in cash. Turning the trap round in the small village square, he headed in the direction of the farm on the edge of the moors. His breathing came short and fast and for a moment he forced himself to settle and remain calm. He must not allow his emotions to get the better of him, whatever the consequences.

James Elkin squinted, raised his hand against the sunlight and watched the small cloud of dust growing closer. Knotted fear tugged impatiently at his insides and his skin tingled with a flurry of alarm – they were coming for the unpaid rent.

The horse whinnied then snorted down its nostrils as Thomas tugged at the reins and came to a halt. Already fear of discovery spilled into his mind and he tried to lick away the dryness of his lips in an effort to keep them apart.

'Morning, sir, would you be Mr Elkin?' he croaked, pushing his tongue inside his cheek in an attempt to disguise his voice and gripping the reins tightly to stop his hands from shaking. Immediately he felt small in stature and the scourge of shame raked his body at his cruel façade. He felt light-headed and unable to function properly. This was his father who stood before him, not some passing stranger; a father who would happily take him in his arms and cry warm grateful tears at his safe return.

'Aye, I am that, lad, and what can I do you for?' he answered, staring intently into Thomas's eyes.

'I've been informed you might be interested in selling some of your land,' Thomas lied.

'Well, you've been informed wrong, lad. Not my land to sell. Wasted your time someone has.'

'Pity, perfect land for what I had in mind. What do you farm?'

Mr Elkin hesitated and for a long time he continued to stare into Thomas's face.

'Corn on top meadow and half the bottom meadow, keep other half for milking cows. They're

325

getting old now though and milk's drying up, can't afford to replace them, mind you. No bugger can afford to buy the milk anyhow.'

'Do you have any other livestock on the farm?' Thomas said, turning to avoid his father's staring eyes.

'Aye, three plough horses, one of those is as daft as a brush, and a few pigs.'

Thomas felt his stomach stir and grimaced at the mention of the pigs. His eyes darted towards the farmhouse and he prayed his mother would come outside. His prayers went unanswered and he held his head in his hands, rocking back and forwards feigning pain. Again, shame and degradation flushed through his conscience and heat welled in his eyes like a hot spring. He wanted to rip the bandage from his face and expose himself for who he really was.

'Best step down a spell, lad, and come inside out the sun if your head's giving you pain. Mrs Elkin will make us some tea.'

Thomas tensed, afraid to move in case his limbs should cease to function. Then stepped tentatively from the trap and entered the familiar surroundings of what had once been his home. It seemed much the same as when he left, yet the sparkle seemed to be missing and things weren't where they should be. The picture of his mother's mother, his grandmother, hung unusually crooked and the curtains drooped, creased and untidy. But most of all the ever-present welcoming smell of fresh baking was conspicuous by its absence. The house had turned cold and lifeless, not lived in, only inhabited.

'James,' a low voice called from his mother's bedroom. 'James, who are you talking to?'

'Just a gentleman making enquiries about the farm, nothing to worry about, lass, I'll just put kettle on.'

Thomas's heartbeat accelerated and hammered against his chest and his hands balled tight at the sound of shuffling from the bedroom. He felt his heels lift and waited for the turn of the handle that always squeaked, followed by the creak of the door. As a child he had covered his eyes when Archie told him it was the sound of a ghost coming to haunt him. Today, he was being haunted not by a ghost but by the sight of the mother he loved. She stepped out, bent and frail, holding a piece of white cloth to her mouth. Her black hair, once glossy and glistening like the wing of a raven, was now streaked grey, and her warm ever-smiling eyes sunk deep and lifeless into her skull. The hot tears soaking the inside of his bandages trickled down his face. She looked at him momentarily, her eyes briefly widening. Then, replaced with a frown she began to cough. He instinctively took a step towards her, to hold her, to comfort her, and then halted.

'Have you had an accident, Mr...?' she said, her voice muffled through the white rag.

'Smith, John Smith,' he stuttered, realising she'd almost caught him out. 'Shrapnel wound – it will heal, but it isn't pretty to look at. I get the occasional headache, nothing serious, fortunately.'

'Our son is in France. He won the Military Medal for bravery, you know. Aye, it were in the paper it were, one of the very first to get it he were. We are very proud of him, the whole village is, and we say a prayer for him in church every Sunday. Archie Elkin, have you met him? He's a corporal now, you know,' she said in a subdued voice, with the faintest of smiles.

'No, I can't say the name's familiar. Whereabouts did he win the medal?' Thomas stuttered.

'In France, we were told, newspaper reporter came and told us. Said he saved the lives of two hundred Australians singlehandedly from a prisoner-of-war camp. We live in hope he returns home safely one day, to run the farm. Getting a bit much for Mr Elkin on his own, and we can't afford hired help any more – young ones are all away fighting in the war.'

Two hundred men, Thomas thought, raising a small smile, might be the whole Australian Army by this time next week.

'We'll have no more talk of war in this house, Lizzie,' James Elkin said. 'Gentleman's got to be on his way, no doubt.'

Thomas purposely hesitated for a moment and the two men stared at each other.

'How would you feel about purchasing sheep on my behalf, and keeping them in the half meadow you no longer use?' Thomas asked. 'Of course I'll give you the money to buy them and share the profits with you,' he added. 'With the war on, wool and meat fetch a good price on the market. Build the flock up for me, perhaps cut one out for yourself whenever you need food. I already have operations doing very well further north,' he lied.

'Aye, it may be something to think on,' James Elkin said, rubbing his chin thoughtfully. 'Means more work though, and with Mrs Elkin poorly it might be difficult.'

'Bring someone in from the village to do the chores until your wife is back on her feet. I'll cover the cost, Mr Elkin, and you can pay me back later. What you have here is just the setup I'm looking for. Think on it, and I'll come round same time tomorrow. Good day to you both,' Thomas said, striding from the house.

It seemed impossible that the farm had become run down in such a short time, and he prayed his father would accept his offer.

He spent the evening in the inn and ate a meal of cold ham with cheese and brown bread washed down with fresh sparkling water. Sleep came fitfully without comfort. Three times he rose from the warm bed and swilled his face with cold water. Finally, at five minutes past four in the morning he gave up the idea of sleep, dressed and walked out into the silence and solitude of the dark moonless night. Opposite a butcher's shop two dogs fought noisily over a worn shoe until a window rattled open and a pot of urine splattered down, they ran whimpering in different directions. Dejected, he sat on a wooden bench and stared across the empty street, wishing he had the means to clear his troubled mind. At last, dawn came and lights flittered from shops, bakers prepared fresh bread and full milk churns on hand-pulled carts rumbled from the dairy.

The wizened old man with a shock of white hair blinked his watery eyes and glanced up at him. Since the war began he'd seen a steady trickle of customers enter his pawnshop. With the magnifying glass in his wrinkled eye socket, he continued to study a pearl necklace. Thomas waited patiently, listening to him mouthing complaints about people trying to cheat him out of his cash with fake jewellery.

'What can I do for you, lad? Have you any German helmets or bayonets? Fetch a good price they do,' he said.

Thomas pulled out the pocket watch and handed it to the man.

'Full Hunter, eh, nice watch. Couldn't give you any more than three pounds, lad. Got a shop full of them I have, take it or leave it,' the man said, handing the watch back. 'I tell you what though, lad, I'll give you twenty pounds for that medal you're wearing on your chest – Military Medal, fetch a few bob that would. I'll give you an extra five pounds if you write down the story of how you won it, and sign it. Don't suppose you'd be willing to sell it though?'

For a moment Thomas considered what it might be like not to have the ribbon on his chest. In the company of officers and senior NCOs it had served to bring him an element of respect he learned to enjoy. The men of his battalion made no secret of the fact they wrote to their wives and parents extolling his bravery, and revelled in the knowledge that he was one of them. With heads held high they stood shoulder to shoulder in the same rat-infested trenches as he did, and drank tea reeking of petrol like he did. If it was fit for a hero, it was fit for them.

'Forty pounds and it's yours,' he said.

'Bah, forty pounds, more than a year's wages, lad. Where's the profit in that?'

Thomas leaned forward with his hand cupped over his mouth. 'Ever heard of a man called General Haig? Saved his life, I did. Fell off his bloody horse and landed in the German trenches he did. I went straight in after him. On me own I was, killed forty Germans and took twice as many prisoners. Gave me the bloody medal himself, he did, pinned it on me chest and shook me by the hand. First one ever made it was, it's all on film, and when the war's over everybody will be able to see it, but you'll be the one with the medal.'

'You bloody liar,' the elderly man chuckled. 'Put it on paper and I'll let you cheat me out of the forty pounds.'

Thomas took the pencil and concocted a fictitious tale of heroics and false names, then signed it, *John Smith*.

He decided against the suit and wore his uniform. It was going to be a fine day. Under a blue sky he guided the trap into the farmyard. A thrush trilled its song from a nearby bush and he tried hard to memorise each note. A tractor coughing and spluttering in an adjoining field brought back happy memories of better days. His heart leapt, she was there sitting outside the front door of the farmhouse wearing a straw hat on her head and a shawl over her shoulders to keep in the warmth.

'Morning, Mrs Elkin,' he called, with his tongue clamped in his cheek.

'Good morning, Mr Smith, or should I say corporal, my you look fine in your uniform.

Archie's a corporal you know, aye that he is,' she said in a wistful voice.

'Thank you. Yes, you told me yesterday. Is Mr Elkin about?'

'He's with the pigs, over there next to the barn. You can't miss them, not with the noise they make,' she nodded.

Wet clammy sweat formed on the palms of his hands and heat burned into his neck. His legs felt like they were clamped in a vice. Move, Thomas, move, he cursed, wiping his sweating palms down the side of his leg. Why am I doing this, why didn't I mail the money and make out it was from Archie? Hesitantly he made his way towards the barn. Noticing the door swinging to-and-fro on freshly-oiled hinges, the broken slat, still unrepaired allowed a shaft of sunlight to pierce the gloomy interior. James Elkin tipped a bucket of potato peelings and leftover scraps of food into the sty and watched the pigs surge forward greedily, chomping and squealing. Thomas shivered. There were only three, before there were five.

'Morning, lad,' Mr Elkin said, looking him up and down and taking in the stripes on his arm. 'Come into the house and we'll have a brew.'

All of a sudden he felt the hackles on his neck stiffen. Her shrill whinny echoed across the moors and he heard the pounding hooves growing ever closer. She stood in all her magnificence, pawing the ground and hurling her head from side-to-side, snorting and blowing. She knew who he was. She lowered her head and charged at him like a bull would a matador, the way they used to play before he went away without her.

When he stepped to one side, she whinnied with pleasure and shook her mane. Gently she buried her nose into his chest and licked at the bandages concealing his identity. He may have fooled his parents with his cruel deception, but the horse was cleverer. He was home and she was glad. The tears crammed into his eyes until he could hardly see, he wanted to stroke her wet nose and murmur familiar words to her, but he did not dare and remained silent.

'Whoa, Ruby, whoa there, good girl, go on, off you go,' his father said. 'I've never seen her do that for nigh on a year or more. She must have taken a fancy to you, lad. Reminded her of someone she once knew, I reckon.'

Thomas tried to blink his eyes clear and watched as she raced around the meadow. Her coat glistened domino-black, her knees stepped high and the thick hairs of her fetlocks bounced and bobbed. She held her proud head aloof and her muscles rippled in the morning sunlight; she looked every inch a pedigree Percheron, and he loved her.

'I told you, didn't I? Daft as a brush she is. Bloody fine plough horse though, best I've had by a long chalk,' his father said, lifting his flat cap and scratching his head.

Inside the house James Elkin raked the embers, tossed another log on the fire and placed the copper kettle on the griddle. Of Mrs Elkin there was no sign. He pulled the curtains to one side and glanced out, a smile creasing his weather-beaten face.

'Been to gravel pit, she has, goes the first Friday

of every month since we lost our youngest lad. Reckon he drowned in pit, we do, aye. She throws a small bunch of flowers on the water to let him know we haven't forgotten him. Grand lad, he was, they didn't come any better,' his father said in a low voice.

Thomas breathed in a lungful of air and held his breath for a moment, afraid to breathe normally for fear he would sob aloud. That had been the first time they had made any reference to him. He wondered how much longer he could keep up the pretence. His saliva tasted sour like vinegar and his guts were twisted into tight knots. He felt his father's quizzical eyes boring through the bandages, as if he knew what lay below, and he cleared his mind.

When his mother entered the room she gave him a wan smile accompanied by a brief nod. Her hair was neatly combed and tied in a bun with a short length of white lace, and she wore her best dress, the blue one that she always saved for church on Sundays. On the table she placed a shallow straw basket holding a single daisy, and he remembered how he would always pick one for her on his return from school. In a white enamel mug standing on the windowsill she placed the small flower facing the sun, as he had always done. Tears glistened in her eyes, and for a moment he thought his chest would burst, and in his mind he paddled around in water wishing he could feel the warmth of her embrace, just once.

James Elkin interrupted his misery. 'We've given much consideration to your offer, Mr Smith, and we reckon we might make a go of it.

334

What you said makes good sense. How many sheep did you have in mind?' he said.

'I'll leave that up to you. I reckon thirty pounds should make a decent enough start, and ten pounds for expenses. Buy what you see fit to manage. I have one stipulation though – get someone in until Mrs Elkin is well enough to manage for herself. No farm can run single-handedly, no matter what the intentions. I'm not in the habit of tossing good money around,' Thomas said, feigning strictness.

'Aye, done as soon as said, lad. You'll get a good flock for that kind of money. I'll get old Fred Needles in to repair the hedges, best be safe than sorry. Young Clare Moore can have the spare room and look after Mrs Elkin until she's up and about. There'll be a few bits and pieces we'll need, nothing too expensive though.'

'Fine, then we have a deal, Mr Elkin?'

'Aye, Mr Smith, I reckon we do,' his father answered, spitting in his palm and holding out his hand.

For the first time in his life Thomas shook the hand of his father. His grip felt warm and firm. A glowing sense of security enveloped his body and he responded. He didn't want to let go.

'Well, there's nothing to keep me here any longer,' Thomas said, counting out the money. 'I'll forward my address when I've settled. Just one more thing, best keep all the profits due to me and plough the money back into the farm, get the place up and running. We don't want to fall short for the sake of a few shillings. Let's hope we can all look forward to a comfortable future.'

Without another word, he strode briskly from the farmhouse and almost collided with Ruby. She stood between him and the pony and trap, barring his way, with her head lowered and her eyes rolling. Her hot, wet tongue travelled slowly across the bandages as though begging him to reveal himself. He tried to smile and grimace at the same time, and this time nothing in this world could prevent the gasping sob erupting from inside his shaking body. With legs as stiff as telegraph poles he made his way to the trap and swung himself into the seat, and cracking the whip he sent the pony into a fast canter. He heard Ruby's shrill whinny and pounding hooves as she made her way to the top meadow and stood watching him leave her once again, her mind confused and distraught. Standing up in the trap he laid the whip across the pony's back, sending it into a headlong gallop and tried to block the sound of Ruby's plaintive cries from his mind.

'Shut up, Ruby, for God's sake, shut up,' he sobbed aloud, as the tears blurred his vision and soaked the bandages.

'Did you see the gait on him, Lizzie, the way he threw his left leg when he walked? It were the same as Thomas did after he fell from Ruby when she were just a pony, strange that,' James Elkin said thoughtfully. 'And the way Ruby was with him, charging at him the way she did, she did that with Thomas too. If I didn't know better I'd say it were him, aye, I believe I would.'

Lizzie Elkin, about to open her mouth to speak, glanced across to the small white enamel mug on the windowsill. The small daisy was missing. A

336

small choking noise came from her mouth, the room swirled and her legs crumbled.

The monotonous sound of the train rolling and clattering over the railway lines towards London fell on deaf ears. Never before in his life had he felt so lonely and miserable, the last few days had tapped a well of torment inside him that he thought might gush forever. Unloosening the top button of his tunic, he pulled himself to his feet and slipped open the window.

'Close the damn window, you stupid idiot, can't you see I'm trying to sleep?' a man wearing a black jacket and pinstripe trousers snapped angrily.

Thomas turned, his eyes blazed red.

'And who the bloody hell do you think you're talking to, you cock-strangling bastard? I'll put you through the bloody window in a minute!' Thomas spat back.

'I say, I'll not take that talk from...' In a brief moment, the man felt himself lifted off his feet and carried towards the open window.

'Maybe you'd rather walk to London, you useless piece of shit!' Thomas roared.

'Just a moment, Corporal, let's not do something you might later regret,' a gentle voice said at the same time as a strong hand gripped his shoulder.

'Aye, happen you're right,' Thomas said, releasing his hold on the man. 'Sit down, you bastard, I've seen better men than you'll ever turn out to be blown to pieces in the trenches, just so useless bastards like you can fall asleep on a bloody train.'

The man cowered and sat back in his seat,

straightened his tie and stared out of the window in silence. Thomas turned his attention to the man who'd intervened and prevented him from hurling the man out of the window. Immediately he noticed the two stars on the epaulettes. The young lieutenant looked up and offered him the hint of a smile and without a word continued to read his newspaper. In the corner an elderly lady sat with a pair of knitting needles and a ball of blue wool on her lap leaned across and patted him gently on his knee.

'Try not to let it get to you, lad,' she said softly. 'It'll all be over one day, and we'll be back to normal, you'll see.'

He stared at her through narrowed eyes. No, lady, it will never be normal again, not for me, he thought.

Chapter Sixteen

In London blackness gripped him and still he viewed the city as a dirty concrete jungle, crowded and claustrophobic, full of smirking men in suits and bowler hats trying to relieve him of his money by offering to sell him items of which he had no need. People shouted and begged from the gullible soldiers staggering around half drunk.

'Spare us a couple of bob, guv. Got a starving family at home,' they lied through the corner of their mouths.

The greater majority of the soldiers had never

been in a city in their lives, and here they were in the capital of the British Empire where money buys anything and everything has a price. Further on he looked in disgust at two ANZAC soldiers urinating in the gutter in broad daylight. The bloody battlefields of Europe were no different from the squalid streets of the capital, except in the trenches there was honour and reason. Pausing outside The King's Head he listened to the sound of singing and raucous laughter coming from inside. A few pints of their best piss might help him escape his devouring guilt and place him in a different frame of mind – and bollocks to the consequences.

'Pint of your best piss,' he shouted at the barman.

'We don't serve bloody soldiers in here, they cause too much bloody trouble, sling your hook,' the fat barman said.

'You heard, arsehole, pint of your best piss.'

'Sod off, you ignorant cunt,' shouted a heavy man with a barman's smock tied around his waist. 'Nothing but bloody trouble you lot. Couple of pints and you want to wreck the place. Best bleeding place for you is back down the trenches where you belong. Go on, get back with the rest of the rats.'

Thomas felt strong hands pinning his arms behind his back and he struggled for the strength to release himself.

'Go on, out of here,' someone grunted.

Outside, he staggered to his feet and leaned against the wall beside the door with his feet wide apart. He arched his back satisfied he'd sustained no serious damage. For some reason he couldn't explain, he felt in a better frame of mind. Rid of the frustrations that brooded inside him, and pulling his cloak of adolescent isolation around him he resumed his journey to Victoria Station. The smell of the trains and the sweet, sickly aroma of oil and steam fired his senses. Together with the piercing sound of the steam whistle, the late evening air gave him a surge of excitement of faraway places and unknown destinations.

Chapter Seventeen

It was the last week of May 1917. They told him it hadn't stopped raining for days and Flanders lay buried beneath a sea of liquid mud, making progress almost impossible.

'Might call the fighting off until the sun comes out,' a fusilier with his head swathed in bandages said, incurring the wrathful stares of those around him. 'Well I think that's what I heard, can't hear much with them bloody great guns booming in your ears day and night. If they ever actually hit anything, the bloody war might have been over bloody months ago.'

Thomas found a laconic amusement at the remark and smiled, feeling pleasure to be back amongst the only thing he understood. He had learned that the people in England showed a scant regard for fighting soldiers and treated the war with a cynicism he found difficult to comprehend, almost as if it wasn't their war. On the journey back to his lines he no longer noticed the dead or heard the screams and moans of the wounded. Now he'd grown hardened and indifferent, his short life tempered against the needs of others, and he no longer thought of tomorrow. It was during times like this that his insensitive feelings disgusted him and often he tried unsuccessfully to smother them. Further on he stopped to listen to a Highlander arguing with a group of German prisoners-of-war.

'What's the problem?' he asked the soldier.

The man turned, his glance darted to Thomas's stripes and he looked desperately for reassurance. 'The wee bastards want cigarettes and I've been told they can't smoke until they're billeted, but they won't have it.'

Thomas un-slung his rifle and shot the closest German dead.

'Take their greatcoats away from them and cut the buttons from their trousers. Let the bastards get wet holding their pants up, they might not be so keen for a smoke then. If any of them start arsing about, shoot the fucking lot of them,' he said, and walked away.

With an arched eyebrow he raised his head and sniffed. It was a good smell, the kind of smell soldiers were born for. Up ahead a mobile kitchen handed out egg and bacon sandwiches to a patient queue of hungry soldiers, and with a contented smile he thought to satisfy his own gnawing hunger. When he heard a shot ring out he crouched down and, turning, saw a second German prisoner drop to the floor. He grinned to himself –

341

the simple things in life are always the best, he thought laughing out loud. The bastards wanted a war, so let's give them one. Let the pigs have a taste of British steel. Life is just a city of crooked streets and sooner or later death comes to us all when we meet at the marketplace.

The incessant drizzle turned to a steady downpour, to express dissatisfaction was a waste of time – complaints never gave a rainstorm reason to cease. Like he'd always known them to be trenches turned into canals and men huddled together, buried in their own thoughts like statues frozen in time. He pulled out his watch and checked the time, and pursing his lips he thought of Sarah and felt the stirring in his groin. He looked down the line of soldiers in the trench. Some dug holes with long handled ladles and bailed out the water. With a short sigh his carnal thoughts drifted away into emptiness.

That afternoon he watched a never-ending stream of men begin picking their way along the trenches in single file. With heads bowed they moved silently, save for the sound of squeaking duckboards accompanied by the inevitable mandatory bouts of cursing.

'Bloody hell, the bloody Canadians are on the move, stroppy bunch of sods they are,' someone grumbled, stepping aside to make way for the steady flow of heaving bodies filing by.

'Yeah, maybe they are, but I'm glad they're on our side. They hate Fritz ever since the bastards crucified that Canadian sergeant,' another voice drifted through the rain.

Heads with enquiring eyes turned and waited.

342

'Canadian sergeant, what are you talking about?'

'Place called St Julian, not far from here. Fritz crucified him to a barn door, used eight bayonets by all accounts through his legs, shoulders, throat and balls. Left the poor bastard eighteen inches off the ground, covered in blood. I wouldn't want to be a bloody German with them around.'

'With a bit of bloody luck there won't be any left after this cock-up. Hello, I reckon the bloody rain's started to ease.'

'Christ Almighty, we might be going over the top later.'

'Doubt it, someone's pinched his lordship's tin whistle. Can't go over the top without a whistle can we? On account we've all gone bloody deaf listening to the big guns day and night.'

A wave of laughter ran down the trench, easing away the tension from anxious faces, men stretched stiffened muscles and pulled their feet from the clinging mud. Thomas slumped down on the firing ledge and smiled. The Tommies had the best weapon of all – black humour. No matter how bad the situation, someone would always see the funny side and pop up with a joke.

Thomas fought against the weight of the pack that hurt his back. The straps chafed into his shoulder leaving painful red weals. He'd never understood the need for all the equipment they humped around from place to place. The sixty-six-pound weight felt cumbersome. Waterlogged, it weighed an extra ten pounds and offered small comfort that at least it could be discarded when the men prepared to go into battle. Then they carried only a small haversack and a rolled

343

groundsheet with a bandolier of extra rifle ammunition over the right shoulder. He shrugged – orders are orders. Tonight it was his turn in the mines and he thought of Stan Banks. He'd miss his good-natured banter. Harry Hardiker, from a small village outside Barnsley, had taken his place. A one-time gamekeeper on a big estate of a wealthy industrialist, he had refused point-blank to join the Barnsley Pals Battalion.

'I'm not running round wet-nursing some city clodhopper,' he told the pie-eyed recruiting officer with a lisp at the Town Hall. So he joined the Rifles.

Several nights ago, alone on patrol, he returned with a brace of pigeons and four rabbits and frightened the life out of the Germans with his animal impressions. The soldiers in the trenches roared with laughter at the sound of small arms fire as the Germans ran up and down looking for the wolf stalking their trenches. The following day, they searched for a pack of marauding bears.

'Hey, Archie, take a look at this silly bugger,' a large man with a nose the shape of a bricklayer's elbow called quietly. 'There, look, see him, by the firelight?'

Thomas raised the Mauser and squinted down the telescopic sight. Some Germans, in their crass stupidity, had lit a fire, and every few seconds a man with a bald head bobbed up and down. With his finger curled around the trigger, Thomas watched the German less than a thousand yards away and wondered how the big man managed to pick him out in the gloom.

'Here, you take him,' he said, handing the man

the rifle.

The big man stepped onto the firing ledge, raised the rifle and waited. Seconds later, he squeezed the trigger and, under a red splash of blood, the dead German slipped out of sight. Within seconds, the fire was extinguished.

'Good shot; you must have damn good eyesight to see that far in this light,' Thomas said. 'Ever thought about joining the snipers?'

'Thought about it I did, once. I'm too bloody clumsy though. I trip over moonbeams I do. Nay, lad, like as much I'd just get in the way.'

Thomas looked at him with a critical eye. He stood over six feet tall with strong broad shoulders, a clumsy looking fellow with dark bushy eyebrows and a short flat aggressive nose. Tattooed on his beefy arm was a fierce looking bulldog with the words Strength and Honour underneath. He offered no hint of a soldierly bearing, yet Thomas immediately judged he might prove useful in the enemy trenches and the mines, especially at close quarters.

'Go and see Moses, he needs men like you in his team. Tell him I sent you, then come back here. Tonight. I want you with me in the mines,' he said. 'Oh, it might be useful to know your name.'

'Blunder, Atlas Blunder,' he said, staring Thomas straight in the face. Thomas didn't reply.

Eight o'clock in the morning at last – the miserable mind-sapping twelve-hour shift was over and just to walk and stretch the legs seemed like a luxury. Better still, to look at eye level and not see wet muddy walls or the dejected faces of men who'd forgotten why they were here. Those

345

who spent time in the trenches often sat and wondered if there really was a place on earth that wasn't surrounded by swirling mud and scurrying rats. With numb minds they searched their memories trying to conjure up a picture portraying a life before all of this, or was it all a dream? The only people who talked of understanding the war and its horrors were those who'd never fought in one.

Apple crouched and dropped a pinch of salt into the boiling water followed by strips of fatty bacon and sucked noisily on his pipe.

'There you go, lad, get it down you. It won't take long to cook,' he said.

The remark sounded double-Dutch to Thomas and he raked his fingers through his hair and smiled, then tugged off his wet socks and gave his feet a brief inspection. Thankful to see his toes still attached to the end of his feet, he dried them with the cuff of his shirt then doused them in whale oil. Thanks to his penchant for stealing clean socks from the Germans, he had been fortunate enough to accumulate three full sandbags. Yet each time he pulled on a pair, it was always the same, a vision of Stan Banks loomed into his mind and he felt ashamed. He shrugged – what was done was done, best he spent his time concentrating on the job in hand rather than dwelling on a situation he couldn't change. Just the same, with no tilt of conscience he ate the boiled bacon with a hunk of black bread and three pickled cucumbers from a jar Moses produced, and as usual refused to divulge the source.

'There you go, lad, coffee,' Apple said, with a

346

grin on his face.

'I reckon you've got the best bloody job in the army – you don't do bugger all except count bullets and shells twice a week,' Thomas laughed.

'Compensation for being blown up, lad, it is. Compensation.'

After he drank the hot coffee he felt better. Then the wondrous gift of sleep gently probed his body and he closed his eyes and sank into the luxury of undisturbed oblivion until nine-fifteen that evening. His internal alarm woke him and he pushed the blanket away. With a laboured groan he slowly swung his legs over the bed, stood with clasped hands and stretched his arms above his head to release the stiffness. The others waited; not in the trenches where they should be but in the farmhouse. They liked the heat from the fire and he didn't begrudge them that small luxury.

That night they entered a different mine and instead of descending the ladder they walked on a downhill gradient for the first forty yards before the tunnel levelled out flat. Further in, Thomas noticed other tunnels snaking off left and right. He didn't count them but guessed there may be twenty, perhaps even more. He also noticed more men than ever before and sensed a feeling of urgency in the air, like people rushing on a tight schedule to finish a project on time. From out of the gloom they saw a small, heavily built man with a ghostly white face carrying a pickaxe in one hand.

'If you would like to come this way when you are ready, boy,' he said in a slow, laborious tone.

The four men looked at each other, shrugged,

struggled to their feet and followed him.

'He's from the east coast, I reckon,' Harry Hardiker said. 'They speak so slow it takes them three days to get their name, rank and number out. If Fritz captured twenty of the buggers, the war would be over by the time they found out who they were.'

The small man carrying the pickaxe stopped and turned around. 'Keep the noise down, boy.'

The faint sound of scraping and men panting for breath signalled they were nearing the face and nimbly stepping to one side they allowed a man heaving on a trolley full of sacks filled with clay to pass. Thomas turned at the sound of muffled footsteps and raised an eyebrow at the sight of a tall, slim man walking towards him wearing an officer's cap back to front and sporting muddy trousers with a dirty white singlet.

'Lieutenant Reddy, old chap, Royal Engineers. Glad to have you aboard. It's going to be a busy show tonight. We're breaking into Fritz's tunnels to scare him off in readiness for a big surprise we have planned for him. Wordsworth here will show you what to do and where to go. You'll be in good hands with him. Good luck,' he said, nodding towards the small man.

'Follow me, boys, and I'll show you your first port of call,' Wordsworth drawled. 'Acclimatise your eyes to the darkness. Can't be using lights down here, Mr Fritz might see us coming, and that won't make him happy.'

'Right, before we go any further check your weapons. We don't want to be fumbling around in the dark,' Thomas said, making sure each man carried out his orders. 'And keep your rifles at the ready.'

Thomas led the way in single file, aware the further they went the thinner the air became. Soon their bodies glistened in a film of cold sweat, and accompanied by a feeling of uneasy fear their breath came in short gasps. Wordsworth stopped, turned his head and raised his finger to his lips, signalling for silence, then moved closer to the wall.

'I can hear them, regular as clockwork they are, stupid bastards – in ten minutes they'll change shifts. If you go in now you'll be behind them and they'll be trapped against the face. Finish them off and wait for the incoming shift, kill two sparrows with one stone, you will. When you've finished, wait for me and I'll tell you where to go next.'

The men stood motionless and watched Wordsworth place his hands on the wall and push. To everyone's astonishment part of the wall collapsed inwards. Thomas and his men made their way inside the German tunnel. Caught off-guard and completely by surprise the Germans stood rooted to the spot with their mouths open in shock at the sudden appearance of the Englanders. Before they could respond Atlas was on them and grabbing the closest two smashed their heads together so hard that he split their skulls. The others finished off the remaining three with knives.

'Drag the bodies into our tunnel, then lie down on the floor and wait for the next shift – they'll think you're taking a rest,' Wordsworth said.

Hardly daring to breathe they waited until eventually they heard the harsh guttural sound of the German shift coming to relieve them. Tense and ready, Atlas rubbed his hands together to calm himself and smiled. Burke and Hardiker pulled back their lips and sneered, working up the adrenaline for the next round of blood-letting. Hate always kills the easiest.

Then without warning a vision of Archie's mocking face sprung into Thomas's mind clear as a spring day. His mind reeled and the feeling of impending disaster slammed into his brain. He swallowed and felt as though his flesh was on fire. Once again Archie had come for him, unrelenting and insistent on revenge. He should have known he would never allow him his freedom and the time spent away from the trenches merely a brief respite, a cruel hoax. The vision grew closer, so close that he thought he could smell his foul breath. The sound of his hollow laughter drummed into his head and threatened to drive away his sanity. He bit down hard and his teeth penetrated the inside of his cheek, the salty blood trickled into his mouth.

Up ahead the six approaching Germans laughed at the sight of their comrades resting and hurled guttural insults. Thomas pushed his thoughts of Archie to one side and sneered at the sound of the German voices. He remembered the ill-treatment handed out in the prisoner-of-war camp as though it happened only yesterday. He recalled vividly the beatings, the kickings, and his imagination played tricks with his mind. He felt the pain searing though his unprotected body and remembered the manner in which they had laughed when the little Australian gave up the ghost and dropped dead from fatigue.

'Fuck you, Archie!' he whispered. 'Fuck you.'

Now was the time for payback. The first German went down stiff-legged with a bullet embedded in his temple, his eyes shrouded in bewilderment. Thomas went forward crouching with the cut-down bayonet ready in his hand. Pictured in his mind was the German who had tried to drown him in the mud with his boot on the back of his neck. In the pale light of the flickering candles he ignored the villainous shadows dancing on the glistening mud walls. Revenge was about to be metered out to the perpetrators of his past miseries. He jabbed out and blood spurted accompanied by a fearful howl of agony and fear when the cold steel blade entered the German's eye. With all his might he pushed until the hilt prevented further entry. The sound of heavy breathing mingled with shrill curses and hideous screams sounded like a sweet symphony soothing his ears. Rivulets of sweat trickled down his back, soaking the waistband of his trousers while he hacked and cut at the Germans like a butcher suffering insanity.

'Bloody hell, boy, what did you have for breakfast this morning?' Wordsworth said, staring wide-eyed and watching Thomas wipe away the wet blood clinging to his face. 'Only two more to go and we're finished. Straight down the tunnel you go, boy. The first on the left and the last on the right. Give me a shout when you've done, and I'll set the charges.'

In single file they moved cautiously further down the tunnel, ears cocked for the telltale sound of scraping from the German miners. By the entrance to the first face on the left they halted and watched the unsuspecting Germans going busily about their business.

'Wait here, these are mine,' Harry said.

Harry, his back hugged close to the wall and implementing his guile learned during his time as a gamekeeper, measured each step and drew closer. With the minimum commotion he fell upon them, and grasping a cut-down bayonet in each hand he ripped open their throats and left them choking and drowning in their own blood.

For a moment Thomas waited, his eyes bulging as he fought to control a peculiar stillness tinged with apprehension inside his body. He shuddered and felt his skin tense. The cold damp air chilled the sweat that oozed from every pore of his body. He didn't want the killing to finish, not yet. Cautiously they made their way further along the tunnel until they reached their final goal. Overhead the roof inclined downwards, forcing them to walk hunched like old women and swing their arms from side-to-side. Eventually Thomas slowed and peered round the corner.

'Bloody hell,' he grunted and stepped back, 'there are nine of the buggers, and the face is forty yards away with no cover. This isn't going to be easy.'

'Perhaps if we charged them we might take them by surprise,' Atlas said.

Thomas hesitated, he needed to think, and for the first time that day he screwed his nose up at the stench of unwashed bodies and human waste.

'No, if we were caught in the open we wouldn't

stand a chance.'

'We need to entice them out, a few at a time, but only the devil knows how,' John Burke said, unable to rid his mind of the consequences of a cave-in. He felt his nerves flutter and pined for the danger of the trenches and open air.

'Aye, I know how to get the bastards out. Well, I think I do,' Harry said thoughtfully.

Three pairs of hopeful eyes swivelled and looked into his face.

'The way I see it is like this,' Harry began. 'We need to give them an excuse to leave the face, something that might give them a reason to investigate, if you know what I mean.'

Thomas hunched his shoulders and waited expectantly for a few seconds, then shook his head. 'And?' he said simply.

'I'll do my wolf call, that'll frighten the buggers half to death and have them out in seconds, what do you reckon?'

Atlas's grin split his face in two. 'Bloody great idea that, lad, bloody great. What do you reckon, Archie? Frighten a herd of nightmares that bloody noise would.'

'Aye, I reckon it might just work. They can't come out in a rush because the roof is too low. Aye, we can shoot at will, let's give it a go.'

'Best use the knives and not the firearms. We don't want to arouse their suspicion and let them think there's a wolf down here that is a crack shot with a rifle, do we?' John Burke grinned.

'It was just an idea,' Thomas snapped, feeling foolish. 'We'll have to go further back along the tunnel. I remember passing trolleys we can use for cover.'

Minutes later each man waited ready in position behind the trolleys. Harry cupped his hands to his mouth and gave out a howl so mournful that Atlas felt the hairs on his neck rise.

'Bloody hellfire,' he said, crossing himself. 'It's enough to make a band of angels piss themselves with fright.'

Thomas strained his ears. The scraping and muffled thumps of falling clay ceased, followed by the lights dimming and the harsh grunts of German voices trailed off into silence. Harry sent out another heart-chilling howl. Atlas fidgeted and tightened his grip on his bayonets then wiped away the cold sweat running down his face. A big man came first, with a large florid face. Between his teeth he gripped the biggest pipe Atlas had ever seen. It would have taken a bushel of tobacco to fill it and a match the size of a burning log to light it. He came stooped to avoid scraping his head on the low-lying roof, and behind him, with their rifles pointed ready to fire, came two more, their movements hesitant and uncertain. Atlas felt Thomas's hand grip his arm. Not yet, wait until they are closer. Then, the time was right. Thomas watched as his three companions rose as one, and clamping their hands over gaping mouths they slid the razor-sharp blades across the soft unyielding windpipes.

'Three down, six to go,' John Burke grunted. 'Quick, hide the bodies.'

With the bodies hidden in the trolleys and covered with tarpaulin they waited. Once again Harry sent the bloodcurdling howl streaming and slithering through the tunnel. The response came immediately, as though impatience had pushed aside courage and valour.

'Hans, Eric, are you there, where are you? Answer me, Hermann, what is happening?' a reedy thin voice quavered.

Thomas lifted his head and watched Harry slip from behind the nearest trolley and move towards the two Germans. Executing a scissors movement, Harry slashed the two blades simultaneously across the unprotected throats. Thomas smiled, he felt nothing, no remorse, vengeance was his, and the taste sweetened the juices running into his mouth. Harry sent out another howl, louder and more pronounced than before. The dimmed lights plunged into darkness and the men at the mine face sank into a frantic despair.

'They must be crapping in their pants by now. Let's finish them off and get out of here. Bloody place gives me the creeps,' Atlas grumbled.

'Aye, I'm all for that,' Harry nodded.

Thomas went first, crawling on his hands and knees, and sensed the damp clay penetrate his trousers and freeze his hands. Through the gloom he could just about make out the four remaining Germans huddled round a single paraffin lamp.

'Right, give them your best roar, lad, then I'll fire off a few shots to confuse them and we'll charge and finish the sods off,' he said, drawing his pistol.

Harry sucked in his breath and gave full vent. Atlas blinked and thought every muscle in his body had frozen, leaving him paralysed.

Thomas loosed two wild volleys, sending out

spurts of orange flame. A German screamed in pain and fell kicking and writhing into the wet clinging clay. Atlas Blunder led the charge and, synonymous with his name, his innate clumsiness became the mother of disaster. His arms flailed like a drunk on a windswept New Year's Eve, and he smashed into Burke and Harry. Thomas stood alone to face the three grim-faced miners armed with pickaxes. Bending at the waist he ducked and avoided the metal prong seeking his neck and slashed out with his knife, ignoring the scream when the blade slit open the German's arm. Then he felt a strong arm clamp around his neck like a vice, squeezing and tightening, cutting off his oxygen supply. He relaxed. I'm coming, Archie, I'm coming. Blackness swirled like a thick mist. He thought of Dilly with a swollen belly. He thought of the daisy pressed between the pages of the stiff covered note-book, and still he felt the firm grip of his father's hand.

'Well done, men, first class,' Lieutenant Reddy said, rubbing his hands together jubilantly. 'A day without a dead German is like a day without sunshine. We'll show them blighters. Now, Wordsworth, show these men out and make them a brew.'

'Right, boys,' Wordsworth drawled, 'you all follow me now and you can have a nice cup of tea like the officer says.'

Atlas leant over, picked Thomas up and hefted him onto his shoulder like a sack of carrots.

'Put me down, I'll be all right in a minute,' Thomas moaned.

'Best you stay where you are until we're out of here. It's quicker this way than waiting for you to flounder around like a cod in a sandstorm.'

Outside in the fresh air, away from the clamminess of the tunnels, the dimness of dawn retreated into the purple-streaked sky and Atlas dropped Thomas to the ground.

'Why didn't you use your bloody revolver?' he said.

'I never had time.'

'You never had time, my arse! Bloody demented, you are. Like an octopus born with seven tentacles.'

Thomas looked up – he'd never grow used to Atlas's strange method of describing events.

'What happened?'

'It was Harry who saved you. One of them was hell bent on strangling the life out of you and the other two were about to bury their axes in your head, but he got there in the nick of time he did, lucky for you.'

Thomas squeezed his eyes tight shut to block out the pain and ran his hand over his head. It felt tender, like an open wound, and he couldn't remember what had caused it. Then darkness slowly closed in around him like falling night and he pictured himself lying in a coffin with Ruby staring down at him. Archie sat astride her back and in his hands was the ever-present noose. He tried to rise and leave the coffin, but he couldn't because he was dead.

Chapter Eighteen

Their arms felt as though at any moment they might wrench from their sockets, John Burke swore beneath his breath and gripped the stretcher tighter. Sweat ran into his eyes and he shook his head from side-to-side. At last the welcome sight of the farmhouse came into view.

'Bloody great heavy lump, that's what he is,' Harry grumbled, looking down at Thomas lying on the stretcher. 'Concussion, that's what the medic said. Looks to me like he's having a snooze, the lazy get.'

'Stop your mithering, you miserable sod,' Atlas snapped. 'I don't know how he gets away with it, though – he must lead a bloody charmed life, anybody else would be dead by now.'

John Burke pushed open the farmhouse door and smiled as the rush of heat struck his face. 'Christ, it's hotter than me dad's arse after a night on the black stuff,' he choked.

'Welcome back, chaps,' Moses beamed. 'Thought I'd make it comfortable for your return. Tea will be served in minutes. Oh dear, whatever has happened to him this time?'

'He's had a knock on the head. He'll be fine in a couple of days, but I reckon it's best we put him to rest,' Harry answered, pulling off Thomas's wet clothes and heaving him onto the bed.

'There's something big going on, I can smell it in

the air,' Atlas said, gazing from the window at the activity outside – thousands of troops were on the move accompanied by hundreds of field guns.

'Jesus, lad, with a nose like that you're sure to know what's going on in Australia,' John Burke said, picking his teeth with his fingernail and spitting on the floor.

'I'm telling you, something's going to happen soon,' Atlas answered, ignoring the reference to the size of his nose. 'They're even laying extra railway tracks. I reckon Fritz is in for a good kicking. And look at that,' he said pointing out of the window. 'A bloody useless staff officer riding around on his horse, the daft bugger. They only show up when something big is about to happen, and when it starts they bugger off again.'

Sergeant Bull informed the section leaders the next day that all activities in the mines were to cease immediately, the men were ordered to stand down. Over the next few days rest periods were extended with a greater emphasis placed on battle training. Even the food improved. The battle-hardened veterans glanced around nervously when the order went out to pay special attention to the cleaning of rifles and ammunition. Atlas's assumption proved correct. Another big push was being prepared.

With nothing better to do Thomas leaned against the doorway of the farmhouse and tenderly touched the bandages around his head. The incessant throb refused to abate and he found it easier not to think. Through the sheeting rain, accompanied by his three section leaders, he watched column after column of soldiers carrying fifty-pound backpacks containing an explosive called ammonal into the mines under the Messines Ridge. When he'd asked Moses for a remedy for his headache, he had looked at him like he was a piece of cat shit on a new carpet and told him the wisest thing to do would be to cut it off.

'They've been carting that stuff in for months,' Harry said.

'A million pounds of the stuff I've been told,' said Leslie Hill, shaking the rain from his helmet. 'And there must be over twenty tunnels in there by now. Been digging for ages they have, Australians, Canadians, British, the whole bloody lot. Even brought in civilian workers from the Manchester sewers. By the way, did I tell you I saw Stan Banks the other day? He hasn't changed. He's running the money pool now.'

'Money pool, what's that?' Harry asked.

'Before they go over the top or on raiding parties, the men pool their money and those who survive share what's left between them,' Moses said, looking across at Thomas. 'Stops the scavengers rifling through dead men's pockets, and those who survive the war could end up very wealthy men.'

Thomas stiffened. 'Where did you see him?' he asked easily, in an effort to conceal his sudden interest, and casually pushing the toe of his boot into the mud he watched the indent fill with dirty brown water.

'By the small copse behind the medical station,' smiled Hill. 'He's chasing one of the nurses. Apparently he spends a lot of his off duty time with the wounded. Always manages to find them

360

treats to keep their morale up. You know Stan, never a dull moment when he's around.'

'Who's out tonight?' Thomas asked glancing at his pocket watch and bringing the conversation to an abrupt end.

'We are,' Harry answered.

'Make sure their rifles are clean and they keep Fritz's head down,' Thomas said gruffly.

'My men keep their rifles clean and do their job without any bloody mention from you, son,' Harry snapped angrily. 'Just remember that in future. And they can stand on their own two bloody feet, unlike you.' Drawing his lips back in a snarl he walked away leaving Thomas burning with anger.

'I want to you to pay particular attention to hill sixty tonight, Private Hardiker,' Sergeant Bull said. 'We need to keep Fritz busy. Off you go, lad, and keep your head down.'

'Right, Sergeant, we'll do our best. Is something big in the air?'

'You'll know all in good time.'

Harry Hardiker knew the exact point where to cross the lines. All the section leaders knew the wooden building the German officers used as a mess was always lightly guarded. It offered good cover in the moonlight and for this reason the snipers always left it untouched. Hill sixty was a hummock on top of the salient offering a perfect vantage point overlooking the allies' lines. Manned by machine-gunners inside concrete bunkers, raiding parties avoided the area as potentially too dangerous to assail without a heavy loss of men. Sergeant Bull wouldn't ask for it to be attacked for no good reason. Already Harry felt he'd lost all earthly connection with hope and the random grey hairs at his temples seemed a reminder that nothing would ever change.

He sat level with the German lines, tempted to disobey the order to attack. No one had ventured past this point before, and he needed time to think. He had the lives of nine men to consider and more than anything else wanted to keep them alive. Finally, he made his decision. He would take three men and work his way up the salient towards the hummock. Three men would keep the Germans in the trenches pinned down and the remaining three would attack and set fire to the German officer's wooden mess as an extra diversion.

'Use grenades on the officer's mess,' he said. 'And kick up a bloody good racket. That should give the bastards something to think about. When we hear the explosions we'll start making our way up the hill to the hummock. Good luck, boys, and keep your heads down. Off you go.'

At the sound of the exploding grenades, Harry and his party of skirmishers began silently crawling up the gradient towards the hummock. He smiled thinly at the sound of rifle fire as the snipers picked off the unsuspecting enemy troops in the trenches. By a small hump offering only sparse cover he stopped and focused his field glasses. He could see movement in the machine-gun emplacement. Eighty yards away he heard the cold threatening metallic rasp of machine-guns being cocked and made ready. He swallowed and ran his tongue over his dry lips. The sound of puffing and wheezing coming from his

362

men panicked him, and he felt the sweat gluing his trousers to his legs. He wanted to tell them to keep the noise down, to stop breathing for the next ten minutes. Don't be so bloody stupid, he silently cursed himself. When the first flare went up and burst overhead, his eyes opened in sheer terror. White-faced he laid belly down feeling like a naked man in the Vatican. Within seconds the whole of the salient lit up.

'Come on, lads, no time to wait for the porridge to cool, let's get them!' he roared.

The fear of death pounded in his ears like a wild storm and he scrambled to his feet and ran crouching up the hill waiting for the hot messengers of death to embed themselves in his tender flesh. On and on, he waited and waited, his legs pumping and his lungs gasping for air, but the messengers never came. Behind he heard a groan as one of his men fell. Mother of God, Mother of God, Mother of God, he cried. Then, despite what had seemed a cessation in time, he was there. And with sweat blurring his vision he withdrew his bayonet he slashed the first German across the throat, who fell back gurgling and screaming, clutching his neck, the blood gurgling through his fingers. Why do Germans scream in this way, he thought, loud and piercing, like a woman? The second man recoiled and, raising his hands in futile protection, stared with wide panic-stricken eyes. Naked fear distorted his features. He looked like a man who'd just licked vinegar from a nettle. Harry plunged the bayonet into his neck and twisted, ignoring the jet of blood streaming into his face and blinding him. 'Die, you German bastard,' he growled.

Overhead more enemy flares drifted lazily into the sky and he remembered the day his father took him to a firework display to celebrate the coronation of Edward VII, in 1901. That was a good day: candy floss and toffee apples were handed out for free and he had made sure he had more than his fair share.

Beneath the shower of flares snaking into the sky the vista of flat country and low ridges surrounded by shabby hills and bare woods nestling sullenly in the rain suddenly flickered to a murky banana-yellow. Then the earth came alive, moving, pulsating as the Germans came to extract revenge. Like grey worms, they crawled their way towards Harry and his two companions. Harry shook his head in despair and swallowed.

'Right, lads, we're going to kill some Germans today,' he said quietly.

They shook hands like friends do, firm and meaningful. Len Turland pressed a photograph of his wife and child onto the damp wall then lying in position checked the machine-gun. Dougie Glass knelt with the belt of ammunition held loosely in the palm of his hand ready to feed the machine-gun. Harry snapped the bayonet to his rifle and smiled grimly. Their blood would not be spilled cheaply.

Sergeant Bull sat on an empty ammunition box in the trench with his head in his hands listening to the distant incessant chatter of the machine-gun for twenty long minutes. As each minute passed, the sound became louder until he thought his ear drums might burst. By the time the British trench mortars homed in on the salient, a great ball of orange flame erupted from the hummock and it was over. His ice-blue eyes melted, and with a shuddering sigh he got to his feet, removed his helmet and walked out into the rain where no one would see his tears. Losses were heavy that night, of the ten men that left, only two returned.

Thomas approached the casualty clearing station three long, wet and miserable miles from the warm farmhouse. The strong smell of disinfectant barely cloaked the nauseating stench of rotting flesh and gangrened wounds. Through the darkness of the evening he saw rows of horse-drawn ambulances lined up outside waiting to bring in the wounded from the trenches, or soldiers convalescing from injuries after receiving treatment at base hospitals. It didn't seem strange to hear Stan Banks before he saw him. The shrill laughter with the Liverpool nasal twang revived recent memories. The smell of undiluted disinfectant increased, stung his eyes and stuck in his gut when he stepped inside the dimly-lit tent. Instinctively he squeezed his shoulders to avoid making contact with the remains of men sitting or lying with confused eyes. One man, wearing a pair of wire-rimmed spectacles, lay looking like he'd fought and lost a twenty-round bout with the world heavyweight boxing champion. He sat shaking and trembling. Where his left arm should be a blood-stained bandage hung limp and dripping blood. His face slowly creased and he gave Thomas a weak smile. It seemed almost apologetic. Further down the row of beds he saw Stan sitting with his back to him, propping up a man in his arms.

'Come on, lad, down it goes. With a name like Horace I'm surprised you're not a greedy bugger,' he said. The remark immediately conjured up a rare smile onto Thomas's lips.

Moving closer, he stood next to Stan and tapped his shoulder.

'Hello, Stan,' he said in a quiet voice.

Stan jerked at the touch and swung round.

'Bloody hell, General No Names here. What's the matter with you, got a splinter stuck up your arse, or is your bloody halo too tight?' he said, not bothering to disguise the sneer.

Horace attempted to laugh at Stan's remark, but the sound came in a series of rapid hisses like a man pumping up a flat bicycle tyre, and the agony spread like a swarm of ants across the area where his face had once been.

'Settle down, lad, we're nearly done,' Stan said, pushing the spoon of porridge into a blackened hole where once a mouth had been.

Seconds stretched into minutes and Thomas felt unsure how to express his intentions. Then, knowing Stan, he decided on the direct approach.

'I owe you an apology for the way I treated you in front of the men. I'm sorry, I know better now and I want you back with the Rifles,' Thomas said quietly.

Stan continued to give his full attention to Horace. He hadn't expected anything like this to occur after the argument in the trenches. He felt the tilt of anger and wanted to hurl a tirade of foul obscenities at his tormentor to repay him for the misery and abject fear he'd suffered in the bottom of some stinking rat-infested trench. At the same time the words were a like a gift from heaven and he wanted to hug Thomas close and accept the offer of peace with an open heart. But that would be too easy. First, there must be dalliance, a show of unbridled bravado to pretend he needed time to mull over the offer. Damn it, he must first have his revenge, it was only fair, and make sure Thomas felt worse than he already did.

The nerve-racking days and shivering nights spent waiting to go over the top had taken its toll and made him more nervous than ever before. His trembling hands had become even more difficult to conceal from others and his self-control battled with a delirium clouding his mind and making him lightheaded until he thought he would faint with fright. Even worse were his constant flickering eyebrows, the sign of a man tottering on the edge of an abyss waiting to fall into a place so dark that he could never expect to return to normality as he once knew it.

Aware that he'd reached the zenith of his fear, he frequently froze at the thought of what he might do next. Perhaps he would run snivelling like a coward while his comrades were ripped to shreds by machine-gunfire and bursting shrapnel shells. All the waiting and thinking in drizzling rain had eaten away his mind the way gangrene devours a rotting wound, unstoppable and all-consuming until, in the end, life ceases. Those who inhabited the trenches day after day called it bomb fever. Whereas with the snipers, things happened fast: hit-and-run raids, night patrols, face-to-face combat with teeth bared, all these he could handle. He liked Thomas, he always had done, from him drew a kind of strength that no one else had ever been able to give him, yet he didn't know the reason why.

'I'll have to think about it, I've got a lady to think of now. We might be getting married soon. We're waiting to hear from HQ for permission.'

Nonchalantly Thomas shrugged to hide his disappointment. Perhaps he'd made a mistake in believing Stan might be more than happy to return to his friends.

'Yes, I understand. Maybe you are better off in the trenches. Good luck,' he said in a low voice.

It was a cruel barb and he knew it the moment the words fell from his mouth, though he didn't understand the real reason he had said them – perhaps it was Stan's offhand manner. He knew Stan suffered with fright at the thought of running scared, more than death or mutilation. Perhaps their time had passed, like rippling water over a bed of stones in a shallow stream, and it was too late to continue as friends.

When he stepped outside the rain had ceased and the moon hung large and full in the dark late night sky. He drew in a deep breath to rid the smell of disinfectant from his lungs. His journey had been in vain and his optimism replaced by a deep sadness he might live to regret within the confines of his shortened life. Under the cloak of darkness his feet found the lurking puddles overjoyed to suck his feet down into the clinging mud and soak his feet to the skin. He shrugged. He had tried his hardest to right the wrong and with all the willpower he could muster he forged ahead through the darkness and allowed indifference to fill his mind.

When he reached the farmhouse he intended to ask Moses to draft him a letter, using posh words, making his parents sole beneficiaries to his stake in the flock of sheep. If he did not return within six months of the war ending, the flock and all profits would be theirs. It wasn't much, but under the circumstances it was the best he could do. If one thing was certain it was that Archie would never allow him to lead a normal life, perhaps even if he had the misfortune to survive the war. He'd spent most nights wracking his brain for the best road to take, knowing deep down it would finally be a darkened road of Archie's choosing.

'Hey, lad,' Stan Banks shouted through the darkness, 'you wouldn't consider being my best man would you? Someone told me it's a job for silly buggers and I thought you would be perfect.'

Thomas met Mary Sanderson, Stan's fiancée. She was pert with rosy red cheeks, and quick witted, which would suit Stan. She worked tirelessly as a sister in the hospital and came from Fleetwood in Lancashire where she worked as a midwife. To their great surprise, and against all hope, two days later they were granted permission to marry in a small chapel untouched by the war eleven miles from the allied lines. HQ in their infinite wisdom, thought it might be good for the morale of the men to see some sign of normality for once instead of the terror of continual fighting. After the wedding, both parties would return to their respective places of duty; a honeymoon out of the question. After that, their life together during the time spent at war would consist of brief encounters only.

When the news of the wedding broke, a wave of nostalgia filled the air and each soldier from the battalion not on duty promised to make every effort to attend. Uniforms were scraped and cleaned of mud, boots polished as best they could and buttons made to shine fit for parade inspection. Word quickly travelled down the lines that a soldier was marrying a nurse, salutes were fired from the field guns and gifts of food and small tokens were brought on horseback by the men of the Household Cavalry. The Rifle Company formed a guard of honour outside the church, and when Stan became overcome with emotion they snatched his hat from his head and jumped on it, sending him into a rage.

'You silly little bugger,' Leslie Hill chided. 'Stop your daft piping and kiss the girl, or I'll take her back to the trenches with me and you'll never see her again.'

The downside was Thomas's dismal and uninspiring speech, and stuttering and mumbling he was booed and told to sit down. When he adamantly refused to take a drink, swearing he was teetotal, they poured cheap wine down his throat forcibly until he was hardly able to stand. Aggressive with drink, he foolishly picked a fight with Leslie Hill, who dropped him with one punch and left him to sleep it off. The next day all was forgotten. Thomas was happy that he and Stan were reunited as friends once more. He still hadn't asked Moses to draft the letter to his parents, but he would do so today. Moses would know what to say. He always did.

By the fire Moses focused his attention on Thomas sitting with his feet in a bowl of hot mustard water and sniffing every few seconds. He smiled when Thomas sneezed.

'So, the scourge of the Western Front has caught a cold,' he laughed, pushing away the pencil and paper. 'Sign at the bottom and it's ready to go, and don't forget not to sign your real name.'

'Thank you, Moses,' Thomas answered in a nasal drone, blowing his nose on a piece of rag torn from an old khaki army shirt.

'You are more than welcome, my good man. Anyway, what's so special about this farm?'

'Ah, you have to see it, Moses,' he began. 'It's set between the rolling hills of the Yorkshire Moors. You can see for miles on a clear day. The farmhouse is roomy with a large open fire to toast you bright pink in the winter. A large kitchen with a black cooking range big enough to cook for the battalion, and in the cold room sides of meat hang from hooks in the ceiling and choice cuts lie on a slab. They were a celebration to eat with boiled potatoes and dark green fresh cabbage reared from my ma's garden at the back.'

Moses smiled a sad smile at the enthusiastic description and for a passing moment felt a brief pang of envy tangled with sorrow. Before him stood a boy whose young life would never run the gamut of boyhood or relish in the pranks of other boys of the same age. Prematurely pushed into adulthood by a series of events beyond the control of his juvenile mind, he still remained too young to be a man and yet too old to be a boy. For a moment Moses looked at him steadily, like he'd never looked at him before, and with a resigned sigh he tossed another log onto the fire and watched the sparks fly.

'You mustn't stay too long, you'll catch a cold yourself,' Thomas droned.

Moses was prevented from answering by the sound of Atlas Blunder and Leslie Hill crashing through the farmhouse door like two rampaging bulls, sending Thomas's bowl of hot water slithering across the floor. Thomas dried his feet and pulled on a clean pair of socks, aware that with Atlas in the vicinity there would be no point in refilling the bowl.

'For God's sake, why don't you two learn to enter a room in a proper manner?' Moses sighed.

'Sorry, your lordship,' Atlas said sarcastically, snorting through his large hooked nose before turning to Thomas. 'I think we've found a new man to take over Harry Hardiker's section – bloody great shot he is, and he plays a whistle set to make you cry.'

'It's not a whistle, it's a flute,' Leslie Hill said.

'Well it looks like a whistle to me,' Atlas snapped.

'Aye, a bloody trombone looks like a whistle to you.'

Any answer to the remark was lost in the sudden crescendo of guns as the allied barrage sent the ground beneath them shaking and trembling. Outside the sky became frozen red with a curtain of gun flashes from the artillery, and once again the countryside became a well of death. Thomas hurried to get dressed and made his way to the trenches. Stan Banks had already taken the liberty of re-forming Harry Hardiker's old section and with a full complement of snipers ready, he waited for orders.

'Stay in the trenches until you are told otherwise,' Sergeant Bull ordered the men.

The next day Thomas met Leslie Walsh, the man both Leslie and Atlas had recommended taking over number three section. Born and bred in Liverpool, he had trained as a musician and played in an orchestra in Bromley. He possessed an easy way of moving, which seemed to re-assure those around him. He neither hurried nor slouched. Moses said it was his musical training that gave him a rhythm in life. Whenever he played the Londonderry Air the haunting tunes rose above No Man's Land and men listened wet eyed, oblivious to the death-spewing guns and the fate that awaited them. When Thomas mentioned that Stan had already formed a section, he smiled readily and said he would be available if ever needed.

'When the war is over and we are all dead, do you think people will remember us?' Atlas said, unbuttoning his top tunic button and staring down the trench.

'Doubt it lad,' Stan answered plunging his trembling hands deep into his pockets. 'We're here as punishment, though only God knows what for.'

Crouched in the trench Moses raised his head and glanced at the boy bent next to him. He looked no older than eighteen. He noticed his slender hands and long tapered fingers, almost like a woman's. No longer able to bear the incessant

373

guns the boy dropped his rifle and cowered to the ground with his hands pressed tight over his ears to keep out the noise. His head twitched from side-to-side as though his neck was made from rubber, and foam slobbered from his mouth. His legs kicked and jerked and he could no longer stand unaided. Sprawling in the bottom of the trench he clawed violently at the filthy mud like he was trying to dig his way to another world.

'Come on, my friend, not long now, it will soon be over,' Moses shouted, pulling the boy to his feet.

The boy lost all control of his senses and hunched like an old woman. He tried to stand. As the sound of mortars and bombs magnified and the twitching increased, his eyes rolled, leaving only the whites visible, and saliva dribbled from his mouth. Men turned to stare with empty eyes and shivered. They had seen it before. The boy fell head first back into the filth of the trench, mumbling and pleading to be shot. Moses stood unmoved and looked up for support. No one cared. This was a battle of survival and only the strongest would survive. The words shell-shock had replaced bomb fever, yet either, mistaken for cowardice, had taken many brave men where maybe a bullet would have served a better end. Sergeant Bull, true to form bobbed up from nowhere and hefted the twitching boy onto his shoulder.

'Come on, lad, this is no place for you today,' he said, and making his way down the trench he pushed him into the recess full of spare ammunition.

'Give him here,' Apple said, sitting the boy in a

374

corner. 'Okay, Sergeant, I'll keep an eye on the poor little sod.'

At ten minutes past three in the morning on a Thursday in June, Moses and three-hundred-thousand men fought against the odds to hold their sanity intact under a pale moon. The shelled countryside now totally unrecognisable turned into a churned ocean of viscid mud. Some men dropped to their knees mumbling a distorted prayer, others lost control of their organs and stood petrified in the stench of their own excrement. The piercing screams of terrified horses brought tears to hardened eyes, causing men to drop their weapons and clamp their hands over their ears. This wasn't a war. No one knew what it was. There were never the words.

The Messines Ridge heaved and belched as nineteen huge mines erupted in the tunnels. Moses stared in disbelief and horror as the deepest hell spewed its worst in front of his very eyes. One million pounds of ammonal in nineteen of the twenty-four mines erupted under the German lines. The ground shook men off balance, sending them staggering with broken legs and falling screaming in pain to the ground. Hundreds of tons of earth plumed into the sky, leaving pillars of black earth and crimson fire hanging like huge thunderclouds blotting out the moon. The savage blast rent the countryside apart, altering the landscape forever. Ten thousand Germans were atomised, thousands died without a mark on their bodies with ruptured spleens and kidneys from the shockwaves, and others were buried alive or blown to oblivion. Moses blinked and looked around for his men.

'Steady, steady,' he called, as men turned away to avoid looking at the senseless destruction and carnage.

'Serve the bastards right. If they have an ounce of sense it will be the last bloody war the Germans ever start, I'll bet my balls on that,' a shaking voice called.

Two-thousand-two-hundred-and-sixty-six artillery guns went into action and the creeping barrage began. Nine infantry divisions surged forward, some so precipitately that they were injured from the falling debris hurled into the sky by the exploding mines.

Moses ordered his men forward; and they went forward as though they were hypnotised by some unknown superior will. Thomas, Stan and Leslie watched from further down the line. German soldiers, dazed by the ferocity of the explosion, walked round in a state of shock, gibbering and mumbling and surrendering by the thousand. The German survivors, too numerous for men to be spared to escort them to captivity, were rounded up by New Zealanders and forced to hand over their braces. When the buttons were removed from their trousers, they were sent back to the allied lines busy preserving their modesty.

'Get your snipers down the slope, and knock out the machine-gunners before our lads are ripped to shreds,' Sergeant Bull ordered Thomas.

The towns of Messines and Wytschaete were captured and the allies advanced down the slope capturing German concrete pillboxes as they went. German counter-attacks were repulsed, leaving nearly twenty-five-thousand allied soldiers dead or wounded. The Messines salient disappeared forever. It had been a great victory but never magnificent. Moses wiped the grime from his face, sighed and re-joined the stream of men passing through the trench. The bloody third battle for Ypres had begun.

Chapter Nineteen

In the days that followed the snipers were kept together and despatched when and where they were needed, Sergeant Bull often put his life on the line and refused to allow them to be used just to make up numbers and plug gaps. Thomas sniffed and ate a tasteless hunk of cheese in a warm wooden bunker vacated by the retreating Germans. Moses screwed the top back onto his water bottle and watched him through tired eyes. On impulse he decided he wanted to know what lurked in Thomas's mind confronted by so much appalling danger and confusion, why should he ignore the threat to his own existence. The impression of memories left by past battles had heightened his grip for self-preservation, and he had no intention of allowing Thomas to bring about his early death.

'What are your intentions?' Moses asked him bluntly, making certain no one overheard his remark. 'Are you contemplating suicide, or can you be relied upon?'

The suddenness of the question took Thomas by surprise.

'What's it to you?' he said, looking up and frowning.

'Because if you endanger my life, or anyone else's in the pursuit of ending your own, I can guarantee I'll save you the trouble and put a bullet in you myself. Do I make myself perfectly clear?'

For a long moment they locked eyes, tension crackling in the air as possibilities and motives tumbled in their minds. Thomas rubbed his face with his hands and pushed back his hair. A man didn't go around making threats unless he had something to hide. Never before had Moses spoken to him in that manner and he was eager to know why.

'Are you afraid of dying?' Moses asked.

'No more than any other man.'

'I am, the thought haunts me day and night.'

Moses stretched his fingers and balled his hands and remained silent, then turned and shuffled away to re-join his section. Thomas watched unable to find the reason for Moses' threatening attitude. Again and again his heart had always wanted to cling to life, Moses knew that. Yet deep down he knew it was futile to try and escape from Archie's clutches. Even from beyond the grave Archie controlled his mind and appeared at will to force him into which road he should take. At times he actually believed he'd lost the power to be afraid. He'd made provisions for his parents, happy in the knowledge they believed Archie was the true hero. He had no problem with that. In fact, after a time he'd come to derive a great deal of pleasure from the thought.

Dilly didn't want him and the thought of having his child call another man father did nothing to prick his conscience. Maybe that was down to his immaturity – by now he'd almost convinced himself it wasn't his child in the first place. Dilly's mother mentioned she wore her heart on her sleeve and he wasn't so stupid that he didn't know the meaning of that. Also, he hadn't forgotten Moses's remark concerning the simplest way to change his identity. Even now he carried two sets of dog tags taken from corpses on the battlefield. He also had identification tags from the body of a German corporal he'd skewered with his bayonet during a raid, although he wasn't really sure why he'd taken them. Perhaps I might take tags from Canadians and Australians too, he thought, they'd never find me in Canada. A few men lounged around trying to catch a brief respite from their surroundings; others shuffled playing cards and jingled pennies as they wagered away next month's pay.

That evening he left the comfort and warmth of his quarters to make one of his regular checks on his men. He found them happy and comfortable in a dry German recess in one of the few remaining trenches inspecting German buttons and cap badges scattered around on the ground after the explosion. With mixed feelings he sat for a moment and took a drink of watered-down rum and grimaced at the taste. Reassured his men were settled, he set out to find Stan. He found him pumping Leslie Walsh about the origin of his surname. Already pre-warned of Stan's preoccupancy with surnames, Leslie told him it concerned the size of his manhood and the less said about it the better.

The following day against all expectations the sun accompanied the dawn and the change in the weather brought a sensation of new life to where death lurked in every crevice. News filtered down the lines that the war was slowly beginning to turn in favour of the allies. The men felt re-born and in a haste to get the job done as soon as possible. Second Lieutenant Bellamy, who hadn't been seen since before the battle on Messines Ridge, sent a runner informing Sergeant Bull and Thomas to attend his quarters at eighteen-hundred hours that night. Thomas stood with his mouth open at Bellamy's appearance. Dressed in a new uniform, he looked as though he might have just stepped from a high-class tailor's shop.

'Good evening, gentlemen,' he said, not bothering to turn and look at them. 'We have been chosen to take a town called Roulers, and after the Flying Corps have dropped a few of their bombs to soften up the Hun, we shall advance and capture the railway centre, key to the Hun's position in Flanders. I know you can do the job – we leave in the morning. Who knows, there may be promotions in the air. Yes indeed, indeed, indeed.'

Thomas swallowed the taste of bile in his mouth. You bastard, he thought. I bet a penny to a pinch of horseshit we won't see you anywhere near the fighting.

'Do you mean we are going in alone, Sir?' he asked.

'No, of course not. We shall be assisted by a regiment of the Irish Rifles and our job is to keep Fritz's head down while those paddy blighters finish them off.'

'Will you be joining us, Sir? After all, it might be dangerous,' Thomas blurted out.

Bellamy visibly stiffened and his face flushed cherry red, spinning round he faced Thomas, sniffed, ran his forefinger across his neatly trimmed moustache and licked his lips nervously.

'Yes, of course I shall be there to lead you. Where else would you expect me to be?'

Sergeant Bull, sensing the situation might quickly get out of hand, interrupted and offered a desultory salute. 'Yes, sir, I'll have the men prepared to move out at first light. That will be all, Corporal.'

Outside Thomas, unable to rid the acid taste of bile from his mouth, glared at Sergeant Bull in open defiance.

'Get about your business, Corporal. Sharply now,' Bull said, cutting off any chance of conversation.

Thomas restrained his rising temper and watched the sergeant bob away.

It wasn't long before rivalries broke out and trouble began. Jeb Mooney from the East End of London made no secret of his dislike for the way in which Irish immigrants conducted themselves in the city.

'God made England in six days,' Mooney declared, 'and on the seventh, he squatted down for a shit and produced Ireland, wiped his arse

381

on Wales and threw the waste north and called it Scotland.'

Sergeant Bull told Mooney he'd better watch his mouth before racial riots broke out, although he smiled with amusement at the rhetoric.

Thomas set his men out at vantage points on the outskirts of Roulers and their steady, accurate rate of fire sent the German garrison scrambling for cover. The Irish Rifles followed up with mortars, then advanced and began a stranglehold in the town. Going from building to building using hand-to-hand fighting they quickly cleared the Germans out.

'Uncivilised the buggers might be, but by God they know how to fight and I'm glad we're on the same side,' Leslie Hill said in admiration of the Irishmen's fighting qualities.

'Yeah, and now the bloody trouble starts,' Mooney said. 'You mark my bleeding words, the buggers will start looting and looking for booze.'

All that remained of the Town hall had been cleared and served as a rallying point, and the locals, ecstatic to be rid of the Germans, happily provided the soldiers with cheese, eggs and bottles of rough wine. Thomas reeled in amazement at the behaviour of the Irish, feeling shocked at the extent of their crudeness and ignorance to get more than their fair share of anything placed before them.

'Leave the buggers to it,' Leslie Hill scowled. 'They are no worse, or better, than the rest of us and die just as easy.'

Thomas saw the sense in the remark, shrugged and left the men arguing while they deloused and washed their clothes. For a time he sat alone with his thoughts sensing the emptiness of the lonely and felt the need for company – company as far away and removed from squabbling drunken soldiers as possible. On the edge of the town he saw house lights glowing dully, and tilting his helmet forward he slung his rifle over his shoulder and moved away.

Behind him food and wine relaxed most of the soldiers, others felt their blood run hot and rapid. First came the melancholy air of traditional songs followed by the odd skirl, and finally the raucous songs rang out. Then the wine worked its mischief and threats were issued and quickly accepted as the Irish fought amongst themselves. Atlas and Leslie Hill watched with scowling faces, growing bored with the Irishmen's tiresome squabbling, and decided it may be time for them to take a hand and join in the action.

'Do any of you pig-ignorant bog-trotters know how to fight without a drink in you? If so, step forward and get your useless Irish arses kicked by an English gentleman, the likes of which pricks such as you lot have never seen before.' Atlas said. 'Before you stands The Great Stromboli, the strongest man in the world, and I'm looking for easy sport – and nothing comes easier than a bunch of thick Paddys.'

Atlas stood with his hands resting on his hips snorting through his elbow-shaped nose, his black curly hair hanging limp like a horse's mane and his huge arms rippled with muscles. As though by an order from God above, silence descended and the world stood as still as the day it began.

'Bejasus,' an Irish voice called out. 'You've got some gob on you for an English tit. Go home to your mammy, young fella.'

'Step forward, you bog-trotting bastard and show yourself!' Atlas roared, strutting between the tables with his chest puffed out. 'I should have known you were a bunch of yellow-bellied bastards.' Atlas watched the big bluff Irishman push his way through the crowd. He was an ugly man with a face like a gargoyle suffering from a bout of acute haemorrhoids. 'What's your name, Irish?' Atlas sneered. 'Or couldn't your whore of a mother think of one?'

'O'Hare, Sean O'Hare, not that it's any of your business, you English prick,' he said, pushing his fists together and cracking his knuckles.

'Well come on then, Mr Rabbit, let's see what you've got.'

With his fists raised in classic boxing style he circled his opponent, first one way and then the other. Jabbing and feinting with his left, he stepped forward, slammed his right foot hard down on the floor and sent his right arm out as straight as a magistrate's stare. His fist landed flush on the Irishman's jaw. Twitching like a tangled puppet he went down like a third-time sinner on his way to hell. Quietness reigned, disturbed only by a stray dog lapping up spilt wine and a door hanging on its hinges.

'That'll do for now, boys,' said the Irish Sergeant Major. 'You've had your fun. We don't want to be fighting each other while there are plenty of Germans to go round. Time to get your heads down and save your energy for tomorrow.

Good punch, lad, well delivered.'

'The Great Stromboli, who the bloody hell was he?' Leslie Hill grinned, watching four men carry out O'Hare.

'Before I became embroiled in this shit I worked in a travelling circus as a strong man and was known as Stromboli.'

'A circus, you mean a real circus? What else did you do? Tell me, what other things?' Hill said, hardly able to control his imagination ignited by visions of big tops, galloping horses, tumbling clowns and most of all the snarling prowling lions.

'I'll tell you another day,' Atlas said, leaving Hill seething with disappointment.

The echo of his steel-studded boots crashing on the concrete pathway brought a wry smile to Thomas's face. After months of floundering through mud it felt strange to walk on a solid surface and he felt a spring in his step. Ahead, the lighted house drew closer and seemed strangely out of place, as though isolated in the darkness of the street. He hesitated for a moment, unsure whether to continue. Somewhere locked inside him caution gripped his stomach and he turned to re-trace his steps. Too late he saw the movement from the corner of his eye, a strong arm wrapped around his face covering his eyes and cutting off his vision.

The acrid odour of sweat stung his nostrils. Twisting his head he felt the knife slash across the side of his neck, opening up the soft flesh from ear to shoulder. Had he not twisted, the knife would have ripped open his throat. He jerked his elbow back and he heard his attacker grunt as the hard bone smashed into his soft stomach. A light shone from an opened door. Blinking away his blindness he heard a shot fired from a revolver. The arm relaxed and slipped from his face and he could see again.

'This way, Monsieur, please, you must hurry.'

Thomas raised his hand to stop the bleeding and staggered through the doorway, and passing through a small, sparsely furnished unlit lounge, he entered a large bedroom with a double bed in the corner.

'Please, Monsieur, lie on the bed. I must stop the bleeding before it is too late. Take off your coat and shirt, quickly.'

Thomas stared at a boy no more than twelve years old and feeling the blood streaming down his body he began peeling off his clothes while the boy rummaged through a set of drawers next to the bed.

'Who was he, the man who attacked me?' he asked, watching the boy unroll a bandage and wipe away the blood with clean lint.

'Another German deserter. They desert all the time. They have no belly for fighting unless they are winning,' he said, expertly bandaging the wound.

'And you go around killing them. Where are your parents?'

The boy shrugged. 'The Germans killed my father two days ago because he would not help them – he was a policeman and tried to stop them from stealing our food. They took my mother a week ago and we have not seen her since.'

'Isn't there anyone to help you?'

'Most have run away to hide in the country to escape German cruelty. I live with my small sister. Alas, she no longer speaks, the war frightens her. There, it is done, you must rest now.'

Thomas lay back and sank into the warm feather mattress, allowing the pleasure of weariness to envelop his body. He felt his muscles relax and time slowly spooled away. For a moment he fought to stay awake then drifted into a deep sleep.

When he woke the bright morning sun beamed shafts of light through a weather-stained window. He raised his hand, blinked and looked down at his body. A black waistcoat with the top button missing replaced his bloodstained shirt and a pair of worn corduroy trousers covered his legs. His eyes swivelled searching for his uniform then jerked with surprise at the sight of a small girl wearing a pale-blue dress. Waif-like, she sat frail and frightened at the bottom of the bed. A flush of colour stained her cheeks and her eyes widened, the pupils dilating as she stared at him through doleful soft caramel eyes.

'Hello, who are you?' he said, feeling a sharp pain sear into his arm. Twisting round, he grimaced at the sight of the handcuff locked around his wrist with the other end fixed to the steel bed. The child smiled revealing dimples used to a better life, and slipping from the bed she disappeared through a doorway. Thomas pulled frantically against the handcuffs, and felt the neck wound open up and begin to bleed.

'Hello,' he shouted. 'Is anyone there? What the bloody hell's going on?'

In turmoil he ignored the pain and struggled to free his trapped hand. Suddenly, the door swung open and the boy entered.

'Undo these cuffs, lad, now, before you get into serious trouble when the soldiers come for me,' he demanded.

'No, Monsieur, I am sorry,' the boy answered. 'It is Françoise. She wants you to be her new papa, and until she is better and learns to speak once more you must stay here with us. Do not worry, Monsieur. We will feed you well and care for you.'

Thomas froze and looked at the boy through incredulous eyes, and feeling his breath die in his chest. He shook his head and leaned back with a sigh. The boy watched wild-eyed, as though he had slid into an unreal world. His trousers were at least three times too large for him and tied around his waist a short length of frayed rope prevented them from falling down. His jacket and cap the kind a train driver might wear, also too large for his slight frame. He exuded a look of determination yet his lucid brown eyes portrayed a subtle glint of fear while he fought to maintain courage that slowly but surely drained from his body. For a moment Thomas felt an empathy with him. They were two of a kind, kindred spirits, both without hope and in the middle of a war neither really understood.

'Don't you have any other family, aunts and uncles, grandparents perhaps? There must be someone here who can help you and your sister,' Thomas snapped rattling the chains. 'And for God's sake take these chains off.'

'We have an uncle in Antwerp, but we don't know his address,' he answered quietly, almost hopefully. 'Will you help my sister to talk again, please?'

For the first time since he ran away to Catterick Thomas felt a brief surge of pity for someone other than himself. He knew the agony of losing parents, the cold twist of vulnerability and the loneliness, all sense of hope draining away to leave a gnawing fear and a fading memory. His over-riding selfishness and desire to die had made him lose all consideration for others. Now his mind told him his troubles were less than trivial compared to the plight of these two young children. A warning bell sounded somewhere in the back of his mind. What can I do? he thought. I'm only sixteen and it isn't my responsibility. Or is it? Should I make it my responsibility and to hell with the consequences?

'What is your name?'

'David.'

'I want to thank you for saving my life, David, it was very brave, and not many boys of your age would have the courage.'

He shrugged. 'Many of my friends have killed Germans, some have been caught and shot, some hanged and left for the crows to eat as a lesson to us, but still we kill them,' he said in a matter-of-fact voice.

'Where do you get your food from?'

'We find it where we can. When the Germans were here we stole from them. Now we will steal from the British to live. Sometimes we steal pot-atoes and turnips from the farmers. They don't

389

mind so long as we don't get too greedy.'

'Undo these chains and I will do all I can to help you, I promise,' Thomas said.

'I am sorry, Monsieur, I must do what I must do,' he answered firmly.

Anger flared in Thomas's eyes. No matter how hard he argued and threatened, the boy was adamant that he would remain shackled until his sister regained her voice. That night Thomas lay on the bed trying to figure a way out of his predicament. She still sat there, Françoise, on the end of the bed, her hair, matted and tangled, hanging in disarray. Her small face, pale where it should have been pink and vibrant, gazed into his eyes with look of forlorn hope. He held her gaze and smiled, slowly she edged toward him, her expression never changing, until she was close enough to climb onto his lap.

Melancholy shook away his resistance and a flow of pity trickled into his soul. Automatically his arms enclosed her small body. He felt her trembling and searched his brain for the right words to ease her pain. Without looking up into his face she slipped her thumb into her mouth, gave a deep shuddering sigh and fell asleep. He stroked her hair and face with grimy caring hands and fought against the tears welling in the corners of his eyes. Silently, and with no small amount of rancour, he cursed the war for the misery it brought to the innocent, like he had so many times before.

David sat with his arms folded across his chest, like a judge in his high-chair waiting to pass judgement, and watched from the corner of the room. His face taut and serious, his brown eyes alert and brimming with hope, the slight flicker told Thomas he approved.

'If you undo the chain I'll show you how to make proper stew,' Thomas said the following afternoon.

'You will escape.'

'No, I give you my word.'

David gave him a bland stare, then pulling a key from his trousers pocket slipped it into the lock and allowed the chain to fall free. Françoise gasped, her breath came in short, rapid bursts, her tiny hands clutched at Thomas's trousers and she refused to let go. With a grin he looked down and lifted her. She smiled, and when he blew gently into her ear she slipped her arms around his neck and held him tight as though he might try to escape.

'Shh, don't be frightened little one, I'm not going anywhere,' he said softly, cradling her head in his hand. He felt the slight tremor and waited for her to push her thumb into her mouth and close her eyes. Warmth such as he'd never experienced before swarmed over his body, caressing and soothing his mind. He couldn't remember the last time anything so tender had reached his inner feelings and touched his soul and it frightened him. No longer did he suffer the grip of loneliness as though he existed in a wilderness hewed out for him alone. Gingerly he lay the child on the bed and gazed down, his one thought was to chase away the fears and vulnerability of an innocent child seeking solace in a turbulent world. For a moment, he forgot about death and rejoiced in the gift of life.

A few minutes spent rummaging through the drawers and cupboards in the kitchen produced flour and a small quantity of milk. With his bayonet he sliced vegetables and mixed them with water and flour to produce a thick soup, and with two eggs and some flour mixed with milk and water he baked a Yorkshire pudding. That afternoon they ate their fill and saved some for the evening.

After the evening meal Françoise sat quietly and allowed him to unbutton her dress and remove the rest of her clothing. With gentle hands he lifted her into the sink of warm water. Playfully flicking his finger, he sent a jet of water into her face. She smiled her tiny smile, the one that tugged at his heart, yet still she never uttered a word. With a small remnant of soap he lathered his hands and washed her clean. Finally, he dried and dressed her and sat her on his lap so he could brush her hair. She remained quiet, her eyes overflowing with uncertainty, and gripping a handful of his waistcoat she sought refuge and refused to let go. Still her nightmares persisted within her, and the ceaseless flood of jumbled memories washed her childish thoughts into a vast sea of confusion that sank so deep they became impossible to reach.

For a while he sat impervious to the demands of time, waiting until she pushed her thumb between her lips and slipped into the sanctuary of sleep. As she slept he prised her hand from his waistcoat, laid her on her small bed and gazed down at her face. Without warning an abrupt rush of guilt poured into his mind and he clenched his fist with a barely suppressed fury.

Tension hammered into his brain and he hardly dared to think of his own self-inflicted predicament. He turned his head away in a quivering sense of shame. His problems were negligible, unworthy of a mention compared to those of the child who lay sleeping in front of his eyes. Yet he lacked the backbone and inner strength to purge from his mind the experience that had caused him to leave the place he never wanted to leave. It was he that had fed Archie to the pigs, no other, him and him alone, and while he lived he must bear the guilt, it was only fair.

She lay still, save for the barely audible sound of her breathing, abandoned, lost and adrift in another world that only the remotest corners of her mind recognised. He leaned forward and covered her shoulder with the thin blanket. Before he could rise, the door crashed open and four military policemen battered their way inside.

'Corporal Archie Elkin, you are under arrest for desertion!' the heavy-built sergeant roared. 'Cuff him, and bring his uniform.'

Françoise stirred, sat upright and ran towards Thomas with outstretched arms. 'Papa, Papa!' she screamed.

'Get that bloody brat out of here,' the sergeant called, flinging the child to one side. Thomas watched Françoise slam into the wall and lie unmoving on the floor. A curtain of scarlet mist dimmed his vision and snapping his head forward he caught the sergeant flush on the nose. He staggered back moaning with blood gushing from shattered bones. Thomas twisted and sent his foot crunching into his groin. When he doubled, groaning in agony, Thomas's knee smashed into his face, splintering his cheekbone. From the corner of his eye he glimpsed the rifle butt coming for his face. Now he was trench fighting the way he'd been taught – no rules and nothing barred. Leaning back, he sent his fist into the man's face and felt the teeth give way and cut into his knuckles. The remaining two men backed away with fear and uncertainty etched on their faces. Thomas crouched, looking for an opening, his outstretched fingers groping for their eyes or anything else to rip open and maim. For a split second he felt the heavy blow cannon into his head and his legs buckled. A second blow knocked his head to one side and he sank, dazed, to the ground. When the first hobnailed boot thudded into his side, he passed out.

Stan Banks winced at the bruises and looked the other way. He'd seen the state of the sergeant and in no uncertain terms made it public that he wished Thomas had killed him. Throwing orphaned kids around wouldn't be forgotten by the men in the trenches.

'We'll deal with you bastards in our own time, think on that shithead,' he sneered at the hawk-faced military policeman sitting in the police station with his feet up on the table.

'What happened, Thomas?' Moses asked, ignoring Stan's threats. 'Where in God's name have you been for the past four days?'

Thomas heaved himself to a sitting position and told them everything, including the knife wound to his neck. They listened grim-faced to his story of the child, Françoise, who refused to speak after seeing her mother taken from her and her father shot down in cold blood by the Germans, and of David, her brother, who tried his best to care for her.

'You have to find her mother. Fritz took her a couple of weeks ago so she could be anywhere, looking after their wounded or more likely in one of their mobile brothels,' Thomas said, wincing through the pain.

'Aye, Sergeant Bull's the man for that,' Stan Banks said, scowling at the military policeman with his feet on the table.

'That's your bloody lot, you've had your five minutes, now sling your bloody hook, go on hop it,' the policeman said. 'He's not allowed visitors anyway. You can see him tomorrow after the court martial when they stick him in front of the firing squad.'

Banks's face exuded an undisguised hate and disgust at the policeman lounging in the chair with the top button of his trousers undone, and lashing out with his boot he sent the chair crashing from under him. Spluttering and roaring obscenities, the policeman fell to the floor. Banks bent down, ripped the policeman's trousers down to his ankles and walked to the door.

'Hey, lad, fetch an officer,' he called to two Highlanders. 'There's a bloody Redcap in here pleasuring himself in front of the prisoners.'

At ten o'clock the next morning, in the bombed-out town hall, Thomas stood to attention before four officers sitting behind two tables jammed together. They gave short thrift to excuses. The verdict was guilty as charged, and he would be shot at dawn the following day. He gave a slow smile and said nothing. Outside, he waited under escort for the battalions of Anzac troops to pass before crossing the road to the police station.

It was done and he felt no remorse. Archie's death had been no great loss to the world, in all probability it was a better place for it. Harsh but true, he mused, then again, maybe not his judgement to make. After all, Archie was now a hero, a winner of a Military Medal, a trainer of an elite band of snipers who terrorised the Germans and saved endless allies' lives. Archie will bring a child into the world through Dilly, dear Dilly, who wears her heart on her sleeve. Where else would a pretty girl wear her heart during a war? Archie held the respect of many men who served with him, ate with him and slept fitfully in the rat-infested trenches by his side. He had even been the best man at his friend's wedding. Archie had done well in his short eventful life, and even his pending execution would go down in the annals of war as killed in action to those unwilling to delve further. Thomas had died fighting for his breath in the bottomless gravel pit close to the farm on the edge of the Yorkshire Moors, so the story would go. He wouldn't be remembered as a hero, or anything other than an unfortunate little boy. He pulled the ragged blanket over his shoulders and lay down to sleep on the stiff bare wooden board. All was well with the world.

In the morning, he was informed by the police his execution had been deferred for twenty-four hours until his death warrant could be signed at

GHQ. He spent the morning playing draughts with a policeman from Rochdale, who had originally signed up for the Catering Corps. Such was the transience of the British Army.

'Here, mate, want a fag?' he said.

'No, I don't smoke.'

'No, and you don't want to start, mate, bloody things will kill you,' he said, closing his eyes tight shut upon realising what he had just said. 'I'm sorry, me and my big mouth.'

Thomas smiled at the unintended pun and turned as Sergeant Bull walked into the police station.

'You have visitors, lad,' he said, pulling the door open. 'We found her hiding in an outhouse after escaping from Fritz, been working as a cook she has, among other things.'

The young woman might have been pretty in the past but today she looked used and haggard. Her black three-quarter-length coat was held together round her waist with a piece of dirty white string and she wore a beret on her head, perched to one side in an attempt to portray a fashion. The sole of one of her muddy shoes was hanging off. In her arms she held Françoise, David clung to her coat.

'Papa,' Françoise whispered.

Thomas looked hesitantly into the woman's face and waited. With a small smile she nodded. He stepped forward and took Françoise in his arms. Her arm slipped around his neck and she pushed the thumb of her other hand into her mouth, closed her eyes and lay her head on his shoulder while he gently stroked her hair. It was a wasted effort closing his eyes – it did nothing to halt the

397

flow of tears springing between the lids and running down his cheeks. He cried in a manly way, silently and without a change of expression. Françoise wiped away his tears with her small hands until his face shone with wetness, and afraid he might lose control he handed her back to her mother. David stepped forward and thrust out his hand. They shook hands, like men do. Thomas raised a breathless smile and recalled the day he'd shaken his father's hand. It was a fine thing to do and he felt grateful for the memory.

'Thank you, Monsieur. I shall show my mother how to make the Yorkshire pudding, and when we eat it we shall always think of you,' the boy said.

Thomas nodded and wiped his face with the back of his hand, pretending the tears were not there.

'From the bottom of my heart I thank you, Monsieur,' the woman nodded. 'I have begged on my knees to your officers for your release, but there is nothing they can do. I tell them it is a waste of a fine man.'

Thomas watched them leave. A fine man, she had said – it was a good feeling.

That evening the signed warrant for his execution arrived. The Provost Marshall accompanied by a padre explained the procedure for death at dawn by firing squad. He would be allowed a good tot of rum to dull the brain or a shot of morphine. He refused both and declined the attention of the padre.

Moses came alone later and asked if he could speak with the condemned man.

398

'You'd better make it snappy. I could be shot for letting you in.'

Moses curled his lip and glared at the cringing policeman.

'We are trying all we can to get the sentence overturned. The snipers are threatening to shoot the officers, some are even asking for Ruby's address. They want to write and tell her you were a good man and that you died honourably. Not that it makes any difference, but I'm convinced you wouldn't want to die with a lie on your lips.'

'Moses,' Thomas snapped angrily. 'I'm being shot in the morning for caring for two young abandoned children who thought they had lost their parents. I fed them, washed them and tucked them into bed and told them bedtime stories when no other bugger gave a damn. What's your reason for dying tomorrow?'

Moses tilted his head and stared at the floor. Thomas was mocking him – fine words disappear into nothing once spoken, but deeds have a way of lasting longer. The logic of a boy had defeated him.

'Very eloquently and succinctly put, Thomas, I applaud you. Are you telling me you held no thoughts of your future when you decided to stay and care for the children?'

'Do I really need to answer that silly question?' Thomas said softly. 'Whatever you think of me no longer matters; it's what I believe that counts. You and Stan are my two best friends, and now you will become my lifelong friends.'

Moses reeled at the words, he tried to pull himself together and his shoulders slumped in despair.

'Time to go, sorry, mate,' the young policeman said.

'Goodbye, Thomas, I salute you for your courage,' Moses said quietly, unable to disguise the choke in his voice.

'Goodbye, Moses, thank you for all the kindness you have shown me in the past. I want you to have this,' Thomas said, holding out the pocket watch.

Moses snatched the watch and strode out into the night – for once, it wasn't raining.

Bully beef, green beans and hot potatoes followed by a whole jar of preserved apricots – a last meal fit for a condemned man. In the morning, a cup of coffee only, they told him.

Dawn crumbled away the darkness. The escort came accompanied by a young pale-faced captain from the Royal Engineers. The night before he'd refused the assignment, and only the threat of going the same way induced him to obey the order. He stood before hundreds of troops lined up and ordered to witness the punishment meted out to deserters. He knew how the men felt. The reason for the condemned man's execution had travelled like a tropical brush fire down the lines. What was the alternative, what was he supposed to have done, ignored the children after one of them had saved his life? Grim-faced they watched Thomas stumbling blindfolded accompanied by an escort. To his right waited a freshly dug unmarked grave. When they tied him to the post he braced himself so as not to lose his balance during the ceremony of shame and thought of Archie. He refused the white cloth bag they wanted to slip over his head leaving him in darkness, and asked for the blindfold to be removed.

'Sorry, mate,' a man with a florid face said fumbling while pinning on the white piece of cloth for the executioners to aim at.

Thomas closed his eyes. His breath, rushing from his chest, pounded in his ears like a winter storm on the moors. 'Walk easy on the plough, Ruby,' he whispered. The padre murmured some unwanted words over the sound of the officer's command to present arms, and he waited.

'Aim!'

'Here, just a minute, you bladdy drongoes, I know this bloke. He ain't no bladdy deserter,' Warrant Officer Digger Barnes called out. 'What the bladdy hell's going on?'

Sergeant Major Ned Molloy stepped in front of the pale-faced captain and glowered at him. Hesitantly, the confused firing squad lowered their rifles and looked at the captain, standing rooted to the spot with his mouth gaping open.

'You're a troublesome little bugger you are, what the bladdy hell have you got yourself into this time?' Barnes grinned at Thomas.

Thomas blinked and looked at the Australian. Something stirred in his heart and he wanted to scream, to tell them to go away. How could they snatch from him what he wanted more than anything else in the world, his freedom from the guilt that kept him awake every night and haunted him throughout the hours of daylight? He stood stunned, his brain scrambling, why was it they failed to understand he longed for death

401

to cleanse him from his sins and pain.

'What the blazes do you think you are doing? I'll have you arrested and thrown into prison, now get out of the way and I'll deal with you later!' the captain roared, coming to life.

Digger Barnes, like most Australians, had no time for British officers.

'You listen to me, you Victorian-bred mongrel. Lay a finger on that boy and I'll see that every Anzac soldier is pulled off the front line by noon. He won the Military Medal for helping twenty-five Australian soldiers escape from a prisoner-of-war camp and you stupid bastards want to shoot him. He's a bladdy national hero back home,' Digger Barnes raged.

The captain's face turned as white as a penguin's bib and the veins on his neck pulsed and throbbed purple. In one flowing motion he swivelled to face the Provost Marshall standing to one side with four military police, and thundered, 'By God, I want these men arrested at once, both of them, and throw them in the cells, they'll be dealt with later.'

The Provost Marshall gulped and remained stationary, salty sweat glistened like tiny drops of rain on his upper lip. He'd experienced trouble with the Aussie and New Zealand troops in the past concerning executions. They refused point blank to participate in the executions of their own men and threatened withdrawal from the war if any other foreign soldier raised arms against them. They had volunteered to fight of their own free will, unlike the British who fought through conscription. At this moment they considered Thomas to be one of theirs.

'I think we had better stand down on this, Sir, and await a ruling from above. Seen this type of thing before, and he means what he says. We picked up three Welsh guardsmen a few months ago trying to cross the border into Holland. Guilty as sin they were, one of them a young lieutenant from a titled family. Let them off scot free they did, said it would bring shame on the regiment,' he said to the fuming captain. 'Three days later they sentenced a soldier from an Australian regiment to be shot for cowardice. Suffering from bomb fever he was, Sir. The poor blighter couldn't even stand up. His commanding officer pulled his troops out of the trenches and threatened to shoot the officer in charge of the firing squad and return to Australia.'

'Did he, by God? Well I'll not stand by and allow a mutiny in the British Army to take place in front of my very eyes,' the captain said, drawing his revolver.

The metallic clunk-click of five hundred rifle bolts pushing a cartridge into the breech stopped him in his tracks and his eyes widened as the muzzles pointed at him, each finger itching to pull the trigger.

'If you want to stay alive to bugger your stable boy again, I'd put that revolver back up your arse where it might do some good,' Barnes said growing angry, and turning to one side he sent a stream of phlegm splattering next to the officer's boots.

The captain turned away with an expression bordering on naked fury.

'Release the prisoner and take him into custody,

403

this isn't over yet,' he croaked, and walked stiffly away.

'Strewth, Digger, you were over the top this time, mate. You'll be staring down a barrel yourself soon, too bladdy right,' Ned said.

'Yeah, well I don't think so. I ain't got nothing against the captain, probably didn't want the job in the first place, but the bastards still do it don't they, every bladdy time. That's not discipline, Ned, that's bladdy blind stupidity.'

By order of the Provost Marshall Thomas was held in custody until the situation was resolved. Aware of the danger concerning the Anzacs' attitude in the past, the Provost Marshal had been given strict orders not to antagonise them. Nevertheless, he wasn't happy at the present outcome. It was bad for discipline for a warrant officer to treat a commissioned officer in such an offhand manner in front of the troops.

'You ever speak to a British officer in that manner again, you fucking stupid colonial sheep shagger, and I'll be only too pleased to put a bullet in your fat ignorant mouth, do you understand?' he growled at Barnes that evening.

Barnes cocked his head to one side, shrugged his shoulders and looked at Ned Molloy. 'What's bladdy eating him?' he said.

The next day a communication came for Second Lieutenant Bellamy. Corporal Archibald Elkin's death sentence had been rescinded by a general staff officer by the name of Montgomery. He was free to return to his battalion with a loss of rank, ten days' leave and one week's pay.

However, not all of the news was good. The

404

snipers were to be disbanded and the section leaders transferred from the battalion. The news on both accounts sent Thomas into a state of depression and he grew morose and withdrawn. Not even the irrepressible Stan Banks could raise a spark of life from him.

Many men were perplexed by his attitude and couldn't understand his reluctance to join in the constant banter. A last-minute pardon from the firing squad was unheard of, yet he walked around like a man with a mouthful of wasps. Rumour had it that he'd received a *Dear John* from Ruby, though none dared to ask him.

'Never been known before,' Second Lieutenant Bellamy said. 'Never heard of a condemned man being released from the pole of death with the rifle sights already lined up on his heart. If anyone should be full of the joys of life it should be Private Elkin. He still lives when many don't. Dear me, dear me.'

Thomas had no desire to ignore their banter or appear rude and offhand. He knew they cared for him like they cared for each other. He was the fresh-faced kid whom death avoided like death itself. 'Soon be going home to Ruby' still rang down the trenches when itchy nerves frayed at the edges, when men gripped their hands to stop the trembling and their whole bodies shook. Now events began to overtake his young mind and despair crept in like an incurable disease, stifling, smothering and blindfolding his reason. He raised the brown jug, held it to his lips and gulped on the fiery contents. The neat rum hit the pit of his stomach, exploded and stole his breath away. He raised the jug again and swallowed, then suddenly felt the jar ripped from his hands.

'You thieving idiot!' Moses roared at him. 'This rum belongs to the men who stand in the trenches shaking with fear, not some halfpenny snivelling fraud like you.'

'Leave me alone, you're not God, and give me back my rum,' Thomas slurred, reaching out for the jug with an unsteady hand.

'I think not. You're not old enough to drink and you're not man enough to hold it when you do.'

'Archie drank you know,' he continued to slur. 'Liked his drink, old Archie did, dear old Archie. He ended up in a pork sausage you know, half the village must have had a taste of him. Wouldn't be surprised if they are all dead by now.'

Moses stared at him and shook his head in despair, his mood suddenly interrupted by Atlas falling through the door.

'You don't want too much of that, Archie lad. Too much rum, not good for your bum, you'll have the shits, you mark my words. I've just heard we're moving to a place called Langemarck in the morning.'

'Fuck off and mind your own bloody business,' Thomas sneered, climbing unsteadily to his feet.

Atlas's face hardened – nobody had the right to speak to him in that manner. 'You've been a miserable little bastard for the past few days, perhaps you're getting a little too big for your breeches, lad. You need taking down a peg or two,' Atlas said. And reaching out he threw him over his shoulder, carried him outside and jerked him up and down until he vomited the rum from his stomach. Then deposited him in a shallow ditch of slurry and left him.

'A bit harsh, old chap, but probably necessary,' Moses smiled. 'Never reason with a drunk.'

Thomas rolled over and lay on his back, giggling in a drunken stupor and trying to remember what had happened to the warm room he had been sitting in. 'Where are you, Archie?' he sang quietly. 'I know you are there.'

In the morning Thomas, Stan Banks, Moses and Leslie Hill gathered to say their goodbyes to the few remaining snipers. Moses suggested Thomas say a few words to mark the occasion of their parting. Thomas stood morose and disjointed from the previous night's encounter with the rum and reluctantly agreed. It seemed the appropriate thing to do.

'Well, men, I can't say all good things come to an end, that wouldn't make any sense, us being here. And I can't say it's been a pleasure knowing you because pleasure seems a bit sparse around here too,' Thomas began, feeling the words come easily. 'Many have come and gone, and those of you that filled their boots were more than good enough. When this war is over I would like to think we were responsible for saving a few lives, but if we saved only one it would be a job well done. Thank you all, and God bless.'

The silence was shattering. Thomas looked at Moses with a worried frown and Moses smiled and nodded. Thomas knew he'd said the right words.

'What about Ruby? Give our love to her. Kept us going through the hard times she has, three cheers for Ruby!' someone called.

They all hip-hip-hoorayed Ruby. Atlas became emotional and when someone offered him a pair of stained underpants to dry his eyes on he failed to see the funny side. He took a swing at his antagonist, missed and toppled into a trench, knocking over four men cooking a sizzling pan of beef sausages and bacon. Within seconds a horde of squealing rats had devoured the lot.

'Here, I think this belongs to you,' Moses said.

Thomas stared at the pocket watch for a few seconds and twisted his face into a wry smile.

'No, I don't want it, it's yours to keep. It never brought me any luck, and anyway it only reminds me of times of sadness.'

Chapter Twenty

At five-to-four in the morning it was cold at Langemarck and the men's heads dropped at the sound of rain pattering down into the trenches. Dark low clouds and a gentle wet wind blew across the besmirched landscape of No Man's Land. Few men had been able to sleep with the dread of the impending attack playing on their tired minds. Some crouched hollow-eyed, others abandoned all hope and the ever present smell of death lingered and shuddered in heaving lungs. Within a few seconds of the shrill blast from the officer's whistle they could be dead or wounded, and those unfit for a stretcher would be shovelled into sandbags. If they managed to get as far as the enemy trenches, would the barrage of field guns destroy the rolls of barbed wire, or would they become snagged and struggle for their lives, becoming easy prey for the German machine-gunners?

There was a glassy quiet and a sudden lapse in the gentle breeze. Thomas, Banks, Hill and Moses now attached to the 12th Battalion, The Rifle Brigade Prince Consort Own, waited with their nerves stretched to breaking point. Soon the creeping barrage would begin its deadly tattoo on the landscape, already naked of any form of life. No longer afforded the luxury of choosing their own ground they held their nerve and waited to go over the top. Eight British divisions waited in the cold lifeless hour before dawn to attack the German concrete pillboxes. Some men glanced across to Captain Sands and prayed for him to sound the whistle before their nerves evaporated from their bodies. Captain Sands, like most tall men, suffered rounded shoulders and with his steel-framed spectacles perched on a shapeless nose he possessed a face not made for remembering. A confectionary salesman from Reading, he tried to be a good officer who tried his best to care for his men, and for this reason they held him in high esteem. With a crash the barrage began at a quarter to four. Men jerked upright and snatched at their breath.

'Hold, boys, hold,' Captain Sands called above the sound of the barrage. Seconds later, he raised the whistle to his thin lips and blew. He was first up the trench ladder, and as cool as a cucumber he waited on the parapet, pulling men weighted down with equipment onto the battlefield. When it was Thomas's turn to go over the top, Captain Sands smiled at him.

'Hello there, Private, you're one of our new boys, aren't you? Good luck, lad, off you go,' he said.

The attack was a rout – fifteen-thousand British soldiers dead or injured and not one yard gained. It took four days of hard fighting to gain a foothold and bite and hold became the order of the day. When the relief troops finally made a welcome appearance those living raised a mute cheer and shuffled away. Captain Sands sent a runner for Thomas.

'I am aware of who you are and your history. Nevertheless it seems a mighty shame not to utilise your skills,' he said in a kindly voice. 'I need you and your companions to scout the country-side and bring in as much information as you can find about the Germans' movements, gun em-placements, stores, and anything that might help us out of this unholy debacle.'

Stan Banks felt the tension empty from his body and released a sigh of relief. One more day in the trenches and he was finished. His mind now a bubbling cauldron of fear, lately he'd tried to rea-son the meaning of war and why should it be necessary to die the way they did. What were they fighting for? Who the hell wants a trench full of dead bodies? What does anyone do with a bomb crater full of brackish water? What possible use is a hill entangled in barbed wire or a field full of rot-ting turnips and corpses in the middle of nowhere?

The next day, after a meal of fried eggs and

sausages and under the cover of a fading twilight, he cautiously led the way along a deep row of thorn bushes towards a derelict farmhouse with gaping holes in the roof. Nothing moved and only the falling rain could be sure of its destination.

'Don't feel right,' he whispered nervously. 'Somebody would have been billeted in there by now.'

'I'll go in first, wait here until I signal,' Moses volunteered.

Moses made his way round the back. A split door hung partially closed and using the weight of his shoulder he slowly pushed it open. Inside a large empty kitchen, the remains of a broken table lay scattered about the floor and a sink full of pots and plates lay unwashed. He crept silently along a narrow corridor stopping only to listen to a faint squeaking noise coming from a room to his left. With his bayonet gripped tightly in one hand he gently twisted the door handle and pushed the door ajar, and waited. The stench of urine and excrement hit his nostrils and soured his stomach and he turned his head away, fighting the nausea rising in his throat. An ear-splitting scream, followed by another and then another chilled his blood and he backed away, slamming the door shut.

Overcome by jangling nerves he baulked at the yellow glow of a hurricane lamp piercing the darkness. A soft footfall on the uneven flagstones stopped him in his tracks and a dark shadow flitted into a room opposite the kitchen he'd left only moments ago. The eerie glow spread from the room into the corridor, revealing the peeling wallpaper hanging from the mildewed walls. His boots echoed on the uncarpeted floor as he slowly made his way towards the light, and he cursed beneath his breath. He wanted to roar out a challenge to bolster his failing courage. He tried unsuccessfully to relax and a surging fear soaked his brain. He stopped and jerked his head round the door frame and snatched a glance into the semi-darkness. His lips parted and he made no sound. For a moment his lifetime refusal to believe in ghosts hung by the slenderest of threads and he stared at the dark shrouded apparition before him. Hardly daring to think he stumbled backwards raising his hands for protection, and in his haste he felt the bayonet slip from his hand and clatter onto the floor.

The dark apparition swayed towards him and his Adam's apple lodged in his throat. With his eyes glazed in terror he pressed himself back against the wall and tried to make himself invisible, to disappear in a puff of smoke like a magician in a music hall. Too late, the shape loomed close enough to touch him and he was helpless. God would not help him now, not after he had denounced him on the battlefield. His eyes widened by the second as he stared into the pale face and dark-brown eyes hovering before him. With a sigh, his shoulders slumped and the breath drained from his body.

'Bloody hell, miss,' he said breathlessly, stooping from the waist and trying to get the colour back into his face.

'Yes, I suppose it is,' the nun said, shaking the dust from her habit and lowering the revolver. 'You are British, thank God.'

Moses stepped into the room. 'I can assure you he has nothing to do with me being here,' he grunted. 'What are you doing here, why aren't you in your church?'

'The Germans came weeks ago and they moved us out to fend the best we could, so we came here. Yesterday they came and took all our food and smashed everything before they left. We have elderly people in our care suffering mentally from the continual shelling and bombing.'

'I'm certain the Germans won't be back tonight and we need somewhere to sleep.'

'We?' she said edgily.

'Don't worry, we are out on patrol, there are four of us, you are quite safe.'

Her expression relaxed and softened. From a thick cord hanging around her neck dangled a wooden crucifix. She raised it to her mouth and pressed it against her lips. Although her face looked young and only faintly lined around her eyes, her hands were wrinkled and her fingernails coarse and bitten with worry. Kneeling, she clasped her hands together and mumbled an incoherent prayer. Moses noisily cleared his throat and looked the other way.

'At the right side of the building there is a lean-to full of straw. You are welcome to share our food in the morning,' she said softly.

The sun stood high the next morning, the sky as blue and fresh as cornflowers in a summer meadow. The rain had ceased at last. Moses watched three nuns appear from the dilapidated farmhouse like a trio of imperfect souls unable to

413

separate religion from science. They came accompanied by a crowd of elderly men and women, stumbling and staggering in their wake, their clothes stained and ragged and looking not unlike adult street urchins. Eyes wide with vacant stares and shivering and trembling with fright, they looked pathetically thin, moaning and calling like mindless children. Stan said he'd once seen people like them when he'd delivered coal to an asylum for the insane.

'They are the local elderly people. Some are ill, most were infirm. Yet the Germans ordered them from their homes and left them to starve,' the nun explained.

Over a brew, Thomas sat and thought of Françoise and David – was nothing that lived exempt from the manmade holocaust? His mind flashed to Dilly and the innocent baby waiting to be born into the same violent world, and the thought saddened him. By midday they had patched the worst of the holed roof and performed odd tasks to make the group more comfortable. Before they left, they handed the nuns five precious tins of bully beef, a jar of preserved pears, half a jar of raspberry jam and two tobacco tins filled with sugar and tea. They knew it wasn't nearly enough, but they had no more.

'God be with you,' the nun said to him.

'I have no need of your God, ma'am, or any other,' Moses answered softly.

'Then I shall pray for you, my son.'

With the welcome change in the weather the men in and behind the trenches stripped naked and

414

attempted the impossible task of ridding themselves of the ever-present lice. Huge empty fuel drums were filled with water and brought to the boil. Thomas and Stan tossed their shirts and trousers into the bubbling mass of uniforms and took pot luck in receiving something back that fitted. Very rarely was anyone fortunate enough to get their own clothes back. It didn't really matter, so long as men could sit quietly without scratching and raking frenziedly at their skin every few minutes. Due to modesty and embarrassment, they deigned to wash their own underwear. Trousers became of paramount importance and priority was given to drying them as quickly as possible. All the men in the trenches possessed an irrational fear of suddenly being caught under fire with their pants down.

For months they attacked and counter-attacked the German lines until the Germans broke and fell back. Finally the men were pulled back to a rest camp and allowed to recover their shattered nerves.

Moses sat down next Thomas, doused in his own thoughts.

'How are you?' Moses asked.

'I'm fine, why?' Thomas answered.

'No reason, old chap, just asking. Passes the time of day.'

Thomas frowned and turned to face him. The one thing that struck him the most about Moses was that he never seemed to change. His appearance and un-forced aloofness remained constant, and if he was ever tired he never showed it.

'Are you tired, Moses?' he asked, already aware

of what the answer might be.

'Knackered, old man, I'm absolutely knackered,' he said in a mimicking voice.

'You don't look it, you always look the bloody same to me.'

'That's because I'm always tired, Thomas. I do believe you are growing up at last,' Moses said, playfully slapping him across the back and getting to his feet.

Thomas turned and looked into the smiling face. He felt good. Moses had never addressed him in that manner before. He wanted to grow up to be like other men, to be like Moses, to feel assured of his being and perhaps gain a better education. Without realising it the call of life beckoned him. He'd met death head-on and survived. He'd offered his body as a willing sacrifice to amend his past misdemeanours, but death had refused him. Then, like it always did whenever he dared think these thoughts, a vision of Archie's grinning face flooded into his mind and, in a rage, he gritted his teeth and rebuked himself for his selfishness and remembered his vow. With downcast eyes he watched a sergeant handing out tin triangles to be tied to the back of a soldier's pack, thus allowing the observers at the rear to see how far he got before he was blown to pieces. They think of everything he mused.

'Here, Sergeant, give me a large shiny one,' he grunted.

Grey skies signalled the arrival of early autumn, yet still the air hovered mild and comfortable. In far-off parts of the world falling leaves would produce a splendid golden-red carpet to herald the

416

harshness of winter. In Flanders, falling leaves were as rare as a glacier in a sun-baked desert. Stan Banks's heart sank at the warm rain spots, and groans reverberated down the length of their trench. Sentries reached for groundsheets just to be on the safe side – better to be prepared when the rain plopped and bounced off their helmets. As quickly as it had started, it stopped. One more time he read Mary's letter before carefully folding it and pushing it into his pocket. All was well, and he could ask for no more. He was happy, and the tremble in his hands had diminished.

Leslie Hill sat content eating chocolate and biscuits washed down with a brew reeking of the fickle taste of diesel oil, although a liberal helping of brown sugar helped to dispel the taste. In his pocket a letter from his feisty wife demanding he get a promotion and send her more money or she would run away with an Indian sepoy she'd met on one of her regular forays to the local pub. He'd already penned a harsh reply telling her good riddance and that he intended to join the circus the next time it appeared on the Northampton racecourse. He hadn't yet worked up the courage to post it.

Thomas glanced up from cleaning his rifle and watched an officer on a Dapple Grey approach from behind the lines. When the colonel reined in, the horse whinnied and threw its head to one side, pawing at the air with its front legs.

'Easy, girl, easy,' the colonel said in a soothing voice and glared down at Thomas through a rimless monocle. 'I'm looking for a Private Elkin. Any of you lot know of his whereabouts? Come

417

along, speak up now, I haven't all day.'

'Yes, Sir, I'm Elkin,' Thomas said without looking up at the officer, and walking over to the horse he whispered and rubbed the animal's nose and mouth with the palm of his hand. 'She has a soft mouth, Sir, and this bit is wrong for her. She needs a straight one, Sir, if you don't me saying so, Sir.'

'Know horses do you, Private?' he said. 'Didn't you used to be a corporal? God, you don't look old enough to be out of short trousers.'

'Yes, sir, I used to be a corporal, and yes I know a little about horses,' Thomas answered easily.

'I'll see it's changed the moment I get back. Now look here, see the large chateau over there, behind the elms?' he said, pointing to the grey building on the dull horizon. 'Be there by four this afternoon, and don't be late. I won't be kept waiting, understand.'

'Yes, Sir,' Thomas answered, rubbing his palms down the side of his trousers and feeling his breathing quicken.

'I wonder what he wants,' Stan Banks said, watching horse and rider canter away on a loose rein. 'Nothing bloody good, I bet. Mary sends her love by the way, thought you might want to know. A colonel eh. You must be becoming important, Archie, unless they're going to put you back in front of the firing squad,' he grinned evilly.

Chapter Twenty-One

The Chateau

For the time of year the sunflowers were the biggest he'd ever seen, even the pear trees laboured against the weight of over-ripe succulent fruits, and sweet peach trees holding golden delights dizzy with juices were enough even to tempt Eve away from the forbidden apple. Everywhere the lulling smell of rotting wood and perfumery of swaying hollyhocks embraced the senses. Only the sight of a snow-white unicorn amid the fields of bright red poppies would be proof that God had breathed his breath and the world was made that same day. Removing his peaked cap he unbuttoned his tunic and ran the back of his hand over his perspiring face, then wiped the sweat down the side of his trouser leg.

For a long time he sat in his filthy uniform in the middle of this newly-discovered world and gazed on nature's response to man's destruction. This was how it was meant to be, the air so pure it should never be allowed to be breathed by man. For another mile he wandered unaware of the time along ragged hedgerows and through the avenue of scents, where flowers growing beneath his feet sprung back dreamily against his touch. All around the songs of wild birds filled his head and he clenched his eyes shut and tried

419

to distinguish one call from another.

Then, in sudden contrast the stone wall surrounding the chateau loomed up black and grimy, divided by two large rusting gates worked in Spanish scrollwork. Above the pillars either side sat two rampant stone lions like frozen guardians waiting for better times. He stopped and gazed up at the chateau and noticed it was badly in need of a cleaning to restore the stonework to a semblance of its one-time glory. In awe, he reworked his mind and out of the fog of his memory the chateau vividly reminded him of the wicked giant's castle he'd once seen in a children's storybook that George Spikes had received for Christmas. The front shaped flat with large windows devoid of drapes and the roof surrounded by a castellated wall, tall enough for men to look over and beat off an attack. To both sides, large rounded towers with slated roofs covered in red creepers pointed sharply skywards, giving the building an air of the spectacular. A dried-out moat provided a home for random tall weeds, and nettles mingled with thorn roses and thistles to flourish unhindered along with bushes teeming with full ripe succulent blackberries. Small outer buildings, some collapsing and in need of repair, others beyond care, lay dotted around tree stumps, cut down to provide fuel during the cold winter nights.

To the left of the chateau, a large silver lake surrounded on three sides by elms and beech shimmered beneath the sunlight, throwing long shadows over the small whirlpools displaying the presence of feeding carp. It was the most wondrous place Thomas had ever seen in his life, and he felt he should not blink for fear he might miss one magical moment.

As he drew closer he saw a freshly painted white boathouse shaded by thoughtfully-placed weeping willows standing on the end of a small peninsula jutting out into the lake. Nearby, a young woman of approximately twenty years of age and wearing a pair of grey tailored trousers struggled to pull a dinghy onto the bank. Her blouse hung partly undone and the white lace strap of her bra slipped down her arm, dangling freely. When he approached, she made no attempt to cover herself and despite his appearance smiled warmly at him, her teeth gleaming white against the gloss of her bright red lipstick. Her honey-blonde hair, grown long and tied back by a black velvet ribbon, danced in the autumn sunlight like a swaying field of golden corn, and a red silk scarf matching the colour of her lipstick lay knotted around her slender neck. His eyes widened and he wanted to pinch himself to prove she was real, and not a trick of his imagination.

'Thank God,' she laughed. 'Help at last. You wouldn't mind giving me a hand would you?'

'No, ma'am, of course not,' he mumbled feeling the heat sear into his cheeks.

With the dinghy finally nestled safely on the bank, he nodded shyly and began to move away towards the chateau.

'Thanks awfully, rather sweet of you. Have you come to see Daddy? I'm afraid he's not in the best of moods,' she said, interrupting his thoughts.

'I've been told to report to the colonel, ma'am; if you'll excuse me,' he said tugging off his hat.

'I'm Charlotte, the colonel's daughter. I hope I haven't taken too much of your time and made you late,' she interrupted again.

'No, ma'am, I've plenty of time.'

A faint course of water weaved and trickled like a mini waterfall down the steps leading up to the chateau, leaving small dirty puddles on the uneven worn stone. Above him, on the upper level, a weedy thin private with a long expressionless face and gimlet eyes leant on a bracken brush with a pail of water by his feet. He jerked at the unexpected sight of Thomas.

'You must be Private Elkin?' he asked, more hopefully than directly.

'Yes.'

'Been told to expect you, follow me,' he said, striding into the building with water dripping from his trousers.

Thomas felt irked and wanted to ask if he knew what the colonel's business with him might be. But the weedy private strode so quickly he struggled to keep up and, biting nervously on his lip, he followed him up an ivory-coloured marble staircase. A stone balcony with more Spanish-style scrollwork matching the heavy gates overlooked a magnificent long dining room, or all sides hung cracked dull-framed mirrors. The walls along the upper corridor showed signs of crumbling plaster, bare of rows of past portraits depicting the severe faces of the former masters of the chateau. An absence of furniture or fittings of any description gave a sense of wilful neglect.

422

The chateau lacked the grandeur it would have once ostentatiously displayed in its days of unbridled finery and pomp – days of narrow-waisted ladies with painted faces cooling themselves with delicate ivory fans, pursued around the ballroom by men cavorting in powdered white wigs to the strains of Schubert and Johann Strauss. The emptiness emitted a feeling of coldness and depression, and he felt like a trespasser setting foot where he had no business to be.

At last the weedy private stopped in front of a pair of double doors standing at least twelve feet high. Thomas looked up in awe and wondered why anyone would want doors so high, unless people from Flanders were exceptionally taller than others. He struggled to remember if he'd ever seen any.

'Private Elkin, Sir,' the weedy private said through the open doors.

'Ah, come in, Elkin. Thank you, Cockshead, that will be all,' the colonel boomed.

Thomas looked up at the weedy private finding it difficult to conceal his smirk. The private's lip curled at one corner and he noisily slammed the doors shut.

'My name's Cookson, you useless stupid old bastard, not Cockshead. I've told you a dozen times in as many days, and now half the Western Front will know and the name will stick forever. How would you like it if I called you Colonel fucking Dickhead? I hope you fall off your horse and break your fucking neck,' he muttered angrily. When he returned to his place of work, he undid his flies and urinated down the flight of steps.

'At ease, lad, sit down. I understand you were a sniper with the Yorkshire Rifles, and a damn good one by all accounts,' Colonel Dickson said standing by a window with his feet apart.

'Well yes, Sir, I suppose so,' Thomas stammered awkwardly at the officer, wondering why he was here.

Colonel Dickson was a handsome giant of a man with broad shoulders and a pansy-purple nose gained from imbibing glasses of fine vaporous wines, one ear slightly higher than the other added to his timbre. His whole person suggested that of a military peacock and he carried a carefully practised swagger designed especially for the ladies of the day. As far as the ladies were concerned, his sharp blue smiling eyes were his first line of attack, a force no female barricade had ever resisted. Other than that, he was thought to be an honourable man and a good officer.

'I keep livestock here, Elkin,' he said in a bombastic voice that might have struck terror into lesser men. 'Pigs, sheep, chickens, turkey, geese and a small herd of Friesian cows, even a few wild ducks out on the lake stocked with brown and rainbow trout. Oh yes, I nearly forgot the goats. All used for fresh food for the staff officers at general headquarters. That's it in a nutshell. Problem is, some bounders are stealing them. Not only that, but they're tearing them to pieces. We suspected foxes in the beginning, but it didn't seem feasible that they could inflict the kind of damage we have witnessed on the animals. German soldiers hungry for a square meal were considered, passing gypsies, perhaps even the locals. Might be anybody or anything, and I want the blighters apprehended as soon as possible. I want you to patrol at night, discover the culprits and shoot the bounders on sight. No mercy, mind you. There's a war on and we can't have the generals going hungry, can we? Course not. You will be relieved of all duties on the front line. This is of great importance to me and I expect a quick result, for obvious reasons. Well, speak up man, what have you to say?'

A cold, moist, damp air blew into the room and the drapes hanging behind the colonel shifted. Thomas felt a mixture of elation seasoned with apprehension.

'May I ask where will I be billeted, sir?'

'Why, here of course.'

Thomas pondered for a moment, wondering if he dare ask another question, and then raked up the courage.

'I was wondering, Sir,' he ventured, 'if perhaps two of us might be better than one man alone, if there is more than one prowler it might prove difficult to catch them.'

'Absolutely splendid idea, I should have thought of it myself, anyone in mind?' he boomed.

'Yes, Sir. A West Indian. He's a very good shot, Sir.'

'A West Indian, eh? By God, one of those darkie fellows, with built-in camouflage they won't spot him in the dark in a hurry. Very good, Elkin, very good indeed, you'll go far in this army,' he said in a loud condescending tone. Squinting, he leaned forward and tapped his fingers on the desktop. 'We're going to get on just fine, young man. By

425

the way, how old are you?'

'Nineteen, sir,' Thomas lied.

'Look more like twelve to me. Be sending them straight from the crib next wearing nappies. Off you go and see Marie Antoinette. She's the cook and she'll give you something to eat. And for God's sake get yourself cleaned up. Can't have you walking around in that state. After you are billeted, come and see me.'

When Thomas entered the kitchen, Marie Antoinette was hollering and cursing in a language he didn't understand, and flapping a wet cloth in a vain attempt to be rid of a troublesome fly. With practised ease he snapped out his hand, caught it, threw it on the floor and stamped on it. She puffed out her heavy cheeks, wiped her face with the damp cloth and smiled.

'Zank you,' she wheezed.

'The colonel told me you might give me some food.'

'Zit,' she said, jabbing a podgy finger towards a brown chair with a wicker seat. The kitchen was enormous and stretched the length of the building. Pots and pans made of copper hung next to cooking utensils of all sizes from hooks fixed to the walls. From the dark-stained beams swung cooking contraptions he failed to recognise. He thought they might be instruments of torture. Four large sinks, three with silver taps and one with an ornate wooden handle used for pumping in the water from an outside well, were arranged beneath rows of spotlessly clean windows. To one side three huge wood burning black ovens stood side-by-side. Two remained unlit gleaming from continual polishing, the other hurled out heat and aromatic smells from bubbling cooking vessels sent saliva running into his mouth.

He waited impatiently, staring at her as she prepared a wooden platter of cheese, onions and black bread. An overly fat woman with brush-stiff black hairs hanging untrimmed from a large wart protruding from her left cheek, her chins too numerable to count. A course of sweat dribbled from her jowls and ran down the loose turkey folds of her neck before disappearing down her cavernous neckline. But it was her eyes that took his attention – they were big and staring, almost frightening, like ripe damsons.

'Eet,' she said, dropping the platter on the scrubbed table and sending the onions bouncing over the table. For fear of offending her he ate in silence, quickly aware she was obviously not a woman a person would dare to trifle with.

When he was finished, he stood to leave and opened his mouth to convey his thanks.

'Zit,' she interrupted and clattered a huge plate of hot bread pudding in front of him.

By the time he'd finished he could hardly move and loosened the band of his trousers for comfort. Whether or not she mistook his action for a sexual attack, she picked up a ladle quicker than a pike taking a baited hook and, without holding back, smashed it against the side of his head.

'Out!' she roared.

Moments later Private Cookson nervously watched him approach and prepared himself for the insulting barrage. Even when Thomas failed to mention his mispronounced name, he kept a wary eye on him.

'I suppose you are staying for a few days and need somewhere to sleep?' he asked.

'Yes.'

'Come back later, I'll clean out one of the back rooms for you.'

Thomas nodded and made his way back to Colonel Dickson's office.

'Ah, Elkin, been fed and watered have you by our gentle, refined cook? By God, don't cross her. Pricklier than a troop of lancers that woman. Now then, about the horse, find the stables and try her with a straight bit, take her out for a spin, do her the world of good.'

The doors to Thomas's mind flung wide open, and with his mouth gaping he sucked in a great breath. To ride the colonel's horse was a dream come true, to feel the fresh wind in his face like he had with Ruby was a thought almost too large for his brain to digest.

'Perhaps I could ride her to the farmhouse, Sir, to see the West Indian I told you about?'

The colonel raised his eyes and stared into Thomas's face. Thomas felt the flush burn into his face, and nervously licking his lips knew he'd overstepped the mark.

'Take it easy with her, Elkin, no more than a fast canter, and be back before dark,' the colonel answered, as though in two minds.

The ecstasy exploded within him, and he wanted to laugh, to scream out loud. At the rear of the chateau he followed his nose and the smell of sweating horses and soiled straw guided him with minimum difficulty to the stables. He found her immediately, her proud head protruding from the top of the stable door.

'Monsieur, how can I help?' Michel, the stable boy, asked.

'Saddle her, and use a straight bit, please.' Thomas smiled.

With each passing second his impatience bit into his soul until he thought he might faint with excitement. Her coat gleamed with a mixture of white and grey hairs and her tail and mane near white. She stood seventeen hands high and rippled with carefully exercised sinews and muscles.

'Isabelle, Monsieur, is ready.' Michel smiled, tightening the girth another notch.

Thomas mounted and waited for Michel to adjust the stirrups to cavalry length. Then, with a slight forward movement of his pelvis, Isabelle responded immediately. Thomas's smile spread into an inane grin and he thought he might lose control of his features. As if Isabelle sensed his delight, she broke into a slow canter and with her head high and her feet hardly touching the ground beneath her, she moved like a well-oiled machine fit only to carry the gods themselves.

Stan Banks saw them approach and his eyes dilated, he felt his buttocks squeeze tight together and his rifle slipped from his grasp. He took off his helmet and held it tight across his chest like a man in shock.

'Bloody hell, what did I tell you? He's gone and done it, he's only gone and got himself a bloody horse, now he thinks he's a bloody officer!' he shrieked, running down the trenches. 'It's General bloody Elkin. We'll all be on parade in a minute,

429

better get a bit of spit on your boots, lads.'

Thomas slid from the horse and made his way into the farmhouse certain that shortly the whole battalion would be conscious of his presence. As expected, Moses and Leslie Hill were the first to show their faces, and Stan lingered outside for a while, afraid to enter. Convinced that Thomas had stolen the horse, he wanted no part in the crime. When Moses told him how Thomas had gained access to the horse, he changed his mind and reluctantly entered watching Thomas through twitching eyes. Thomas was brief and to the point.

With a pinch of guilt cooling his pleasure, Moses laced up his boots and glanced at the brooding face of Stan Banks. Maybe it was only right that Stan should join Thomas at the chateau. He was married now, and with a young wife to think of it seemed reasonable to assume that he wanted to be out of the front line and away from almost certain death. Thomas had tried his hardest to explain that the war had no bearing on his decision to take Moses and not him. He knew Stan was the best fighter of the four. In the trenches he was ruthless. It was like watching a butcher at work, slicing up a carcass ready for hanging in the window. But this operation was different. It would require stealth and cunning. It was possible they would have to sit quietly night after night waiting patiently for the culprit, or culprits, to appear. Stan couldn't sit quietly for any length of time without breaking out into a monologue concerning a surname, or how many kids he and Mary were going to have and what he intended to name them. Nevertheless, as expected Stan took it badly, and jealousy raised its time-old green head. With a face as black as Newcastle coal, Stan stalked out of the farmhouse simmering with anger and looking for trouble.

Leslie Hill sat and listened thoughtfully and in his wisdom suggested it could only be wolves.

'Best to set a trap for them buggers,' he said. 'You don't want to be coming face-to-face with one of those at night, especially if the poor little bugger's hungry. That's what wolves eat you know, other animals. Entitled to their grub they are. Just like we are, you remember that.'

'I will, Leslie, and the second it gets its teeth round my throat I'll offer to share a tin of bully beef with it,' Moses grinned, checking his ammunition pouch. 'Do me a favour and keep an eye on Stan.'

'Bugger off, you sarcastic sod,' Hill retorted, walking out with a large smile on his face.

Private Cookson, true to his word, had cleaned out two back rooms of the chateau overlooking the rear meadows and the livestock. Each room, once ornate guestrooms, contained a double bed with down mattresses brought from the quarters where guests had once spent comfortable nights during happier days. The rooms were warm and comfortable, with long drapes to block out the muted rumble of guns from the front.

'This is Private Cookson,' Thomas said by way of introduction.

Cookson sighed with relief and nodded his gratitude at being referred to by his correct name.

'Kenneth, that's my name,' the weedy private smiled.

'Absolutely splendid name,' Moses said, extending his hand.

'Aye, bloody sight better than Cockshead,' he laughed. 'Follow me, I'll show you where the copper boilers are and you can wash those filthy uniforms. Old Dickhead's a bit funny about his men's appearance.'

Kenneth brought pitchers of hot water and soap, and the two men stripped and scrubbed each other clean with rough sponges they found under the sink. Later, they asked Cookson for a pair of scissors and trimmed each other's hair, and using their fingers as a comb they made themselves as presentable as possible.

Alone in his room, Thomas gazed wistfully into the mirror set above the sink. His once youthful face held a sickly pallor, save for the black shadows that stained the skin beneath his eyes, which stared back, blood-veined under their heavy lids. Even in the sanctuary of the chateau, far away from the lunacy of the trenches, the madness felt close, like a shadow confined to a permanent dusk. In a bid to distract his devils he fumbled with his thoughts and pre-occupied himself with his minor ailments.

Sores and boils abounded on his back and thighs, and an occasional searing cramp in his legs caused him to wince and stretch out his limbs for relief. Worst of all was a persistent cough that racked his chest and produced mouthfuls of thick yellow phlegm. From the mirror he moved to the window and embraced the vista of multi-shades of

432

green pastures overlooked by rows of trees already shedding their leaves in deference to the approaching winter. For him to return to the way he once was, the way he wanted to be, time would need to stand still.

Mid-afternoon the next day Thomas walked with Moses out into the meadows behind the chateau. He closed his eyes and inhaled the country air. All seemed so peaceful and yet so uncommonly unreal that it became almost threatening, as though a thousand field guns waited impatiently to rent the air and cast their reverberations upon the outer cortices of his brain. In the distance he heard the faint tolling of a church bell and listened to the sound of his own breathing. For a moment, no more than a brief fleeting interval, he attempted unsuccessfully to wash away all thoughts of war and brutal carnage from his mind. Caught in a dream of his own making, he hardly listened as Moses told him how he had been raised in a building similar to the chateau called a manor. Then with rising interest he listened enthralled to his friend's dulcet tones extol tales of a privileged childhood, with no thought of malice.

Happy to be of the same frame of mind they rounded up the livestock and herded them into a nearby pasture close to the chateau. From their rooms overlooking the pastures they could keep a sharp eye on anything causing a disturbance.

Kenneth scratched his head and frowned at Thomas's suggestion he take a horse-drawn cart to the area where the Pioneer Corps buried unwanted litter and rubbish. His job was to collect as many empty tin cans as possible. Nevertheless, he was more than happy to escape the dreary employment of sweeping around objects that collected dust with amazing regularity.

'As they say in the army, if it moves salute it, if it doesn't, paint it,' he grinned.

While he was away a young lieutenant walking arm-in-arm with Charlotte introduced himself as Lieutenant Cheeseman, the colonel's aide. Thomas held grave doubts over what he called fraternising with officers, and felt ill at ease when the colonel and his daughter joined them during an afternoon break by the lakeside. It was like the meeting of a dinner jacket with a rough leather jerkin, and Thomas writhed in the clutches of intimidation.

Moses, however, thought differently and turned his attention to Charlotte. 'May I ask what you are doing in such a hazardous environment for such a charming young lady?'

For a second she stared at him with raised eyebrows, visibly surprised at his eloquence. She hesitated and then turned her head away without answering.

'Answer the question, my dear,' her father said, watching her closely.

'I work for a London newspaper. I'm doing an article on the psychological effects that modern warfare has on the men serving in the trenches. I believe you might refer to it simply as shell shock. Does that answer your question?' she answered, breathing heavily through her nose.

'And what conclusions have you arrived at, might I enquire?' Moses continued.

434

'Do I have to talk to this man, Daddy?' she pouted. 'He's black, for goodness sake.'

Moses stiffened.

'He is a serving soldier in His Majesty's army,' the colonel reminded her coldly.

Her eyes blazed like hot coals and she turned to face Moses. With her fists clenched white she reluctantly responded to her father's wishes.

'I have a considered opinion that some cases often referred to as cowardice are unfounded, and a man's refusal to fight is not always intentional but brought about by a form of nervous disorder and a loss of co-ordination due to the trauma of the battlefield. May I enquire as to your function in this war?'

Thomas tensed, confused by Charlotte's reference to the colour of Moses's skin, and he watched Moses squirm. Moses wasn't accustomed to confrontation, let alone the vitriolic directness she hurled at him without mercy. He preferred to pass on his opinions, unquestioned and without argument, whether others wanted to hear them or not. He could hardly tell her he was employed to shovel shit out of trenches.

'I am employed where the authorities deem fit, miss,' he said, looking out over the lake to avoid her eyes.

'How very convenient, Mr Moses, how fortunate we are to have such versatile people at our disposal,' she answered haughtily.

'Moses Pendleton, ma'am, Private Moses Pendleton, at your service,' he answered with a curt nod of his head.

'How dare you, you impertinent man?' she

435

hissed though clenched teeth.

Thomas saw a coldness appear in Moses's eyes that he'd never seen before, and the whole point of the conversation eluded him. He stood stiff-legged for a moment, as if at attention, and his right hand twitched and nervously patted his leg. For a moment he thought Moses might turn and verbally cut her down like he'd seen him do on numerous occasions to people who irked him. Instead, he turned and walked away without a word. Thomas frowned and glanced across at Charlotte, feeling as if some light had gone out inside him. She returned the frown with raised eyebrows, blinked slowly and with an unspoken act of dismissal turned her head away. He suddenly realised that people such as he only spoke to people such as Charlotte when spoken to.

Kenneth, although completely intrigued as to the use of the tin cans, willingly volunteered his services and helped Thomas and Moses punch a hole in each tin. Passing string through the holes, they tied three cans together. Then they tied the string onto lengths of thick twine from the gardener's shed and strung this to the trunks of the trees surrounding the meadow. Anybody, or anything, making contact with the twine would set the tins rattling warning of their approach. Kenneth scratched his head in bewilderment and swore it was the daftest idea he'd ever heard of. Finally, Moses marked the distances from the chateau to the meadow and they adjusted their rifle-sights. That night Moses elected to sit on the roof of the stables. Thomas remained at his bedroom window with the Mauser resting across his legs.

Throughout the night they maintained a sharp vigil pushing tiredness to one side. Soldiers serving in the trenches learned quickly how to sleep with one eye closed and the other open, one ear readily cocked and the other deaf to the world.

A wild array of birds orchestrated the arrival of dawn and the sky streaked pink against dark blue. Moses yawned, stretched and blinked simultaneously. He scratched his head and hoped his hair would soon grow back. As a child he'd read the story of Samson and Delilah, and the thought of having no hair caused him a certain amount of anxiety. Thomas filled the earthenware bowl from the water pitcher and with a sudden gasp sluiced cold water over his head. With his thumb and forefinger over the bridge of his nose, he snorted and cleared his nostrils making a noise like a deflating balloon. The night watch had produced nothing, apart from the occasional hoot of an owl and the inevitable faint rumble of far away guns.

Marie Antoinette never allowed her eyes to wander from Moses and hastily dropped the plates of fried eggs and black pudding onto the table, taking great care not to make contact with him. Utterly convinced that his colour was caused by an incurable disease and ignoring all advice to the contrary, she kept her distance and threw away each plate he ate off.

'Eet,' she ordered.

With bulging overfed stomachs, Thomas and Moses stepped outside and felt the cold breeze sending a low murmur from treetop to treetop. Moses shivered, picked up his rifle and followed

Thomas for an extensive tour of the surrounding countryside. The last few days had proved difficult for him and the raw morning chill caught his face. He regretted his decision to leave the trenches and become subjected to the bare realities of racism, and then he smiled with a little dry twist of his mouth. He should have grown used to people by now, people with minds readily corrupted by stupidity and ignorance as though it were a fashionable flair to be displayed without shame.

Whatever attacked the animals must have come from somewhere nearby, perhaps a snug lair hidden away in the crowded countryside. Tall elms fronted a small wood and a worn path looped its way through the trees and circled the lake. Overhead the rasping sound of rooks mingled with the gentler call of nesting pigeons. Occasionally the path gave way to clearings and Thomas, familiar with country lore, searched for tell-tale signs of animal presence: flattened grass, snapped branches, defecation and perhaps the bones or remains of victims. For hours they searched diligently and fruitlessly.

'We'll walk round to the other side of the lake and sit a while. Might catch a glimpse of something,' Thomas said hopefully.

Moses shrugged silently and dropped in a few yards behind him.

On impulse he turned. Whatever it was that smashed into his shoulder sent him crashing into the lake and for a brief second he smelt the rancour of its foul breath. Instinctively he reached out to hold the gaping jaws away from his face. Kicking and struggling they both sank down into the cold water beginning to cloud as he fought to escape. Razor-sharp claws scratched and ripped frenziedly at the front of his shirt, and water poured into his mouth and nose cutting off his air supply. The fear of drowning pierced his mind and he wanted to cry out, a pain like a searing red-hot poker forged into his shoulder. Whatever it was that gripped him refused to let go and shook him from side-to-side like a wet rag doll, and the water turned blood-red. In blind panic and fearful for his life he kicked out with all his might and felt his strength fading. His mind became overcome by the paralysing terror of a violent death in the jaws of something he couldn't see.

Then the scratching and ripping stopped, and he rolled over and floated face down to the bottom of the lake. Something grabbed at his arm and he tensed, waiting for the pain to start over again and keep him underwater. Propelled upwards, he looked at the blue sky and gasped for air, his lungs refused to respond. A thundering blow cannoned into his back and the blood-red water retched and spurted from his mouth and he gasped and groaned out loud, feeling as though his chest was about to burst.

Thomas left him half in the water and half on the bank and prised the dead animal's jaws from his own hand. His index finger and the finger next to it on his left hand hung by a twist of gristle, and blood poured from the claw gouges running down his face and across his forehead. Against the edge of the lapping lake the carcass of a German shepherd dog floated partly submerged, with the bayonet still embedded in its neck. With his good hand he pulled the dead dog onto the bank and, sinking to his knees, stared at his loose dangling fingers.

Marie Antoinette bandaged his fingers and bathed his wounds, adamantly refusing point-blank to touch Moses for fear of turning black. Her damson eyes turned to ripe plums fit to burst when the colonel told her she was being silly and insisted she treat Moses as well as Thomas. If anything, it made her worse, and in a fit of uncontrollable pique she began hurling cups and saucers across the room interspersed with home grown obscenities, until he beat a hasty retreat and sent Cookson for a medical officer.

'Well done, men,' the colonel said. 'You bagged the blighter good and proper. Only right you stay a couple of weeks until your wounds heal before you return to the trenches.'

'The trenches, why do they always say back to the trenches?' Thomas said to Moses later. 'Like we're rats and belong there.'

'Maybe that's how they see us, as rats that belong in the trenches. Perhaps they view me as a black rat. Who knows what the upper middle class thinks?'

Thomas frowned at the remark and recalled the stories Moses had told him of his upbringing in the large manor, where he played freely and rode horses throughout the day and at mealtimes gladly sat at the earl's table to be waited on by servants. It was the first time he'd referred to himself as a black man, and it was obvious that Charlotte's offhand dislike and reference to his colour had left

440

him in a state of constant disdain.

Kenneth brought hot food to their rooms to save them from the histrionic ranting and utensil bombardments of Marie Antoinette.

'I'll be sorry to see the back of you two. Straight back on that bloody broom, that's where I'll be, what a bloody life, eh?'

'Have you never seen any action, lad?' Thomas asked.

'Action, aye course I have. Trouble with me is, every time I fire a rifle I get a nosebleed. Three times they put me on a bloody stretcher and carted me off to one of them hospitals where they cut off everything with a drop of blood on it. Silly buggers thought I'd been shot in the head, and I thought, bugger me. They're going to cut it off. The daft buggers realised in the end though, and sent me up here to ponce about for his lordship.'

Overjoyed at the temporary respite from the trenches, they ate their food and counted their blessings. At the close of day they sat in silence and watched the sun wander off to perform its mandatory duty on the other side of the world leaving them to prepare for the grip of approaching winter.

On his bed Thomas lay staring at the decorated ceiling and felt the stirrings of purpose in his belly. For a brief moment he attempted to imagine life without the horror of war. He tried to push the feelings away, but they refused to shift and clamped firmly on the rim of his mind. He ran his fingers across the scabbing scar by his left eye. If he'd lost his eye he would surely be finished with the army and forced to return to England to face an uncertain future, and worst of all the gallows. Suddenly he heard Moses suck in his breath and, putting his plate down, he placed his forefinger to his lips motioning for silence. It was faint at first, hardly audible, then it grew louder and Thomas had no need to strain to listen, the sound of the tins clinking and clanking reached his ears easily enough.

'A fox or a badger most likely,' Thomas said.

Moses never received the opportunity to respond to Thomas's supposition. His blood ran cold and his breath caught in his throat at the sound of a prolonged eerie howl stretching through the gloominess of dusk. He picked up Thomas's rifle and peered down the telescopic sight.

'Good grief,' he whispered.

'What, what is it?' Thomas frowned.

'Dogs, they must have escaped from a German dog pound and be close to starving by now. That's why they're after the livestock. Lucky for us the noise from the cans have frightened them away. But they'll be back for sure,' Moses said.

Thomas fingered the wounds on his neck and face and looked at his bandaged fingers. There was no way the two of them would be enough, they needed help. With his present injuries to contend with, it would be weeks before he would be fit enough to participate in any form of activity with a rifle. He needed the snipers.

Colonel Dickson stared at Thomas. 'How many did you say?' he exploded

'Twenty at least, Sir, maybe more. They have

442

formed a pack, and sooner or later others might well join them.'

'What do you suggest? How about we leave a few poisoned carcasses? That should get rid of the blighters.'

'Might kill a few, Sir, but still leaves the remaining livestock in danger. If I might make a suggestion, perhaps we should bring in a few more snipers, Sir, and kill the lot in one go.'

'Splendid idea,' he said, thumping the table. 'Why didn't I think of that? How many do you think we shall need?'

'A dozen, Sir, at the most. I can get Hill and Banks here later today. Sergeant Bull is on the Menin road. We'll need him to do the organising, he's good at that, Sir, and he'll know the whereabouts of the other snipers, Sir,' Thomas said.

'I'll write a letter to all ranks stating you are to have everything you need.'

He left Moses to guard the livestock in case the marauding dogs returned and made his way back to the trenches on foot. His damaged hand was in no condition to control a horse as lively as Isabelle. As he drew closer to the front his heart sagged and the temperature dropped, and he wanted to cover his ears and block out the sound of the guns. The tall elms and willows that had gently rustled over the sparkling lake submitted to the bare cold malevolent killing fields, where men died on the whim of another. The unrelenting throb of his partly severed fingers almost drove him to slice them off there and then and be done with them. He showed the letter to Captain Sands and waited.

'Of course, take whomever you need. Glad to see anyone get out of this hellhole for a moment's respite. When you return, come and see me. Might have need of you sniper chaps myself. Good grief, you look awful.'

'Yes, Sir, thank you, Sir. I will, as soon as we return,' Thomas nodded.

He found Stan munching his way through a bunch of raw carrots and drinking a bottle of German beer. He looked well enough and the colour had returned to his pale face. His hair was combed and parted down the middle and he was freshly shaved. Married life had obviously changed him, his trembling hands now reduced to a spasmodic twitch.

'Hello, Stan,' he said, startling him into dropping the bottle of beer.

'Bloody hell, General, did you have to do that?' he said, watching the liquid froth and run away between the duckboards. 'Jesus, look at the state of you, some bugger drop a bomb on you?'

'Where's Leslie Hill? We need you both at the chateau,' he answered, ignoring the questions. Stan insisted on calling it the big house, swearing blind a chateau was something you wore on your head, and nothing would force him to alter his mind.

Fired with the thought of escaping from the filth of the trenches he clambered over the edge, his weasel eyes glittering like newly polished diamonds. 'I'll find him, lad, don't move. The big house eh, lad? Sounds grand that does. What's the scoff like? Pig's head with an apple stuffed in its mouth? That's what them donkeys eat.'

Leslie Hill's mouth dropped open, and overcome with emotion he feasted his eyes on the unblemished countryside touched only by the coolness of an impending winter. He slowed to a halt, pulled off his helmet and gazed around, unable to halt the tears blurring his eyes, he was in paradise. Where else could he be? Even when he racked his brain for an answer he couldn't bring to mind the last time he had seen a tree in its entirety, not blackened by fire and gun-smoke or with pieces of human flesh hanging from the boughs. He couldn't remember anything as nature intended it to be, and at that moment it didn't matter. On reaching the lake beyond the elms, he ignored the cold and walked into the water fully dressed until he submerged from sight. Stan stripped down to stained underwear and dived in after him, shouting and laughing like a child.

As the weeks passed they were joined by all that remained of the company of snipers: Sergeant Bull, Atlas Blunder, Leslie Walsh and his flute, Walter Smith from Preston and Harry Kershaw from Morecambe. The rest, including Harry and John Burke, were never mentioned or heard of again. One day spirits rose when the indomitable Corporal Apple Crumble turned up with a donkey cart loaded with flares and hand grenades, and a special surprise: a crate of twelve Mauser sniper rifles fitted with telescopic sights captured from a German trench.

It was like old times watching Sergeant Bull bobbing up and down in his inimitable style as he scouted the pasture used during the night to pen in the animals.

'Good thinking, lad,' he said, 'stringing out the rows of tin cans. They make a grand warning system they do.'

Despite their arguments both Moses and Thomas were told by Sergeant Bull in no uncertain terms that they would take no further part in the proceedings due to their extensive wounds. One look from the sergeant's piercing eyes warned them it was fruitless to argue.

On the third night Thomas sat by the open window of his bedroom overlooking the pasture and meadow and watched the moon drifting in and out of the dark clouds. His fingers hurt like hell and with the pain came a shortened temper and a muddied mind. He untied the bandage and studied the wounds. The bones were separated and would take months to knit together properly, and even then they might never function properly again. He drew his bayonet and placed his hand palm down on the top of a set of drawers, and positioned the blade over the damaged fingers, closed his eyes and pushed the blade down. His breath came in short bursts and he groaned, surprised at the lack of pain and blood. With a towel wrapped round as a bandage he tucked his hand under his right armpit for comfort, like he had done when Mr Webster caned him for scratching his name on his desktop.

First the flares fluttered into the dark night, illuminating the meadow and pasture like huge falling searchlights, followed by the crump of the grenades. The sharp staccato of controlled gunfire poured into the unsuspecting dogs, and barking

446

and yelping in pain they jerked and died. It was over in a matter of minutes and the thin starving corpses of man's best friend were quickly collected and burned. Thomas watched sadly at the fire crackling and spitting until only charred bones remained.

'Well done, men. An excellent job performed with military precision,' Colonel Dickson enthused. 'Get a good night's sleep and come and see me in the morning.'

The following morning Sergeant Bull lined up the men in the best orderly fashion they could muster and waited for the arrival of Colonel Dickson. They stood weary and red-eyed, carrying war fatigue like a non-removable badge pinned to their souls and displayed for all to see. Tired of war and degradation, and lacking in hope, they waited patiently and uncomplaining because they were expected to.

'My God, I've never set eyes on such a bunch of rabble in my life. Don't they ever bother to wash and shave, Sergeant?' the colonel said, walking up and down the line of men and staring at the tattered unkempt uniforms with hardly a button between them.

'Where would they do that, Sir? These men are front-line soldiers, the last of a company of veteran snipers, Sir,' Sergeant Bull said, his manic eyes staring fit to explode and blow his head from his shoulders. 'Dirty they might be, rabble they are not. You'll find no finer men on the Western Front, Sir.'

Leslie Hill swivelled his eyes and bit his lip, and he gazed at the sergeant, this was the first time

Sergeant Bull had ever spoken of them in this manner. He felt the flush of pride heat his face and forced back his shoulders. Pushing out his chest he pulled himself upright and crashing his right foot down he stood rigidly to attention. Stan Banks followed suit, then the rest of the men. Thomas turned with military precision and smartness to Sergeant Bull.

'Company present and correct, Sergeant!' he bellowed like they would at Catterick.

'Thank you, Private Elkin,' Sergeant Bull nodded and turned to face the colonel. 'Company ready and awaiting orders, Sir,' he said, snapping up a textbook salute at the colonel.

Colonel Dickson sucked in his cheeks, stared down at his boots and felt the spur of shame rake his conscience. Now was the opportunity to portray a veneer of decency to real fighting men who looked upon officers as immoral vultures who preyed on the minds of young fools. The only battle he'd ever fought was to convey the correct amount of fresh eggs to GHQ each day. He cleared his throat, and pulled himself to attention, and returned Sergeant Bull's salute.

'Stand the men down, Sergeant. Tell Cockshead to prepare rooms and hot baths for the men and inform Cook to give them all they need to eat for the next seven days,' he ordered.

'Cookson, Sir,' Sergeant Bull said.

'What?'

'Cookson, Sir. His name is Cookson, not Cockshead.'

'Really, then why didn't the blasted fool say so?'

'I'm sure he had his reasons, Sir,' the sergeant

said scornfully.

For seven short days they ate until they could eat no more, while their dirty uniforms boiled in the scullery under the watchful eye of Marie Antoinette. When she set eyes on Stan Banks, she snarled in disgust, threw him into a tub of hot water and scrubbed him with a kitchen scouring brush while he howled in protest and told her he was a married man.

Chapter Twenty-Two

'I want you to re-form your sniper company. I'll leave you to decide how it should be done. By all accounts you once did a fine job, so let's hope you can do the same for us. Dismissed,' Captain Sands said to Sergeant Bull.

'Well, get to it, lad,' Sergeant Bull said to Thomas in the trenches. 'We've business in Polygon Wood tonight.'

'Polygon Wood?' Stan Banks said, elated at last the snipers were together again. 'Never heard of it. I know what a polygon is though, it's a figure with more than four sides, I think.'

'Thank you for that, Banks, I'm sure it will make everything worthwhile now we know the meaning of the word,' Sergeant Bull said patiently. 'After dark our job is to make our way through No Man's Land and tie explosives to the German barbed wire. Keep the explosives at least nine inches off the ground to keep it dry. In the morning we'll be going in first after the artillery bombardment. Our job will be to blow up the barbed wire and skirmish with the enemy to give the Aussies a chance to get at them. Good crowd the Aussies. Let's give them all the help we can.'

To refer to Polygon Wood as a wood would be a misnomer. There were no visible trees, only a few blackened stumps left from numerous previous assaults. A German stronghold, it needed to be cleared to make way for the assault on Ypres.

'All set, Stan?'

'As I'll ever be, Archie lad,' Stan said, shifting the backpack of explosives over his shoulders and slipping over the parapet. With the camouflaged hessian pulled over his helmet, he began working his way over the dusty terrain. Every few yards he stopped, allowing Thomas to pass him while he regained his breath. They repeated the procedure until eventually they reached the rolls of barbed wire, and immediately began tying explosives above ground as ordered, both aware if the scheme worked, thousands of lives would be saved from enemy machine-gunners. Glancing left and then right Thomas watched the rest of the snipers complete their task and start crawling back to their own trenches. Finished, Stan turned, gave the thumbs up and started to do the same. Two hours later they were all safely back and drinking a strong brew.

The bombardment started and continued non-stop through the night. Sleep became impossible, and once again men's eyes grew heavy with fatigue their bodies racked by tiredness. Gripping their rifles tighter they called upon an untapped energy. Those experienced from their time in the trenches retained the ability to sever their minds from their bodies and stared like zombies dislocated from reality into a valley of darkness. When the time came they would be ready.

At last dawn brought good weather and a dull sun shone overhead. Greatcoats along with all other unnecessary clothing were quickly discarded.

'Like Blackpool in June, that's what it reminds me of,' Apple joked, wrenching the lids off ammunition boxes with a claw hammer.

In the background, Walsh competed with the guns and piped *It's a Long Way to Tipperary* on his flute. Some joined in, grateful for the diversion, others stood quiet, unaffected by either the guns or the tune. Then there were those who stared at photos of loved ones and pressed their lips to the creased squares of thick paper. The younger ones stared at pictures of unknown wives and sweethearts taken from the tunic of an unknown fallen comrade. In their troubled minds it offered a morsel of comfort, a tiny sense of belonging. Dying never seemed so painful in the company of a pretty woman, regardless to whom she belonged.

'What did you do for a living, Apple, before you signed up to become an international playboy with the British Army?' Atlas called out.

'I had a shooting gallery on Blackpool front, eh t were grand it were.'

'Oh aye, and what were the targets?'

'Tin cans, lad, tin cans. What the bloody hell did you think they were, bloody Sitting Bull and his Red Indians?' Apple snapped.

'I had a go on them buggers once. Bloody barre
were that bent when I pulled trigger bloody corl
went straight into me ear. Deaf as a hungry dog's
belly for days I were.'

'Aye, lad. We must be using the same bloody
guns, I shot a Hun four times last week at point-
blank range and he didn't have a scratch on him
just got up and scarpered he did. I reckon Apple
takes gunpowder out of cartridges to make a
brew with,' Stan Banks said.

'Bollocks,' was the only response Banks heard
amidst a roar of laughter.

The ear-shattering bombardment maintained its
waterfall of exploding metal towards the German
lines. The Germans sat in their secure concrete
dugouts smoking cigarettes and drinking coffee
until the bombardment ceased and the Allies
began their attack. Then they would go out into
the trenches and mow the advancing enemy down
with their machine-guns. Unless the troops had
access to a clear pathway unhindered by barbed
wire, it would be another bloody slaughter.

Captain Sands sat on the firing step reading
poetry from a book written by Keats over the top
of his spectacles as though he was waiting for a
kettle to boil. At last the bombardment ceased
and observers peered though slits between sandbags. Visibility was zero, everything hidden
behind great clouds of smoke and dust. Now the
time had come to see whether the bombardment
had triggered the explosives on the barbed wire
Thomas went first and under the cover of clouds
of dust they made their way towards the wire
The gaps they encountered were few and far

between but not wide enough for a full blooded attack and dropping grenades next to the explosives, they retreated a few yards and waited. From somewhere, lessons had been learned and instead of a full frontal charge the attackers came in small groups, and assaults were made from the flanks pinning the Germans down.

'At last some bugger at HQ has grown a brain,' Stan called, grinning and relishing every moment of the Mauser fitted with the telescopic sight, as German after German disappeared in a frothy cloud of blood.

'Yes!' Thomas shouted over the screams of dying and injured men. 'After a thousand yards we'll stop and dig in, then wait for the counter-attack.'

And that's what they did. Bite and hold they called it. Repel the counter-attack and attack again. Thomas gathered his men together.

'Take out the pillboxes and machine-gun nests and the bastards are finished. Come on, lads, let's see what the bastards are made of!' he roared, getting to his feet in full view of the enemy. 'Well come on then, what are you waiting for?'

With the same shortened bayonet he'd used in the mines at Messines Ridge in his hand, Thomas closed in on the German trenches. Moses turned his head skywards and closed his eyes. Convinced Thomas was about to receive the only thing he ever wanted: a glorious death, to cleanse himself of guilt over his brother. Half-a-dozen Germans cowered, dropped their weapons and threw their hands up in surrender. A grizzled old German officer in a tight fitting uniform cut them down with his pistol. Thomas slashed at the officer's throat and with a grimace he thought of Archie.

'That's for you, Archie, that's for you,' he shrieked.

Inside the dugout he picked up a spade and buried it in the first German's skull. Like a man set adrift from reality, he cut and battered the four occupants cowering in the corner. When he came out he was soaked in blood. His mouth hung open as he panted for breath, his eyes crazed like those of a rabid animal. Thick streamers of snot hung from his nose and spittle dribbled from his mouth.

Moses stared with pity in his eyes and a great sadness surged over him like an incoming tide. Stan Banks's arrival brought the short cameo to a halt.

'Bloody hell, you look as if you fell out of an abattoir. You need to get yourself cleaned up. Gave old Fritz a right kicking this time, didn't we?' Stan Banks said, wiping the blood from his bayonet on a dead German. 'I reckon tomorrow's going to be another day like today.'

It didn't turn out to be a day similar to the day before. But a day they'd experienced many times in the past. The rain sheeted down. Dust turned into mud and mud evolved into a clinging quagmire. Artillery became bogged down and without a firm platform to fire from became useless. Once again it became a war of attrition, man versus man in close hand-to-hand fighting, no quarter asked and none given. The assailant would smell his victim's stale breath as he pushed his bayonet into the yielding flesh.

'Right, boys, one more big push and we can have a day off. This time we're going in with the Canadians,' Sergeant Bull called down the trench, attempting to muster morale into the weary men.

'What's up? The bloody Aussies had enough and pulled back for a rest, why haven't we? We can't go on forever,' Stan Banks grumbled.

'Yeah, Stan's bloody right, what's this place called we're supposed to take now while up to our necks in shit and mud?' Atlas Blunder complained.

'Poelcappelle, and I don't want any more talk like that. The quicker it's done the quicker we can go home to Ruby,' Sergeant Bull snapped angrily.

'Poor old Ruby, she'll be ninety by the time we've finished arsing around here for Chrissake,' Leslie Hill muttered, staring down at his boots. 'And my old woman will be a dipsomaniac by the time I get home.'

'Yes, that's if we ever get home alive,' another disgruntled voice came from the far end of the trench.

Sergeant Bull knew how the men felt. He felt the same – tired and weary of pulling their bodies through the clinging mud, muscles cold and aching, stopping every ten minutes to clean their rifles and change the hessian used to keep the weapons dry. The camaraderie was rapidly disintegrating and the steady banter absent from the everyday chatter. 'Our job is to work the flanks and knock out the concrete pillboxes,' he called out. 'We'll use hand grenades. We'll go in pairs, one to throw the grenades and the other to keep an eye out for snipers. This is going to be a hard fight, lads, so stick together and good luck. Moses, you're with me.'

Thomas looked up quickly. Moses glanced back and shrugged. He had always gone into battle with Thomas by his side and pairs always preferred to remain together. Sergeant Bull ignored the shrugs and grimaced.

'Come on, Archie boy, we'll crack a few heads between us,' Atlas grinned, listening to the slurp as he pulled his foot from the mud.

At twenty minutes past five in the morning, the creeping barrage opened up and Thomas and Atlas began making their way towards their objectives. The conditions were worse than anything they had experienced since the Somme, and men disappeared in water-filled shell holes never to be seen again as the battalion pressed forward. Atlas's legendary eyesight proved a God-send. He seemed to possess the ability to tell the colour of a chameleon's eyes from half a mile away.

'There, Thomas,' he said, nodding his head and raising his rifle. Thomas was still searching when Atlas sent the German to the bottom of the shell hole with a bullet in his temple. He despatched four more German snipers before Thomas had laid his eyes on any of them. Further on, they stopped, their way barred by a wide stream with two hundred yards of marshland on the other side.

'Wait here, I'll go on ahead and make sure it's clear and find a place to cross. Wait for my signal,' Thomas said, wading knee-high across the stream.

Atlas, as brave as he was, could only lumber under the best of conditions. He would make a

456

perfect target for the keen-eyed German snipers. Cautiously Thomas made his way through the marshland before dropping to his stomach and crawling towards the lip of a shell hole. With a bit of luck it might be empty and he could call Atlas to join him. A few feet away he strained his ears. Nothing. He pressed forward. About to slip into the trench, his heart skipped a beat and his breath stopped in his lungs at the sight of a German's head. Slowly it reared up from the shell hole and stared at him from less than two feet away, the face pale with red rosy cheeks and a flawless complexion, the eyes soft grey and wispy gold hair sprouted from beneath his helmet. He smiled a small smile revealing slightly protruding milk white teeth. The smile was friendly and warm, like the meeting of two old friends.

'Hello, Tommy,' he said.

Then, with a high-pitched scream, he disappeared from sight and slithered into the shell hole mumbling something about God, and vanished over the opposite edge leaving one of his boots and his backpack entrenched in the mud. Thomas closed his eyes and felt his heart hammering against his chest. In a mild state of shock he felt certain he was dreaming. At last he caught his breath and, raising his hand, signalled for Atlas to join him. From across the marsh Atlas came in a cloud of spray like a migrating water buffalo with half-a-dozen crocodiles on his tail, and fell head first into the shell hole. In the backpack they discovered an orange, a tin of dates, half a black sausage, a pack of playing cards made in the USA with pictures of undressed women on the back

457

and a photograph of a woman who might have been his mother.

'I like dates,' Atlas said, downing them in two gulps. Next he devoured the black sausage leaving Thomas with the orange, a picture of a middle-aged woman and a pack of playing cards. 'I like oranges as well,' he said.

Thomas handed him the orange and put the picture back in the pack, stuffed the cards into his tunic pocket, Moses or Stan would find a use for them.

Stealthily working their way round the back of the first concrete pillbox, they hesitated before taking stock of their position. Before them rows of concrete pillboxes were cleverly situated to provide a deadly crossfire, making any form of headlong attack tantamount to suicide. Inside they saw the movements of gunners preparing for the impending attack.

'Christ, our lads don't have a chance in hell of getting past that lot. We've got to try and get inside and turn the bloody gun on the Germans to give them a bit more time,' Thomas said.

'Good idea. Right now the troops are held up by the marshland. There were hundreds of them looking for somewhere to cross while I was down there. Do you think there'll be something to eat in those pillboxes?' Atlas asked.

'Yes, might be a couple of dead Germans,' Thomas grinned.

'Yeah, well I better go first then, before you get there and eat them all,' Atlas chuckled, moving away.

The entrances to the pillboxes were down four

steps cut into the earth, each pillbox contained a gunner and a loader. Atlas killed both in seconds. The only access available from which to use the sniper rifle was through a slit in the bunker overlooking the salient concealing the German snipers, as soon as the Germans realised they were being attacked from the rear they quickly started to fall back. Atlas carried the heavy machine-gun onto the roof of the box and started raking the remaining pillboxes behind them, while Thomas picked off anyone foolish enough to show himself. Within minutes the Allies had broken through and were looking for blood. Shouting and screaming they ran over the enemy trenches, intent on taking no prisoners. An exhausted lance corporal oozing sweat and spattered with blood stared at the carnage.

'Touch me, mate, and tell me I'm alive. Do I look like I'm alive?' he asked a dazed sergeant.

'Yeah, you're still alive, all right, lad, well done.'

No one took any notice of the scavengers taking watches and rings from warm dead bodies, ripping open pockets and searching for anything of value. Some even pulled boots off the corpses. They had learned long ago that there is no honour in death. There is death, and there is life, nothing in between. In Flanders death meant no more than a thrust of a bayonet or the squeeze of a trigger, or a boot squashing a rat's head.

Nine days later the snipers sighed with relief and moved back to a place called Vlamertinghe, a large tented rest and recreation area that served as a quiet area. Those numbed and shattered into silence by the sound of artillery were left to recover their senses. Wounds healed and most broken nerves remained broken forever. Men played football and cricket and slept in beds without their boots on. The luxury of sitting down to a meal without the company of a horde of squealing rats of all sizes scratching and clawing to get to the food was unheard of. They used knives and forks instead of the tip of a bloodstained bayonet, and kept their table manners impeccable in a bid to prove that they were men and not animals. They ate slowly, and methodically, without having to listen to hundreds of frogs and toads croaking through the night in the water-filled shell holes of No Man's Land. In a bid for sanity, some even denied the trenches had ever existed.

'Wanted to spend a bit of time with the missus, but the bastards wouldn't let me. My bones are aching for some slap and tickle, and I can't see me lasting much longer without the five-fingered widow,' Stan Banks moaned.

'The five-fingered widow?' Atlas said frowning. 'Who's she? I've never met a widow, you know.'

'Well, you'll be meeting plenty if you get out of this shithole,' Leslie Hill laughed. 'You'll be able to take your pick, mate.'

Thomas listened to the ever-present banter with a smile. To him it was an education in life, like being in a school for adults only. Everybody had a story to tell, some sad and some worse than sad, but all were told with a dry humour that brought a smile to the face.

'I've been out with a widow you know,' Harry Kershaw from Morecambe said with a serious

460

face. 'Married at the time she were. Seemed like her hands were on the end of rubber bands. I didn't know where they were going next I didn't, never left a button on me undone.' Sergeant Bull smiled a satisfied smile. Already their morale had begun to rise.

Thomas ran his fingers through his hair and cast his mind back. Dilly, Marie and Catherine seemed a million years ago, and Sarah the same, almost as if they were merely a figment of his imagination. His mood dipped when he conjured up a picture of his mother and father, and Ruby of course. There was always Ruby. Most of the Western Front knew about her by now. With a crooked smile he wondered how they might react if they knew she was a horse. For over fourteen months he'd served at the front, yet it seemed like he'd spent the whole of his life immersed in a trench. Chilly fingers began to probe their way into the uncovered crevices of the men's uniforms to invite a shudder. Winter loomed and threatened.

It was mid-afternoon when Moses wandered over to where his comrades were sitting. His attitude was languid and he seemed completely bored. 'If I spend another day here I'll die of boredom,' he said, sitting down on a creaking bench.

'Hey up, lad, here comes bobbing Sergeant Bull looking like a cat that's just been condemned to drown in a vat of fresh cream,' Atlas said.

'Private Elkin, follow me, at the double,' the sergeant snapped.

Thomas pulled himself to his feet. He felt his mouth dry, and his tongue felt as though it were glued to his palate. He paid no attention to the

461

stares and frowns of those around him and dropped in behind Sergeant Bull. There was a rattle in the sergeant's voice he had never heard before and in the back of his mind knew something was wrong.

'Something wrong, Sergeant?' he asked in a tinny voice.

'See the big tent with the automobile outside? Someone's waiting in there to see you. Best you don't keep them too long.'

Thomas clenched his fists. By the entrance to the tent, a military policeman stood at ease. Immediately, his eyes homed in on Thomas's pale worried face as though he already knew who he was, and his eyes narrowed into a sneering smile.

'Button up your uniform, Elkin. Colonel Simmons is waiting inside for you. On the double.'

Thomas felt a stab of coldness bury itself deep into his subconscious. He needed no prodding, already he knew he was about to serve himself up to the law as the murderer of his brother, and that all avenues of escape were slammed shut. The day he had always dreaded had arrived.

Colonel Simmons was a small man with fine wispy grey hair that moved and bounced with every word he spoke. His face shone pink and his lips were thin and pursed. To some he might appear nondescript. Seated behind a portable table he watched Thomas through large watery eyes that blinked so slowly the movement must surely have left him blinded for a number of seconds. To his right a corporal sat armed with a pencil and notebook ready to take down the proceedings.

462

'Thomas Elkin, you are under suspicion of being responsible for the death of your brother, Archibald Elkin, impersonating the said soldier while under-age and being in possession of his uniform. What do you have to say?'

Thomas heard his own gasp whoosh from his chest and he broke into an uncontrollable fit of coughing, feeling the stretching in the pit of his stomach. He stared into the hazy mass that had once been the colonel's face, and fear and confusion blurred his eyes and senses. How could they know after all this time, how could they know?

'There must be some mistake, Sir. My name is Archie Elkin. It's here in my pay-book,' he stuttered.

Colonel Simmons shrugged. 'Bring in Private Davis,' he called to the guard standing outside.

Thomas forced himself to breathe easily and remain perfectly still, his face impassive. He needed to clear his mind and deal with one thought at a time. Moses's words echoed through his brain and he grasped at their meaning with both hands. He had witnessed a death but never committed a murder. Now at this moment the words offered no form of solace or peace of mind. The sound of the tent flap drawn to one side shook him from his incumbent thoughts and he turned his head.

'Do you recognise this man, Private Davis?' Simmons asked.

'Yes, sir, that's Thomas Elkin, brother of Archie Elkin. They live just a half mile from my village.'

'You are absolutely certain?'

Thomas felt the saliva rise in his mouth and swallowed, the thought of the gallows swayed

463

into his mind. He recognised Jed Davis immediately. The brother of Josie who he'd discovered lying half undressed with Archie in the barn.

'Yes, sir, that's Thomas, not Archie, I'm certain. Where is the bastard, Thomas? Ran away like the useless bloody coward he is, eh, and left you to do his dirty work, as usual?' Davis said vehemently. 'When I heard the name mentioned I thought it was him. It's Josie, she's with child, a daughter, and she says it can only be his. Pa's put her in a place for unmarried mothers. You tell your brother that when I find him I'll bloody kill him with my bare hands and feed him to the dogs, you remember that.'

'That'll do for the time being, Davis, wait outside,' Simmons snapped, leaning back in his chair waiting for Davis to leave. 'Tell me where your brother is, Elkin, and I want the truth!'

'I don't know,' Thomas stammered weakly, attempting to gather what little strength he had left. The response was negligible.

'When was the last time you saw him?'

'I can't remember.'

'When was the last time you saw your parents? I know you have taken home leave twice.'

'I can't remember.'

'Can't remember? For God's sake, get a grip of your senses, man. How did you obtain your brother's uniform. Don't you realise your life is at stake here?'

'I can't remember.'

'You are a traitor, Elkin. A traitor to your country and a traitor to your parents. I will ask you one more time, where is your brother? I put it to you that you have killed him and taken his place in an effort to conceal your crime.'

Thomas's hands trembled and he felt a rage rise within his chest so strong he thought he might be the victim of lunacy. He told himself he must not lose control, and yet he already had. They wanted him to fall to pieces, to blurt out all he knew and more, to admit to coldblooded murder, and tell them about the pigs and how they ripped his brother's body to pieces. Fear pierced his guilty conscience and fate held the address of his final destination, the gallows. But although he was innocent, an English court of law must prove him guilty in accordance with the law of the land. Moses had told him so. But why should he die for something as rotten and vile as Archie Elkin?

'No, Sir, I did not kill my brother,' he said calmly.

Colonel Simmons sighed, clasped his hands together and rested his elbows on the tabletop. Blinking slowly, his watery eyes settled on Thomas's face. From records he was aware of the Military Medal that Thomas had won freeing Australian prisoners-of-war and of the sniper company that had helped save countless soldiers from death by German machine-gunners. He held no personal grudge against him, and if anything he would reluctantly admit he admired him. However, his job was to find the truth and nothing could be allowed to interfere with the course of justice. The British constitution respected the rights of every man, and boy, and he would receive a fair hearing in accordance with

465

the enormity of his crime.

'Thomas Elkin, I am of the opinion that you have committed a crime of which you must stand trial in the law courts of England. Therefore, you will be taken to the 1st Army HQ at Aire under guard, and from there you will be accompanied to England and handed over to the civilian authorities to stand trial for the murder of your brother, Archibald Elkin,' he said in a monotone voice. 'Corporal Barnes, place him in handcuffs and keep him in confinement overnight.'

The corporal pushed the pencil into his tunic pocket and closed his notebook and, standing to his feet, pulled a pair of handcuffs from his tunic and snapped the bracelets over Thomas's wrists. Cuffed to the rear bumper of the open-top automobile, Baines threw a groundsheet over his shoulders and left him to the mercy of the chill autumn night air. The sneering Military Policeman, Private Theakston, who stood guard outside the tent, quickly settled himself comfortably in the back of the vehicle and fell asleep.

That night Thomas spent much of the time unable to sleep due to the throbbing pain tormenting his arms as the handcuffs ground and chafed into his wrists. With his back to the vehicle, he had no way of adjusting his position. The slightest movement brought more agony and he dare not close his eyes and relax. Instead he envisaged a lifetime in prison, confined between four walls until the mind could take no more and he would end up mad, or perhaps when he reached hanging age they would take him outside and pull the noose around his neck. His parents would learn of his crime against their son, everyone would know, and for the rest of their lives they would suffer the sneers and snide comments of those who were once their friends.

Tears welled in his eyes as he conjured up a picture of his mother's fragility the last time he saw her. She wouldn't have the strength to survive the everlasting shame, no matter how strong his father was. The tear ducts burst open and a rage of hot unstoppable tears flowed freely from his face. Frantically he struggled to loosen his hands, ignoring the searing pain as the cuffs ripped open his wrists. The notebook ... he wanted the notebook in his tunic pocket that held the crushed daisy he'd taken from the windowsill of the farmhouse. He wanted one last contact with his mother.

It hadn't been Stan Banks' intention to stare at Sergeant Bull, not from the corner of his eyes like he normally would, but full on. Sergeant Bull fidgeted aware of Banks's interest in the whereabouts of Archie. Finally, Stan plucked up the courage and spoke.

'Where's Archie, Sarge, nobody has seen him since he left with you yesterday?'

'None of your business, lad.'

'Aye, maybe it's not, but I'm making it my business.' Stan gulped, realising what he had just said.

'Don't lay your mouth on me, Banks, ever. Do I make myself understood?'

'I asked you a civil question. We all want to know where Archie is,' Stan persisted, growing angry.

'We have been through a lot of shit together, and me and the men are not about to let him disappear without knowing the reason why.'

Sergeant Bull reined in his anger and allowed his temper to cool. It was a fair question asked in a straightforward manner. If he'd wanted to he could have eased Stan Banks's curiosity, or certainly have raised it to a higher level. He remained tight-lipped. He'd been ordered to take Thomas to the Provost Marshall's quarters, and like all good soldiers he obeyed orders. He knew nothing more.

'We're moving out tomorrow to a place called Droglandt, an airfield used by the Royal Flying Corps. You'll receive training when we get there. Tell the others to be ready to leave first thing in the morning,' Sergeant Bull said, turning away.

'Here, get this down you,' Corporal Baines said undoing the handcuffs and handing Thomas a mug of steaming hot tea. 'Bloody hell, what's happened to your wrists?'

'I had a bad night,' Thomas mumbled, grabbing the mug.

'Theakston, you fucking mean minded arsehole, get some bandages and bind the prisoner's wrists, and keep the cuffs off until I tell you different, understand?' Baines screamed at the sleeping guard. 'I've had enough of your antics, you cruel bastard. Watch your step from now on or I'll put a fucking bullet in you myself.'

Theakston pulled himself from the rear of the automobile accompanied by his fixed sneer. He was a coward, and to make matters worse he knew

468

it. He envied the men who waited in the trenches for certain death. He envied their coolness in the face of the enemy and the manner in which they went over the top. To him they were Hectors, Lysanders, Alexanders, men of consummate courage like ancient heroes written in legend. So, riddled with self-hate and wretchedness he tormented his prisoners and never squandered the opportunity to show them that he was their master, happy only when they suffered and bent to his will.

With a snigger he looked at the wounds on Thomas's wrists. 'They'll have plenty of time to heal where he's going.'

'Corporal Baines,' Colonel Simmons called, 'we'll be leaving within the hour, make sure the prisoner's fed and allowed his ablutions.'

'Yes, Sir,' Baines answered. 'Listen, Elkin. Promise me you won't try any funny stuff and I'll leave the cuffs off.'

Thomas nodded and kept his face blank. He wanted to tell them all they could do whatever they wished and that he didn't give a shit. Instead, he refrained from a futile display of bravado and remained quiet.

One hour later, to the second, they began the journey to Aire and the end of Thomas's life as he'd known it. Colonel Simmons insisted that Thomas sit in the front next to Theakston, who drove, while he and Baines, armed with pistols, remained in the back. Thomas felt exhaustion suck the marrow from his bones and he slumped back against the stuffed horsehair seat, his body cried out for the release of sleep.

'If you try to make a break, Elkin, I will have no hesitation in shooting to wound,' the colonel said. 'Be assured, you will stand and answer the charges against you, do you understand?'

Thomas ignored the remark and stared dead ahead as they pulled even further away from the front lines. The previous evening he had willingly allowed his body to be drained of all hope. It was time to pay for his crime and he was fast approaching the end of his tether. Gone were the nerves of iron, the will of steel. Replaced by a trance-like state of lethargy and moral insensibility, even the spattering rain held no interest, or diverted his attention from the darkness brooding deep inside of him. He felt spent, like a used match drifting in the wind.

'Over there, man. By that wrecked farmyard. Get a move on. We can stop and raise the hood on this blasted contraption. Damn weather,' Colonel Simmons grumbled.

Theakston dropped into a lower gear, pulled off the road and headed for the part-roofless building. By now, the rain had increased and Thomas raised his head and looked up into the sky, allowing the moisture to caress his face and cleanse the congested sweat and thick grime from his skin. Suddenly, he felt better, as though the rain had washed away his guilt. He felt clean and free of the past, and closer to God than at any other time in his life.

'Right, everyone inside,' the colonel ordered. 'You included Elkin. Out of the rain, can't have you catching a cold.'

Thomas felt the rumble in his stomach followed

by the laughter exploding from his chest. For Chrissake, he thought, they can throw us into trenches to get our heads blown off, they can order us across No Man's Land to be mown down by machine-guns, and they can demand we live in trenches like pigs in our own shit with rats for company, but allow a prisoner to catch a cold? What a catastrophe that would be. Bound to go down in the annals of warfare for future generations to ponder over.

'Something struck you as funn...' the colonel said, cut off mid-sentence by the sound of the gunshot and the bullet entering his heart.

From nowhere the appearance of three German soldiers took them completely by surprise. Thomas automatically dropped to a crouch. Watching and swaying as he chose his target, with his fingers outstretched like claws he launched himself at the German in the middle. Reflexively, he reached out for the German's eyes and felt his fingers press into the sockets. The German dropped his weapon and, screaming in agony, fell kicking and twitching to the floor, clutching at the remains of his crushed eyeballs. Lashing out with his feet, Thomas sent his foot into the groin of the German to his left. The man grunted, stood his ground and squeezed the trigger of his rifle, the bullet flew harmlessly over Thomas's shoulder and into the face of Theakston sending a fountain of blood gushing from his eye. Theakston groaned and slumped to the floor. Thomas slammed his fist into the German's face. As he staggered back Thomas wrenched the rifle from the floor and put two bullets into the man's brain. Spinning round,

471

he saw the third German on top of Baines with the point of his bayonet about to enter his throat. Baines's eyes sprouted terror and blood dribbled from the corner of his mouth as he bit into his cheek. He mumbled something incoherent Thomas couldn't understand as the point pierced the skin and blood bubbled to the surface. Thomas did not dare fire in case the German slumped down and sent the blade into Baines's neck. Instead, he reached out from behind, and placing one hand on the German's jaw he jerked the head round until he heard the crack of the neck snapping.

It was over. Baines lay gasping and wheezing for breath, thankful for his life. Behind him lay the dead bodies of the colonel and Theakston, whose cowardice would never be proven or brought to the fore. He would be feted as a brave soldier who died in action. Thomas gazed at the carnage with a soulless stare and shrugged. In only a matter of seconds, five out of seven men had died and once again he wasn't included in the body count. Baines pulled himself up and sat on the floor, and with his arms wrapped around his knees he rocked from side-to-side like a child and began to weep uncontrollably. In a moment of unguarded gentleness, Thomas leaned forward and placed his hands on his shoulder.

'Come on, lad. It's all over now. Get yourself together,' he said softly.

'For God's sake, where did you learn to fight like that?' Baines sniffed. The two men locked eyes in silence for what seemed an eternity. 'Yes, you're right. Time to move on,' Baines said. 'Come on, let's get out of here. Where'd they come from anyway?'

'Most likely deserters trying to find their way home from this shithole, and who can blame them?' Thomas shrugged, making his way to the automobile and climbing into the front seat.

Baines slipped in beside him and fired up the engine. Thomas stretched out his legs and pushed his shoulders back to ease the ache in his arms.

'What are you doing, Elkin?' Thomas frowned and turned his head. 'On your way, lad. You'll go no further with me. I owe you my life, I'll clear this mess up and no one will be any the wiser. Go and find your regiment, or whatever it is you do, and good luck. Hey, who knows, I might even get a medal out of this,' he laughed, grating the automobile into gear.

Nightfall had stolen over the land when Thomas pedalled into the rest area on the bicycle he'd stolen from an irate Scotsman. Sergeant Bull saw him first and stiffened with surprised.

'Everything sorted, Private Elkin?'

'Yes, Sergeant, I reckon it is.'

'Good. Let me give you some advice lad. Don't dwell too long on the past. It won't do you any good. Tomorrow is always more important than yesterday, remember that. Now join the rest of the men, we move out in the morning.' Sergeant Bull nodded.

Thomas derived a brief comfort from the words, then realised they weren't empty and meaningless. Somehow, Sergeant Bull knew his secret.

'You know?' he said quietly.

473

'Not much goes on round here I don't know about,' Sergeant Bull answered. 'I know what kind of person you are, Elkin, and I believe your problem was not of your making. Best forget the past and start a new life, let the rest take care of itself. And I'll tell you something else lad, you'll not catch me staying in Blighty after this bloody war is over.'

'Where will you go?'

'Canada, that's the place for me. Land of opportunity and freedom away from the horse-faced bastards that run England. Already been too much blood spilt for that lot.'

'Do you think I could go there?' Thomas said feeling his spirits rise.

'Come and see me when this bloody mess is over, and we'll have a chat.'

When at last he laid his head on his pillow he felt relief flood into his veins, and once more he contemplated life over death. That night sleep came quickly, but not unaccompanied. Archie came with a vengeance as if seeking retribution for his brother's unpremeditated escape from the clutches of the law. He came so close with his malevolent bloodshot eyes staring like a madman that Thomas thought he could smell his beer-stained breath and cowered beneath the thin blanket. He tried to call out to tell Archie to leave him alone, but the sound stayed trapped in his throat when he felt the weight on his shoulder. He shot bolt upright in naked fear.

'Hey, lad,' Stan Banks said softly. 'Settle down and try to get some sleep.'

He blinked and lay back without uttering a word, feeling Stan pull the blanket over his still body.

Chapter Twenty-Three

1918

Christmas at Droglandt was as Christmas should be, the celebration of the birth of Jesus Christ. Church services, evensong and carol singing were delivered with reverence and controlled gusto. Small trees were decorated with lights and Christmas parcels arrived from Blighty for the lucky ones. In the pilots' mess Leslie Walsh performed with his flute and brought a sombre silence with a haunting version of *Silent Night*. Later, he accompanied Sergeant Bull's singing of the Christmas favourite *Oh Come All Ye Faithful*, leaving not a dry eye in sight.

For Stan it was a posting made in heaven. No more sombre nights and days spent sharing filthy trenches with hordes of squealing rats. No more chewing on tinned food accompanied by the nauseating stench of human excrement. From now on they sat at tables and ate like a normal human being. Of the pilots he stood in awe, and with respectful eyes he stared in unbridled admiration as they waited like knights of old for the call to aerial combat, dressed in cap, goggles and large pairs of leather gloves. Most, still in their teens waited for their first trip into air warfare. A jollier bunch he had never seen, always happy and laughing away the horrors of the war as they smoked their pipes, drank coffee by the gallon and acted as though they were already grown men. The war as Stan had known it seemed far away.

The 28 Squadron was aptly commanded by a Canadian whom everyone addressed as Major Billy, a man with a reputation for bravery and the distinction of a flying ace with over twenty kills to his name. Just to even matters up, Thomas, Stan and Moses put on a shooting display of their own. They stood at four hundred yards and with apples as targets the young pilots were left with their mouths hanging open in astonishment at their speed and accuracy. The pilots responded with a show of aerial musketry in their Sopwith SE5as, and a mutual respect quickly sprang up between the men of the air and their protectors on the ground.

Of the original forty snipers only Thomas, Leslie Hill and Stan Banks remained. The rest, including Moses, were relative newcomers. Those who died had served bravely and paid the ultimate price for being born into the world at the wrong time and led by men unfit to do so. Most were never found to be put to rest in the eyes of God. Apple kept the records of their names and places of their demise. A padre billeted outside the airfield in the village and Sergeant Bull arranged a service to bless those who no longer served with them. Moses refused to attend, still unsure of the meaning of Christianity and adamant that he would never seek God again. God would have to seek him and ask forgiveness for allowing the killing fields to exist to return him to his faith. The men murmured quietly between themselves. Some disagreed and some gave a non-committal shrug, muttering that religion was a personal matter between man and his soul, but Moses was steadfast and the nine men prayed without him.

'Who's he, Sir?' Stan asked pointing. 'That man over there with the bandages on his head and playing around with the golf club.'

'That, old boy, is Lieutenant Singh, one of our best pilots,' the young pilot chuckled. 'And they aren't bandages on his head, that's his turban. He's a Sikh and it's a sign of his faith.'

Stan looked nonplussed, why would anyone who was sick, regardless of his faith, wear a turban on his head instead of bandages?

Thomas sloshed cold water over his head and face and rubbed hard with his hands. His hair had grown long and he reminded himself to visit the cook who doubled as a hairdresser for the squadron. Today he and Stan were manning the Vickers on the west side of the airfield, and he glanced through the thin grey light of dawn, feeling pleased at not seeing the drizzle of cold rain. It was early April 1918 and soon spring, his favourite season, would be upon them. He had put on weight and now stood at over six feet. Time had healed the scars on his neck and face to just faint white jagged lines and the loss of his fingers was never a factor. True, Archie visited most nights, more enraged than ever, but he waited expectantly and pushed him to one side.

The sharp rapid clattering of cold aircraft engines warming up disturbed the vibrancy of a fresh spring morning. Overhead a skein of migrating geese honked a warning that better weather was on its way. Mechanics waved and signalled, and teased the aircraft onto the grassy area used as a runway ready for take-off. The young pilots ran their perfunctory tests before they gunned the engines to full pitch, and with a cheery smile and friendly wave sent the flimsy aircraft bouncing across the field on pram wheels before pulling back on the stick and left planet earth trailing in their wake. Thomas looked up and saw the rapid orange flashes as the pilots tested the guns and circled while waiting to be joined by the remainder of the squadron. Shortly, they would fly off in their familiar arrowhead formation, seeking the excitement of a mid-air joust with Fritz. Their life expectancy in the air was no more than eighteen hours.

'Hello, Stan, you're early. You didn't shit the bed last night did you?' Thomas grinned, slipping into the fox hole.

'Did you know that a nom de plume is a borrowed name? It says so in this dictionary one of the pilots gave me. Why would someone want to borrow a name?'

'Guns tested?'

'Yeah, did it while you were still dreaming of Ruby.'

At last the sun peeked shyly from behind a dark cloud and the wet leaves of the beech trees glistened and floundered in a small breeze. A flock of starlings dipped and fluttered in unison from a small copse to search for the first meal of the day. Another ten minutes passed. Thomas checked the time on his pocket watch and looked across the airfield. As usual, Sergeant Bull was precisely on time. And jumping from the driver's seat of the five-ton armoured lorry mounted with a Vickers naval gun he approached the fox hole. After a detailed check of the Vickers machine-gun he snatched the dictionary from Stan's hand.

'You're on duty, Banks. If you want to read you should have joined a library and not the army,' he snapped angrily, leaving Stan glaring after him as he bobbed towards the lorry and drove away.

'Sometimes he gets on my bloody tits,' Stan grumbled.

Thomas ignored the complaint and searched the sky for any sign of German intruders. Stan placed his thumb on one of his black front teeth and jerked it back and forth.

'I reckon I've got the makings of toothache,' he said. 'Do you reckon there's a dentist in the village?'

'A dentist? You need a bloody coalminer to remove one of your teeth.'

'Arseholes.'

Thomas grinned and shaded his eyes with his hands. At first it looked like a speck on the horizon. Then as the seconds passed by it grew larger and became a dot of red and white in the Wedgewood-blue sky. Stan looked up then made a dive for the gun and pulled the cocking lever into position like he'd been taught. Thomas knelt with the canvas ammunition belt resting in the palm of his hands, ready to feed in two-hundred-and-fifty rounds of .303 bullets every thirty seconds.

'Aircraft approaching!' Stan roared, ringing the heavy brass warning bell.

With his thumbs pressed ready against the firing buttons he watched through expectant eyes as the shape drew closer, weaving from side-to-side and reducing height as it approached. Then he saw the large black menacing crosses painted on each wingtip and on the side of the fuselage.

'Come on, come on, just a little nearer, you murdering bastard, I'm waiting,' he whispered loudly.

Thomas remained still, like a statue, keeping his eyes firmly on the ammunition belt. The moment it expired he would feed in another, the way Sergeant Bull had taught him. Don't rush, lad, keep it quick and easy. A jammed gun's no use to anyone, the sergeant had said, and Sergeant Bull never told lies. Stan's thumbs pressed down on the buttons and the rapid chatter of outgoing hot metal tore towards the oncoming aircraft. As he fired the vibration sent his helmet slipping forward over his eyes. He leaned his head back to prevent it obstructing his line of vision. Thomas began to laugh as Stan jerked his head first one way and then the other like an Eastern belly dancer might as he fought to regain his line of sight.

The orange flashes from the aircraft wiped the smile from his face as a stream of bullets danced and spurted towards their fox hole. Something tugged the cuff of Thomas's uniform and he felt his boot knocked to one side, and then with a great rush it was upon them, the engine squealing and roaring like a hundred maddened

480

banshees, the shadow, like a great passing bird, blocked out the sun. Then it was gone, winging its way to the safety of the drifting clouds. Stan stared angrily into the bottom of his helmet with the strap entangled round his ears.

'Fucking thing!' he roared, and madder than a sack of snakes he threw the helmet out of the fox hole. 'It's about as much use as a leaking kettle in a drought.'

The hole in Thomas's cuff showed where a bullet had missed his hand by a fraction of an inch, and the heel of his boot had been shot off, taking part of the sole with it.

Later they stood and clapped when the squadron returned, smiling at Lieutenant Singh as he jump off the wing of his Sopwith wearing an oversized flying helmet over his turban.

'Oh dear, dear!' he exclaimed. 'I've had such a wonderful time up there today.'

All of a sudden, for only a fleeting moment, it didn't feel like a war any more. It was unreal and amusing. With a quizzical grin on his face Thomas watched the pilots laughing and joking. It was as if they had just spent the evening down the Bull and Bush playing darts for half pints.

Outside the air hung still and silent, the only sound to prick his ears coming from the ever present dampened thump of the guns somewhere far away on the front line. In the wooden hut Thomas sank onto his bed and for the first time in months recalled his vow of death. Why he allowed the mental process to cogitate he failed to understand, and in a daze attempted to dismiss the thought from his mind, yet like always it persisted. Most nights he summoned up the strength and courage to push away the torment Archie heaped upon him without the slightest hint of mercy. For a time it felt as if the agony had diminished. Perhaps he thought Archie's eternal quest for revenge was at last fading.

News of the Germans' retreat to the Hindenburg line meant the Germans were losing the war, particularly with the advent of the American presence. His newly-found courage deserted him and steadily the horror of existence after the war built up in his mind, the once almost forgotten flames of his extinction fanned his imagination. He must die, he must keep his promise. Like an eternal curse the lifeless face of Archie sprang into his mind, his eyes empty and staring, his lips cold and blue and his neck swathed in a deep open gash held only by threads of dried skin. Thomas squeezed his eyes shut and again struggled against the overriding burden of guilt flowing through his veins like lava from a volcano. Now, after all he had been through why couldn't the past sever itself from the shackles of his soul?

On 1 April 1918, The Flying Corps were awarded the title Royal Air Force and pilots celebrated as much as Major Billy would allow. Completely fascinated by their attitude, and realising they were mainly upper-class former schoolboys with an insatiable zest for life on the ground as well as a complete disregard of danger in the air, Thomas enquired why they never used parachutes.

'Ah, now there's a question,' Pilot Officer Daniel said. 'The beggars seem to think we will abandon the fight too early and jump, the saucy bounders. Damn airplanes are only made of wood wrapped in Irish linen and take off and land on pram wheels. I say, why don't you let me take you up for a spin? We've got a few twin-seaters, and I'm sure the major wouldn't mind too much. Be here after lunch about half-past one.'

Thomas's eyes narrowed and he nervously rubbed his hands up and down the sides of his legs, 'I'd like that,' he said.

'Bloody hell,' Stan Banks said, growing pale in the face. 'You've got some nerve going up in one of those death contraptions.'

Moses winced and feeling unsure of Thomas's motives watched him with suspicious eyes. He was aware that front-seat gunners often fell out of the aircraft when the pilots were forced to take evasive action. Thomas pulled on flying boots and a flying helmet and climbed into the front cockpit of the Bristol F26, known with affection as the Biff. Daniel smiled when he saw the Mauser rifle in his hands.

Suddenly Thomas felt the surge of an animal instinct for self-preservation, and gritting his teeth forced his eyes to remain open. Already he regretted his foolhardy decision and apprehension leapt into his heart tormenting his imagination. The flimsy aircraft bounced and rocked over the airfield as though it were ready to collapse and judder into a thousand pieces, leaving him lying broken and helpless. He gripped the sides of the cockpit with white-knuckled hands as though to hold the aircraft in one piece, convinced that the machine would never leave the ground. Suddenly, the bouncing ceased and for a moment he thought they had stopped in the middle of take-off.

He sighed with relief when the aircraft rose smoothly over the treetops, below the ground pulled away at an angle his brain failed to comprehend. A cold wind pulled at his face muscles distorting his features and he closed his mouth to catch his breath. He relaxed his grip and peeked cautiously over the side. It felt good, different, better than a fun ride at a fairground.

Over the trenches of the Western Front he looked down on men that looked like slow-moving ants. Huge field guns stood like toys in a row and the trenches resembled a maze of furrows ploughed by a loose horse and plough. He smiled with pleasure when the plane banked and dropped away to port, turning his stomach over and over on the descent to the safety of Mother Earth. When Daniel gunned the engines open and pulled back on the stick, the machine responded magnificently nosing up into the clouds, forcing him down into the seat. His smile grew wider and he wanted to laugh out loud, he wanted people to see him looking down on a flock of starlings flying below him. The plane banked and the world opened out as they passed through vapours of drifting clouds, he raised his hand to wipe away the moisture from his goggles obstructing his view. Finally he released his feelings and screeched with childish delight as the ground rushed towards him as they approached the airfield. He waved madly at anyone watching when they skimmed over the buildings and zoomed out of sight to gain altitude.

Suddenly, without question or condemnation, he released his grip and placed his hands on his lap. His saliva turned bitter and sour in his mouth, and solemn faced he waited for the aircraft to bank one more time allowing him the opportunity to slither from the seat and plummet to the earth below. Now would be a good time to end his life. Suddenly, from across the sun he saw the black spot, like an approaching bird growing larger. For a moment he felt a tinge of dread and again his hands reached out and gripped the sides of the aircraft. He watched the spot draw closer then gain altitude and circle overhead like a menacing bird of prey, the black crosses on the wing tips and fuselage turned his dread to naked fear.

Without warning, Daniel banked away to the port and started to climb to meet his adversary head on. Panic clawed at Thomas's senses. He grabbed at the machine-gun mounted in front of him as the air became filled with tracer bullets. Daniel pulled back on the stick, and with the engine screaming in protest Thomas felt himself forced back into his seat and struggled to control the mounted machine-gun. At last his fingers hovered over the firing buttons and he fired two short bursts, he pressed again, nothing. His guns jammed, here he was, a novice in the art of aerial warfare, then feeling cold yet perfectly calm he reached for his rifle and rested it on the fuselage.

The German aircraft, black and venomous, whizzed over their heads and banked, then turned to face them just below their flight line. Daniel, realising Thomas's intentions for a split second held his line, and at two hundred yards Thomas raised the rifle, aimed and squeezed the trigger. The German pilot jerked back and looked around him as if expecting to see a second aircraft, then slumped forward. The nose of the aircraft dropped, and cart-wheeling and spinning out of control headed down out of control.

Daniel circled overhead and watched the aircraft smash into the ground then explode into a ball of orange fire. With a grim smile he pulled back on the stick, climbed and turned eastward.

Thomas eased his near-freezing body from the cockpit and fell to his knees as the young pilots surged towards him, offering their congratulations.

'I say old chap, damned fine piece of musketry that.'

'Just a lucky shot,' he stammered.

He spent some time struggling to right his mind and failed to understand their excited emotions at what he'd just achieved: one dead German. In the trenches he'd killed twenty in a quarter of the time. Nevertheless, the kill was attributed to him and his name was entered in the squadrons' records book for eternity as having shot down an enemy aircraft. When he finally found himself alone he sneered with a barely suppressed anger. He had just allowed the best opportunity of ending his life to pass him by. He had been ready to jump from the aircraft, until the untimely event of the German turning up to scupper his plans. There was no way he could have left Mullins to the mercy of the enemy aircraft.

It was a mild evening when he left with Moses, Atlas and Stan Banks to celebrate his notoriety in the air in the small village on the edge of the airfield. The countryside basked in drowsiness. Overhead the sky hung soft pink with flounces of gold and pale blue. As they walked Sergeant Bull's words of a new life in Canada filtered through his mind. A new beginning away from the horror of war, he had said. Perhaps it might work for him.

At the inn they would often take a drink and sing bawdy songs with anyone present, including the locals who never missed the opportunity of a free drink, and he would sit quietly in the corner and sip lemon water. It was the happiest any of them had been during their time on the front, a cushy number, they called it. Clean, dry clothes, three hot meals each day, and a real bed to sleep on. They even dared to hope that they might see out the war on the airfield. Major Billy seemed happy with their input and Atlas gave him lessons on how to be a crack shot with a rifle. He'd taken on Stan a couple of times to no avail and took his defeats in good spirits. When Moses offered him advice he quickly declined without giving a reason and walked away, leaving Moses staring angrily after him. Yet, still Thomas couldn't completely escape from the haunting appearances of Archie. Like the moon, he came at night, jeering and taunting as the noose swayed and threatened in his hand.

'If I should die,' he said to Moses, while the others were getting drunk and throwing horseshoes at a metal spike stuck into the ground, 'what would happen to everything I own? My money and my pocket watch for instance?'

'It would go to your next of kin, unless you

make out a will,' Moses said, looking at him from the corner of his eye. 'Why, you are not thinking of doing something stupid again are you?'

'I don't have a next of kin, so I'm going to make out a will and leave everything I own to you. I have thought about this often, it's what I want,' he said solemnly.

'Don't talk about such things, I don't want to hear it,' Moses said sharply.

From the corner of his eye he watched Thomas and wondered what had prompted him to ask the question.

'No, I want to. You are the nearest thing I have to family now. I can never return home, I trusted you to keep my secret and you did. And anyway, you are my best friend, along with Stan. I've decided.'

And that was that. Moses knew that once Thomas made up his mind about anything, nothing would shake him into changing it, so he remained silent. Eventually growing tired of throwing horseshoes, Moses, Stan and Les Hill joined a group of off duty pilots inside the inn. Thomas remained alone outside deep in thought.

The distant drone of the three approaching aircraft did nothing to necessitate their attention. Aircraft took off and landed at short intervals throughout the day while starting or ending missions. The first bomb erupted, lifting Thomas clean over a low slate wall. Clambering to his feet he saw the black German crosses on the wingtips. The second and third bombs crashed into the wood-framed inn sending up a mass of red and orange flames licking avidly at the falling dusk and lighting up the sky. Thomas hesitated for a split second and with a seemingly scant concern for his own safety rushed into the inferno of flames and choking smoke. He saw Moses first, and heaving him onto his shoulder staggered out and left him gasping for air on the damp grass.

Inside the burning inn Stan Banks felt the flames attack his body and groped at thin air while searching for the exit, Thomas grabbed his arm and led him outside then returned into the inferno. Beneath a pile of burning timbers he found Atlas lying with his eyes closed and stared at the blood pumping from his body where a wooden beam had impaled his chest. All around flames licked at the charred remains of men caught leaning on the bar before the explosion. He looked down at his burning trousers and in a panic began slapping furiously at the greedy flames rapidly spreading over his uniform.

Chapter Twenty-Four

It was only a misty vague outline surrounding the distorted and hazy features of what might have been either man or woman. The charred body jerked at each recurring prick of pain as though he'd fallen into a pit of wriggling porcupines. It did not scream or remonstrate, and suddenly without reserve it knew it was a woman because she was gentle, like his mother, so he retained a vision of his use and allowed it to settle in his mind.

'Hello, Archie, my name is Rose, Nurse Rose,'

she said in a soft voice, pushing a wisp of straggly hair back inside her fresh linen headdress. 'I'm going to attempt to cut away the burnt clothing from your body. It will be very painful, so if you want me to stop, just nod your head.'

She sounded distant and detached, yet the precision of her words gave him a feeling of great comfort, and if he had been in a position to relax he would willingly have done so. He couldn't see the helplessness pitched in her caring eyes, nor the unrelenting pain that cruelly clutched and twisted at her insides. Ever since the doctors had surreptitiously placed him in her care the warring conflict of uncertainty flooded her ever-mounting doubts for his survival, and she didn't know where to begin. It was that simple. Twenty months she'd spent on the front and she thought she had seen all the pain and suffering that the damnable war had to offer and that nothing again could ever be worse. But she had never seen anything like the shape before her and for a fleeting moment despair conquered hope. She had never been witness to a living cinder.

Her breath smelt of fresh coffee, warm and reassuring like the comforting drift of a mild sedative, and for a passing moment he imagined he could smell the slight brush of crushed roses. Whoever it was had come to ease the pain and quell his suffering with her small warm hands. He could feel them, he was certain. Bathed in a riotous discomfort he listened anxiously for the sound of her voice, her soft lilt, the warm touch of her hand on his arm, but then his mind faltered remembering that her name was Rose,

Nurse Rose she had told him.

Dr Colonel Richard Travers glanced at his watch and shook his head. It was nine thirty-five in the evening.

'He won't last the evening. God, I've never seen anybody in such a condition and still remain alive. How the devil can you be sure of his identity, he doesn't have a square inch of skin on his body, best all round if he were left in the fire to perish,' he said to a white-faced Sergeant Bull. 'Who managed to pull him out?'

'It were the locals that pulled him to safety before the building collapsed, but we reckon it's him all right. He's a tough little bugger so I wouldn't write him off just yet,' Sergeant Bull answered quietly, wincing at the form twitching on the table.

Nurse Rose began by using a pair of metal tweezers to gently tease away the charred fabric, but it was useless, a complete waste of time. With the burned skin still attached, his flesh fell away in small pieces leaving small blisters of blood. He tried to call out as the pain suddenly became unbearable, but no sound came from his mouth, only short rasping gasps interspersed with primitive groans. The nurse pulled back, unable to halt the flow of tears trickling from her once bonny blue eyes. Now with eyes that were just a short step from lifelessness, she looked at the blistered flesh and knew that slowly but surely she was killing him. She put down the tweezers and called for the doctor.

'He needs to be immersed in a saline bath to remove the cloth and fabric burned into his flesh.

491

If I continue as I am for much longer, he will die of shock,' she said, clasping her hands tightly together and lifting them to her lips.

'Yes, I understand, nurse, do whatever you deem necessary,' the doctor told her.

He turned away, glad he possessed the seniority to pass on the case for someone else to treat, yet his gladness came tainted with a deep unnerving guilt. Since first casting his eyes on the charred body he had wanted him to die as quickly and painlessly as possible. Even if he survived and healed, he would never again resemble a man.

Hours later, with the help of an unwilling assistant, they lowered him slowly into a harness made of white canvas, a little at a time – they were in no hurry. Even if he should survive, they could only offer minimal treatment and, in all probability, he would never walk, talk or see again.

When he was half-submerged she tried desperately to gauge the amount of pain he suffered. It was impossible and she quickly realised he was in agony each time his body came into contact with anything of a solid nature. Her hand closed over her mouth and she swore a silent oath to herself that she would keep him alive no matter what. Aware he'd received his injuries saving his friends, she assured herself he was man deserving of the gift of life.

He felt the rising pain engulf him in a closed corridor of agony setting his bones on fire and slash through his veins, igniting the craving for death. He wanted to die but couldn't tell them. If he could they wouldn't listen to him. In their innocence they would prolong his agony in ignorance of his mindful pleading. Leave me to die, leave me to die, please, his mind screamed.

'I suggest we spend a period of fifteen minutes each removing the debris from his body. That way no one will lose patience and begin hurrying. We must assume that he is in great pain at all times and act accordingly, is that clear?' she said to the three volunteer nurses before rendering a sedative much stronger than recommended.

It took three heartbreaking days by the angels of mercy to remove the black crust from his body. Off-duty nurses gladly dedicated themselves to his well-being and instantly surrendered their rest periods to assist in any way they could, cheered by his gradual recovery. Over the following weeks his condition improved slowly, and careful treatments of antiseptic oils and paste promoted a slight healing of the skin.

'In his condition he might easily suffer a relapse and the body would then cease to function. It's going to be touch and go for some time,' the doctor said.

Stan Banks stood shaking outside the tented field hospital and clasped his hands together to control the intermittent trembling. He had changed inwardly, perhaps more than other people might notice. Gone was the fast backfire of banter and rapid repartee for which he was famous, and no more did his voice reverberate down the lines with quick-fire jokes and nuances of the day. It wasn't the scourge of guilt that had moved him to a new existence. It was the encumbering hang of shame. Through the canvas of the tented hospital he could hear the sharp rasp of breathing and he felt afraid to enter, afraid of what he might see. His own injuries were minor and had responded rapidly to treatment, leaving just a few almost invisible scars to fade away with the erasure of time.

Inhaling deeply through his nose, he plucked up the courage to raise the flap and stepped inside. Unprepared for the shock he staggered back, groping for support to prevent him from slipping to the bloodstained bare grass floor. With eyes tight shut he turned, fighting against the darkness clouding his senses. The bile rushing into his mouth tasted sour, like vinegar, and he thought that he might lose control and retch. The stumpy body laid bright pink, devoid of skin, and surely couldn't be living. Nurse Rose ignored his response at the sight of her charge. She'd witnessed the scene on many occasions and understood. She applied a thick layer of cream to the twitching body, and glanced up with a knowing smile.

'He's sleeping, it's a good sign,' she said.

Stan opened his mouth to speak and his breath came heavy and fast, leaving no room for words. Frenziedly, he raised his hands to his forehead and squeezed the skin as though trying to erase the sight from his troubled mind. But it remained and he felt trapped in a flush of self-inflicted pain.

'How do you know, how can you tell?' he mumbled.

'Oh, we can tell,' she said, widening her smile. 'Do you know him?'

'Know him? Yes, I know him. I owe my life to him, perhaps even more. We came over together from Blighty and have been friends ever since. He

494

was best man at my wedding, did you know that? We were best friends, we were. Yeah, the best of friends, that's what we were. We lost Atlas, bloody good bloke he was, I can tell you. Les Hill's in a poor way too, but he'll pull through,' Stan Banks said jerkily, clenching his fists and gripping his hands together to stop the violent shaking.

'Well, that's good news,' she said, gently laying a piece of muslin over her patient's eyes.

'He won't be able to see me now when he wakes up, miss. He'll want to see me, you can bet on that. We're best friends, miss, didn't I tell you?' Banks said on the verge of vomiting.

'Yes, I believe you did,' she nodded with a knowing smile. 'I thought you knew – he'll never see again, his eyes were burned out in the fire.'

As though he was made up of loose bones and spongy flesh, Stan sagged and knew he had to get out, away from the sight and sound that turned his legs to smoke and choked the very existence of his body. With trembling hands he clumsily exited the doorway, lurched outside into the fresh air and threw up. A young lieutenant on crutches hesitated and asked if he needed help, reeling away without answering Banks made for the rear of the hospital and with his head in his hands wept.

It was his fault – if he hadn't gone into the inn when he did this would never have happened. If he'd shown more consideration and remained outside with Thomas he might have been in a position to help. Somehow it was always the story of the simple man – if this, if that. The light in his heart dimmed leaving only the shadow of what might have been, and he promised himself he would repay his friend, and vowed solemnly he would never again leave his friend's side.

Weeks turned to months and gradually the charred body improved. Better still, parts of his skin re-grew, and with the help of skin grafts a red blotchy form of crinkled skin formed over his body. Still unrecognisable and unable to hear or speak, they dressed him in pyjama bottoms and a baggy cotton shirt. Sergeant Bull visited on a regular basis, as did Stan.

'Jesus Christ,' Leslie Hill mumbled through quivering lips. 'How can he be alive? I won't be coming again. I prefer to remember him how he was.'

Even Major Billy made the effort. A few pilots reluctantly turned up, but horrified at the unrecognisable body they vowed never to come again. It was nothing personal, they said. Each day they risked fire and burns from crashed aircraft and maybe it was superstition that kept them away.

The moment the doctors agreed to the release of Moses from a hospital further down the lines, he made his way to see Thomas. Late one evening, accompanied by the never-ending cacophony of croaking frogs, he stood outside the field hospital and stared at the silhouette beneath the flickering acetylene gas lanterns inside the tent. He felt no warmth in his body. The disintegrating sand of his being slipped through his fingers and his hands felt frozen and were tinged white around the knuckles. He had to confront him. Yet he shivered in the harsh coldness of what he might see. His heart shrivelled hard like a walnut and he loathed himself for his cowardice.

'Stay as long as you wish, but do not cause him any stress, he is weak and needs rest. If you do you will suffer the wrath of the nurses. They say once he was quite a handsome young man,' Nurse Rose said.

'Handsome? Yes, ma'am, he was handsome, inside as well as outside.'

'I shall convey your words to the nurses,' she said in a soothing voice and left.

Moses listened to the hoarse rhythmical breathing forcing air from scorched lungs.

'Hello, Thomas,' he said softly, leaning closer to Thomas's ear.

For a moment the body twitched slowly, then more pronounced than before as though it had something to say. Moses turned away as the mists of emotion swept like a tidal wave of affection into his breast, the words in his heart choked before they could be uttered. He wanted to stay, he wanted to leave, and he wanted to tell the poor wretch before him he loved him like a man loves his brother, so he did.

Chapter Twenty-Five

Armistice

It was November 1918 and the Great War finished as abruptly as it had started. German troops made their way back to Germany with the knowledge they hadn't won the war, yet still denied they had lost. Stan Banks stood in the fantasy of quietness on the empty battlefields and thought the silence might turn him insane. The deafening absence of field guns, fused with the heart chilling memory of screams of the dying pulverised his senses. In a daze he lost all idea of time and direction and wondered if he could ever live in a world of normality again. It was widely rumoured that many men lost their grip on reality at the silence and, turned into trembling hulks forever unable to lead a normal life. Alone, he stood grim-faced and bent, surveying all he had fought for, and he sighed. A few miles of blackened fields in a foreign country full of rotting flesh, stinking shit and bloated, satisfied rats. Mary would soothe him when his hands shook and his eyes shrunk into their sockets in fear of pain and mutilation, but the feeling refused to go away and always returned. Like Monday following Sunday.

Stan and the indestructible Leslie Hill were the only two remaining men left alive from the original group who had left Catterick a million years ago in 1916. Between them they shared the considerable sum that had accumulated in the death pool, the money pooled by the snipers before each battle.

The doctor and Nurse Rose pondered on the best way forward for their patient. Maybe it might be best if he were repatriated back to Blighty to convalesce when he grew stronger.

The doctor thought it a wonderful idea and readily agreed for an ambulance to take his patient to the airfield at Droglandt to receive DCM, the Distinguished Conduct Medal for the bravery displayed while trying to save his comrades during the fire. Major Billy agreed to make the presentation. If the doctor could spare the time he promised he would be honoured to attend. In any case, Nurse Rose promised to attend regardless. Darkness hid the shameful vista of the barren wastelands from the reproaching eyes of Mother Nature waiting to heal and change the dirty brown to a rich vibrant green. As always, she would shortly appear in her eagerness to repair man's foolish mistakes and ease away the scars of stupidity. Perhaps one day she wouldn't, and would leave mankind to boil in its juices.

When the weather blew wet and cold the ceremony was cancelled until the following day, at ten in the morning.

When he woke Nurse Rose helped him dress in his simple makeshift clothes and fixed the leather mask over his face to hide the horrific distortion and scars. Late that morning, under a cool sun, she placed the charred body in the wheelchair and allowed Stan to propel him slowly to the presentation point. Major Billy and those pilots not on essential duties stood in line, waiting to come to attention in honour of Private Archie Elkin MM. Stan walked proud and erect, his hair neatly combed and wetted tight to his skull, his uniform full of its complement of buttons and freshly sponged for the occasion. He stopped before the station commander. Beneath the mask he could hear the breath coming in short, loud gasps, each sounding as if it might be his last. The leather mask bare of eyelets meant the mouthpiece puffed and fell as he fought for air. A young pilot new to the squadron closed his eyes tight and refused to watch the ceremony for fear of being sick.

'Aircraft approaching, aircraft approaching,' the warning drifted across the airfield, accompanied by the tolling of the bell. Shocked eyes quickly shifted skyward at the solitary German aircraft skimming low over the treetops about to make Germany's final attack in defiance of defeat. Years of habit mixed with an instantaneous reaction flowed into man's automatic act of self-preservation, and each ran and dived for cover. Stan Banks left his charge unattended and like the rest ran for survival. Alone and exposed in the abandoned wheelchair the body twitched and jerked in spasms. Overhead the aircraft passed like a silent black bird. Still the warning bell tolled.

Death came in a gentle manner. Painless and all-consuming like a man might have wanted. The bomb landed with a muted 'crump' and blew the body into the air as though lifted by an invisible hand, and smashed it against the wooden walls of the operations hut. A broken rib delivered the fatal blow, piercing the heart.

Moses clung hopelessly to his senses, stunned by the intensity of the moment. Frightened by the glimpse of what lay before him, he shook his head and waited for the pain. It came, as he knew it would, and he closed his eyes against it seeking not answers but questions. With a gasp he sank to his knees, and looked up at the sky.

'Why? You evil bastard, why? You are no God. You are wicked, and they should have nailed you to the cross with your son. Why do you always punish the innocent?' he roared, reaching out with

500

his arms and breaking down into gut-wrenching sobs.

Stan Banks backed away. Each black particle of coal dust ingrained on his shocked face glistened in the paleness of his skin and his blood shrivelled and dried in his veins. He recalled the soft voice, a shy glance, a warm smile, and still he felt the presence of his young friend who had given all and asked for nothing in return. The same young friend he'd deserted when he needed him most. He turned and shuffled away. Some might say at least he had survived the war. Bent and broken he made his way from the airfield and was never seen again, just another faceless casualty in the magnificence of war, just another name chiselled into cold marble and soon indistinct from memory.

The sight of the red flesh splattered against the wooden sides of the operations hut turned Moses from a normal level-headed man into a physically trembling wreck with a scrambled brain. He allowed no one to touch the remains and buried what was left in a makeshift grave beneath a group of swaying beech trees. Alone, in a spot where nightingales sang and waited for nature to heal the squalor and degradation of the trenches, he knelt in stunned silence, his eyes dead and hopeless and his breath quick, like a panting dog. Days later, he was diagnosed as a victim of mild shell shock.

Finally, it was over and all hostilities ceased until man made ready for his next folly, and Moses struggled to find a valid reason to return to a broken England. Instead he gained part-time employment with the Commonwealth War Graves

Commission assisting to find and bury the dead. He remained, cared for by a young French nurse called Bernadette in a small two-bedroom cottage with a red-tiled roof and running water next to a bombed-out church. Over the passing months, he slowly recovered to his normal mental state and at last toyed with the idea of returning to England with Bernadette as his wife.

Leslie Hill returned to the small village of Duston on the outskirts of Northampton. On the sweeping bend of the main road, next to St Luke's church he stood in his unbuttoned uniform with his feet apart and watched his wife step from the bakery. His eyes welled and he felt the heave of his chest. She stopped and turned, and the anxiety fled from her face, and a long absent light shone in her eyes. She did not swoon or faint. Yet relief and happiness sapped the strength from her limbs and she sank to her knees. She had never looked so beautiful.

Early one wet winter morning in the year 1920, a smartly dressed official from the War Graves Commission in London made a surprise visit to Moses's small cottage with an unusual request. It had been proposed that the body of an un-identified soldier from World War One be exhumed and returned to London for burial in Westminster Abbey to symbolise those who gave their lives in battle and whose bodies were never recovered. He was charged to exhume the bodies of six men from the cemeteries of the Western Front, transport them to France and lay them to rest at the chapel at St Pol.

Armed with a shovel he diligently searched beneath the swaying beech trees for the spot he felt certain he'd laid the remains of the charred body of Thomas, until his hands blistered. For a time, he stood alone beneath a cloud of despair and questioned the very reliability of his memory when his efforts unearthed no sign of the remains. Moving to another group of trees he frantically began his search one more time, thinking perhaps his mind played tricks. Overcome by fear for his sanity, he moved from spot to spot in the hope of discovering his friend's burial site, until his mind began to deteriorate and he sank into a deep depression. When Bernadette found him he was on his knees with his face upturned to a grey sky, cursing God in heaven for the multitude of sins he had committed in the name of Christianity. He refused her pleadings to return to the comfort of the cottage.

Less than an hour later, exhausted, he finally exhumed the remains of the mutilated corpse, and beneath a torrential cloudburst struggled to his feet like a man way past the end of his tether. She led him back to the cottage and nursed him through his delirium. For three days and nights the past became crystal clear in his mind and he re-lived the past two years. Although his soul fought against a complete recollection of memories she listened to his ramblings and pieced together the secret of Thomas Elkin. On the morning he woke he lay with his eyes open, he no longer trembled and she cradled his head to her chest and said the words he needed to hear.

'He is gone to a place of rest now,' she reassured him. 'Perhaps Archie came for him and they finally made their peace; time to let him be.'

Moses mulled over Bernadette's words. Maybe her assumptions were correct, yet often in the stillness of time he imagined he caught the echoes of Thomas's voice and thought he might be returning to near insanity. Then finally common sense triumphed over foolishness, and he left his sickbed to prepare the six coffins containing the remains of the unknown soldiers.

Brigadier General Wyatt randomly chose one of the six coffins. Moses waited till after dark and transferred the charred body into the selected coffin. That same evening he and Bernadette left for Brighton, and on the south coast of England they purchased a small two-bedroomed flint stoned cottage with a thatched roof just off the lanes.

From the chapel, the coffin was transported to Boulogne and then to Dover aboard HMS Verdun. After an overnight stay at Victoria Station it was drawn in procession with full military honours to Whitehall. Moses stood with hands clasped and head bowed and watched King George V unveil the cenotaph at eleven o'clock in the morning on the eleventh day of the eleventh month. Two minutes of silence followed. Then from the cenotaph the coffin was carried to Westminster Abbey and passed hand-over-hand by one hundred recipients of the Victoria Cross to its final resting place in the west nave and buried in soil brought from France.

Slowly Moses turned away and raised his collar against the biting wind channelling through Whitehall. In his mind he felt the warmth of satisfaction of knowing he could do no more to honour his young friend. Should he and Bernadette ever be blessed with children, he would tell them the story of Thomas Elkin, the soldier who saved his life. A worthy ambassador for the unknown fallen.

Chapter Twenty-Six

Cromwell Bull, ex-sergeant of the 3rd Rifles sat by the roaring open fire in the inn overlooking Torbay and read the front page of the local paper reporting the story of the internment of an unknown soldier about to be laid to rest in Westminster Abbey one more time.

'Never bloody happy unless they have a drum to beat and a trumpet to blow,' he declared to the man sitting by his side sipping lemonade. 'I wonder who the poor bugger is in the coffin.'

'I don't suppose anyone will ever know the answer to that,' Thomas Elkin said. 'But I reckon it's time we made our way to Southampton if we're going to make the boat to Canada.'

Cromwell Bull neatly folded the newspaper, pushed his hair back with short stubby fingers and smiled. All they had planned couldn't have worked out better. The burning inn had provided them with the opportunity they had been seeking for months. History would never know that after saving Moses and Stan Banks, Thomas had re-entered the burning building and made his way through the rear door. Further down the road on the outskirts of the airfield he hid in a disused farmhouse. With the knowledge the war was all but over and with a dull satisfaction he watched the RAF bomb the Germans to a standstill. Alone he had managed to survive on anything edible and looked into the reserves of his strength. He could never return to the farm on the edge of the Yorkshire moors, he knew that. Never again would he feel the firm comforting grip of his father's handshake or the warm embrace of his mother's arms. On more than one occasion he opened the hard-covered notebook, and extracted the pressed daisy. He felt a strange intimacy embrace his body and held the daisy to his lips and imagined the fresh smell of the moors teasing his face. And Ruby, always there was Ruby. She displayed no flashes of temper nor made unreasonable demands. She had given him the only thing she had to offer, her inescapable and unconditional love and affection, how could he ever forget her. 'Walk easy on the plough, Ruby,' he murmured, ignoring the tears streaming down his face. 'I won't be coming home lass, not today.'

When finally, at last, the big guns fell silent and the blackened environment lay like a playground for those practiced in the art of hideousness and evilness, he made his way to England with a Field Artillery Battery. The sky hung overcast with a drizzling rain when they finally reached Folkestone, a small crowd eagerly waited on the quayside. Some waved flags and cheered as England's returning heroes made their way slowly down the gangplank.

The gaunt hollow-eyed men who stepped

ashore were not the same happy rounded men who had left laughing to the stirring strains of a regimental band and kisses blown from sweet soft lips. That had taken place many long months before. Now they came like men devoid of purpose. Each wore an assortment of clothing nothing like the smart uniforms they had left in. Sheepskin jackets and skin coats purchased from local French and Belgium farmers, or ripped from mutilated corpses scattered and rotting over No Man's Land. Instead of caps with gleaming badges they wore dirty bloodstained scarves tied around their heads. Their clothes cut and ripped for comfort, and caked in thick dried mud.

Back in civilian life some would be fortunate enough to have jobs to go to. Others, those not permanently affected by the horror of war would go from house to house selling bootlaces for a living. The more unfortunate would knock on doors and ask for second-hand clothes, perhaps a slice of dry bread and dripping. The faces in the crowd changed from ones of happiness to bewilderment and horror, and for a moment felt afraid of these men, the same men whose only aim had been to endure or die without complaint all that their peers had set before them.

After disembarking at Folkestone, Thomas had travelled alone along the south coast to the fishing town of Torquay, Devon, and waited, as pre-arranged, for Sergeant Bull to join him. Once settled they quickly found work on the fishing fleets bringing food to a hungry nation. Here, at last Thomas had found the freedom he'd always sought. Since the day the war ended Archie never

507

again appeared in his dreams or haunted his once troubled mind. It was as though he had suffered enough, and the debt was put to rest, paid in full. As for Cromwell Bull, well, he wanted more from life than repairing bicycles and dangling from a church bell rope twice a week.

'Aye Archie, lad. Let's be away. Between us we've saved more than enough money over the past two years to start a small automobile repair business in Canada. Time to start a new life,' he said.

Thomas chuckled, wiped his mouth with the back of his hand and gave the ex-sergeant a sideways glance.

Archie, Thomas, what's in a name?

Acknowledgements

Janice always. For her undying patience in helping me to put this book together. Without her I would never have got started.

Emma Morris for her computer skills.

And in memory of SAM, my yellow Labrador and constant companion during the writing of this book, now sadly passed away.

The publishers hope that this book has given you enjoyable reading. Large Print Books are especially designed to be as easy to see and hold as possible. If you wish a complete list of our books please ask at your local library or write directly to:

Magna Large Print Books
Magna House, Long Preston,
Skipton, North Yorkshire.
BD23 4ND

This Large Print Book for the partially sighted, who cannot read normal print, is published under the auspices of

THE ULVERSCROFT FOUNDATION